DR RAJ PERSAUD is a Cc
a consultant at the Bethlem
in London from 1994–2008
at the Institute of Psychiatr
the premier research and t
in Europe. He was also Res ... at the johns Hopkins
Hospital in the USA and the Institute of Neurology at Queens
Square. His training in psychiatry since leaving UCH medical
school in 1986 has been entirely at the Institute of Psychiatry and
the Bethlem Royal and Maudsley Hospitals.

Unusually for a psychiatrist, he also holds a degree in psychology, obtained with First Class Honours, and eight other degrees
and diplomas, including a Masters in Statistics. He was awarded
the Royal College of Psychiatrists' Research Prize and Medal,
The Maudsley Hospital's own Denis Hill Prize, and The Osler
Medal. The Royal College of Psychiatrists recently also awarded
him the Morris Markowe Prize.

In 2004 he was appointed Visiting Professor for Public
Understanding of Psychiatry at Gresham College, and he was
asked by the Royal College of Psychiatrists to edit its first book
aimed at educating the public on psychology and psychiatry. *The
Mind: A Users Guide* was published in 2007 and reached the top
ten bestseller list. All of his five non-fiction books have been top ten
bestsellers. His writing is in several established textbooks, and he
has approaching 100 publications in journals such as *The British
Journal of Psychiatry, British Medical Journal* and *The Lancet.*
Recently he was elected Fellow of University College London
and the Royal College of Psychiatrists. He is patron or supporter
of numerous mental health charities including, at various times,
OCD-UK, The Manic Depression Fellowship, Association of
Post-Natal Illness, Childline, Action Aid and The Samaritans.
The *Independent on Sunday* newspaper conducted a poll among
members of the Royal College of Psychiatrists and the Institute
of Psychiatry to discover who were the top ten psychiatrists in the
UK. Dr Raj Persaud was the youngest doctor to make it into this
esteemed list. *The Times* newspaper also placed him as one of the
Top Twenty Mental Health Gurus in the world.

He is now joint podcast editor for the Royal College of

Psychiatrists and also has a free app on iTunes and Google Play store entitled "Raj Persaud in Conversation". This includes a lot of information on the latest research findings in mental health, plus interviews with top experts from around the world.

He left the NHS in 2010 for full time clinical private practice in Harley Street. He has been chair of the judges of one of the world's most prestigious prizes for popular science writing – the Aventis Prize for Science Books – in 2002 awarding the prize to Stephen Hawking.

Praise For *Can't Get You Out of My Head*

Dr Persaud has woven the facts about stalking that are important for everyone to know into a gripping story of fixation and violence… *Can't Get You Out of My Head* captures the obsession that drives some stalkers to ever more desperate and bizarre behaviour in pursuit of their victim.
– Dr Troy McEwan – one of the world's leading authorities on the psychology of stalking – Lecturer in Clinical and Forensic Psychology, Centre for Forensic Behavioural Science, Australia.

An entertaining romp through the weirder frontiers of VIP protection, notable for blending into its story-line an array of serious information about the problem of stalking.
– Dr David James – Consultant Forensic Psychiatrist and co-founder of the UK National Stalking Clinic.

In this fascinating novel Dr Persaud reveals the core of these obsessions and what it means for their victims.
– Professor David Canter – Emeritus Professor, The University of Liverpool, and inventor of Investigative Psychology.

Raj knows his subject; the typologies, the behaviours but ultimately the fear, the terror and the complexities of being stalked…ordinary people are living this terror on a daily basis.
– Tracey Morgan, Survivor & Campaigner.

CAN'T GET YOU OUT OF MY HEAD

Raj Persaud

SilverWood

This is for my parents, Lakshmi and Vishnu,
the greatest support act on tour

Published in 2015 by SilverWood Books
SilverWood Books Ltd
14 Small Street, Bristol, BS1 1DE, United Kingdom
www.silverwoodbooks.co.uk

See pages 384–387 for full music credits. Selected lyrics by kind permission
of EMI Music Publishing UK Ltd and Sony/ATV Music Publishing (UK)
Ltd, Fabulous Music Ltd, Peter Lawlor, BMG, Alfred Music Publishing,
Music Sales Ltd and The Hal Leonard Corporation

ISBN 978-1-78132-448-6 (paperback)
ISBN 978-1-78132-449-3 (ebook)

British Library Cataloguing in Publication Data
A CIP catalogue record for this book is available from
the British Library

Set in Adobe Garamond Pro by SilverWood Books
Printed on responsibly sourced paper

The Suzy Lamplugh Trust

The Trust was established in 1986 after the disappearance of twenty-five-year-old Suzy Lamplugh, who went missing while working as an estate agent. She was never found, and was legally declared dead in 1993. Suzy's parents, Paul and Diana, wanted to make people aware of their personal safety and founded the charity to educate everyone, from schoolchildren to people out working on their own, on how to stay safe. Today it campaigns, educates and supports people to reduce their risk of violence and aggression.

The Suzy Lamplugh Trust also runs the National Stalking Helpline, offering guidance and information to thousands of victims of stalking every year. If you have been affected by stalking, call 0808 802 0300 or visit www.stalkinghelpline.org for more information on how to get help.

iDU

iDU was developed by Professor David Canter in collaboration with law enforcement agencies. This free security app instantly and securely stores photos of people you meet in a private database only available to you and authorised law enforcement. The intelligent privacy software safely stores your images with the date, precise time and location and any notes you want to add, so even if your phone is destroyed or stolen the photo is already stored securely. No commercial organisations or other institutions are involved in this app or have access to any of the information stored.

The app can be freely downloaded at www.idu.onl

When you are more famous than God,
how long before you get crucified?
– Fixation, Fame, Insanity and Assassination

Part 1

It's Worth Being Shot At

It is worth being shot at – to see how much one is loved.
– Queen Victoria, 1882, after an assassination attempt.

1

Remember just who you are
Where do you go to my lovely?

*Erotomaniacs are relentless, Philippa! They have a psychotic delusion
that the person they are stalking is in love with them. They never give
up. Released from prison, they'll go straight from the detention centre
gates to the victim's house.*

The ovation erupted beneath him.

Such acclamation!

But not for William's warning.

The Prime Minister's speech was ending, and William, high
on the balcony which floated halfway up the exquisite Egyptian
Hall of Mansion House, heard something dangerously out of
place. Now it was lost within the thunder of the applause.

The stalker? Had he decided to attack? Spaced along the
balcony on either side of William, armed police were examining
each guest at the banquet, checking every possible line of ambush
on the Prime Minister and his Foreign Secretary. Their earphones
would be filled with crackle from marksmen and spotters
surrounding the building.

William's hands moistened as he gripped the handrail.
Listening hard for the danger, he kept his eyes glued on the
Secretary of State for the Foreign Office.

The previous evening, the youngest member of the Cabinet,
while swishing a silk ballgown, had granted him a private viewing
in her drawing room.

'What do you think goes with this? The Louboutin pumps or
the Cavalli ankle straps?' she had asked.

Pulling back a slit in the elegant frock, Philippa Foot revealed
some slender thigh.

'Look, your safety is our primary concern…'

'Do you always sound like an airline announcement, William?'

'Pip, can we please focus on the stalker? He's so mentally messed up he won't realise how dangerous this is.'

'Yeah, yeah…then he hasn't got much chance of getting through Gerrard's men, has he.'

She had clicked her fingers.

'Pay attention, William! What about the Balenciaga glove sandals?'

William thought he'd heard something from her bedrooms above them, but he was distracted. As she bent over, glowing creamy skin was exposed where her zip was undone. He had to wonder: was this whole scene a provocation, put on for the benefit of someone lurking upstairs, impatiently waiting for him to leave?

Rumours had begun to pursue the Foreign Secretary, through the gossip columns, as to exactly why she was getting divorced.

'So we've agreed,' he had fretted, 'if he turns up at Mansion House…'

'*If*? You told the AC the psycho was *definitely* going to make contact then. He's been grumbling about it all week.'

'Why is Gerrard involved at all?' William had asked sullenly. 'The Assistant Commissioner wouldn't usually dirty his hands with a stalking case…'

'Earth to William – because I am who I am, you muppet. And the police are *bothered* by you. Shrinks make 'em nervous. Honestly! Think about it, you keep getting stuff right while they're stumbling about guessing.'

William had insisted this stalker would make his first physical contact at the Mansion House ceremony, but the Metropolitan Police still couldn't understand how he made his predictions. These prowlers weren't ordinary criminals – most forensic psychiatrists found obsessives banal because of their focus on one goal. All of life distilled down to a single desire. William, however, *envied* their clarity. His own mind was forever waking up in unfamiliar mental territory.

Like now.

With flaming red curls that shimmered ambition, Philippa regally paraded in front of her mirror. Supremely confident, she was taking her place in history – the youngest female on the frontbench – easily in her stride. She had claimed to William that she was bored silly by the idiocy of politics. But she never stopped playing mind games.

'C'mon, Pip, Gerrard is not an emotionally talented man.'

Their eyes met in the mirror. She smiled and her impudent lips moistened, the same way as when she'd disclosed to him her strategy on selling the war in the Congo to the public. The *exact* same pout as when she'd confided that her soon-to-be-ex-husband would be livid if he had any idea how much her ballgown had cost. As would her Cabinet colleagues, who were constantly battling to de-emphasise the party's links with privilege. Well, they would all know once the dailies commented on it.

William had harboured a suspicion, as he floundered in the rising tide of silk which was hemmed in by her collection of alpine heels, that she was in some weird way dressing up for her stalker – for her date with destiny.

Anonymous threatening messages had been arriving for months, but Assistant Commissioner Gerrard Winstanley had dismissed the rambling incoherent notes as too muddled to be of real concern. The Foreign Sec, he'd protested, received loopy letters every week. Why had William, hired as a consultant by a worried Foreign Office, picked these out for special attention?

Leaning out, brown hair flopping forward, he surveyed the high-powered banquet clinking below in the lustrous hall. Edging towards the windows, security bolted despite the stifling August evening, he kept his scrutiny cemented on Philippa, the imperious Foreign Secretary.

As she hadn't looked up to the gallery the whole evening, William wondered if she was still exasperated by his sartorial shortcomings – or because he'd amused himself with the Prime Minister.

'How old are you?' she'd hissed in his ear during the security briefing. She played with her necklace when she was annoyed. She started flicking it after her glittering entrance in the flowing ballgown the moment she saw what he was wearing. 'What on earth do you look like?' she'd added.

'I'm thirty-three and NHS psychiatrists don't go to black sly, sorry, *tie* balls that often.'

'It's *white* tie,' she snapped, irritated by his verbal tic. 'And you're meant to blend in,' she continued as she eyed his decidedly wash-and-wear dinner jacket. She gestured at the Assistant Commissioner, resplendent in his white tie and tails.

Gerrard, now in his early fifties, had been quite the hero as a younger officer, daringly intervening in a bomb disposal operation that had gone horribly wrong. A resultant scar licking up under his collar added to his hard-man good looks, which were topped by an enviably thick thatch of salt-and-pepper waves.

After Louise Mensch, while still an MP, had hit back at abuse from Twitter trolls, there was new pressure from above. Nothing was to be left to chance when it came to the stalking and harassment of female public figures. But like so many of his colleagues, Gerrard was not convinced that psychiatry had any real place in police work – just look what had happened in the Rachel Nickell case back in the nineties, he kept reminding Philippa in front of William.

William had given up pointing out it was a *psychologist* who had been involved in the Nickell shambles, not a psychiatrist.

The audience were regaining their seats. William knew the standing ovation was always going to be the essential psychological moment of most distraction in the room. So he had guessed immediately what any unexpected noise meant. The Egyptian Hall provided a natural acoustic drum for any disturbance on the roof. And that's where the scraping sound only William seemed to be hearing was coming from.

'Listen!' he whispered fiercely, tugging at Gerrard's tailcoat.

Gerrard frowned – then froze as the noise from above became more insistent.

'*Your* stalker's on the roof?' the Assistant Commissioner asked indignantly.

2

Like the circles that you find
In the windmills of your mind

She couldn't breathe.

The terror had sidled up, crawling out from underneath whatever dark stone it had been lurking. Then its pincers struck, throttling her. It was the most desperate moment for Dread's first panic attack. She was marooned inside a stadium buzzing with 93,000 adrenalin-soaked fans as her vocal cords coiled tighter and tighter.

She had become so bored repeating her household anthems that she'd fallen into the habit of no longer really being there on stage. But suddenly she was hyper-aware – ensnared in the headlights of thousands of eyes.

It was all bewildering – where was she again? And what on earth was she doing here?

The 'now' echoed back at her. Another colossal concert on an interminable world tour. She couldn't remember where they'd got to, or what stack of stadiums remained to be serenaded. Knowing which country they were in would be a start. She couldn't make out the spectators but she *felt* the swarm out there. And there were more serious torments than trying to work out where the gigantic arc of luminosity was.

How come she now felt so tiny against the giant Ferris wheel she'd demanded for her stage?

And why was her voice unresponsive?

Her mind faltered. Teetering above the arena on the towering carnival ride, her legs began to slide. She couldn't steady herself. A whip writhed in one hand, in the other a sweaty microphone slipped. Shock was distorting her sense of time. Inside, everything had become very, very slow. And outside it all seemed jerkily sped up. At least she recognised the demon for what it was – panic. Other performers had thought they were having a heart attack.

Or a seizure.

Or about to go mad.

It was the last unspoken taboo of swaggering rock performances. And no one in the press was going to be silent for long about this catastrophe. Beneath her was a gathering the size of an entire town – several times larger, she reminded herself unhelpfully, than Romford where she'd grown up.

Her chest was thudding louder than the drummers below. Only an immaculate sense of timing kept her from being thrown off. Reeling almost above the level of the stadium roof – a bit of rock 'n' roll showbiz tomfoolery – the colossal gleaming lattice wheel had been designed by the same people who'd constructed the London Eye. They seemed malevolent to her now, because their gigantic spiralling loop mercilessly stranded her far above any possibility of help. The swaying platforms, suspended high up here, on which she and her dancers cavorted declined the protection of railings.

That would have ruined the video.

She was supposed to be flicking her bullwhip, but only her throat was doing the cracking. Battle as she might, Dread's voice refused to respond.

The amphitheatre began to erupt with its own dazzling laser display. Sunset surrendered to a fusillade of pyrotechnics.

Her entire career had been painstakingly scaffolded on an intolerance of imperfection in herself and others. How absurd now to be praying ardently for *something* to go wrong. That the rotating Ferris wheel would grind to a halt; that something, anything, could happen to create a distraction.

The audience had almost disappeared from sight, but Dread was never truly alone. TV cameras and zoom lenses were splattered all over the concourse.

The podium quivered with the once-reassuring punch of the music. Now the pulse tripped her treacherous stilettos.

I can dive from this height, she thought, *crash on to the stage below and bounce off into the welcoming arms of the audience.*

What a way to go!

But will the floodlighting keep up? she wondered. *Will my Follow Spot arc through space and capture the plummet?*

Riding the perspiration from her quivering thighs, the lacy sides of her thigh-high boots slid down.

Even her feet had vertigo.

The Ferris wheel agitated into action again, gliding her downwards towards the worshipping horde. She croaked to the end of her latest hymn to west coast rock, tottering from the bottom rung. Solid ground level boards heaved reassuringly with dancers and musicians. Were they deliberately ignoring signs of distress in their lead singer? Fizzle instead of flamboyance; goosebumps and gushing sweat in place of glamour. What were they waiting for? A distress flare?

But even that cry for help would have been bleached out by the cascading stage fireworks. There was no one to turn to. Dread had cracked the whip mercilessly with everyone here, bullying them into shape. Nothing would offer them more pleasure than watching her flop – live.

She could just make out the sound engineers, gesticulating at their headphones. She should have been able to hear them talking to her via the desk mikes, but instead, nothing.

She'd frozen. But she knew they'd be thinking that her microphone and the monitors had possibly gone down. She could see them frantically switching channels and re-patching her mike to try to reach her. *Houston, we have a problem*, she thought.

The crowd was a foaming ocean of adulation. However, among the band, dancers and acrobats, Dread only received cold shoulders. On stage she experienced more concentrated hatred than anywhere else on earth. The Ferris wheel impatiently accepted her and violently swung her away from safety.

The musicians, now nearly two hundred feet below, were glaring at each other, bemused that she hadn't started the next song as rehearsed.

What was she up to?

Behind her tears she saw the drummer roll her eyes and her drumsticks. She then nodded to the bass player, who shrugged back. They had decided not to wait for Dread. Slightly late to the prompt, they struck up the next number "Everybody Wants to Rule the World", originally by the UK band Tears for Fears.

This was the song the Care for Congo organisers wanted her to deliver at what was going to be the largest charity concert in history. It was just two weeks away at Hyde Park, before a multitude of two million people. What would happen if she suffered a panic attack then? Was that why she was so terrified now?

It was coming in waves, a giant tsunami of terror crashing down on her again and again.

Guns 'N' Roses had sparked a violent ruckus right in the middle of a performance at Montreal's Olympic Stadium in '92. Axl Rose declared he had a sore throat – a whining announcement that cued rioters to overturn cars, smash windows, ignite fires and loot stores. Dread had overtaken Guns 'N' Roses in record and download sales eons ago. Montreal's Olympic Stadium boasted a capacity of 50,000, but the Rose Bowl Stadium in Pasadena – ah, that was where this was – dizzied beneath her 93,000 pairs of eyes.

There wasn't a more perfect way for her to destroy herself. Every other rock star she'd ever overshadowed would be sobbing with mirth at the last rites of her career – which is what this concert had become. Everything that had ever mattered came down to whether she could hit the right notes in the next few seconds.

After this, she mightn't be able to go out for the rest of her life. Press and fan hysteria would follow her wherever she sidled, because Roger had predicted this was going to happen – that she wouldn't be able to keep it together.

End it all up here, now, and she would be relieved of the interminable pain of a lifelong obituary. The prospect beckoned of elevation to a legend. But only if she could reach out from beyond the grave and retain dominion over what they alleged about her afterwards.

Macabre fragmented plans swirled through her mind. An insistent shard was even projecting how they would film her life story. No wonder she was so messed up – she needed to get off this rocky merry-go-round once and for all. She just could not let him win.

Catching the prompt, she caressed the microphone with her lips. One last prayer for her snarled vocal cords.

3

Swing low
In a dark glass hour

Whoever was up on the roof began a bizarre howling. Bangs followed and what sounded like someone leaping from ridge to rafter. High-arched ceilings amplified the feral scrabbling as armed officers fanned to the exits towards the crown of the building.

'Haven't you got people up there?' William asked, incredulous.

'In case you hadn't noticed, we're a bit stretched, what with the anti-war demos from here to Trafalgar Square,' the AC snapped. 'SECO checked the roof was clear and locked it down.'

He sounded rattled. Irritated that William had got it right? Again?

'ASU is coming in, Sir,' a sergeant reported from his walkie-talkie.

'The chopper was meant to cover the roofs, but it got pulled over to Parliament – you stay here,' the AC growled at William. 'It's most probably some of those damned beatniks who've gone up there to protest.'

It was an absolute certainty the howler was the Foreign Secretary's stalker, but there wasn't time to explain before Gerrard whirled towards an exit, and an armed group clanged out. The briefly opened window allowed the baying to scurry through to the hall, louder and more insistent.

Looking down, William saw consternation developing among the guests. Philippa was gesticulating up at the gallery in response to the Prime Minister's obvious grumbling.

William's concern grew as the bumping and clattering from the roof rose to a crescendo. They really needed someone who knew about mental illness out there. Below, officers chattered urgently on walkie-talkies by the Prime Minister's side, and Philippa's head was bent over her mobile.

William's handset buzzed. Philippa was texting him!

Is it true snipers get more head?

Another text.

H9.

He couldn't work out this new code. The evac plan would be in full swing. Was her message a clue he was supposed to remember from the briefing?

He texted back a question mark.

Gerrard hadn't specifically told him *not* to go out on the roof. And he *was* part of the Fixated Threat Assessment Centre team – even if the AC was making it painfully clear he was very much the new boy. William pushed the exit window open and levered himself out. There was a metal fire escape winding up and down, so he crept upwards.

'Gerrard?' he hissed.

No answer. Where the hell was everyone?

On the base of the vertex, it was surprisingly blustery. Feeling precarious so near the edge, he crouched. Was that the shadowy figure of the stalker? No, it was a flag rising in the breeze. It was eerily quiet up here, bar the wind moaning around pinnacles disappearing into the gloom.

He loathed heights, and the pavement below was an unexpectedly long way down, the street jammed with flashing blue lights and running uniforms. He was so high up that no sound reached him. It felt surreal. Had the stalker been muzzled already?

Someone arrived by his side, and William nearly tumbled over the parapet. The police marksman dropped to one knee, taking aim across the roof while William crouched, palpitating, scanning the horizon. As his eyes adjusted, he could make out shadowy figures from the protection squad spread everywhere.

William called up a mental image of the area maps Gerrard had deployed to explain the security perimeters. To his left was Threadneedle Street, where the Bank of England peeked from behind the corner. On his right was the British Arab Commercial Bank Headquarters bathed in yellow light, and further over was the dome of one of the finest of Wren's churches, St Stephen Walbrook.

The rising clatter of the arriving helicopter made it even more difficult to be sure what was going on. An intense shaft of white light bounced down on to the parapet. The aircraft drifted uncomfortably close and William's glasses nearly blew off. He clutched his specs.

A second later there was a flurry of sharp cracking sounds.

The snipers had opened fire.

William ducked instinctively, but the firing stopped. There was an electronic squawk and the sniper beside him padded away. Other figures stood up, beginning to walk purposefully between the slopes of the roof.

William shivered. Had they shot the psychotic patient? Was this the funeral march for someone suffering from a severe delusional illness?

He stood, trembling slightly.

About 200 yards from him came shouts. The search party looked at their feet. Some more yells and the officers dived for the floor in a cascade, disappearing from view.

William swivelled.

A shadow was hurtling straight at him with the thumping sound of feet, a metallic clang rattling confusion. Ear-splitting snapping cracks peppered the murk while the helicopter search-light struggled to catch the weaving figure.

Something stirred below, pulling the psychiatrist's eye line downwards – shimmering red dots from rifle laser sights crawled over his own torso.

William hit the deck.

Whining pings bit the air beside him, forcing his head further into his hands. A tang of sweat and a flapping, panting shadow passed overhead. He looked up and was blinded by the glare of the searchlight. The helicopter's piercing beam illuminated a blur that leapt into empty space. William gasped, reminded of old vampire movies.

'He's jumped?' he croaked.

Uniformed figures scuttled to the side of the roof, and the psychiatrist got shakily to his feet and joined them. Automatic rifles were trained on the blackness.

They stared into the abyss, then across the gap. The British

Arab Commercial Bank's roof was scattered with lunar crags, and it was continuous along a series of further buildings, including Barclays. Nothing stirred across the white walls. The helicopter beat the air as its searchlight tracked up and down the street below. In his mind's eye, William pictured the stalker's shattered body smeared on the pavement, trapped in the chopper's beam.

But all he saw were the shadows of the night.

'What the hell are you doing? You nearly got creamed!'

'What?' said William.

'You got in the way of us dropping the target!' Gerrard arrived, bellowing.

'Why were you shooting? Whenever this stalker turned up, I was to get first chance to negotiate with him, remember?'

'All your goddamn rules go out the window when a terrorist is trying to assassinate the Foreign Secretary,' the AC snarled.

Was it Gerrard who had rewritten Philippa's rules of engagement? Or was there some agreement with her which William wasn't party to? The helicopter drifted, hunting along the skyline, its clattering lessening.

'Did you see that? I think he had wings!' William couldn't believe what his brain had told him he'd seen.

'It was a wing suit!' Gerrard said, scornful at William's terror and bewilderment. 'That's how he got here.'

He turned to indicate a panoply of material and cord being disentangled by officers behind him. It was a discarded parachute.

'What's a wing suit?'

'It's exactly the MO of those anti-war demonstrators. Bunch of bloody handgliding eco-warriors. And there are all these tall buildings to launch down from.' Gerrard gestured at the Shard and the Gherkin. 'And if he's flying a wingsuit and using a back-up 'chute, he could be anywhere by now.'

But when William inspected the void below there was surely no way any jumper could survive. Whatever device you were skydiving with, there wasn't sufficient altitude to permit a landing, but there was more than enough height to dismember you from a fall.

Down and to the left, the ministerial cavalcade, surrounded by a forest fire of police lights, had begun to ease away. Philippa was heading back to Maida Vale and her home.

'ASU say there's nothing showing on infrared,' one of Gerrard's sergeants shouted.

'Tell 'em to spread the perimeter,' said the AC as he looked up and waved the chopper towards the Barclays building like an agitated football manager urging his players forward.

William's phone buzzed. She was texting him again.

Is our stalker barking mad?

Followed by: *Is he off the woof yet?*

Then: *Is this a paws?*

Then that bloody code again: *H9.*

He must find out what it meant. He imagined Philippa in the back of the hushed limo awaiting his response. A near-death experience probably turned her on. But almost being shot and facing the stalker had left him shuddering. He'd pretend to be too busy saving her life to text back.

'Okay, let's suppose that was the perp...' Gerrard turned to William, rubbing the scar on his chin. 'What the hell was it all about? He risks being shot just to jump up and down on a roof?'

The psychiatrist gulped for air.

'He doesn't think gravity or bullets apply to him, so he's got no fear,' William answered, halting between breaths. 'There's always a link between the most intense love and death. Think of Romeo and Juliet...'

'Romeo and Juliet? What on earth are you blithering on about?'

Gerrard turned away to his officers.

'Our shrink says it's all because our target's ego surfing.'

A chief superintendent followed Gerrard's backwards thumb and muttered something. The uniforms guffawed. William wasn't sure what joke had been shared but he did grasp that the officers were giddy with relief. To them it was getting clearer, nothing too dangerous had actually happened.

But the leap had been into death – and the suicidal were the most deadly stalkers of all.

'Listen, Gerrard, first came the notes, now there's going to be the gifts.'

'Come again?'

'If he's survived this, he's going to escalate,' warned William.

'What? Arrive by jet pack?'

'It could be he'll start sending her presents now, packages. It's possibly the next phase, and some can be really nasty – bits from cadavers, or dead animals, so we need to warn her...'

Gerrard coiled a confiding arm around William, pulling him aside.

'...including vials of blood or semen,' continued the psychiatrist, struggling against the policeman's grip. 'Obsessed fan Ricardo López mailed an acid squirting letter bomb to pop star Björk's London home...'

'These people...' Gerrard gestured at the procession of limousines below '...they don't want their pretty little heads bothered by this crap. So, no, we will *not* be disturbing Ms Foot with your alarmings.'

'But Gerrard...'

'We scan and search every package and letter arriving at her offices and homes. It's all in hand.' Gerrard pushed him away dismissively and returned to his officers.

William suddenly realised that up here they were free of the prying eyes of the press and dinner guests. Maybe that was why the rules of engagement had been tossed off the ledge.

4

All for freedom and for pleasure, nothing ever lasts forever
Everybody wants to rule the world

And then it came to her.

Let *them* sing it!

Dread thrust the microphone away from her and waved it at the audience. Their roar broke over her.

Welcome to your life.

She beckoned the stadium to sing into her mike.

There's no turning back.

She might be punch-drunk, but she could still swing. The giant Ferris wheel gingerly approached its apex. Everyone gets off here, the rasping entrails whispered.

We will find you.

The extended arm of the crane, on which a grape bunch of TV cameras was suspended, hurtled towards her then braked abruptly, the multiple lenses shimmering at her from only feet away. Even the camera crew was screwing with her. She fought a momentary temptation to dive into space and cling on to them – a departure even the musicians below might notice.

Already the audience was tiring of this new game, squirming in exasperation with their neighbours' lack of rhythm. Dread flinched. Would her voice return from the rest? Another bolt of inspiration. She would sing one line, and allow them to respond. They would chant back and forth. She would challenge them to a battle.

Turn your back on Mother Nature.

A pause, but then they got it, and they came back stronger than ever.

Everybody wants to rule the world!

The Ferris wheel rolled again and deposited her back at the

bottom. Voice was back, sort of, but now limbs, of all things, were reluctant to rejoin the party. What the hell was she to do? Part of her was begging to prostrate herself, flat on her back, right now, right here on the stage, embrace the solid landing and give up. But the other side, the dark menacing side, whispered, *You bottled your chance of the quick escape at the top of the wheel.* Now all the exits were closing down.

Huge breath and she ceremoniously flung the whip to one side. It slithered across the stage, and the bored tiger, limited by its gleaming steel chain, pounced on it. Barely glancing at the big cat, the pop star leapt outwards with a high kick. A startled gazelle in the opinion of the beast, too well fed to be tempted. Departing from the choreographed routine, she cavorted down the ski slope, cartwheeling. The dancers fell back bewildered, ad-libbing a joyful skip.

Nothing ever lasts forever.

The nickname the roadies give to the part of the centre stage that projects into the audience is 'ego ramp'. This thin platform tongue stretches out from the mouth of the theatre, relishing the sea of devotees crowding it.

Skirting the corners of Dread's eyes were the security staff in the dry moat between the ramp and the straining horde – their walkie-talkies raised to their mouths in concerned unison. Her chief of security's billiard ball head was rolling back and forth, spinning, trying to glean what on earth was going on.

Did I break your concentration? she questioned with grim satisfaction. *No one takes me for granted. Anything Avril Lavigne and The Jonas Brothers can do, I can do better.* One-handed cartwheels while clutching the microphone, followed by a high no-handed flip, mocked them all.

The spectators were fixed on her prancing head-over-heels antics. But on stage, the dancers and musicians exchanged drained looks and gestures with the uniformed army in the trench. What *was* she up to?

Everybody wants to rule the world.

She skidded to the end of the ski slope, to the siege that was the mob below. Inwardly grimacing, she teetered as she peered into a fifteen-foot drop. The blackened floor of the amphitheatre was a chasm, falling away on all sides. A moat of dead space, a few yards across, guarded her stage from barricades penning back spectators. Could the lights and cameras reach her in that deserted crevasse? Had she found a refuge in the midst of the glare?

There's a room where the light won't find you.

A cascade of camera flashes and mobile phones shot up like periscopes.

Without hesitation she rolled forward in a final graceful somersault to the sanctuary delivered by an instrumental interlude in the song.

The world spun into a blur.

Silence.

She had abandoned the safety that the stage offered.

A hundred thousand pairs of lungs held their breath.

A raven leap into the heart of thunder.

Both feet collided with the amphitheatre floor and her arms outstretched like a gymnast completing a routine. Sawdust erupted into a cloud of dust, and a stab of pain through her heels revived her.

The scrum bayed at their prey and very quickly oxygen rushed in. Back on stage the troupe edged forward, one eye from each peering over the rim, the other checking the video screens for her progress. A spear of light found her and she sparkled – a diamond discovered at the bottom of a shaft.

It was just like the old days. Fans' hands were stretching out desperately between the slats, trying to touch her. She reached back, fondling fingertips, feeling life. Down in the moat she realised that diving off the stage meant she had found her flock again, her meaning.

Her security head ran out into the gully in an attempt to block two TV cameramen who had been dispatched to get in close to this new source of action, their equipment hoisted onto their shoulders. One lens panned the jeering trampling crush, while the other was shoved in unexpectedly close to her face.

Hundreds pressed in, bearing down on her from all angles, testing the barrier. The crane camera was lowered over the melee, posting writhing images on to the giant screens fixed across the stadium. Fingers and phones pointed upwards at themselves, and the three sets of cameras began to film each other.

On the podium there were desperate looks – mounting horror at the departure from the routine. Had she fallen or jumped? Was she injured? Had the crowd broken through the barrier and surged over her?

No one had set up the lighting for this shot.

Agonised gestures and shouts came from the stage, but their instruments didn't falter a beat. Searchlights picked her out and camcorders blinked. Her lustrous image was projected on to the giant screens which flanked the stadium. She was down there, but up here as well. She was everywhere.

And nowhere.

Everybody wants to rule the world.

A shrill splintering sound. Something inside the barrier fractured and barked. Bodyguards swirled at the howl of objecting metal.

Dread was too busy nuzzling the closing lines of her song to notice.

Two sentries sprang to her side and tried to restrain her, but she didn't want to be brought back. She fought with them, her smallness ineffectual against their strength. They gradually lifted her on to their shoulders, frantically dragging her towards the side stage door.

They stopped abruptly.

The melee had grabbed her hands. Being pushed up on to the shoulders of her uniforms had brought her level with the rim of the fencing. Some spectators lapped over the edge. She felt herself being pulled into the scrimmage, bobbing and sinking. She bounced above, and then below the waves of humanity, floundering against an insistent undertow.

Her sense of life became fear, so she resisted, flailing against the tentacles pulling her in.

And then, how she'd got here came back to her. In the early days of the pubs and small clubs, when the fans were just a hand's length away, she used to think, *See Mum – I can do it. Yes, I can. I can make them want me. I can make them want us.*

As her career gained altitude, with every increased vastness of venue they'd all disappeared below. Falling further and further away, shedding payload like a rocket burning into the sky. But now everybody was back. Face to face. Back to the beginning. All over again.

She was slipping from the bodyguards, her sweat-soaked body greasy to their frantic clutch. It was tug-of-war, stretching her body over the top of the fence with a few on her side and 93,000 on the other. A pair of hands immobilised her arms in a vice, scrunching her long once-elegant gloves so they began to split. Shadows in the swarm embraced her – there was a reek of chafing oily skin.

But you can't treat me this way, she wanted to protest, *don't you know who I am?* Outrage filled her as she was sucked into the middle of the spiral, disappearing fast from her beach.

I can't stand this indecision.

And then she was gone.

5

Flowers every day
The cops they tell her to stay
500 feet away

William gazed around the fragrant luxury of Philippa's bedroom as Gerrard raged. It was a world away from his institutional National Health Service doctor's flat that was only really intended for nights on call.

'Have you any idea how much our budget is going to be squeezed now? I'm going to have to fill this street with uniforms. Simply because the stalker got in here.'

'Gerrard, relax, we've got him. Look...'

'Did you *listen* to the speech at Mansion House? She *gutted* us with her cuts,' Gerrard fumed as he closed the door on the Scene of Crime Officers and drew the bedroom curtains. In the sudden silence and gloom, Gerrard adjusted his ultraviolet lamp and pushed his forensic goggles on. The shimmering lenses reflected fluorescing pools of light bouncing off the bed from the UV torches.

William surmised that the AC was in deep trouble because the stalker had penetrated his tight security and enjoyed free play in the Minister's bedroom.

They stared at the roses the intruder had strewn over Philippa's duvet. Given how unsettling it must have been to walk in and find them there, Philippa was, unsurprisingly, incandescent. She had left for Parliament before they had arrived, but William could feel her fury at them in her absence.

Yet there again, he thought, beneath the outer armoured shell of bravado and defiance, Philippa was experiencing the psychological terror of being stalked. It was a kind of mental rape, which the police still didn't seem to get.

But Philippa had the benefit of Foreign Office Security

Protection – would she ever wonder what it was like for an ordinary woman who didn't?

'He decided to scatter the roses so it would be more artistic. More spontaneous,' said William as he gingerly circumvented the bed, crouching down, examining the room from alternative angles. 'He didn't want to leave,' he added.

'How do you know this?' Gerrard asked, inspecting the bedclothes.

William didn't answer as he scrutinised the wardrobes and cupboards. One brimmed with high heels in floor-to-ceiling clear plastic drawers. Another revealed mountains of leather handbags, lovingly wrapped in tissue paper. A musky, expensive odour wafted up from groomed hides when he pulled away the wrapping and peered into one.

The AC shook his head. 'The purses have all been checked and nothing was disturbed, but he rummaged through these drawers over here. Some, ah, undergarments are missing. Government papers she reads at night were undisturbed on the sideboard – nothing "Official Secrets Act" is missing.'

William ignored Gerrard's comment; it was the contents of the handbag which piqued his interest – a bathing cap, packet of mints, spray can air freshener, toothpaste, mouthwash and a toothbrush.

Suddenly Gerrard was by his side. 'So she likes to be prepared when she travels?' he asked suspiciously.

Hastily, William replaced the crocodile flap, recalling the other pieces in the jigsaw that was the Foreign Secretary's psyche, such as the amount of water Philippa had swigged during the banquet, and her short fingernails.

The pattern should have been blindingly obvious from the beginning, but he'd been distracted by the force of her attraction. In a strange way the stalker was exposing her dark side to him. And although he'd only been in her bedroom for a few minutes, William had worked out that she had secrets which he doubted even the prowler had twigged.

William wasn't surprised there was a clandestine side to Philippa's life. Despite their long conversations, she hadn't asked him anything about himself beyond the superficial – a clue that she had things to hide and didn't want to invite prying. People reveal how much they want to disclose about themselves by how little they ask about you.

'He isn't ready for proper contact yet,' said William. 'This, in his eyes, is the slow build, the curtain raiser.'

William examined drawers which had already been pulled out.

'You think you can reconstruct the scene?' Gerrard asked.

William shrugged. 'Pretty well. A certain type of stalker likes to break in and move stuff about so the target knows they were there. Sometimes just things in the fridge, so maybe only the wife realises, and when she complains the husband thinks she's mad.'

'But they don't take anything?'

'One I knew would break in and wash the dishes. This kind of thing can be very disturbing and the police don't take...'

'Listen, if all he's doing is washing the dishes, then when he's finished at her place, send him round to mine,' Gerrard smirked.

William shook his head. For him, stalkers held no amusement.

'In January 2012, when thirty-two-year-old Frank Tufaro travelled from the US to a remote Devon home, he broke in carrying a £3,000 ring he intended to give to the pop star he'd been obsessed with since he was a teenager but had never met.'

'Yeah, yeah, the Foreign Sec insisted I endure your Kate Bush seminar. Remember?'

William ignored him. 'However, after exploring inside, he left of his own volition when he found Kate wasn't in.'

'And how does all that help us?'

'It's kind of poetic. The roses. After all the precautions this particular stalker took, double gloving and everything, every letter, every note, forensically clean...here in her bedroom he could feel how close he was to her. Smell her perfume...'

William was thinking to himself that obsession is like a disease: it takes over the body.

'You almost feel sorry for these wack jobs, don't you,' the AC said contemptuously. But William was preoccupied with the fact an erotomaniac wouldn't keep their identity hidden, nor maybe even steal underwear. Was this a case more of morbid infatuation?

'Gerrard, this is the place where he drops his mask of sanity because he's now almost touching her, so he pricked himself spreading the roses, only he didn't realise it…'

'Yeah, yeah…my dick is so big it's in the next room making us drinks.'

William was resigned to Gerrard's assessment that the psychiatrist considered the police, indeed practically everyone, beneath him intellectually. This had all started when the psychiatrist had thrown up his arms on first arriving at FTAC to discover some of the police lower down the chain of command had been cataloguing and keeping the actual correspondence, quite correctly, but randomly discarding the envelopes in which the mad notes had been arriving, after forensically screening them for DNA, fingerprints and other physical evidence. Now William recalled that particular argument with a wince. Philippa had roundly told him off afterwards for humiliating her officers.

'But the envelopes reveal a key clue as to the mental state of the stalker and how dangerous they are.'

William remembered how he had begun.

With long-suffering patience.

'You what?' Gerrard had defended himself. 'There was nothing on these envelopes but a printed address.'

'Oh yes there was.'

'Oh no there wasn't.'

'It's a thing on all envelopes. C'mon, Gerrard, think.'

'You've lost me. There's postage and, in this case, a printed address for Philippa, which doesn't help us much. That's it. There was no salivary DNA under the stamp either.'

'Nooo, this is useful to anyone screening crank mail for dangerously hostile motives in the sender, because this is a signifier that is practically always on post sent by an individual.'

'Will you stop playing silly buggers and get on with it.'

'It's a thing called a postmark. Postmarks include a date and corresponding post town to give an indication of when and where a particular item was sorted. Postmarks are always on letters with stamps because the Royal Mail needs to signify the stamp has been used, and cannot be reused.'

'And how does that help us? It doesn't narrow the address of the target that much. Besides he could've mailed it miles from his home to cover himself. Knowing the sorting office won't help us nail the bastard.'

'All true, Gerrard, except it's the pattern that unlocks this one. Always look for a pattern. If all the letters arrive with the same postmark, indicating they've gone through the same post office or sorting office, then that tells you he's obsessing about his target, writing letters, then popping down to the same local postbox. It's a kind of almost homely routine. But, if the postmarks are all different, as these ones here are, then that's a different scheme. It reveals wherever he is – going shopping, commuting to work, travelling on holiday – spread across a wide geographical range, he's fixated on the target, and he *can't get her out of his head*. So he's dropping letters in postboxes all over the place. It's a measure of obsession, and a predictor that he's going to make physical contact. Oddly enough the presence, or absence, of actual threats in such correspondence doesn't appear to foretell accurately whether the infatuation is going to turn into more dangerous pursuit behaviour.'

'You've lost me, mate, but if you want to keep all the envelopes from now on, you be my guest. Where are we going to get the extra staff for this new exercise in futility?'

Philippa and William had flared at each other across the table in Downing Street, strewn with crank mail, while Gerrard fulminated.

'What?' William had asked her after the fractious meeting.

'Try and be less of a complete arse with the police, otherwise…' Philippa had seethed as she left, flicking her necklace. She would also twist the ribbon of jewels around her fingers, a mannerism which seemed to be prompted particularly by William's presence.

Tullia d'Aragona, William's head of department and a former psychoanalyst, had explained the gesture as suggesting the Foreign Secretary unconsciously wanted to strangle someone.

But that was all weeks ago, and now the psychiatrist triumphantly believed he had been proven right. The proof was the roses on her bed. So, up here in her bedroom now, William pressed on.

'…maybe because of the gloves, maybe because he was too distracted. And we – sorry *you* – now can get a DNA match off that speck of blood on the thorn. And we've got him.'

William could hear his voice cracking under the strain of keeping everything strictly scientific. Once the stalker was apprehended, would Philippa have any further use for him?

'You're banking there'll be a match in a database.'

'There's a fair chance.' William nodded. 'He certainly seems to know the system pretty well. I think he's probably had some kind of prior with forensic science.'

'How'd you reckon that?'

'Well, the American law enforcement establishment used to believe there were two main kinds of people who are a threat to public figures, and the US Secret Service termed them "hunters" and "howlers".'

Gerrard's goggles jerked up. He was beginning to see the significance of the stalker's baying on the roof of Mansion House.

'Hunters are supposedly deadly serious and fully intend to kill or harm. You've heard of Robert Bardo in the US?'

'Yeah, he stalked some actress, didn't he?'

'Rebecca Schaeffer, who starred in a sitcom, *My Sister Sam*, from 1986 to 1988. Bardo was infatuated with the childlike character she played, but when she turned to raunchier roles, he felt betrayed, so he shot her in '89. He's supposed to be a classic hunter, but in fact he had written hundreds of letters to her, and tried to get on to the film set where she was working – just like a howler. When he tried to visit her at Warner Brothers Studios, he was carrying flowers and gifts, but also had a large knife hidden on him.'

'But he was really a hunter?'

'The Americans got it all wrong with their classification system. Bardo *started* out a howler, and *then* became a hunter.'

'So which one is our guy?'

'A howler is meant to be someone who sends messages, intending to get a reaction from a public figure or perhaps draw attention to themselves, but he never follows through on the threat. So, you see, when he was up on the roof, howling, this stalker was sending us a communication. He knew that we'd promptly recognise the technical meaning of "howler" in the field of stalking. For some reason he wants us to know he's also on the inside of the knowledge circle, perhaps trying to show off he's more of an expert than the rest of us.'

'Semen fluoresces too...'

'Only the blood is the stalker's.'

Gerrard examined the torch, as if hoping there was another adjustment that could be made to its beam of unseen energy. It had, after all, inadvertently revealed the history of the Foreign Secretary's recent sex life. But also, of course, that the stalker had left a bloodstain.

William quickly checked another handbag. Sure enough, inside was the same kit. This had nothing to do with being prepared for travel.

'Okay, okay, how'd you know he didn't do anything more sordid here?' Gerrard demanded.

William grimaced. He had a sudden flashback to Philippa running through costume options with him in the living room. She had waved away a pair of shiny patent leathers he was handing over.

'Not those. Those are for bedroom use only. *Those* over there. Honestly!'

William tried to refocus. He had been banging on that this stalking was obsessive lust, but Gerrard seemed to be hoping it was terrorism. Presumably because that would procure him more helicopters.

'Oh dear, you're just not getting him, are you,' William said impatiently. 'This is a courtship and you've got to understand what stage we've reached in his mind.'

'Okay, listen up,' Gerrard said. 'We're going to send the bedspread and the flowers for testing, but we're going to file them under a codename, so just you and I know whose they are and... for God's sake, why are you lurking by her bags?'

Gerrard was presumably trying to fathom how the psychiatrist could have foreseen the minuscule accident of the interloper pricking himself on a thorn. It wasn't usual to perform a UV scan at this kind of crime scene, and Gerrard had at first resisted the psychiatrist's perplexing demands. But it was pure coincidence that the ultraviolet had shown up the stalker's microscopic blood clot on the thorn of a rose. William had wanted to bathe her bed in UV light because he wanted to settle, for his own purposes, whether the gossip columns were right about the delicious Philippa's bedroom politics.

She was linked via press insinuations to a variety of alpha-males in Parliament and outside. But Philippa confided that it was her billionaire husband's divorce lawyers who lay behind the hearsay, so they had money to throw at the mission of smearing her. Whoever the unidentified sources were of the innuendo, her adversaries in Parliament, and there seemed to be as many in her own party as on the other side, were busy using the whispers to plot her political demise.

She was taking hits from all sides.

Now, if he was lucky with the DNA databases, forensic science was going to tell him just who she'd been fooling around with.

It was gossip column gold.

But he had to carry on the act that he had envisaged the stalker screwing up. The police believed he was some kind of weirdo psychic as it was.

'Gerrard, the only thing on the duvet which belongs to the stalker is the blood, trust me. But we're going to have to ask her about that as well.' William gestured to the wall behind Gerrard.

The AC spun round.

'What?'

'There's a picture missing and I think our stalker took it.'

William had been following the trail of ebony framed black and white photographs all the way from the living room. Each one was of the Foreign Secretary adorned by a celebrity.

On the ground floor, plainly for public consumption, were images of Philippa beaming out as Mandela seemed to be almost nuzzling her hair, and Obama looking pleased with himself for making her laugh. In the atrium was Hollande nervously checking on his current partner as the Foreign Secretary cosied up to the French President. Clinton was writing something down – her private number perhaps?

'She never said that anything on the walls was taken!' the AC said.

'She won't have noticed,' William responded. 'She was probably too preoccupied with the roses on her bed.'

'How d'you know it's missing? Neither of us have been in here before.'

Up the stairs the dictators marched, Middle Eastern and African potentates, arms folded, and here Philippa was more demure, embarrassed perhaps to have just signed some weapons deal? Those pictures must have been from when she spent that frustratingly long time at the Ministry of Defence, before securing promotion to the Foreign Office.

Black and white photography didn't do her justice. It didn't capture the flecks of burnt sienna in her hair, though each frame did reveal she had found yet another fresh way of blushing, nearly always with her gaze.

'If you look at these other walls you can see they've been arranged according to a pattern, and that would mean there should be one there. But look, a hook with nothing on it.'

When they had reached the landing and approached the privacy of the upper floors, William had noted who she felt genuinely intimate with. Actors, elite athletes and Formula One drivers jostled to get into her bedroom. And here in the inner sanctum, sweaty and hairy-looking rock stars obligingly screamed something for the camera, while Philippa grinned mischievously into the lens.

He might be newly recruited into FTAC, the elite unit designated to protect high-profile public figures from stalking intimidations, but were there hints from the Mansion House evening that she might be progressing William from purely identifying and neutralising the culprit into more general hand-holding?

That night had been a key turning point in the mind of the stalker, but in a way, had it been one for Philippa and him too?

'Trust me, he's taken a picture, and it's important to find out which one it is. *Who* it is.'

'Okay, you ask her…she likes you,' Gerrard said.

William brightened at the thought: this was valuable intelligence.

'She says you remind her of Hugh Grant in *Four Weddings*.'

His craving for her appeared to be surviving the onslaught of the totalitarian regimes storming the staircase.

Then he sank into gloom again.

The SOCOs had found no signs of forced entry, so one theory would be that the intruder knew the layout of her home well enough to bypass her extra security. William was beginning to wonder if he was a former intimate. Because, of all the different types of stalkers, ex-lovers were the most likely to become violent in any future pestering. But until now, this pursuer had seemed either more psychotic, or suffering from some kind of sexual deviance.

'So let me get this straight: the reason this punk, who hasn't put a foot wrong to date, pricked himself in his agitation was…'

Gerrard ruffled his resistant hair.

'…that he shared the excitement of the voyeur,' William explained. 'Peeping Toms have an itch that can never be scratched because they believe something is forever being hidden from them.'

And then there was the contents of the handbag. William needed a peek at her kitchen to confirm his qualms that Philippa was covering up something from him, and perhaps even hiding it from herself. But how to engineer that inspection elsewhere in the house without arousing the AC's suspicions?

Especially as the psychiatrist was getting a sense that Philippa didn't forgive easily – just like her friends on the stairs.

6

Fire in the sky
Smoke on the water

Dread glimpsed the camera crane flying low and long over the throng, probing each face, frantically trying to locate her. The whirlpool of the audience encircled her, spectators rising up in their tiers, mountainous waves threatening to crash down and pulverise her.

She wrestled to lift a waving hand. *I'm over here!* The searchlight, which normally found her so easily, scurried helplessly across the amphitheatre, a terrier that had lost its owner.

The cameras towed away in the melee continued to broadcast, their transmitted images rocking the big screens. A blow from the side painfully twisted her head away and she lost the flicker of what they were displaying next. She wondered groggily where the blow had come from – one of her fans? Seriously?

The fighting for possession of her became increasingly desperate. A faction realised she was frightened. So this wasn't another stunt. Now the hard hands squeezing her found resistance. Others worked to prise the gripping fingers, then wild punches thumped the air. A clammy, fleshy reek pinched her nostrils. The baying scowls surrounding her seemed to vomit something sticky in her face.

Blood!

But was it her own?

She was drowning in a salty sea of fleshy tissue. Expecting to slam into the stadium floor at any moment, she braced herself, imagining being trampled on. But then she was grabbed by her Alexander McQueen costume, and it ripped as she was flung away. She gazed numbly at her own limbs, which flopped about like a fish out of water.

Dread was being clawed apart.

The band's industrial sound reverberated back at her from the ground, competing with her thoughts. It was impossible to concentrate on calling for help when rodent hands scurried up and down her legs. Her body was being invaded by crab-like parasites probing to enter.

The radio pack, tightly wound against her and strapped to the small of her back, was being worked loose by scratching from all sides. The earpieces abruptly lost sound. Moulded tightly to her canals, when not picking up frequency, they shut out the world.

Besieging her were angry baying faces and thumping fists, but everything fell surreally silent.

Two thoughts.

First she'd be raped. Then killed.

Warm body fluids and beer spattered the air. She was sinking for a final time, staring up at a crushing army of legs menacing towards her. Instinctively she shielded her head with her arms from the inevitable stabbing of all those feet...

Without sound, none of it seemed real.

There's magic in my eyes, I know you've deceived me, now here's a surprise.

From somewhere close by, a new lyric whispered, *I can see for miles and miles...* The voice fluttered the lines, strangely disembodied from the chaos overwhelming her, *...and miles and miles.*

She was zeroing in on the source when her earpieces were ripped through her hair, and the clamour of the stadium broke over her.

What the hell were those words? Strong, clear and menacing. But also intimate. She couldn't make them out above the shriek of the mob and the yells of her panicked security guards.

Fingers were scurrying, frantically undoing the clasps, clips and clutches that kept her body gripped by fashion. The radio pack was finally prised loose and she twisted and turned to evade the creepy crawlies. Still in time to the beat, her brain refused to accept that the concert had jumped tracks and was skidding off the turntable.

I can see for miles and miles and miles and miles.

41

7

Nothing is more dangerous
Than desire when it's wrong

The speck of blood on the rose thorn had produced a match on the DNA database. As the crime scene specialists were now finishing up their forensic examination of the target's location, the AC and William were being shown into the council flat of the blood's donor, who'd been identified as a man called David Lewis.

Surveillance revealed that the stalker was out. And because Gerrard Winstanley was convinced that David Lewis must be involved in some kind of political conspiracy, rather than being just the mere "love obsessive" William had diagnosed, the plan had changed to keeping tabs on the target rather than arresting him.

William had felt Gerrard's disappointment when David turned out to be living alone in a council flat, and wasn't part of a buzzing Al Qaeda cell with fertiliser bags coming and going. But the AC now wanted to keep the stalker under observation rather than blow his head off.

None of it made sense to William.

This stalker must be high IQ, and expert in academic criminal psychology – his awareness of the whole hunter/howler distinction proved that – and he'd told them as much with his behaviour on the roof of Mansion House. He was also probably at least an acquaintance of Philippa and familiar with her home. Cognisant enough to get in without forced entry, and so relaxed while there that he'd taken the time to scatter roses artistically over her duvet. The bedroom crime scene was covered in the kind of psychological fingerprints that suggested he'd been there before. But was he also psychotic enough to jump up and down on the roof of Mansion House, and then suicidally fly off the side? For no apparent rational purpose whatsoever?

The psychological profile just didn't add up.

William made the mistake of confessing his confusion to Gerrard, who leapt on the psychiatrist's doubts triumphantly. Good old-fashioned police work by matching DNA samples from the blood speck on the rose thorn was, of course, the answer, he declaimed. Not psychobabble.

So, thirty-six hours after Mansion House, the police and William had slipped in for a reconnaissance while David was camping outside Philippa Foot's constituency office along with the permanent ragtag army of anti-war demonstrators.

The police telephoto lenses had revealed an unremarkable-looking apparently middle-aged man, bedecked in political badges, straggly beard, hunched under a ragged baseball cap, silent among the chanting protesters, slouching resolutely in the middle of the rabble, making the only photograph possible one from the helicopter high above. Gerrard, however, was pleased that he could weave the aircraft into his report on how they caught David.

Security agencies had infiltrated the anti-war groups so comprehensively that the stalker was doubtless currently surrounded by more plainclothes double agent officers than bona fide demonstrators. Yet none of their hidden cams had got a decent picture either. William became full of foreboding about stalking the stalker. Forensic psychiatric analysis indicated you intervened rapidly – the longer you waited in this kind of case, the more dangerous it became.

William felt his way into the heavy blackness of David Lewis's lair. There was only a brief window of opportunity to gather data which would reveal David's true mental state. The AC was in constant radio contact with the officers currently keeping David under surveillance. He was parading up and down outside the Foreign Secretary's constituency abode, oblivious to the forensics team covertly entering his own residence to gather evidence.

But the moment their target got fed up demonstrating and turned for home, they would be alerted and have to vacate fast, ensuring he didn't return too quickly and bump into them before they had time to get out.

Which would be awkward.

Assembling evidence before any psychotic's detention was a chance too remarkable to pass up. In cases like the Norwegian mass killer, Anders Breivik, and the American Unabomber, Theodore Kaczynski, many people were slaughtered, but the court-appointed psychiatrists still fought with each other afterwards, clouding the diagnosis – partly because they were too reliant on prison interviews with these disturbed and manipulative minds.

David had removed the light bulbs in his flat and taped black bin bags to all the windows. He'd also soundproofed the rooms so noise was swallowed by the blackness.

High intensity beams from the police torches criss-crossed the gloom, throwing slanted shadows around them. Gnarled objects loomed up out of the nothingness, and William would flashback to searing images from previous cases.

But as more searchlights came to bear, the illuminations would transform into something more mundane. The furniture was shabby but, so far, there wasn't anything like, for example, the homemade acid bomb that Ricardo López filmed himself making, the video of which he then posted to the pop singer Björk in 1996 before killing himself, while still on camera. Indeed, there wasn't even any filming or surveillance equipment decorating this spookily desolate place.

'You never explained how you'd worked out he'd be fifty-five years old,' said Gerrard.

The AC's voice was muffled behind a handkerchief. Following the accuracy of yet another of William's predictions, the AC now seemed to be taking the prospect of dead animals and cadaver parts decorating the flat more seriously.

'I didn't say he'd be fifty-five, just that he'd in all likelihood be over fifty. If you know his precise age, then that must have shown up on the database with the DNA match. But what database was that? And what else d'you know about him?'

But Gerrard wasn't answering. So the police were keeping things back from William, just as the Foreign Secretary was. She had been evasive about the missing picture. *The plot thickens*, William decided.

Gerrard had claimed that the forensics lab was experiencing difficulties decoding separate individual DNA profiles from the mixtures of various other body fluids found on the Foreign Secretary's bed, hence the continued delay on those results. The possible implications of this discovery for a more furtive side to Philippa, William found too disturbing to dwell on. He had to get her out of his head.

But the lab could definitively confirm that David Lewis had indeed been in the bedroom, yet all he'd left of himself was the fleck of blood when he'd unknowingly pierced himself on the rose thorn.

'The DNA can't target his age – so how did you?' Gerrard persisted.

'His notes to Philippa might have been thought-disordered and rambling, but they were beautifully punctuated,' replied William. 'So he clearly hadn't suffered from a lack of education. I suspect he may even have been schooled abroad – somewhere the old way of teaching grammar was still used, such as a former colony.'

William's mouth dried up. There was a warm sticky smell that had a metallic edge, a human smell of neglect. William knew it well from entering flats where a patient suffering from schizophrenia had died weeks before anyone noticed.

'Ralph Nau, who stalked Olivia Newton-John, once cut open a cow that had died on his family's farm, and spent the night sleeping inside the animal's body,' William muttered to himself more than anyone else.

'If he was schooled abroad then there's even more reason to wait and see what he does,' Gerrard said eagerly. 'A quick arrest might block us tracking down the rest of his overseas collaborators. We want the cell and its connections, not just this cog.'

'But a love obsessive works alone,' complained William, exasperated. 'Anyone else would be competition.' He was almost relieved to discern in the torchlight piles of newspaper cuttings featuring Philippa. And none of them in Arabic.

Gerrard demanded to know why the windows were blacked out.

William shrugged. 'Schizophrenics who've become convinced

the aliens, the intelligence services or just the neighbours are transmitting messages, rays or voices into their brains do this kind of thing. They're trying to protect themselves.'

The light bulb removal had been a new one on William, though he didn't say so. And when some of the officers went back outside to secure more powerful illumination, William stopped a constable from pulling back a blind. If anything was disturbed, David would know.

William also wanted urine samples from the bathroom for lab analysis, but results from the onsite dipstick indicated that the stalker had been imbibing Chlorpromazine as well as a cocktail of Class A drugs. Substance abuse elevated the risk of violence to Philippa.

'If he's on medication, then some doctor must have diagnosed him,' said William. 'But it's a strange choice, a positively ancient drug for psychosis. That might indicate he's been receiving therapy for an inordinately long time.'

'And you claimed the treatment your boys dish out works!'

'And you never told me which database he came up on.'

'Why soundproof the place?' Gerrard asked, continuing to keep his cards close to his chest. 'He's obviously worried his conversations with fellow conspirators will be overheard next door.'

William hid his frustration with the AC's delusion. *Could I persuade Gerrard to try one of David's tablets?* he wondered.

'Nooo, people who begin to hear voices are often convinced they're emanating from outside their gnomes – sorry – homes. Leading to excessive or irrational soundproofing.' William gestured at the black taping outlining the windowsill. 'This could be an indirect sign of auditory hallucinations. Patients often deny the symptom to doctors, fearing they'll be committed to hospital.'

'I see,' Gerrard said. 'He *looks* like a conspirator, he *behaves* like a conspirator, but we mustn't let that fool us!'

An inspector, more attuned than William to the AC's fixations, said, 'But at least this means we could bring the chopper in, and he won't hear it.'

Gerrard clapped him on the shoulder in hearty approval.

The AC must be banking that the fugitive at large could help save his helicopter fleet. The Prime Minister had put the Foreign Secretary's usual spin on "efficiency savings" during the Mansion House speech. Everyone was going to have to make sacrifices to fund the war in the Congo, and Gerrard might have to lose one of his beloved helicopters. Longer term, they were all going to be replaced by drones. Gerrard had been muttering about it ever since.

Now he was mouthing to himself, checking David's bedroom.

Then they found duct tape and handcuffs.

'It's a rape kit,' William interjected before Gerrard could draw any hasty conclusions. The psychiatrist was directly reminded of similar tackle found in the car, and on the person, of a man who attempted to break into film director Steven Spielberg's home, and who had even claimed to security that he was the adopted son of the film director as another way of trying to get inside.

The AC half grinned. *He still finds me an entertainment,* the psychiatrist decided, but rape, along with all the other disturbing phenomena the constabulary and psychiatrists encountered daily can brutalise. William loathed the casual way his colleagues in medicine and the services joked about this terrible stuff. Yet he also understood it was a defence mechanism.

Then Gerrard spotted pictures of Philippa plastered all over one bedroom wall, and the grin vanished.

'The duct tape and handcuffs aren't necessarily to rape Philippa,' William said. 'In the case of Jonathan Norman, indicted of stalking Steven Spielberg back in 1997, the stalker had planned to rape Spielberg after breaking into his home, and use the restraints to force the director's wife to watch...'

William trailed off as Gerrard gestured. All the photographs were from celebrity glossies, and every one had her mouth cut out.

Multiple snapshots of Philippa mouthlessly gaped at them.

'What the...' exclaimed Gerrard.

William went in closer to inspect how David had removed the mouths. Were they surgically etched, or hacked in an agitated state?

'Just because you act mad, doesn't mean you *are* mad, as Dr Paul Bowden testified in the Dennis Nilsen case. Keeping heads in the fridge and getting the bodies out from under the floorboards for the occasional cuddle, or worse, might seem mad, but in fact Nilsen wasn't.'

The officers traded weary glances as William pursued yet another mini-dissertation. At times like these he appeared to be talking to himself. Gerrard got on the walkie-talkie to check David was still far enough away they didn't have to evacuate his flat. He almost seemed to demand the target should come home now so that William could then be duct taped and bundled out.

'On the other hand, just because you can plan scrupulously and seem normal on the surface doesn't mean you're sane. To some degree, it's the opposite. Which killers engage in the most painstaking planning? By and large, it is the psychotic ones.' He shook his head at the team of operatives installing tiny hidden cameras into the wall sockets. 'Aren't you concerned he might have anticipated that, Gerrard?'

'Huh?' responded Gerrard. 'Do you honestly think he jumps up and down howling like a…a wolf, and is bothered about covert surveillance technology?'

'What, with the radios in every room to drown out microphones and the lights taken out? What kind of image are the spy cams going to get? I told you, he's got some kind of prior relationship with the science of stalking.'

'Maybe, but we're setting up a unit next door to use Backscatter X-ray which doesn't need light and can see through walls. We're going to get the evidence that he's connected, no matter how hard he's tried to hide it. And if you're so clever, Doctor, explain all these chopped up pictures of Philippa.'

But William didn't know why David had disfigured Philippa's face, though he could tell that David had been careful and thorough as he had edged her lips.

Then they found graffiti scrawled across another wall.

It read, *Who screws that pretty angel?*

'There! You see? He *is* planning to rape Philippa!' Gerrard triumphantly pointed out the words, and the psychiatrist wondered what the hell had happened to the terrorist cell theory from a few minutes ago.

Again William had to shake his head.

'Actually, it raises a question as to how interested in Philippa he really is.'

'Why?'

'Because the sentence is an anagram of *The Actress Gwyneth Paltrow*.'

Gerrard stared at the words and then back at William.

'Relax,' William said wryly. 'I'm not some kind of autistic savant who can unlock a word puzzle in seconds – this kind of crap is all over the Internet. And Paltrow was the victim of a case that didn't receive that much attention because her legal team took it to an obscure court in California to avoid press attention. Dante Michael Soiu was a fifty-one-year-old unemployed man who began sending the actress bizarre mail such as a vibrating penis with the words *Cause I love you* written on it. He got arrested after visiting her family and her home on several occasions.'

'Yeah, but did they really need a shrink to work out he was a few fries short of a Happy Meal?' asked Gerrard, returning to the slashed pictures. 'Why the mouths? I thought these weirdoes always went for the eyes.'

Oh dear, a little knowledge is a terrible thing.

William realised that Gerrard was recalling a case the psychiatrist had recounted in a recent briefing for the constabulary: Michael Perry had become fixated with actress and singer Olivia Newton-John ever since her movie *Xanadu* in 1980, developing various bizarre delusions, including that she was imprisoned and needed liberating by him.

Perry apparently became convinced that Newton-John sent messages to him through her eyes, possibly by them changing colour, and that she was responsible for dead bodies rising through the floor of his home. Camping out near where she lived in order to pursue her, he eventually murdered five of his relatives, including his mother and father and an infant nephew, by shooting them through the eyes. It was alleged that when he was apprehended, there were seven TVs in the room with him, each tuned to noisy static, but with eyes he had drawn on their screens.

Michael Perry's case wasn't relevant to this one in William's opinion. Instead he was developing another theory, but decided to keep it to himself for now, given how easy it was to confuse the police.

The vast majority of people suffering a psychotic illness were, for various reasons, harmless. But cases like these, grabbing headlines, featured disproportionately in the press, distorting views of the dangerousness of mental illness. Basically every case needed a meticulous psychiatric assessment before jumping to conclusions.

Dante Soiu had believed that Gwyneth Paltrow's spirit visited and talked to him. While out shopping he'd hear Paltrow whispering romantic messages, talking to him from her pictures on the front of celebrity magazines in the racks at supermarkets.

'The longer any stalking goes on, the more likely the stalker is psychotic – this we already know. What we don't know is if we've found David's real hideout.'

'What are you talking about? Look around you!' the AC exclaimed, exasperated.

A burst of static from one of Gerrard's lieutenants' handsets, and the plain-clothes officer turned to them abruptly.

'Sir, David Lewis has called it a day outside the Foreign Sec's place. He's returning now – we've got to leave stat!'

The team began to filter out hastily.

William was being hustled away when he became distracted by the pasted up pictures of Philippa gently stirring in the air. David had only bothered to stick the top part of each clipping to the walls, so the bottom halves were being gently fanned up and down, glinting in the torchlight as officers hurried from the room.

She seemed to be staring and frowning at him.

At the doorway William put a hand on the frame and turned back to Gerrard, resisting being pushed.

'We can't leave right now.'

'What? Go, go, go!'

'Where is that missing photograph from Philippa's room, and where is the underwear he took?'

8

Lipstick cherry all over the lens as she's falling
Girls on Film

Unexpectedly, Dread was free. A current tossed her back over the broken barrier into the arms of the security staff. Her torso felt different, as if she had left part of it behind in the stampede. She had lost one of her long white gloves, but from the bruised feeling all over, it could have been a limb. Right at the end of her other arm, her hand was still knotted over the microphone, but she was so numb, there was no reaction to the taut grip.

Bringing the microphone to her lips brought sharp pain. She grabbed her elbow and screeched in agony. The audience bellowed back.

She looked at her hand. Something dark and sticky…

The security scrum placed her gently on the ground and turned to shore up the leaning barrier, heaving against it with shoulders and backs while tons of human pressure steamed up behind the small group.

Walkie-talkies were deployed.

'Dread is down! We need an ambulance crew out here! Dread is down! Repeat, Dread is down!'

Some dazed and injured fans were helped over the fence and taken away, limp, in the hands of the crew. Everyone was panting at a frenetic rate. The surge forward crashed too many people against the barrier. The railings groaned, then, screaming in fury, began to collapse.

Kwame, a towering black man who headed security, sprang out and scooped Dread to his side like an American footballer clasping a ball.

'Hang on!' he bellowed as he darted towards the sanctuary of the doors at the side of the stage.

It seemed a very long way away.

The bulging fence dividing them from the mob felt like it was toppling. She could sense the crowd gathering behind breaking over, like waves beating at a weakening flood defence.

The barricade over to Kwame's side rippled, the apex following them. Now it ripped, skin peeling back, revealing people gushing through. Splintering metal parts showered them; the shrieking drowned the electric guitars. Kwame accelerated as the bodies spilled on to the floor behind him.

Using his other hand, Kwame shoved those scratching at them. Grabbing his neck to help him carry her, Dread hitched herself further up his chest as he gathered speed, digging his way through the wall of humanity. Behind them, hundreds of fans were exploding through the barrier.

She wanted to shout, 'Careful! Look behind you!' but her voice failed her yet again. Kwame hurdled bodies that flailed across the floor as she bounced like a rag doll.

The other security staff formed a wall of protection as they scampered alongside. Backstage crew held the refuge door open, their beckoning frantic hands reaching out to help bring them in. For the first time, Dread believed they might make it.

Glancing back, she found herself staring into a face. Some unearthly aerial demon had caught up with them and was looming over the head of her soaring chief of security. Its bulging irises focused on the back of Kwame's head and it was about to swing something down on him when its swollen eyes darted to her and its elbows paused mid arc.

Kwame was tall. This demon hovering over him and about to wallop his oblivious head was either gigantic, or flying like a vampire.

Dread thrust the sharp end of the microphone crazily and felt it penetrate something spongy. A wordless yelp and the figure fell behind them, clutching its face. The microphone left her quivering fingers, rumbled, then died. The other fans fell over the demon's body, and it disappeared under writhing limbs.

9

The hunter gets captured by the game
I was in your arms, and I knew I had been captured

Two more police vans arrived. Their roof light bars flickered, then died. William peered at his watch through the dripping rain, wiping its face to uncover it was now three o'clock in the morning. How many more officers were going to have their leave cancelled by Gerrard?

A caravan of police vehicles converged in a circle around the psychiatrist.

'Roll up, roll up, come inside, come inside, welcome my friends, for this godawful show that never ends,' William mumbled, hunching against the drenching. He felt part of a carnival troupe, complete with jugglers and dwarves, fidgeting as they waited to enter the big top.

At this desperate hour the streets resembled a freak show, in particular the motley mixture of reporters and pedestrians pressing against the crash barriers. Who loitered out in this torrent just to watch legions of police criss-crossed by shivering crime scene tape?

Only an audience for the grotesque. And they looked the part.

A canteen truck surrounded by bored officers, trying to warm themselves up with tea, should be dispensing popcorn.

'Really?' William spluttered. 'Really?' This circus was beyond his comprehension.

He vainly pulled his coat collar up against the steadily falling sleet. The police were handling the case catastrophically – they had planted the helicopter on the ground right here.

So they even had their own elephant.

The Assistant Commissioner was moving away from the

journalist he'd been briefing on the far side of the aircraft. David Lewis, their quarry, was burrowed in his shambolic council block flat, about to be flushed out by a gun-toting squad wielding tear gas. The throng of police, press and public were like hushed theatregoers awaiting the grand entrance of the star turn. William was becoming concerned – was it possible that David was orchestrating this?

Was he in fact directing the spectacle more than the authorities realised?

'Frances Wright. She's a war journalist,' said Gerrard as he indicated the reporter's sodden army jacket. 'She pitched this documentary idea to me: the war on the streets, how some parts of London have become no-go areas…good, huh?'

Gerrard Winstanley was now gripped by the vice of starring in his own TV show.

'If she's a war correspondent how come she's not out in the Congo?' William hissed back.

'She was. Frances Wright has flown back just for me!'

William weighed up the reasons the AC was turning the operation into a media extravaganza. Was the reporter Gerrard's ace, to be used against Philippa's helicopter culling? The rest of the press village, cordoned off down the road, strained to hear any titbit.

William shook his head soberly. 'Gerrard, patients suffering from psychosis, presented with a choice between an apparently clear exit or massed ranks armed to the teeth, are more likely to hurl themselves at the security lines, grabbing anything that might count as a weapon. This may not make for a good opening shot…'

But Gerrard had already turned his back.

William edged to put the cabin of the helicopter between him and the reporter. But this made him more visible to the entrance to David Lewis's flat, a quarter of a mile away across a vast car park the police had emptied. Was David peering out at him right now?

'Don't forget we might need a quote for later,' said Gerrard, turning his back on the psychiatrist. 'Let's just try not to make the answer to every question "because of his mother".'

'The experiment requires that you continue,' William muttered under his breath.

'Isn't that a line from Stanley Milgram's *Obedience to Authority* experiments?' The journalist had slunk up on William. He jerked round to stare at her. She was suspiciously well informed. The damp sparkled around her dark eyes so they seemed to glitter, but William could also detect a light burning inside. Obsession.

He now recalled that he knew her. Well, he didn't *know* her, he knew of her, and he'd seen her at a BAFTA awards ceremony he had attended with the Minister. Philippa had chattered relentlessly at him throughout, distracting him from the podium formalities.

But he recalled Frances accepting her gong in a slinky sequin top which she dropped off her shoulders when she got to the stage, revealing a grim T-shirt underneath emblazoned with: *The National Security Agency – the only part of Government that really listens'.* The image above the stencilled protest advertised the Foreign Secretary wearing wrap-around mirror shades and flourishing a machine gun.

William remembered, in the pop of flashguns at the podium, an arresting elfin-like face with limpid eyes stealing mischievous glances, as if Frances was hoping someone would liven up the evening and out-prank her.

As she dodged the photographers while trying to get back to her table, the journalist had waved her fist, with an enticing giggle, at a gaggle of reporters brandishing boom mikes at her, in some kind of obscure media in-joke.

Yes, this was that left wing journalist who always appeared cack-handed, Philippa had explained sourly, but who was indeed a razor-sharp interrogator. Her comment suggested that the Foreign Sec had been a target in the past. Apparently Frances would let the boom mike bob into shot to create an aura of bumbling chaos which lowered her subject's defences, but the shambling was fake.

He remembered that the Foreign Office table had all turned to frown at Frances as she strode past them to her seat.

'That hair-cut is so lesbian,' Philippa had whispered.

'Yeah,' Frances said, now looking a lot less charismatic and more like a drowned rat, 'isn't that what the people who believed they were administering deadly electric shocks to an actor were told when they looked uncomfortable about proceeding?'

She must have been researching him, burrowing about in his academic publications.

'It was a famous social psychology experiment in the sixties? Yes? C'mon, Doc,' she persisted, 'they didn't know it was a bit of theatre and the actor was safe. They thought they were killing him, didn't they.' She moved away as Gerrard waved her over.

'This Eurocopter 145 is one of three we have in the Met. Any fugitive is usually more obvious from these eyes in the sky,' the AC boasted as she reached him. 'This is the actual one we're using for the Care for Congo extravaganza in Hyde Park. If you want a dry run over the park before the big day, let me know.' Gerrard seemed desperate to regain her undivided attention. 'You get a great view now of all the construction and I can explain our crowd control strategy.'

'Is he the shrink who's advising you on this case?' asked Frances, gesturing towards William.

The psychiatrist kept his distance. William was wary of journalists – they only ever descended on the hospital following a suicide or, much more rarely, a homicide.

The press relentlessly contributed to a negative and inaccurate image of psychiatric disorder. The patients usually recovered with the correct treatment (which was increasingly difficult to get hold of on the NHS), and were largely harmless. But reporters' interest in mental illness was only ever piqued by the rarer cases such as this one, where menace was implied. This kind of reporting contributed to a enduringly distorted view of what psychiatry was really about.

'I can't go into that, Frances, but you know enough about the Mental Health Act to appreciate that detaining some psychiatric cases requires medical signatures on the paperwork. I don't anticipate any problems though – our friend will come quietly,' said Gerrard.

'So why the heavy artillery?'

Frances gestured at the riot squad and the CO19 Armed Response Vehicles.

Because David Lewis, your stalker for tonight, is obsessed with the Foreign Secretary's underwear, was the answer William mentally provided. *Got quite a collection. And it's all catalogued most neatly. We just don't know where, but we're not gonna let that bother us.*

Gerrard shrugged. 'Just routine operational policy. Now, I think if we get back to the chopper. Those zooms on the cameras of your colleagues over there – what can they magnify to? Ten times? Twenty? Eh?'

Frances continued to scan William through the sleet.

'Now this here on the skids is one of the video cameras. It's a rotating ball, so it can peer in any direction, and it's fitted with broadcast quality video – a camera with zoom at 1,000 times magnification – *1,000* times!'

Frances wasn't interested. 'Has this anything to do with that chap who turned up on the roof at the Mansion House speech? The anti-war protestor?'

'Frances!' Gerrard puffed. 'I can't confirm or deny, but…the sister chopper to this machine was deployed in that incident.'

'So, what with the Prime Minister and all those foreign dignitaries being there, the Saudis negotiating that deal with the Aerospace people that week, and this disturbed character gatecrashing – must've put the wolf among the sheep.'

William, only half-listening, was getting more agitated about how the night was developing.

The quasi-military presence, rank upon rank in full riot gear and armed officers on the Marylebone streets, could feed directly into David Lewis's current delusional system. His probable fantasy that he and the Minister were fated for a blissful marriage would lead David to deduce that only a conspiracy of massive proportions was keeping them apart. And this "army" would be exactly what he'd expect.

'Is that why the chopper and CO19 are here?' Frances pressed. 'I mean, this feels more than just a simple fixation.'

Frances clearly hadn't fallen for Gerrard's press spin about the event. In William's opinion the AC still didn't grasp that detaining the mentally ill was not quite as straightforward as banging-up ordinary criminals. There was longer-term treatment to consider too. Because no matter how long you put David away for, without proper psychiatric input his psychotic ideas would fester and harden.

Many stalkers continued to pursue their victims from inside a prison cell, using contacts on the outside to continue the harassment. William knew of a case where the stalking had gone on for forty years.

'Is this a political thing? Is this guy part of the campaign against the NATO air strikes in the Congo?' Frances machine-gunned the AC with questions.

Before the journalist had turned up, William had tried to remind Gerrard about the case of Günter Parche who'd stabbed tennis ace Monica Seles during a match in 1993. He needed Gerrard to see how tenacious and committed obsessives could be.

'He was fixated on Steffi Graf and wanted to assist her career by eliminating a key rival. He served less than six months in prison, and just before the attack he buried a suitcase full of pictures of Graf in his garden. He must've been anticipating a long gaol term.'

'Was this before digital?' the AC asked with a sneer.

'...and by 2005, it was reported that he had once again begun decorating his flat with pictures of Graf. Only now he was adding photographs of her family – her husband Andre Agassi and their two children.'

Gerrard retorted, sharply amused at his own wit, 'These, er, how did you classify them? Incompetent suitors…yeah, that's right. You're always telling me stalkers are just "incompetent suitors", or then there's the "intimacy seekers", so to get a date what do *you* do, Billy Boy? D'yah borrow some tips from 'em? Do you offer candy or a puppy?'

In fact, studying stalking had changed William's mind about affiliations. If he ever had any daughters, he would tell them never to have anything to do with men who were jealous, demanding or controlling.

And that was good general advice to anyone who wished to avoid finding themselves with ex-partners refusing to let go.

The pursuit of unattainable perfection was the stuff of courtly love and medieval romance. But, was there really any difference between the "intimacy seeking" stalker and the romantic who wouldn't take no for an answer? After all, what had been praise-worthy in another age had recently been redefined as criminal and inhuman.

Stalking only exists as a concept in countries where women have equal rights. In societies where they don't, women are legitimate targets – stalking fodder with no recourse to help or redress. William doubted that Gerrard would understand, or particularly care.

'Is this why the Foreign Secretary is reported to have been wearing a bulletproof vest under her designer wear?' Frances had reloaded her clip of questions. 'And is this why her official diary is now off limits to the press? C'mon, is this a celebrity or a political thing?'

William refused to answer. But Gerrard and he had rowed about precisely this point in the police car on their way here.

'He's most likely acting alone. He's obsessed. When you devote yourself to someone 24/7 like he's doing, one man can look like a whole organisation, but he's most likely a disturbed loner,' William had insisted from the rear seat, trying to be heard above the drumming of the rain on the vehicle roof.

However, Gerrard had refused to countenance this. 'He's collaborating with others, he must be. No one can achieve all this alone!' Sitting up front, Gerrard had declared this to his driver, ignoring William in the back.

The AC was so convinced he was right that he had purposely let David know the net was closing in on him. The theory was that the fugitive would take fright and make some kind of contact with his fellow conspirators. But no email or phone or any other kind of message had leaked out or seeped into the flat. Gerrard was betting heavily on this last turn of the card, but the chopper in the car park was hardly subtle.

'There's almost no doubt he's a recluse, I tell you!' William had insisted, virtually elbowing his way into the front of the car to get Gerrard's attention. 'Too obsessed with his idiosyncratic sense of purpose for anyone else to be able to work with him.'

One gleaming wet army boot resting on the landing skid of the helicopter, the journalist seemed much more part of Gerrard's team than William had ever felt.

'What about the rumours of death threats to all those that perform in Hyde Park, particularly Dread?' Frances asked the AC. She was broadening her attack. 'Is this part of a general rounding up of undesirables before the big day?'

William could sense Gerrard's irritation. The AC, in full gleaming regalia, his peaked hat swaddled in protection from the rain, seemed to be swelling up with frustration.

'What about the special precautions over security at the Care for Congo Concert? Are you confirming the existence of FTAC, the so-called VIP Stalker Squad, and that this doctor is one of the team?' Frances was back at William's side. 'This *is* Dr William James, isn't it, the psychiatrist the Met keeps for stalking cases? And you can deploy him to sign into Belmarsh or Broadmoor anyone you don't like the look of without due process? Right, Gerrard?'

Gerrard contained himself with a professional smile.

'The Fixated Threat Assessment Centre has never been a secret, Frances,' he soothed. 'You in particular shouldn't believe everything you read in the *Mail on Sunday...*'

William recalled with a shudder the front-page banner headlines *Blair's Secret Stalker Squad*, continued on pages three and four with an editorial attached.

'...FTAC is a police unit jointly manned by NHS psychiatric staff...'

'But, Gerrard,' Frances interrupted, 'the pressure group, Liberty, argues that this secret unit represents a new threat to human rights. That the Mental Health Act is being used to detain people the Government finds "inconvenient". Where there's insufficient evidence for a criminal prosecution...'

William could hold back no longer. 'FTAC doesn't detain anyone, it just gets help for mentally ill people who've fallen through the net...'

'You want to know how come the helicopter doesn't move about too much to get stable images?' interrupted the AC, deploying a firm hand. Frances looked back, disconsolate, then made a phone gesture at William.

'This is the Thermal Image Sensor, FLIR or Forward Looking Infrared. It uses body heat to secure an image, which means it sees as clearly in the middle of the night as if it were midday.'

'Midday, you say…' Frances was making all the right noises now, but William could feel her eyes on him.

'It scans to an accuracy of point one of a degree, and converts the digital information into a black and white picture, which you can see on that monitor there next to observer two sitting behind the pilot.'

Frances scribbled furiously. Like William, she wasn't wearing anything to protect her head, so the streaming rain stuck her hair down. She looked like an earnest young Shirley MacLaine with her pixie short haircut. But the way she cradled her notebook protectively from the rain told William she cared a lot about words.

'You're going to let us film all this, yeah? Next time out, right?'

Truth was, Gerrard desperately needed there to be a conspiracy. If this army of his met with only one deluded patient, the AC could end up looking a bit of a fool.

'And it's only in the last few weeks that, thanks to my initiative, the Met has been issued with night vision goggles, so units on the ground can benefit from enhanced optics in the dark.'

William lifted a shivering hand through the sodden mop on his head. How to explain that the higher IQ psychotics, like Anders Breivik, think their plans through to the nth degree? Breivik had the presence of mind, when starting his rampage, to bring an official looking sign, warning passers-by of the smell of cleaning drains, covering up the odour from his explosives. David Lewis created a similar impression, and for someone like this, night vision goggles are hardly a concern.

The reporters on the opposite pavement had now got so bored with the endless waiting that they began streaming a live rock concert in sunny California on their iPads. William caught brief glimpses from the reflections. Was there a giant Ferris wheel on the stage? And a pacing tiger?

It gave him an idea – when you find yourself in a circus, you'd better get an act. William opted for juggling with knives.

'C'mon, Gerrard,' he said. 'You worked in SO14, the Royalty Protection Unit. You *know* that FTAC performs a vital service for the police. Practically every day there are inappropriate communications or approaches to the Royal family and it's calculated that approximately eighty per cent come from people with a mental illness.'

Gerrard sighed, irritated. 'Look, the US Secret Service reports that in the last fifty years, eighty-three subjects were involved in the assassination attempts of US Presidents and other prominent public figures. Over fifty per cent were near-lethal approaches, and they were all apprehended near their targets with a weapon. So how'd you expect us to respond?'

He was arguing with William, but looking at Frances as he spoke. Her eyes flicked between them.

'Last time I checked we were living in the UK,' William responded.

'Okay, okay – let's stick with the Royal family. From the 1980s until now there have been almost 600 successful breaches of their security – incidents where the stalker broke through a security barrier or perimeter, bringing them into close contact with royalty, and no one's been killed.'

Gerrard was triumphant.

William was nodding.

'But eighty per cent of those making inappropriate contact have some form of mental illness, and the commonest is delusions of royal identity – that you are the rightful heir to the throne – which is about a quarter of those identified as mentally ill.'

'I don't get your point,' Frances said.

'He's explaining why the Government should spend so much on his pet project, the clinic for treating stalkers and victims,' Gerrard explained. 'Why there's a psychiatric dimension – that's right, isn't it, Dr James?'

'Without treatment, nothing will change!'

'Doctor, you're so keen to protect these sufferers from mental illness from us in the goon squad, but when I was in SO14, Royal households were forwarding roughly 11,000 inappropriate, barmy or threatening letters per year to the intelligence division.'

'That many? In a year?' Frances sounded incredulous.

'Yes, and those are just the ones the Royal household feels are bizarre enough to forward to the protection squad. That's just the tip of the iceberg.'

Frances was getting the scale of things, taking Gerrard's point. Seeing the real danger.

'Bottom line, *we're* responsible,' continued Gerrard. 'So apologies if we can't be bothered with your psychiatric classification system, Doctor. Which, by the way, keeps changing.'

William was dismayed. He could see that the AC was convincing Frances.

'That's not...'

'A T-shirt was thrown at the Queen by a Maori demonstrator in 1990,' Gerrard interrupted. 'That could have been a bomb. Marcus Sarjeant fired blanks at the Queen in 1981 during the Trooping of the Colour, but he'd tried to get hold of real bullets.'

Gerrard continued as he ticked off the incidents on his fingers.

'You really don't get the point he's making, do you.' Frances was looking unbelievingly at William. 'This is some kind of test, right?'

The AC's teeth showed as he grinned in satisfaction. He stabbed an emphatic finger. 'An aerosol was sprayed in Prince Charles's face in 1994 by an anti-monarchist in Auckland. It could have easily been acid. Then, Ian Ball shot four people who were trying to protect Princess Anne. These may be interesting case histories to you...'

'Ian Ball was diagnosed with schizophrenia, and that's important if we're going to properly evaluate risk!'

'And David Kang, who fired a starter pistol while rushing at Charles in 1994, appears to have been hoping to be shot,' Gerrard continued triumphantly. 'While in 1989, Diana was indecently assaulted by a man who also, it's said, had schizophrenia – whatever *that* is!'

Frances turned to William. 'Look, Doc, don't you get it? Out here in the real world it's shoot first, psychotherapy later.'

Gerrard leant in to William. 'It's not going to happen on *my* watch that we lose any public figure to one of these...these... completely unpredictable *maniacs*.'

10

She's got all the friends that money can buy
Well, you can buy your friends, but I'll hate you for free

Kwame dabbed a wound on the side of his face with a bandage someone had thrown at him.

'How many dead out there?' one of the crew raved. 'How many injured? Kwame! We need medics down here, stat.'

'It looks worse than it is, everyone calm down!' the head of security bawled back. 'Stay focused! I want an orderly dispersal, so man your posts. If spectators wanna leave, allow them out! But don't herd 'em, don't start a panic.'

Kwame held his walkie-talkie up to Dread's face, wanting her to listen. Panicky voices were relaying the anarchy spreading to the edges of the stadium.

He lowered his voice for her.

'If they get up on that stage, not only is this concert over, but they're gonna get on to that blasted wheel of yours. Then we're definitely gonna have problems. After what happened with Alonzo's suicide jump, it was a nightmare getting Health and Safety to allow us to continue using it. Well, kiss goodbye to it forever if this doesn't stop here. You started this, Dread. Only you can finish it.'

Why was he bringing up the bizarre demise of their ex-lead guitarist now, of all times?

Seriously?

Like she needed the vivid images of his shattered body under the wheel to return? She had finally managed to exorcise them from constantly intruding only recently. His head had burst open, spread like smears from a dropped strawberry someone had stepped on.

Kwame Appiah's high visibility vest was speckled with dark stuff that looked like it was once inside a person. She backed away, shuddering, her ears still ringing from the stadium blast. He reached out and held her arm tightly, his hand closing over the wound. She suppressed the urge to yelp in pain. The twitch of agony in her face told him she'd understood.

Hands appeared from the sides and wound around her waist. She pulled away, thinking they were bandaging her or checking the wound.

But a fresh radio pack was being attached. A brand new surge of terror rushed through her at the thought of returning to the arena.

The irony! She'd *faked* panic attacks on the TV talent show that had launched her. Back then the anxiety act had secured audience sympathy. When she'd won, she'd cast aside the little girl lost look and become the creature she truly was. Invulnerable.

But this was not part of the game plan. This was *real*.

Dread grimaced a lopsided smile, turned on unfeasible heels, and tugged her shredded boots back up to her thighs. Darting back along the side of the ski slope, scaling it easily from inside the performer's sanctuary, she bounded on to the milling off-stage area. She had no idea what she was going to do – what she was looking for was the way out.

Shadows rushed past and a new microphone was thrust towards her. She grabbed it instinctively and whipped on and up. But, uh-oh, this can't be right – she was trying to run from the platform and the terror it held. Backstage crew pushed her in the direction of the blaring lights and patted her on her back as she passed.

'Go, girl, go!' they whooped.

No one seemed bothered that her earpieces had gone down, or that she'd have to rely on the stage monitors to get feedback.

As Dread veered on to the platform, the band and dancers turned to ask with body language, *What the hell is going on?*

She motioned at her ears and shook her head at them, then turned to face the adversary. The riot collectively squinted – was it really her? The last they had seen of her she was disappearing into the mob. They believed she had gone for good.

Then an earthquake of adulation. The resurrection was there for all to behold.

Married with a lack of vision.
Everybody wants to rule the world.

The voice was back! Listen to this! Ignoring the turmoil on stage, she faced the enemy. Legs apart, hands lifted aloft, fingers arched to maximum as if kilowatts were jolting through her body.

She glimpsed the rampage spread out before her, the heaving and spilling horde. Wild eyes stared up at her. Kwame was right: only she could regain control of this vast arena. The assembly below, intent on self-destruction, became gradually distracted by her.

She stepped backwards without looking and gracefully twirled on to the hinged Ferris wheel's pulpit. It shuddered and spun her up into the night sky, and the rabble put aside their ragged mutiny. They were fascinated by the rise of the new phoenix; something on her tattered garments held them spellbound.

She herself was entranced by the homecoming of the voice. Flying so high above them, eyes closed as in meditation, arms outstretched, impaled on a cross by the piercing searchlight, she hung her head as Christ had done on Golgotha.

Fleeting impulse to suicide. It would be so easy. Just take one little step and she could join Alonzo forever and be free of this nightmare. The setting sun's rays enticed her. *Come on now*, it seemed to whisper, *I'm going and so can you.*

Join me…

Through her half closed fluttering eyes, over the heads of the crowd, for a split second the sun and land seemed joined by a bridge built outwards from both bodies. Then it was gone, and the horizon began to swallow the orb hungrily, accentuating the crimsons which now blushed her shuddering shoulders.

Below, everyone was reverentially gawking upwards to her heaving body, X-rayed behind the translucent billowing outfit. Her gradual stillness built the suspense: what was she thinking? What was she going to do next?

Her disciples hushed and wondered.

From the images of herself on the colossal TV screens, Dread could now discern what they were hypnotised by: fluorescing blood scarring her glamorous frills, dramatic lines of red on the skin of her arm where the glove had once been.

Ironic that she would forever remain the only person to appreciate the greatest performance of her life fully, because only she would ever know what she had gone through to deliver and finish.

Kiss, Axl Rose and the Rolling Stones, you may strut and you may snarl, but who offers you absolute annihilation? You can smash your instruments into smithereens on stage, but you have never splintered yourself. Dread had spilled right to the teetering edge of self-destruction just for their entertainment, and plunged off the precipice.

Her eyes opened, lustrous because they had been polished by a stifled weep and polychromatic as the sun waved goodbye in them. The reverential multitude broke their silence with a gasp.

Live on stage, they had never seen this special effect before.

Everybody wants to rule the world.

And right now she did.

11

If you believe it
Don't keep it all inside

The Assistant Commissioner's mobile buzzed. Recognising the voice, Gerrard straightened, frowned and handed the phone to William.

'It's for you, the Secretary of State for the Foreign Office.' He sounded testy.

'William?' Her tender, breathy voice warmed him more than his coat. William struggled to maintain the aloof and remote persona he cultivated whenever hanging with the police.

'Oh, hiya, Pip.'

'So? Where are we?' she demanded. 'Is he...are *they* in custody?'

'We're, ah, minutes away now. It's just a matter of timing when the police break into his, ah, flat.' William moved away from the group and lowered his voice conspiratorially. 'Gerrard's been showing some journalist one of his precious Air Support Units. You know the Met has three of these Eurocopter 145s. We all went up to Lippitts Hill for that unbending...sorry, *spending* review you were involved with.'

Given his stomach-churning fear of flying, William had ducked round behind a hangar to retch after they clambered out of the test flight, but he figured she hadn't noticed.

'So let us guess, William...' Her voice cracked with intimacy. 'You're surrounded by a bunch of cops towering over you and not listening to your advice. Your obsession with detail is, as usual, being overlooked.'

Towering? He wasn't *that* short – five foot ten only looked short next to Gerrard.

'Er, you're on the button, yes. He's got the rest of the press out here as well, hoping for a photo opportunity.'

'Okay, now try not to get too upset. We rang and used the AC's mobile, rather than calling you directly, so that he would pass on his phone to you. We thought it might buy you a bit more credibility with him and his gang.'

Her habit of using "we" instead of "I" had alerted William from their first meeting to her sense that she was a political movement, and not just a person. That she had recently begun converting part of her home over to being the local constituency office just confirmed to William that the boundary between her person and her office was getting smudged.

'Thanks. Look, the question Gerrard hasn't asked himself is how come David Lewis started to send you signed photos of himself immediately after we, supposedly surreptitiously, entered his flat?'

'You said it was because he believes we're already in a relationship.'

'Yes, yes, that was one *theory* which fits with erotomania, another...'

Philippa was losing patience.

'William, listen up! After the Lord Mayor's Banquet debacle, the...' She hesitated. 'Anyway, the senior security people sent the message down that this had to be wrapped up, and quickly. It's become downright embarrassing for the Government.'

Embarrassing certainly, but as William knew, they were unremittingly terrified by stalkers because this group of personality disorders possessed a unique ability to be disruptive. Before email there had been a disgruntled constituent who had rigged several fax machines to keep all the receivers in Parliament continually busy – it had effectively shut down governing the country for the day. And then there'd been the obsessive who kept mailing in white powder that looked like anthrax, grinding the civil service to a halt for a week.

That one, though, was still a state secret.

'Philippa...' His exasperation showed. 'D'you know when the fixated are probably most dangerous? The week before their court case starts, that's when. Because they figure they've got nothing to lose, so that's when a large number of stalking murders happen.'

'If it were just us, we'd give you your lead,' she mollified. 'These nights out with you have been all that any girl could want,

69

and more. I mean, at Mansion House it was dinner *and* a show.'

'Gerrard's the kind of policeman who makes sure of hitting the target by firing away and then calling whatever he hits "the target"!'

'You might want to play the politics a little better. I mean, was it wise to go out of your way to annoy the most powerful man in Britain?'

'Gerrard?'

'Oh, for God's sake, William! No, the Prime Minister.'

'Oh, you mean the Theodore Roosevelt thing before the Mansion House speech.'

Philippa launched into an uncanny impersonation of William's voice.

'President Theodore Roosevelt's life was only saved by the thickness of the speech in his pocket after anarchist John Schrank fired a shot at point-blank range at the president just before Roosevelt delivered an address. The fifty-page oration in Roosevelt's jacket pocket, covering his heart, prevented the bullet doing any more damage than a flesh wound.'

'B-but it really was the only example in history where a politician's speech hadn't bored people to death!'

'William, for a shrink your timing is all wrong. Anyway...'

William tensed up, sensing they were at a crossroads in their relationship.

'We'll leave you alone now. We had an interminable meeting at the Cabinet Office, so then we escaped back to Maida Vale for a press briefing about the church renovations following that last spate of arson attacks. Anyway, we've got to get back to Parliament to prepare for a meeting about the latest developments in the Congo.'

William intuited that she was trying to tell him something between the lines. Was his connection with her drawing to a close? Maybe his hold over her didn't, in fact, lie in her fascination with his reading the minds of her colleagues. Any pull he had seemed to reside solely in the menace posed by the stalker. Affairs of state were beginning to distract her again as this threat was about to be extinguished.

'Whatever you may say about David, his arrival means my

ministerial entourage has become decidedly impressive now! Bigger than the PM's. But your shadowing me, constantly going through the diary, controlling what I can do and what I can't, is just *too* much. Am I going to be allowed to get back to my schedule after tonight?'

'Listen, Pip, I need to ask you something. And I know I've asked it before, but please, please think very carefully before answering.'

An impatient silence down the line.

'Right, the thing is with stalkers, in fact with anyone really, once you've been intimate with someone...'

'You're asking, *again*, if I know this person?'

'It's important because it changes things completely, Pip. Once people have been...ah...y'know...carnal knowledge...with someone, the risks of violence go up dramatically – particularly in a stalking scenario.'

It was more than that, though. When precisely the stalking occurred for the first time was also crucial because the timing revealed the motivation for stalking.

'I have never seen this man before,' she said coldly. 'Never.'

'I mean, if you knew him even casually it helps us allocate the risk.'

'Yeah, yeah, I remember that was in one of your academic publications – I was showing it to a friend just the other day – how we're all more likely to be killed by someone we know intimately...'

'Two women are murdered every week in England and Wales by their partner.'

'Look, he's definitely not my type. Call us later. Hope to see you soon and good luck, and be careful.'

William handed the mobile back to the Commander.

Once the Foreign Secretary's security detail had started to exceed the Prime Minister's, William detected she'd developed a taste for halting central London, making foreign dignitaries wait, requiring buildings to be evacuated and searched. Indeed, she was now getting high on it.

'So she didn't mind you poking about in her kitchen?' Gerrard's glinting eyes met William's.

Of course she didn't. Because it was the psychiatrist who had identified this stalker's notes as being particularly ominous, so his warnings had galvanised all the extra safeguarding. This had transformed her from bored doodler at meetings into a Prime Minister in-waiting.

In an oblique way, the stalker, or at least the threat he represented, rendering her important beyond her wildest dreams had inspired her to bid for the top job. Philippa's newly formed addiction to all the extra motorcycle out-riders and imperious traffic hold-ups meant the psychiatrist's counsel must have cost the state six, or even seven, figures in additional expenditure.

No wonder Gerrard was peeved.

'Of course not. Bloody hell, Her Royal Highness is always upping *your* budget!'

The psychiatrist knew that his excuse for opening the pantry cupboards in her Maida Vale home had been feeble, but he had confirmed his suspicions. Gerrard may not have known what to make of the piles of tomatoes, but he was presumably starting to twig there was more to William's curiosity about Philippa's lifestyle than just official security.

'I still don't understand, Dr James.' The AC's tone was as pleasant as a sugar coated razor blade. 'Could you walk me through which of the diagnoses you were describing back at the police station briefing our Mr Lewis falls into?'

Gerrard, aggrieved by the call from the Minister, was putting him on the spot in front of Frances. On the other hand, maybe there was still a sliver of a chance he might get Frances to persuade Gerrard to take a different approach. Even at this eleventh hour.

'Oh please, let me, let me!' Frances bobbed up and down with her hand in the air.

William's heart began to pound. He hated giving his opinion only to have it binned straightaway. He knew he appeared to be nervous. In fact, he was resisting an urge to jabber something irretrievably vicious and ultimately ruinous.

'There are five types,' she began. 'Do tell me if I'm not word perfect, Dr James. It's the Resentful Stalkers that keep Dr James awake at night. They're the ones who are driven by a grievance. They frighten or intimidate as part of a quest for justice or revenge which takes over their lives. It's the sense of absolute righteousness that is so worrying.'

Frances had, though he didn't recall seeing her at the briefing, pushed in. She was curbing his vicious urge with a remarkable display of memory. Trouble was, though her repeating the mini-lecture he'd rattled through many times was intended to help, her mimicry was also galling. Did he sound like that? Had Philippa and Frances been comparing impersonation notes? Should he correct her and say that Resentful Stalkers were, in the main, not violent, but turned to it when they saw no other option?

'...Rejected Stalkers who are controlling jealous types start stalking an ex after the breakdown of an intimate relationship. They're after reconciliation, revenge or a fluctuating mixture of both.'

She glanced at him to check how well she was doing. He nodded.

'The Intimacy Seekers are pursuing a relationship with someone they've become keen on. Many are convinced that their affections are, or will be, reciprocated despite obvious evidence to the contrary. If you don't intervene, they don't give up. Then there are the Incompetent Suitors. They too stalk to try and establish a relationship. Unlike the Intimacy Seekers, this lot are just social incompetents looking for a date or a sexual encounter but not having a clue how to go about it.'

'Isn't that half the male population?' Gerrard asked with a snort of derision.

'One visit from you boys in blue and they'll happily desist – and move on to a new victim,' Frances said coolly. 'Finally there are Predatory Stalkers who are staking someone out in preparation for a sexual or violent assault. But they are very rare.'

'Okaaay.' William was rather touched that she had listened so carefully. However, he had developed a sneaking suspicion that she was in a hurry and wanted to bypass his rather academic discursive delivery. She was punching out his standard sermon – an edgy need lay behind her words, but for what?

'Look, this motivation stuff is absolutely crucial. The earliest of the classification systems for stalkers was pioneered by the Los Angeles Police Department Threat Management Writ, sorry,

Unit. And the LAPD has a higher concentration of celebrities in its jurisdiction than anywhere else in the world.'

'So is this an Intimacy Seeker? Has he got this erotomania then?'

'In fact…' William ignored her, '…the LAPD system doesn't look at motivation in sufficient depth. Erotomaniacs suffer from a psychotic delusion that the person they are pursuing is actually in love with them and it's a massive conspiracy that keeps them from their loved one.'

'So you doctors are all just throwing darts at a board?' Gerrard, eyebrows raised in mockery, seemed to have addressed the comment at the journalist.

William was flashbacking to schooldays. All he needed now was for the riot squad to start up the familiar playground chant:

Your dad's in the loony bin! Your mum's in the loony bin!

'Not all stalkers are erotomaniacs, but the average length of duration of a pursuit for most groups – erotomaniacs, love obsessionals, call them what you will – is over ten years.'

William glared pointedly at the massed ranks over Gerrard's shoulder.

'And one of the reasons the hounding and persecution can go on for so long, and elude police intervention, is that this group – according to research – tends to be absolutely focused on their goal. They don't stop, even after they've destroyed their own lives. Law enforcement underestimate them.'

'But, Dr James, I thought all stalkers were basically bad, sad or mad,' Gerrard said.

That playground again. In retaliation to the chants – William had never been physical – he would blurt out the most awful things to his tormentors. It was his only way to get them to stop hitting him. He'd learnt how to find out their worst insecurities. But, ironically, it was he who would always end up in front of the headmaster, defending some verbal grenade he had thrown which had got his tormentors' parents on to the phone, complaining about him.

He was transported back to something he had long pushed behind him: how his flight into medicine and psychiatry had started. But then he became aware of Frances studying him, and he steadied himself.

'Look, the whole point of assessing stalkers is to grasp their motivation. This is the only thing that unlocks how dangerous they are.'

Gerrard gestured to Frances, as if to say, *Who will rid me of this troublesome priest?*

'Consider the so-called Rejected Stalker. This is usually someone who has been dumped and refuses to accept the relationship is over,' said William. 'They persist with phone calls or visits, or gifts, and refuse to take no for an answer.'

'Oh, yes,' Gerrard added, 'wasn't there a case just like that recently, the Laura Ashley murder?'

'Yes. Asha Muneer. She worked at Laura Ashley and was stabbed so brutally with a kitchen knife by Gulamyr Akhter in a frenzied attack that the blade broke. She was impaled thirty-two times, including one wound that cut right down to the bone. This was after he became deeply embittered by rejection.'

'She was found floating in the River Kennet,' added Gerrard, a flicker of pondering in his eyes. Was he considering how a helicopter could have saved her?

'Before the murder, Akhter made more than 620 calls to Asha, an average of thirty-four a day in the days leading up to her death,' said William. 'So her stalker had ticked the two-week threshold box – just as David Lewis has. Once stalking goes past two weeks, it is likely to persist way into the future. That is the tipping point at which you should call the police. Leaving it any longer becomes increasingly dangerous.'

William weighed if Asha would be alive today if those close to her or she herself had known about the two-week rule – it definitely needed more publicity.

Gerrard interrupted his reverie. 'How could any shambling, introverted, isolated, incoherent…ever imagine that a member of the Cabinet might be interested in him?'

Whom was he referring to? William loosened his collar to respond, but a senior officer interrupted.

'Sir, the Backscatter X-ray and thermal imaging indicate that he's up and agitated. He appears to be shouting at the voices in his head.'

William visualised the £100,000 American refrigerator-sized

machine that would be producing the X-rays. The gleaming clean technology would be a stark contrast to the grim decrepitude of David Lewis's council flat.

'Which of all your different types of stalkers is the one that's after Dread?' Gerrard suddenly asked William. 'Unlike Mr Lewis, her one's as famous as she is now – and she's the most celebrated pop star in the world.'

William stared bleakly through the rain. Dread? Which one was Dread? Well, obviously he knew her image. She leered from hoardings all over London, but beyond that? He could feel the journalist's eyes on him, more intent than ever. Were Gerrard and she playing good cop, mad cop with him?

This singer's stalker certainly wasn't David Lewis, which was all that William cared about. The sort of person who stalked a celeb was usually different from the kind who went after a politician.

'He's leaving her anonymous notes,' Gerrard said. 'This is one – *All for freedom and for pleasure, nothing ever lasts forever.* An obvious threat, eh? Anyway, her stalker is sending her lyrics from pop songs. What does this one tell us then? Which type is it? *Like the circles that you find, in the windmills of your mind.* Is that an erotomaniac then? And what about this one? Even I can work out what the nutter means here: *The hunter gets captured by the game.*'

William tried to ignore Frances's laser beam stare. He felt she could see right through him. Much like Gerrard's Backscatter X-ray machine.

'Before I could comment, I would need to know a great deal more. Like what songs the lyrics come from, the overall context,' he replied, irritated.

'The context is Dread came to fame on the biggest TV talent show on the planet,' Frances chipped in.

William just looked blankly back at her.

'Surely you've heard of *The Weakest Lip-Sync*?'

William shook his head. He didn't watch TV.

'Round after round the audience kept voting her back in against the panel's protestations,' she continued. 'It had turned into the drama of that summer. To prove Roger Moirans wrong (the Simon Cowell of the show), she struggled on stage against the most awful panic attacks, and yet somehow, right at the end, she always managed to pull herself together. In every show she was pitted against Roger Moirans's mounting and very verbal fury with the great British public. And as the votes piled in at the end of each broadcast, he'd throw his arms up in embellished despair.'

'The other starring players were the viewers who seemed to keep voting for the then painfully shy and awkward Dread, just to see what would happen in the next episode,' Gerrard chipped in. Together they sounded like voiceovers on a documentary about Dread. William could sense they had kind of bonded over a mutual hatred. And Gerrard had at last stumbled on to a subject from which he was spared the psychiatrist quoting obscure academic papers.

'And then, after she'd won,' Frances went on, 'something happened to Dread. She transformed from a fragile trembling innocent into the most arrogant artist ever to flounce an awards' ceremony. The audience had created a Frankenstein, but they didn't seem to notice.'

'Yeah, that first single she released was a real shocker,' agreed Gerrard.

'One of the first hits following the talent show win that launched the pop star had been the lavatorial chant "Friggin' in the Riggin'". Dread had controversially covered the foul-mouthed Sex Pistols hit,' Frances explained to William.

William wondered who, or what, on earth were the 'Sex Pistols'.

Gerrard threw his arms out and indicated the graffiti-strewn walls of the council housing estate.

'That's another of her stalker's lines.'

Lipstick cherry all over the lens as she's falling.

For the first time, William took note of what was sprayed across the glistening concrete.

'And that.'

William followed the gesture.

Fire in the sky, smoke on the water.

'They're all over the world, not just London, you know. And no one knows who's doing it. Any opinions, Doctor?'

It seemed to the psychiatrist that the author of the menacing messages to Dread was most probably in the grip of psychosis, so was reading deep and special meaning into the lyrics. The fan believed the songs were about him – or her – and was trying to tell Dread that her intimation was received and understood.

As for the missives spreading all over the world, the most likely explanation was that others were picking up on the first message. They were harmless copycats.

He shook his head. 'I'd have to listen to the whole song. Maybe the hidden meaning is embedded not just in the fragment of lyric, but has something to do with the particular way the music or that specific lyric is performed…it's always the pattern we need to look for, across all the lyrics. Examine the pattern. Always.'

'Sir,' said an officer, 'apparently he just made a call to the constituency phone line in Philippa Foot's home and tried to have a conversation with voicemail. He really lost it and started swearing at the machine.'

Waving the officer away, the AC turned back to William.

'We're going to be in charge of security over this massive pop concert in Hyde Park and we need intel on what these lyrics are about. So we're gonna bring someone on to the team who can give us answers, not maybes and not theories.'

'You'll need someone who knows about pop music,' added Frances. She sounded disappointed in William. 'All the messages are from songs that were in the charts. Quite good ones originally, until she screwed them up.'

'We've had half the record industry bopping through my office trying to explain what the pop lyrics refer to…'

Gerrard was enjoying this conversation at his expense with Frances, William decided. There was something about the journalist's acumen that enticed the psychiatrist into trying to impress her.

'A lot more than the crushing emptiness of Dread's own lyrics,' Frances drawled.

'Over there! Those lines.' William pointed to a scrawl splattered across an estate wall which read, *Nothing is more dangerous than desire when it's wrong.*

'Those words come from a love poem John Hinckley Jr wrote to Jodie Foster, who he was stalking. He also attempted to shoot

President Ronald Reagan to demonstrate his love for the actress.'

'It's one of Dread's song lyrics,' a nearby inspector confirmed.

Frances chipped in, 'No, it's something she covered from a band called Devo.'

Gerrard's gold striped cuffs flailed at the graffiti. 'You do know it's more of these wackos who are behind the spate of church fires in London? Dread's fans are taking revenge on those religious extremists who accused her of blasphemy.'

William was concerned to get back on track with Philippa's stalker and disentangle from Dread's.

'Gerrard, the Predatory Stalker is the most worrying kind. Because the stalking is not the key act, it's just a curtain raiser. The pursuit is like casing the joint, the preparation for the attack, which is often a rape. Or murder. The harassment in this case is about information gathering, details which will be used to...'

Several walkie-talkies erupted and the Chief Super intervened.

Our boys monitoring sound think he's preparing to leave and we should go in now. They believe he might be arming himself.

'Right, Dr James,' Gerrard said, all twinkling gone. 'We haven't got the luxury of time for your academic pontificating. We've got to make a life or death decision now. And I've got to catch those church arsonists before Hyde Park, otherwise who knows what they and the God Squad will do there.'

William was aware of the recent church burnings, but how come he was suddenly to blame?

'Go! Go! Go!' snapped Gerrard.

Almost instantly there was a series of blinding flashes, followed by sharp bangs which echoed across the street as the entry squad rolled exploding NFDDs into David's flat. The whole scene seemed to expand and then contract. Gasps and exclamations rang out as the gathering, which had been straining to stare down the cordoned-off street, stepped back instinctively.

'Stay down! Armed Police! Armed Police!'

Muffled shouts drifted down the street on the wisps of smoke.

And then gunshots.

'*No!*' mourned William.

Two reverberating reports, and then a pause. Followed by another two. William flinched. Had he read it wrong? Was David indeed involved with something more than his delusions? Frances was grinning strangely as she cowered by the chopper. *She's a war junkie*, he decided, *hopelessly addicted.*

Whatever was going on, the Noise Flash Diversionary Devices hadn't delivered what the police had been hoping for.

'Oh, bloody hell,' breathed Gerrard, dropping to his knees.

12

If you look closely it's easy to trace
The tracks of my tears

'Can you hear the gunshots?'

KT Mean, six foot of gorgeousness and anger, was perched on the dressing table and flicking the table legs with the back of her high heels. Thigh-skimming tall boots and sheer top threatened overspill, yet she could, when she put her mind to it, radiate the kind of diffidence associated with prepubescence.

As one of Dread's two backing singers and her sister, Mean's voice had carried the concert when Dread's own vocal chords hadn't showed up. And while a bit husky, she remained able to field a torrent of high pitched indignant appeals to their mother.

Dread was conserving her own throat – still terrified her rasping would give the game away. She wondered what their other sister and backing singer, Kristal Miffed, was sounding like. If her voice wavered now she might be summarily replaced for the big one in Hyde Park by either of her two sisters. Indeed she could end up second fiddle for the rest of the world tour.

'You do realise the religious nutters with the rifle-rack pick-up trucks are now sprayin' our fans with lead? Listen!'

KT Mean tossed her auburn mane in the general direction of the stadium floor as she spoke to their mother, Anne. But Anne was more interested in the bedraggled state of her other daughter, Dread.

Everyone paused, but all that penetrated the dressing room walls were the now familiar sounds of rioting in the distance. Dread, who was still reeling, was lying in the dentist's chair as her assistant, Hannah, began reapplying her make-up. But the lead vocalist was dwelling on the mere two weeks to Hyde Park. She was never going to make it...or she was going to flip out in front of five billion people...

'Kwame confirmed there were shots fired,' Mean grumbled, waving a walkie-talkie at them.

'We're in America, like, *hello*!' Hannah said as she resumed working on Dread.

'An' it's not 'er fawlt.'

Anne, original Essex accent front and centre, opened the door, checking to see if the sound of ordnance was hiding behind it. Deafening commotion from the set being disassembled and packed away for the next leg of the world tour entered and rattled the furniture. 'After all, two ornithologists...'

'*Anthrop*ologists, Mother!' Mean lifted her hands in the air.

'Oh, that as well! Anyway, anfropologists come across a tribe in the middle of Souf America dancing to drummers banging out Dread's songs, but they've never 'eard of Jesus Christ – I mean – 'oo was to guess the story would take off?'

Dread sneaked a look around. Had anyone realised she'd had a panic attack on stage? Wait, maybe the fact that she might have killed a member of the audience should be further up her list of priorities...

'Listen, shit happens when you party naked,' said Mean, 'and the story didn't go global until Madam here announced, "Guess that means I'm more famous than God" at her press conference.'

Dread's lips silently formed the words in time with Mean's pronouncement.

'And then all hell broke loose with bread mumblers accusing us of blaspheming, and now every concert is a battleground. It's only a matter of time before someone gets seriously hurt.'

Dread flinched. Someone *had* got seriously hurt.

'Mother, what happened on stage was so freaktarded! You've got to do something!' continued Mean. 'Her dipshit performance was several pants short of an orgasm – c'mon!'

Mean became almost tearful with fury. 'And I ab-so-lute-ly refuse to do her tweets again for 'er. She's gonna have to explain what happened 'erself. The web has gone wild over this.'

Anne straightened a black and white framed photo of Bono that was drooping on the wall. Against the intense bulbs garlanding Dread's mirror, it threw a sharp elongated shadow across the portraits of other stars who'd played the venue –

a silhouette resembling a dagger, reminding Dread, again, that her microphone, which she had embedded in someone's skull, was still to be accounted for.

'Don't worry, love, Dominque'll do it. When anyone in publicity does the tweets they sound more like Dread than Dread,' Anne said, coming over and checking the row of mobiles, BlackBerrys and walkie-talkies that were lined up on the dressing room table beside Mean. 'You're going to have to calm down, KT.'

Dread hated that Anne's aitches were coming back. Her Essex accent always returned when she got nervous – which was OK, except that it meant her clipped attempts at BBC 1950s announcer became ever more evident when she relaxed again.

'And anyway, Dread storming off stage in the middle of a set is the least of our problems right now. The insurance clauses are a nightmare if we gotta cancel just one date after what happened to Alonzo.'

So Anne thought she had done it in a fit of rage? Dread felt like she had been smacked across the face again by the mad fans.

'I don't Adam and Eve it!' Mean exploded. 'You *always* take her side. What has she gotta do…'

Hannah moved round to put Dread's body between her and the agitated sister as if revealing a portrait to a sitter. Anne raised a hand to staunch the flow of breathless critique from KT Mean and clenched her fist, like she did when she wanted the studio musicians to stop messing about, as if she was gripping a leash.

'Dread, darling,' she reluctantly turned to admonish her youngest, 'you *do* need to be more careful. You were definitely channelling Naomi Campbell out there.'

Dread, dazed and preoccupied with distant sounds, jumped whenever anyone passed by her dressing room door.

'You did see the doctor, right? KT, she saw the doctor, right?'

Mean nodded. 'He said there were a few cuts and scratches but nothing major.'

Anne bent down to inspect Dread's arm closely. 'Is that going to scar?' she asked.

'No, the doc said it should be okay.'

When are you all gonna mention my little stabbing encore? My murder on the dance floor which is going to bring the curtain down on my career? Dread wondered to herself. *Maybe everyone's keeping it from me because they don't want me to freak out.*

'Darling, I would love to stay and look after you,' Anne told Dread, 'but Kristal's gone missing, which with all these strange messages is creeping me out…'

At the stage name of her middle sister, Dread finally made an entrance.

'Kristal's gone missing?' she repeated slowly.

'It speaks!' whooped Mean, flicking her hair back and clapping. 'But come on, Mother, Kristal's bound to be making out with any male celeb from the South…she's perfecting her redneck accent for her assault on Nashville.'

'Redneck? Last week it was Southern Belle.' Hannah didn't look up from Dread as she spoke. 'Is she serious about breaking into Country and Western? Isn't she going to have to change her stage name again? She's only been Kristal Miffed for…'

'Yeah, it's called Hick Hop,' replied Mean as she waved her mother out. 'It's okay, Mum. We've got it covered. You run on. We'll even round up a posse to track Kristal. But all that's happened is she's fallen asleep under some cowboy.'

'If you're sure? I'll go and find Kwame then. We need to have words.'

'Yeah, and for bitchtit's sake, get Dread to listen to the final edits. I've had to get a CD put in her limo!' bemoaned Mean. 'So please make sure she pays some attention to it on the trip home. We need her to sign off on it. Tomorrow! First thing!'

'Okay, you'll pin your ears back, right, Dread?' Anne said energetically.

No response. Dread stared up in a trance through Hannah's busy hands.

'Do you see what I mean, Mum? She's somewhere else most days now.'

Anne prodded Dread with a purple-tipped talon, and it was then that Dread remembered.

She must've been nine years old. It was a tense cello competition and she had missed four bars of the music. She'd been exhausted and panicked, so her timing went fugazi. Her mother, to the horror and delight of the parent-packed audience, had stormed on to the stage, screaming, 'How dare you embarrass me! How dare you! You're 'avin' a laugh, aintcha?'

She had then poked Dread with a fingernail. And when they were on their way home, she ranted a threat into the rear-view mirror that had seemed very real to the nine-year-old clinging on to her cello case, cowering in the back seat.

'Young lady, you're staying in until you get it right! In fact, you're staying in *for the rest of your life!*'

Ever since, Dread had obsessively over-rehearsed. And in one sense, from that moment she had retreated inside, never daring to venture out again. Strange to have forgotten that for years. So much had happened since.

But maybe that was all intermission.

Anne was bending over Dread, checking her pupils for signs of Class A, pressing her thumbs firmly on the skin below Dread's eyes, forcing the sockets wider. The pop star flailed and protested, but she was ineffectual against Anne's iron grip.

Dread was saved by Hannah's intervening hand.

'Anne, like, what are you doing? I'm going to have to do her all over again!'

'Check with Dominique. For the press conference she wants her looking how she was on stage, messed up all over,' Anne commanded and walked to the door, straightening Bono again, where she paused.

'Y'know, the way we ended tonight? Okay, it was different, but...listen to 'em!' Anne gesticulated at the ceiling and the distant rumble of the swarm. 'I mean, there's something about curtain down, abrupt and unexpected like, which seems to get 'em wanting more. Like they can't believe it really is over. Oi fink it's the best ending we've ever done. Dread, you're a genius. I'm going to find Kwame.'

She was gone before Mean could respond.

'Why does no one notice she hasn't even got proper dread-locks anymore?' Mean hollered after her mother. 'I mean, why is she still called Dread, anyway? Why do we keep remixing other people's songs now Alonzo's gone? None of this makes any sense!'

None of it did make any sense to Dread. Her thoughts were

so shrieking loud that Dread could hear them echoing off the walls.

Is it possible I killed someone in front of 93,000 fans and a platoon of TV cameras, yet no one noticed?

13

Everything you know is wrong
...I'm the lie
But you wouldn't stand near me if you didn't want to die

Smoke billowed up from the council block housing David's flat and silhouetted shadows inside jerked about as shouts penetrated the gloom. The rain had begun to peter and the clouds hung low, waiting for dawn.

More serrated gunshots sounding like they were ricocheting down the street pushed everyone over. The media went down fighting, flashing away. High intensity light for video cams threw apparitions on the walls, while officers edged behind lampposts, street signs and bollards for cover.

'Small arms fire, one weapon!' an officer to the right of Gerrard shouted at him.

'Yeah, but where's it coming from?' replied Frances as she backed away, crouching low with an armed officer escort.

The walkie-talkie reported that none of the officers charging into David's flat had been hit. They thought the slugs were coming from another part of the estate. Probably drug dealers panicking that the police raid was for them. They'd soon realise it wasn't.

There was a hiatus. Nausea checked into the back of William's throat.

Whoever was shooting stopped.

'Oh bloody hell!' Gerrard snarled as he gave the go ahead for the raid to continue.

Brilliantly lit explosions came from David's flat as more NFDDs were thrown in.

Instinctively, William looked around to explain to Frances why these, in his opinion, were the wrong tactics, then remembered she'd been shepherded away. At the very least, David Lewis would anticipate this move.

NFDDs produce an extremely intense flash of light which over-saturates the retina, leading to temporarily blindness and creating a very strange sense as if the whole world is "paused" for several long seconds before vision and brain and other senses gradually began to work again. They had left William panic breathing in a corner during his Riot Squad training, much to the amusement of Gerrard, who'd enquired if the psychiatrist was suffering from morning sickness.

'And what effect are they going to have on a psychotic deluded person?' William had demanded.

'They're harmless – they'll just disorientate him and leave him unable to react when we go in,' Gerrard had countered. 'I suppose you think we should roll in some anti-nausea pills first.'

'Say again? Come back! Come back!'

Officers on the walkie-talkies were trying to make sense of information coming in from all over the estate.

Nothing much seemed to be happening. The cloud from the NFDDs drifted over them.

Uniforms emerged from the ground floor flat, manhandling a large dark package. As they limped forward, it became a dishevelled and terrified looking bearded man in plastic handcuffs. Stumbling between his burly captors, he began to pedal with flailing limbs, taking in the ranks of vests, helmets, shields and truncheons encircling him. As the command group approached, the crowd began to rise halfway, murmuring in expectation.

The prisoner party stopped just beyond the periphery of the helicopter blades. Gerrard theatrically stood his ground and looked the prisoner up and down. Satisfied, he jubilantly beckoned William over. The man fell to his knees, overwhelmed with despair, epileptic-like shudders vibrating his body.

'He was no hassle at all, Sir,' said the lead armed officer, sheathing his Glock handgun. The AC smiled from ear to ear at the press corps. Then, troubled that the helicopter might be obscuring the angle of view for the press, he tap-danced around William so his figure would be better placed in the frame.

'You see, Dr James,' he said triumphantly, 'these methods overwhelmed the subject and ensured he came quietly.'

On cue, flashbulbs lit up the early morning sky as photographers fought for the best angle. The video crews trained their lights on the group surrounding the prisoner, so the aircraft radiated proudly, luminous in the glare.

William put a hand up to filter the dazzle. He admitted to himself grudgingly that as far as press coverage was concerned, Gerrard had choreographed the entire operation flawlessly. The AC's toy would decorate the front pages tomorrow and long into the future, when the fact that it had never even moved had been forgotten. Yet it would remain embedded in the collective unconscious that it was the mechanism by which a threat to the Foreign Office Minister had been neutralised.

Was Frances a part of this charade? William had begun to have higher hopes for her.

The face before them was a quivering crumple, tears glistening from wild rolling eyes. The fugitive kneeling in prayer hadn't even noticed them, just the surrounding guns. His back was to the cameras so the gobbling breakfast audience tomorrow wouldn't see his face, allowing the photo to be published without legal objection.

William's eyes locked with the bent and beaten figure.

No one really looks at anyone anymore, he considered.

Frances stooped forward from under the helicopter rotor blades and produced a boom mike on an extendable pole. William had a suspicion it was she who lay behind Gerrard's clever orchestration of the evening. It had all been just a bit too slick, too media savvy for PC Plod. She was helping the AC attain his goals, but what was she gaining access to in return? William looked around. It was a spectacular cast – ranks of uniformed riot squad, armed CO19 officers and a platoon of decorative senior officers framed Gerrard, while press fired away and the restive crowd all encircled him.

It was quite an audience.

He'd have to keep this as cropped as a sniper's crosshair.

'Well, Dr James?' Gerrard said, teeth flashing.

'Well,' William responded, his voice cracking, 'there is only one difficulty. That isn't David Lewis.'

14

Come on baby let's start anew
'Cause breaking up is hard to do

In the teeming corridor, Kwame could see Anne sidestepping the stage crew, dancers, musicians and animal trainers who were packing up for the next stop. He and Dominique Schnapper were racing for Dread's dressing room, but Anne pulled them aside into a large room: a wardrobe area.

'We need 'er to get 'er 'ead space sorted before we put 'er in front of the press.' Anne's aitches were gone again.

'*Mais oui*! *Les hacks* could eat us alive on this one,' said Dominique as she waved the cellophane-wrapped press pack she had prepared.

Anne caught sight of the head of wardrobe tending to glistening material spilling from a trunk.

'Hiya, Damaris!'

Between the various road cases were mannequins of Dread herself. Kwame couldn't remember exactly why Dread was the most used model for fashion mannequins worldwide; was it because she was infamously a size zero? Or was it size 4? He was confused by the whole thing, and all the numbers that got endlessly flung about, so he had learnt to switch off once the sisters got on to their favourite bugbear.

But to Kwame, looking around it felt as though Anne's daughter – or a regiment of daughters – was listening in.

Anne beckoned Kwame and Dominque to move in closer so their conversation wouldn't be overheard.

'A press conference is not a good idea when we don't know the full extent of the collateral damage,' Kwame grumbled in the slightest of Jamaican lilts which officer training at Sandhurst had bullied down, leaving him with a delicately spiced upper class accent.

'*Merde*! It's already been called! *T'es rien qu'un petit connard!*' Dominique turned on him.

'Anne agreed and we can't cancel it now! *Espèce de couille molle.* As your Public Relations exec, my job is to seize the initiative and take advantage of it!' She waggled her finger at Damaris in the distance. 'Damaris! I need to have a word about the wardrobe for the press conference.'

Damaris, the head of costume, looked up and flapped back.

'Anne, this staged entrance of Schnapper's, with Dread coming in from behind the press room and with the lights off, is just adding extra risk.'

'*Mais non, non,* Kwame. We need to maximise the shock of the fans suddenly seeing her, battle-scarred but defiant,' Dominique insisted. '*Ta gueule.*'

'And you don't think that could backfire? Taking advantage of injuries and criminal damage?'

'Okay, okay you two!' Anne intervened.

Before she could go on, Kwame held up a hand and pointed at the ceiling. He wanted them both to listen. Above the roar of the dispersing multitude they could just make out the beating rotors of a distant helicopter.

'That's Dread's private chopper. I called Arnold in to help airlift the wounded to the nearest medical centre. Local emergency services are already deploying their two air ambulances. The road ambulances are having difficulty getting through the traffic and there's a lotta injured out there.'

'*C'est fantastique*! That's a great PR line – we donated our own private aircraft to assist. We can use this!'

'Ms Dominique Schnapper,' Kwame breathed while his hands, the bulbous shape of enormous raw Wagyu steaks, marbled from all the impacts they had suffered, shaped a grip around some victim's neck, 'I called Arnie in because we don't want victims stressing. I've had no reports yet of anything life threatening, but we don't know what's going to pan out over the next few hours. Let's focus on getting safely out of here, not distract ourselves with…this…*sideshow*!'

'*Mais non*!' Dominique interrupted. 'Flipping out on to the stadium floor is unusual, even for Dread. We are going to need a story to explain how she ended up in the pit. *Bordel de merde.*'

'C'mon, Dominique, you can do this in your sleep. Throwing in a new acrobat turn and leaping off the stage had the horde eating out of her hands.' The aitches were back – Anne was feeling more confident.

'Everyone's going to assume that's the new move...' Dominique was thinking and planning ahead. *'La vache.'*

'Yeah, we need a new dance craze to follow up on the success of The Twitch.'

'Listen!' Kwame insisted. 'It's wall-to-wall bodies huddling in BacoFoil heat retention blankets out there on the stadium floor...'

'Mais oui, I distributed them. Zey are going to look *formidables...sensationnels...*gleaming away in le black and white photos on *les* front pages *demain.'*

'Okay, but we need to find out where the hell Kristal is!' Kwame interjected. 'She may be part of some story that comes back to bite us.'

'Mais non, non, non! Kristal goes missing several times on an average day. *Je m'en fiche.'* Dominique was dismissive. 'She's left for Nashville most *probablement.'*

'This is not a typical day,' Kwame sighed.

'So we're still on?' Dominique was backing for the door hopefully, thumbs and forefingers of both hands connecting in an optimistic "A-OK" gesture.

'Yes,' confirmed Anne.

'C'est magnifique.'

Anne motioned to follow Dominique, but Kwame caught her elbow.

'There's a couple of things we need to talk about...' Kwame glanced at the publicist's disappearing back and lowered his voice. 'We found another of those crank notes.' Anne's face betrayed that she knew something bad was coming. 'It was the usual picture of a mutilated Dread with song lyrics added on top. We found it in her dressing room a short while ago.'

'Oh bloody hell, let's take a look at it.'

'Can't... I left it in there.'

Anne began to scurry in small circles.

'Why the Donald Duck would you do that?'

'I've been talking to a stalking expert, Dr Han Fei, formerly of the LAPD Threat Management Unit. He advised that we leave it and see who reports finding it. Often the person who "accidentally" discovers it is the person who placed it there in the first place. This is particularly true if it goes unnoticed for a prolonged period.'

'Have you seen 'er in the dressing room? The lights are on but no one's home,' Anne said worriedly. 'Let me get this straight: this is exactly the same kind of communication as all the others?'

'Yes.'

'You mean the same printed words on top of a horrible disfigured image of Dread? Her body and face are gashed using some kind of image software?'

'Yes, just like all the others.'

'But we agreed they were too disturbing. We stopped showing them to her, remember?'

'Yes, I know, but…'

''Ave you thought about the impact on 'er, just before a press conference?'

Kwame shook his head. 'From now on, if security finds a note we're supposed to photograph it, crime scene it, then wait and see who first reports it. We're to keep a record and build a classification.'

'But where in the dressing room is it? I've just been in there and I didn't see anything.'

'It's under a glossy on the dressing table in front of Dread. And for someone to penetrate her dressing room, it's got to be an inside job – and they're the most difficult to track down.'

'Inside?' Anne blinked.

'Anne, wake up and smell the coffee! Your daughter ain't the most popular person on the music scene. All and sundry in pop detest her.'

'Everyone hates everyone – that's celebrity! I saw it myself, first time round.'

'Yeah, sure, but look, it's the inner circle that's now under suspicion.'

'Inner circle? We're a family unit, for God's sake!'

'Like the band? Didn't you *see* out there? Everyone on stage hates her guts. And the arguments off stage about the band's direction ever since Alonzo…'

'Kwame! You're gambling with my daughter's sanity! Suppose she finds the note herself? Have you any idea what that could do to her?'

'That's the reason we're gonna have to start hiring some more forensics.'

'Our security budget is already more than the US President's!'

She abruptly turned her head and rested it on Kwame's chest, placing both her hands on it as if listening to his heart.

'Oh, Kwame, I don't know how we would cope if…'

He took hold of her hands and gently pushed her away. His eyes flicked to check that Damaris hadn't seen Anne's gesture.

'Anne, we've gotta be careful. You said yourself that the girls are likely to react badly to your first relationship after the divorce. Especially as it's with me, someone who's on tour with them.'

'Yes, yes.' Anne pulled some strands of ash blonde hair back from her forehead. 'It's just that at times like this I need a cuddle and I look over and see you and…'

'I know, but Dread's in a strange place right now – she's burbling on about killing someone out there. I keep telling her that nobody has been recovered, but she's on the edge. Let's not destabilise things any further. And can we please try and pull the press conference?'

'She seemed fine to me. Besides, I've left her with Hannah,' Anne protested.

'You put a lot of faith in a make-up artist.'

'C'mon, Kwame, the great ones like Hannah, they kind of evolve into personal shrinks.'

'Yeah, but she's not a professional whatsit, is she. And what kind of name is that anyway, Hannah Arendt? Where's she from originally? How'd you recruit her? What was the screening?'

'Look, not many people know this, but it was Hannah who got Dread through the nightmare of *Weakest Lip-Sync*. Without her I don't know what would have happened. We kind of owe her everything, so you are to leave her alone…not only because she's absolutely trustworthy, but she's…'

'Your spy on the girls, yeah I know.' His voice was now so low as to be almost indistinct.

'Well,' she said defensively, 'Hannah was how I rumbled the dance troupe for cocaine, and she was how I managed to scupper the girls' plans for an impromptu party with those Arsenal forwards the afternoon of the Wembley gig.'

'Okay, okay, just so as you know, loyalty is going to be a key issue over the next few weeks. We're gonna have to think carefully about who we can trust and…'

'Hannah is absolutely unimpeachable. Leave her alone! She's been with us from the start. And I know what you're like – you start harassing people and then they decide to wimp out.'

'Only 'cos they're guilty of something.'

Then it must have clicked with Anne what Kwame was getting at.

'You've been running new checks! On everyone?'

'Extra background scrutiny, and they're gonna continue until we catch this stalker, OK? So prepare for some nasty surprises.'

'Yes, of course Dread comes first.' Anne straightened and smiled at him. 'Okay. So what were you saying about forensics?'

'I had a quick check of the barrier that was meant to keep the crowd back, and there's a possibility it didn't just break by accident. We're gonna have to call metallurgic experts in. Because if the fencing was rigged to fail, then someone was banking on the crowd breaking through. In which case, their plan was that Dread would get injured, or worse.'

15

You come and you go
Leaving just your picture behind

'That *is* David Lewis!' spluttered Gerrard, unfolding a copy of the photograph that had been mailed to Philippa's office.

William sighed and stepped forward. He put one palm behind the prisoner's head, and using his other hand pushed his thumb and first finger into the eye sockets. The fugitive tried to dodge with shrieks of protest, and the surrounding police surged forward in horror.

William yanked upwards, and it looked as if the top half of the man's face had come away in his hands. A second skin resembling a moulting snake was held up in the streetlight.

'It's the kind of false bald head and forehead they use in movies,' William explained to Gerrard. 'Now we know why he sent Philippa that picture – he wanted us to be looking for the wrong man.'

Newly revealed grey hair flopped over the prisoner's worried eyebrows.

More shouts came from David Lewis's block. William jumped on to the side step of the helicopter to gain a better view.

The council flats looked like they had been designed by the East German Police Station school of architecture, but they still embraced a trellis, and a shadow was inching precariously over it to the top of the building. It scuttled across the roof and out of view. Beneath were more flashes, like silent explosions detonating in his flat. But those couldn't be the NFDDs.

'I suspect *that* is David Lewis,' William helpfully pointed out as he mentally kicked himself.

Their target could have another motive for sending the signed picture to Philippa's office. It wasn't from a delusional belief that she fancied him and he shared her celebrity status. That is what an erotomaniac would do. Instead, was he playing at having the disorder rather than actually suffering from it, and for William's benefit?

This was most peculiar and possibly a first example in the history of psychiatry. But could he usefully share this conclusion with Gerrard Winstanley, who was already infuriated with the vagaries of psychiatric diagnosis?

The riot squad set off at a thumping speed down the street and police vehicles began wailing, the light bars on their roofs flicking shadows.

'Well, who the hell is *that* then?' the Assistant Commissioner snarled, pointing to their prisoner.

'He's not important, he's a distraction,' William shouted back. 'He's in shock and too disorientated to be questioned, thanks to the NFDDs. David factored that in when throwing you a hostage. He predicted *precisely* how you'd go in.'

William's curiosity was piqued by fresh weals on the captive's face. He peered closely at the marks and at the strange garb. It had buckles and belts all over it. These had been undone, so now straps draped down the man's trembling body.

An officer handed William an old fashioned World War II gas mask. It was this which had cut into their captive's face and caused the marks. Had the stalker been prepared for all possible raid tactics?

'Lewis had an old flashgun attached to an ancient camera which he rigged to set off multiple flashes. The sudden bright light disabled our night vision technology and it's then they think he got away,' the office explained.

'You realise what this means?' said William as he fingered the heavy clasps. 'David fashioned a special suit so that he and the man were buckled together. When one moved, the other did as well. It would have looked, on the X-ray machine, like it was one person rather than two. That's why you thought there was a sole occupant in there. That's why you stopped looking after you found this guy. You heard David's voice but he was using this body double as a decoy.'

Enraged, Gerrard blared above the high-pitched clamour of

the chopper engines exploding into action. 'You said he was too mentally ill to have any collaborators! That this was a one-man operation, because when you get this deluded no one else will share your beliefs! So what do you call this, then?'

'They were strapped together! I don't call that collaboration – more coercion,' William screeched back. 'Maybe this *was* collaboration of a sort – in which case he may not be that psychotic,' he mused, more to himself than the AC.

An officer grabbed Gerrard's arm and bellowed into his ear.

'He's getting away! We're being blocked by the crowds so we're going to have to take the chopper.'

'If his stooge was collaborating then it would mean…'

William was startled at the implication. 'It would mean that when we went into the flat, we assumed that David was outside Philippa's. But he wasn't. It was this chap. We were setting up monitoring devices, yet all the time *he* was monitoring *us*. He was presumably under the floorboards. He heard everything we said!'

William recalled that the discovery of mutilated magazine pictures pasted on the walls of David's flat, Philippa with her mouth cut out, had reminded Gerrard of William's homily on the case of Michael Perry. That stalker had become fixated with Olivia Newton-John, developing various bizarre delusions, including that she was responsible for dead bodies rising through the floor of his home.

Had David Lewis signposted, to anyone capable of reading the signs, where he had been hiding all along? Was he testing William on his own home turf, his expertise, and was the psychiatrist being found wanting?

'Never mind all that now! Come on,' Gerrard ordered sharply as William was bundled into the cockpit. 'He's gone after the Minister – got to head him off fast!'

16

And fiery demons all dance when you walk through that door
Is There Something I Should Know?

'*Konnichiwa*! Relax, everyone, all is going to be fine – I'm here now!' Nishido Kitaro skittered in, swinging his cape with an expansive air, a slim computer under his arm. 'Is this the after-party?'

The toothsome smile of her keyboard player would normally charm Dread, but tonight she pondered what lay behind it. Even the jaunty angle at which his shuttered shades were perched on his black straight hair annoyed her.

'This is not the after-party, it's the suicide pact!' Mean looked even more exasperated.

'Dominique, she ask me, you do tweet-tweet? So I come consult with you!'

Sullen silence greeted him.

'So how is Dread gonna account for that abortion of a concert?' Mean demanded.

'That not what I write about.'

'Why not?'

'It's soooo twenty minutes ago,' said Nishido as he tapped the keyboard on the tablet and flourished the screen to Mean.

'Why, what's happened?' Dread craned to look.

'You haven't heard? *Doji*! Biiig news leak! Biiig News! Dread playing wedding of Wilfrid Sellars-*san* and Charlotte Perkins-*san*. It all over Internet – main spectaculation seem to be how much Dread-*san* being paid for wedding singer.'

Everyone looked over to their lead singer.

'I don't believe it! You're going without the band, aren't you, so there's more dosh for you,' said Mean as she waved a walkie-talkie admonishingly at Dread. 'I'm going to find out the fee and tell 'em. How are they gonna feel then?'

'No need,' explained Nishido. 'It here on web. Five to ten million.'

'But you need the make-up team to come with you, right?' Hannah had taken a step back, like she was withholding mascara to ransom. 'I mean, it's about the look, right? The idea is to put Charlotte to shame on the appearances front? Right?'

On the one hand, Dread could detect the artful handiwork of the press relations team, spraying chaff to confuse the media after the concert riot. On the other hand, this was high stakes spin control.

'For an *hour?*' Mean was leery.

'That's dollars, not pounds,' Dread responded defensively, relieved the true figure hadn't got out.

'He *like* Dread, like chart single. He move from number sixteen to now he just inside top ten of the world's – *kanemochi* – richest men,' Nishido confirmed. 'And she get to visit his own ultra-secure private island – Petit Nevis – seventy-one acres with own airstrip.' Nishido displayed a picture of the lush green island floating in a sea of azure on the screen.

'Does it say where the leak came from?'

Dread squirmed deeper into her chair – all leaks were authorised by the diva, everyone knew that.

'You're not taking the jets. We need 'em for the tour,' Mean said firmly.

'Actually, he's sending his super yacht for us,' Dread retorted.

'Oh wow!' Hannah could see the possibilities. 'Given Charlotte is your…'

'…number one celebrity feud partner,' interrupted Nishido, reading from the screen.

'Ah yes, Charlotte Perkins – queen of the power ballad. What were you thinking accepting the gig? She's just trying to humiliate you,' Mean said. 'She landed the big fish and you're just a bit player at the wedding of the decade.'

'What wedding song you come up with?' Nishido asked wickedly.

'What about Kanye West's "Gold Digger"?' suggested Hannah.

'Or "The Lady Is A Tramp"?' murmured Dread.

'"Like a Virgin"?' queried Nishido.

'You're not going to take the money and then sing something really inappropriate, are you?' The light was dawning for Mean.

'*Yabai*! This going to be so cool.'

Nishido began to disappear out the door.

'How many Dreads does it take to change a light bulb?' Mean growled.

'I've heard this one,' Hannah responded. 'It's doing the rounds on the fan forums. It's one. She holds the bulb and the world revolves around her.'

The walkie-talkies beside Mean babbled the police frequencies.

...Got a group of approx 100 fans...from the concert...running south down West Drive...please advise...possible 415...

As if on cue, Dominique Schnapper entered the room like a cold front, varnished nails brushing through her long brown hair. She was furious. '*Merde*! Please, Dread, we sack Damaris! She has lost the Alexander McQueen that you are supposed to wear at the press conference.'

'But it's basically in shreds!'

'*Exactement*, Hannah!' Dominique snapped furiously. Then she saw Dread's face. '*Mais c'est bien! Fantastique.*'

Dominique grabbed Hannah's hand. 'You make her look worse, not better! She looks like she has just done fifteen rounds with the rioters. *Parfait!* I wanted this, *exactement*! This will be the front page of every newspaper tomorrow. Dread fresh from the fight, hair matted with blood. Brave, defiant. What a coup!'

17

Ain't no mountain high enough
Ain't no valley low enough, ain't no river wide enough
To keep me from getting to you, baby

William tussled with his headset until the co-pilot reached over and pulled his glasses off so the headphones could be lowered. Plugging the lead in filled the snug cockpit with agitated static-drenched voices.

Beating out a rasping pitch, the helicopter accelerated upwards. West London spilled out below them, illuminated by the blue and red flashing lights of chasing police cars.

William floundered about for something to grip, trying to steady his nerves as he peered over the side of the aircraft then flinched away from his window. He was beginning to detest this particular stalker. The pursuit was developing into the psychiatrist's worst nightmare – swooping over London with Gerrard yammering in his ears. And the infernal pilot kept straying way too close to high-rise buildings on all sides. Part of William now hoped the armed units would just open fire on David Lewis and be done with it.

The Nightsun searchlight hoovered up the darkness below the chopper, replacing it with glaring white. The police were setting up multiple roadblocks below them, and bleached figures turned to shield their eyes before scurrying away from the ring of light.

'Those marks on his face!' William's distorted voice inside the cans sounded more professional than he felt. 'If they were wearing gas masks it means they knew they were going to be raided. If he walked around strapped to that other guy then he surmised you were using Backscatter X-ray next door.'

None of the uniforms arguing with each other in the back looked up.

'And that shows he's able to get inside another person's mind and make plans accordingly,' continued William. 'That's why he took the light bulbs out – he couldn't trust his co-conspirator to remember not to switch the lights on. People with psychosis are supposed to be particularly weak in that kind of anticipation.'

William was now wondering whether they could be dealing not with an erotomaniac, but with a Resentful Stalker. Resentment could arise out of severe paranoid beliefs about the victim, where stalking was a way of "getting back". The initial motivation was the desire for revenge to "even the score".

Resentfuls present themselves as victims, justified in using stalking to fight back against an oppressing person or organisation. The stalker feels they've been maltreated, and they're the victim of some injustice or humiliation. It is an intriguing one because in point of fact – superficially at least – the stalker doesn't want a relationship. It just looks that way from the outside.

But William must try not to confuse the police further.

The helicopter abruptly changed direction, heaving William from one side of his seat to the other.

The AC and Superintendent were bellowing into their headsets, directing their troops on the ground. There was more visible alarm at this level of officialdom than William had ever seen before. The senior officers were in serious trouble. They had let the stalker – gauged to represent a serious threat to a Cabinet Minister – slip through their fingers.

Again.

'We're going to move back towards Westminster because this chap's most likely to be heading for the Minister there,' said Gerrard.

'Why d'you think that?' asked William, dumbfounded.

'Because it's the obvious destination. His collaborators will have had her home in Maida Vale watched. They'll know the Minister's left there for Parliament, so he'll know where she is. And she's heading for the House of Commons.'

William shook his head vigorously.

'No, no, no! Try to get inside his head and think like him. He figures that is precisely what you'd deduce, so it's the last place he'd target.'

'So where's he going then?'

'Philippa's home in Maida Vale. He'd have been fantasising about her and him there.'

'But that makes no sense. He must know that we'll have doubled security there!' The AC couldn't hide his consternation. 'Especially since we cleared the demonstrators out of her street.'

Tall buildings were beginning to fill the skyline.

'Hold it! Let's hover here for a moment,' Gerrard commanded the pilot. They lurched to a suspended standstill. He turned to William, his face tight and harsh.

'Maida Vale is in the opposite direction to Westminster, so we've got to get this right. Explain to me why he's going to her home rather than her office.'

'He thinks she'll have made it a safe refuge for him.'

'Sir, Parliament makes more sense. It's where she's heading,' argued an officer by Gerrard's side. The helicopter pilot turned his head slightly to look at William.

'It's the wrong move. He's going to her home.'

'But what harm can he do there?'

Everyone was now gawking at the psychiatrist and the Assistant Commissioner.

'Okay, let's review a brief list,' William said. 'Stalker Margaret Ray kept breaking into David Letterman's Connecticut home, often just days after being released from gaol for trespassing on his property. She slept in his place when he was away and drove around in his cars. When arrested in one, she claimed to be his wife and the mother of a non-existent son. She killed herself in 1998.

'In 1999, Athena Rolando slept in Brad Pitt's clothes in his Hollywood house and stayed there for ten hours before being arrested. By the way, she was carrying a book on witchcraft.

'Earlier, in 1996, Robert Dewey Hoskins broke into Madonna's mansion, Castillo del Lago in the Hollywood Hills, on several occasions. When asked to leave by her assistant, he threatened to cut Madonna's throat if she did not marry him. He was shot twice by Madonna's personal bodyguard in the arm and the stomach after the stalker tried to take the holstered gun off him. He received a ten-year sentence. I could go on, but is anyone spotting a pattern here?'

Silence but for the helicopter's rotor blades clattering.

'They go to the homes because they believe they have an intimate relationship with the quarry. A stalker like David Lewis is much less likely to go to her office because that's where the rest of the world goes, the ones who haven't got the special connection with Philippa he believes he has.'

More silence. Indecision filled the air and William sighed.

'Look, okay, let's go to Parliament. If it turns out to be the wrong call, then I'll put in my report that, in my view, it couldn't be predicted where he went, and it wasn't a bad decision given the circumstances. I'll back up the Met, no matter what.'

Gerrard glared at him.

William waited, letting himself think back to Philippa's home. Not just to what he'd surmised from their jaunt in her bedroom after the stalker had roamed around there. William didn't want to go back, though – the place held too many bad memories; too many reminders of opportunities he'd missed to initiate something with her properly.

Philippa had seemed to be cosying up to him once in her ministerial limousine as they pulled up outside her grand Maida Vale terrace, but then the construction site opposite had distracted her. A disused church, which had been an early victim of the chapel fires epidemic, was being converted into a luxurious modern house, the embryonic form sporting a slew of scaffolding with tarpaulin draped across it. Philippa had been impressed at the sheer "balls", as she put it, of the newly arrived Russian oligarch buying up houses on either side of the church to knock through walls.

'It's like he just doesn't care about rules, he remodels the world to fit his design,' she breathed in awe. 'Did you see those pictures in the tabloids of the safe the size of a room where he's gonna store some of that gold of his? The engineering alone to cope with all the weight has been pioneering.'

'Groundbreaking,' William had replied dryly as he replayed in his mind the awe in her voice: *he remodels the world to fit his design.*

Sergei Bulgakov, a gold-mining tycoon, had been the toast of the town after breezing in, riding a cold wind from the Urals of sudden disfavour with Putin.

Philippa had obsessed about how her house price might be affected by his landing on the whole opposite side of her street, and his remodelling bug had jumped the road and infected her. The constituency secretary later confirmed that the oligarch's architect had been invited to give an opinion on the design possibilities of her place. The psychiatrist realised it was this Russian who had inspired Philippa to reshape her house, the cover being she was moving the constituency office in, boosting her public image of the round-the-clock Member of Parliament.

William was suspicious about Philippa's motives. Maybe she had cleverly got the party to pay for a bigger press conference space, allowing her to court journalists twenty-four hours a day. As she was divorcing her first billionaire, perhaps she was already inspecting another one for her collection.

'Those images are just a con the press has fallen for,' William had muttered, vainly trying to divert her from her latest distraction. 'He's showing those photos so any burglar, taxman or state official searching his house for sequestered gold will end up looking in the wrong place. He's got some real location for his bullion, and it ain't there. After what just happened in Russia, he's learnt he's going to have to move the stuff fast at short notice.'

It also came back to him that Dread – that glacial model who'd appeared in a spate of advertising hoardings across town – had caused him another moment of unease. Philippa had seemed intrigued by the pop star. The shot, that he recalled as being particularly pornographic, had been taken from above. Dread gazed up into your eyes – innocence and knowingness playing across her face. A man dressed in a priest's outfit had his head buried in her bosom, and she had his hair clenched in her fist. Her back was arched, ensuring her pert behind strayed into shot. The remnants of some kind of orgy spilled across the altar of a church, rendering the debauchery even more sacrilegious. He now recalled Philippa had gestured to it from the limousine that day with the comment:

'Now that's what's known as foreplay, William.'

What was she getting at? he'd wondered. Enticing people into a state of desire was a way of controlling them, he'd argued with her.

'Okay, we're going to her home,' the AC announced. The

officers got on to the radios, adjusting the search.

'How'd you do that?' A new voice startled William. Then he realised it was the pilot.

'How did I do what?'

'You have to switch channels if you want to speak to me so they can't hear us back there.' The pilot flicked a switch on the dashboard in front of them. 'There you go...so, how'd you do that? Get Winstanley to change his mind and go with your destination? I've been flying him for years and *never* seen that before.'

A pair of flickering ambulances raced down Harrow Road in the opposite direction to their line of flight.

'Could we move a bit further away from the BT Tower?' William pleaded.

What if he had got this wrong? *Psychiatry is about probability, not certainty,* he thought.

'Everyone will work hard to avoid regret so that's what I did just now. I helped him glimpse his possible concern in a few days' time.'

William spoke confidently, but inside he was wondering about his ability to manipulate. Everyone demanded a diagnosis, a category, a box in which to dump people, stalkers, whoever.

'The experiment requires that you continue,' he muttered to himself. The pilot looked over quizzically.

But the fact was none of these pigeonholes captured anyone properly. Life was too complex, so the diagnoses were often pragmatic. You had to know the limits of their usefulness. The police, the press and Philippa craved diagnostic labels as a form of certainty. But he knew the truth was scarier than that.

A whole lot scarier.

18

And you keep it just for fun, for a laugh, ha-ha-ha
Where Do You Go To My Lovely?

'This is such a new image for you, Dread. It's going to be on the front pages of every newspaper around the world tomorrow. Brave, defiant. People are going to look at it and do a double take. They are going to want to read on.'

Dominique Schnapper was turning the room upside down in her frantic search for the stage dress.

'Okay. But you don't want horror ER lurid. You want tasteful beaten-up, right?' Hannah interjected defensively.

'She appears fresh from the fight, clothes torn, hair matted with blood – we're gonna be the lead story on every news bulletin!' Dominique turned on her heels and searched the room vigorously, flinging clothes behind her.

'What are you doing now?' Hannah asked warily.

'Looking for *le* Alexander McQueen she was wearing out there...'

'But it's ripped up and covered in muck!'

Items of haute couture fluttered past them. It was a rainstorm of high fashion.

Hannah skilfully caught a blouse in mid-air that was in danger of dive-bombing Dread's bouffant. Keeping a vigilant watch on Dominique, she quickly added a surreptitious daub to Dread's eyes.

'*Exactement*! She has to wear that when we go out there for the press.'

Dominique's radio transmitter, which was clipped to her lapel, buzzed. She glanced down at it.

'I think it's a great idea,' said KT Mean as she slipped off the dressing table, sending a cascade of papers and magazines fluttering to the floor and grappling with Hannah. 'Where's the bitchtits's dress? You've hidden it!' she shouted as they scuffled over Dread's prone body.

'Say again?' Dominique commanded into the receiver with a sharp hand raised to stop the fighting behind her.

'*Mais non, non*. We're taking her round *le* back, stage lights go off, and she appears from behind the press. Dramatic surprise, the spotlight goes on. You must get the entrance right – it's absolutely crucial that it's a complete blackout. Do you understand?'

Dominique's whitened knuckles gripped the walkie-talkie.

More snap, crackle and pop, and then Kwame's voice, inflated with static, barricaded the room.

'It's not safe. Groups of breakaway fans are roaming the building. The press conference is cancelled. The evac plan is active now. We're getting out!'

19

Hungry like the wolf
Mouth is alive with juices like wine

Alarmed crackle on their headsets, then a burst of urgent shouts.

A police car, a matchbox toy from this height, screeched up outside Philippa Foot's house. Two officers emerged and galloped back from where they had come. The helicopter searchlight chased them, while the police guards outside her front door also set off in what the watchers in the helicopter could now see was a pursuit.

A shadow skulked from a narrow alley and dodged frantically. Even from up here, William could recognise David Lewis. Something characteristic about the fidgeting way his body moved – William had noted it when David was climbing the trellis. It even had a name in medicine: akathisia, a side effect of psychiatric medication or psychosis causing sufferers to shuffle back and forth, yet the cause remained controversial.

'David Lewis,' he said, pointing downwards.

Everyone's eyes were locked on the shadowy residential streets through which the silhouette was running hard, skipping with an added twitch every now and again. He rounded a corner, back into Philippa's road, and headed straight for her house.

David eluded the first two officers who came at him with a feint and a dodge, then another police car almost drove right into him. David leapt on to the bonnet and hurdled the windscreen, slamming on to the roof. Uniformed arms reached for his feet from below. As more police cars slid into his way, he hopped on to them, swinging over car roofs then jumping down, scuttling across bonnets, leaving dents in his wake.

William could hardly bear to watch. Any moment now David was going to tumble off and get crushed under a wheel. The police kept chasing stalkers down, and it kept ending mortally. FTAC was supposed to herald a new health-focused approach.

The helicopter twisted in the wind as David's dancing form skipped the arms that were reaching out to him.

He reached Philippa's front patio. Street parking suspension notices because of the Russian's building works flapped in the downdraught. As the chopper came in lower, they shredded, flying away. *The residents are going to be pleased*, reflected William as his mind went walkabout.

Knees bent expertly, hands akimbo as an additional arriving car tried to block Philippa's front gate, David flew on to its bonnet. It ploughed through the opening, dislodging bricks from a low wall, and took him precariously right up to the door of the house. Protection squad from indoors began pouring out of the front door. As the uniforms converged on him, David, back arched, was stretching up to a balcony on the first floor. He hung in the air for an eternity, fingers slipping from the edge, before gravity insisted and he fell heavily on to the roof of a police car.

He was suddenly oddly still and several officers grabbed for his torso. Galvanised, David rolled one way and then another, but finally he was spread-eagled on the roof with a bevy of blue sitting on him.

In the headphones, the AC's voice was appalled.

'My God, he doesn't ever give up, does he.'

David looked up at the helicopter, and a quiver pulsed down William's spine as he found himself looking right into the berserk man's eyes through the close-up on the video screen in the cockpit. The frenzied figure heaved his body back and forth, and somehow, despite all the tethering, he wobbled to his feet. Face chalk white in the helicopter's searchlight, he bellowed upwards.

As the chopper twirled, William noticed that the large sheets of tarpaulin covering Bulgakov's scaffolding opposite had begun to flap agitatedly from their downdraught.

Gerrard leant forward.

'Damn, damn, damn!' he cursed. 'Where are the press when you need them? This is the perfect photo opportunity. There he is, tackled to the ground by officers right outside Philippa Foot's home. Goddamn!'

111

David had now been brought to his knees, but he was still shouting upwards. William strained to listen. Was it his imagination, or had he just caught his name being shrieked?

On the channels came: *He's really losing it down here, Sir, making all sorts of vicious threats to your psychiatrist. Is there any chance we could medicate him? If he keeps resisting us this violently he's going to do himself, or someone down here, an injury.*

Gerrard reached forward and prodded William.

'Shouldn't you give him something to calm him down?'

William sighed.

'We've been through this before. It's not safe to wield a needle out here, so far away from any resuscitation equipment.'

Just then one of the Bulgakov sheets of tarpaulin, flicked by the gale force of the helicopter's rotors, ripped at its moorings. Metal leant away from the construction site across the street, swaying punch drunk. A hefty sheet broke free and skated across the road, rippling like a flat seabed creature.

It slipped up the vehicle where the police were wrestling with David, enveloping them. All the helicopter's passengers could now distinguish were shapes fighting beneath the billowing expanse.

The pilot pulled away, but the downdraught of the move meant several other gigantic expanses of fabric frayed away, flowing over to engulf the melee.

Writhing shadows under the flapping canopy were etched out by the searchlight until the police finally began gathering up the material, pulling back the shrouds.

They stared at each other.

David had vanished.

20

You'll be dead before your time is due
We gotta get out of this place

'Hello, hello? Robert? Hello? Yeah, just finished the presser. Well, if you can call it that.'

Dread's eyes were wide with fury as she barked into the phone.

Kwame snapped it from her fingers. She glared at him and turned to find another from the entourage, but they weren't behind her. Kwame shepherded Dread into the passageway, motioning to his team waiting outside. They promptly formed a human barrier between Dread and the journalists chasing her out of the Rose Bowl's conference room.

Hannah became trapped behind the barricade of sentries and waved a make-up brush forlornly at them as Dread was hauled away by her bodyguard.

Kwame pushed his pop star ahead of him as she gesticulated angrily. 'We can't ditch the press conferences!' she shouted.

But her bodyguard was as close to livid as Dread had ever seen him. He waited until they had rounded a corner before turning on her.

'I let you have half of one, which is more than was wise. Groups of breakaway fans are roaming the building. It's not safe. And we've got another serious security problem, Dread, so listen up. There was another note left here today by *that* stalker. And now we can't be sure what's going on – none of the forensic experts we're consulting have ever come across anything like this before. We're in unknown territory, so right now I'm thinking *nowhere* is totally secure.'

He grabbed her black short clinging Versace cocktail dress by the shoulder and began dragging her. She didn't want it to rip, so, reluctantly twisting, she had to start loping along to join his quickening stride. They had abandoned the tattered remnants of the "concert-dress-stratagem" back in her dressing room. While her new ankle-high boots were more practical, their tall heels still impeded the pace Kwame wanted to go at.

'Listen, if I'd known we were going for a run instead of a press conference, we could've gone with a different wardrobe scenario,' she retorted when he kept impatiently shoving her.

They were snaking through the clanging backstage corridors of the Rose Bowl, squeezing past roadies balancing equipment on their shoulders and skirting the dance troupe in states of excited undress.

Kwame had dispatched a patrol of eight security personnel, four in front and four behind. Down parallel corridors on either side of them darted other teams of security personnel, running interference.

Bursts of static from Kwame's walkie-talkie were followed by him rasping back, 'Bravo Zulu, Bravo Zulu, over.'

At hallway crossroads he paused and checked both sides before scampering on. Throngs dashed past just yards away, heading in other directions too fast to make out who they were, while screeches rebounded around them. Dread slunk in a bit closer to her bodyguard.

Dressing room doors had been left ajar. Endeavouring not to make it obvious to Kwame, she peeped at news bulletins from accusing TV screens on the walls inside. A flickering strobe effect took hold as they cantered down the echoing corridors. As they slipped past each doorway, if several TVs in a row were tuned to the same channel, a whole segment would make some kind of jumbled sense. The glimmers began to merge together to provide a sputtering portfolio of images, sandwiched confusingly with adverts.

But jeopardy flared up right at the end of the spectacular concert at the Rose Bowl. We are getting reports that a fight broke out between the security staff and some sections of the crowd who attempted to mob the stage...

There were various views of Dread dropping from the stage and disappearing from view. Now another person jogging with a camera, breathing heavily as they turned to run away from the mob. *The viewers are surely seasick from the bobbing images,* considered Dread, feeling a flare of her panic returning. But she also knew Dominique would be arguing that it all added to the sense of drama and would be pleased.

No bulletin, so far, carried anything about a fan being stabbed in the face with her microphone.

As they descended further through the stadium, the dressing rooms disappeared. Soon it was just Kwame and Dread pounding for the exit, and the eerie wails became muffled behind them.

'Your limo's waiting for you. The sooner you're outta here the better.'

'So there was another threat. So what?' Dread asked irately.

'Because this note was found in your dressing room. You know what that means?'

Dread looked blank. She saw him sigh inwardly and knew what he was thinking – *God, was she hard going.*

'It's someone on the inside,' he explained patiently, 'not the outside, as we previously thought. And very, very few people have security clearance to get into your dressing room.'

'Whatya talking about? My dressing room, my so-called "inner sanctum of peace", it's like bleedin' Piccadilly Circus with visiting celebs,' Dread complained. 'They come, they go – and so do their hangers-on. Any of them coulda left it there.'

He shook his head. 'Look, before you talk to any more press, the advice we've had from the forensic psychologists is that the guy might be getting a buzz out of his notes being discussed publicly.'

'Oh, you want me to stop talking about it? At the interviews? Stop telling this loser I'm not afraid of him?'

'The headshrinker thinks it may also be something to do with the "More Famous than God" stuff. Maybe a cult with many members, some in the media. So how much can you trust that Robert Recorde?' he asked, almost not touching the stairs as they descended. Dread skipped along, keeping up because she never lost a race.

'He's in the Congo covering the war. You know that, so what are you getting at?'

They burst through swing doors, and there ahead was the stage door.

'Okay, he's a TV news journalist. Are you absolutely sure he's not just having a fling with you in order to land the story?'

'*Everyone* has a fling with me in order to land the story,' Dread said coolly. 'And right now he's pissed off that my concert has pushed him off the news agenda.'

'Hmmm, I'm concerned that you returned his call at this moment. I keep warning you. You can't trust anyone.'

'Robert isn't like that. He's into hard news. He's seething that hundreds of thousands have died in the Congo and it's still celeb stuff that grabs the headlines.'

She recalled from the dressing room TV screens grainy shaky images of her straining into a microphone. Cut to a shot of screaming girls running drunkenly to and from the melee while the rabble on the stadium floor throwing punches clouded and then resolved into pin-sharp terror. Staring eyes and bleeps and then more prolonged bleeps obscured expletives.

Exactly how could the crisis in the Congo compete with that?

'I thought you were checking Robert Recorde hadn't dumped The Dread before you had a chance to axe him,' Kwame said dryly. 'You looked a bit panicky in the press conference when you were asked about him.'

Dread grinned. 'It's complicated. Men! Can't live with 'em... can't shoot 'em.'

'Lemme guess, the plan's changed and now you need a kiss and a cuddle, so Robert is back on.'

'For the time being, yeah.'

'But he should start to sweat if that single begins to plummet down the charts and we need a bounce from a gossip story that it's over between you.'

'If I were him I would get everyone I know to download it hand over fist. You gotta problem with that? Now show me this skanky note.'

Kwame appeared undecided, so she glared, hands on hips, chest heaving and glistening from the exertion. Surely he knew better than to resist when her voice reached a certain pitch and tone.

He pulled it from his pocket. There was an image she had seen before in the very early letters before Kwame stopped showing them to her. It was a lurid picture of her being mutilated with knives, axes and saws. The words printed in black capitals in a gothic font across the bottom read:

You gotta stand trial
Because all the while
I can see for miles and miles.
I can see for miles and miles.

She put her hand to her mouth and Kwame grabbed the note back.

'What is it?'

'It's...it's...' Her chest heaved and she felt the glimmerings of panic returning, whispering in her ear.

Kwame's hands gripped her shoulders.

'It's just a song lyric from one of your remixes, right? *The Who* is the original group, right?'

Dread shook her head.

'When I fell into the crowd in the concert, Kwame, someone in the mob whispered those exact same words to me. And then a pile of them tried to kill me.'

21

Although she may be cute
She's just a substitute

Gerrard placed a hand over the microphone and leant over to William.

'What the heck are you doing?'

'I'm answering the question. This strategy to catch David with a published personality profile will only work if he knows we're properly credentialed,' William replied.

They had press released William's personality analysis of David Lewis and, to everyone in FTAC's surprise, the profile had launched a media feeding frenzy. The only other story vying for the headlines that morning seemed to be rioting during an LA pop concert. Both screamers had pushed the war in the Congo off the front pages.

'You're screwing this up. Get a grip,' Gerrard hissed.

The press conference had begun to go off beam when the journalists insisted that stalking celebrities was a completely new phenomenon. William's natural irritability with this kind of ignorance wasn't helped by his exhaustion, having been up all night chasing David Lewis.

'According to Frances, the media always wants a story to be brand new. Who cares about this Eddie what's-his-name?' Gerrard's hand was cemented to the mike.

It seemed like every press and broadcast hack in the country specialising in crime was squeezed into the small room. Paddington Green Police Station was fitted out for detaining terrorists, not press conferences. William faced a barrage of TV cameras and telephoto lenses pointed at him over the heads of the press at the front.

The argument had begun about the Robert Redford film

The Natural. Many had seen it, and now the journalists thought they were experts. Frances was nowhere to be seen, which was a bit of a mystery as she seemed to be becoming Gerrard's media strategist.

'It's a fictional account, only loosely based on what is often regarded historically as the first truly dangerous celebrity stalking case,' said William.

Gerrard reluctantly removed his hands from the microphone.

'The real life sports star whose biography formed the basis of the movie was Eddie Waitkus, a Chicago baseball hero stalked by baseball fan Ruth Ann Steinhagen,' stated William to the press. 'When Eddie moved to another team in 1948, Ruth felt betrayed. That's a common theme in stalking which turns dangerous. She had been amassing cuttings on her idol since the age of eleven, and even laid a place setting for him at the dinner table.'

'So, Doc, she was mad as a box of frogs?'

William ignored the intervention from the floor as he continued.

'She eventually checked herself into a hotel where Waitkus was staying on one of his first return trips to Chicago. She left him a cryptic message inviting him to her room.'

'And this is the note you can still read yourself on the Internet? That's what you said, right?' asked a journalist.

William ignored the question. 'When he turned up, she shot him with a rifle at point-blank range. She immediately called the hotel reception and explained what she had done. She was arrested, found insane and sentenced to a psychiatric hospital where, after just three years of treatment, including electroconvulsive therapy, she was released.'

The room erupted.

'Three years?'

'Is that *all*?'

'That's crazy – are you sure you have that right?'

William held up supposedly calming hands, but they shook from nerves at the tumult he appeared to have provoked. He pulled them back down and tucked them under his armpits. It was a characteristic pose. Professor Tullia d'Aragona, head of his department at the Institute of Mental Health, was always motherly, pulling his hands out. She would know what to do now if she were here.

'The fact Ruth had called for help straightaway, indicated the psychiatrically disturbed nature of the crime, and that it was different to, for want of a better word, that of a *common* criminal.'

Gerrard gesticulated to him to start winding things up. The press were utterly confused.

'Doc, didn't the careful planning mean this Ruth character had a clearer mind than the shrinks realised?'

'Doctor, surely Ruth should have gone down for life?'

Gerrard leant back to the officers behind him. 'If I hadn't been forced to let him talk to the press...' His face was gnarled with thunder. 'This new strategy to catch the stalker relies too heavily on his briefing!'

William surveyed the room with dismay as pandemonium broke out. The AC leant in on him, muttering in his ear, 'Chaos, uproar and anarchy, your work here is done.'

Gerrard held up an arresting arm to maintain order.

'Apologies, but the doctor has to go now. He has a lecture to deliver and he's late.'

This was news to William. 'Wha...' he started to protest, but he was bundled out by an inspector while questions sang past his ears like bullets from a chasing posse.

He was frog-marched into the car park, finding with some alarm a text message from Tullia confirming that he did indeed have a lecture scheduled this morning. He was also handed a large case which, he was told, had been specially delivered.

More pressing was the crisis of what the hell he was going to talk about at the lecture. Senior faculty at the Institute believed stalking was a police matter and therefore beneath them. Others considered the field to be about common criminals rather than science – a behaviour, rather than a diagnosis; a tabloid preoccupation, rather than medicine; a social construct, rather than anything substantive. Sociology, rather than psychiatry – the list of objections went on and on.

And William hated public speaking, second only to flying. This was because of the tightrope he balanced on, constantly avoiding venomously blurting out what was really on his mind.

As he opened the rear door of the police vehicle designated to take him to the Institute, he was disconcerted to find Frances coiled up like a cat on the back seat.

There was something about her eyes... Backing away, he jarred the catch of the case open against the door, scattering the contents. T-shirts, CDs and mugs flew everywhere. He scrabbled on the ground, retrieving paraphernalia that had rolled under the wheels.

'You do overcomplicate things with all this stalking malarkey, y'know.'

He could hear her voice, muffled as he crawled by the door.

The objects rolling on the floor were emblazoned with curling hair entwining a resolutely phallic microphone, and various slogans. These included *Lost My Dread*, *InfraDread*, *Were you Bottle-Dread?*, *Best thing since Sliced Dread*, *Dread Spreads*, *I'm not Well-Dread*, *Thorough Dread* and *Knock 'em Dread*.

'Basically you've got people with problems who see getting into a relationship with someone who appears to have solved all of theirs as a...solution. It's cinchy,' Frances continued.

Why is she so interested in me? he thought.

William realised with horror that many of the accoutrements spilling out of the case were in fact sex toys, luridly sporting Dread's branding. He levered himself over the wheel arch of the car, not quite sure how to put the giant phalluses spilling across the rear seat back in the case while looking unconcerned.

Frances leant forward, holding a large pink veiny rubber penis between disdainful thumb and forefinger, eyebrows raised.

'I agree they're better than men – they never poke you in the back at four in the morning to check if you're in the mood.'

She retrieved a lacy thong and looked at him, pseudo-smiling.

'So Philippa's sent you shopping for her?'

Before William could object, she leant in and whispered, 'You were up in her bedroom so we both know she's hiding a dirty little secret.'

William was stunned. Could Frances know about the contents of the handbags? Or even what the UV lamp had illuminated on the Foreign Secretary's bed? He froze. He didn't want to give anything away by reacting.

'You don't like Philippa Foot because she's rich and supports the war. Can't you think of her as an ordinary woman having a hard time with a stalker?'

Frances snorted. 'Ordinary women being stalked don't have FTAC and Foreign Office security as back-up.'

'So you don't feel anything for what she must be going through with this stalking?'

'Look,' Frances said patiently, 'organisations working with stalking victims have a tendency to be irritated by any attention given to the problems of the rich and famous. It's ordinary people with no power or money and nowhere to turn for help who constitute most of the victims. You know this, Dr James.'

'But Philippa's all too aware, from her own personal experience, that power's no protection against the psychological damage that stalking causes to its victims.'

'Yeah, right,' she said without conviction.

He shook his head. 'It's something of an irony that Philippa's found herself being stalked. After all, it was she who had pushed the tightening of the anti-stalking legislation through Parliament.'

'You manipulated her into doing that?'

'No, her interest went back almost a decade to when, as a newly elected MP, she was approached by a constituent whose daughter had been stabbed to death by an ex-partner. Stephen Griffiths had stalked Rana Faruqui and threatened her for an extended period, and despite various incidents being reported to the police, including spying on her at night, breaking into her home and photographing her, they did nothing. Griffiths eventually stabbed her to death with a hunting knife. Discovered in Griffiths's car after his arrest was a "stalking kit" – rope, chisel, crowbar, rat poison, syringe, axe, saw, knives and a truncheon, plus books about stalking.'

Frances looked disconcerted.

'So you were kind of pursuing her from way back, eh?'

'She vowed at that point to bring about a change in the law. And when she was appointed to the Cabinet, she was as good as her word.'

'This is some kind of test, right?'

Then his mobile erupted. William hadn't had any sleep all

night and tiredness was settling like a fog over him. He was going to switch the infernal interruption off when he realised it was Philippa. Had they caught David using his new strategy already?

But he'd taken too long to answer and the call had gone to voicemail. He was now being offered the menu option of hearing the message. His shaking fingers fumbled for the buttons, and he pressed loudspeaker by mistake.

'Is this Bozo Number One or Bozo Number Two?' Philippa's voice was cold as it bounced off the doors of the car. Frances raised an eyebrow.

'Is this the idiot who blocks all attempts to get on with the job and catch this madman? Is this the dipshit who is making my life a misery and who is now stopping me doing my job as a Cabinet Minister? Both you *and* Gerrard! I simply cannot believe it! I've only just been briefed on what went wrong in the raid on David Lewis's flat. From now on you let your betters make the decisions. If you continue to obstruct this investigation I'm going to have you terminated!'

Somewhere in the distance William was aware of a click as the Minister disconnected the phone. He looked up at Frances. She was holding up a banner that had fallen out of the case.

It read: *Restraining Orders are really another way of saying I love you.* The pop star's logo of Dreadlocks underlined the words.

But the banner which truly disturbed William was the one lying on the seat between them:

Stalkers Have Feelings Too.

Oh. My. God! This deranged diva was making fun of her stalker. She was too out of her head on fame to realise just how incredibly dangerous that was. But why had none of her team consulted with a psychiatrist?

'Something not quite right with our Minister for Foreign Affairs? The victims of stalking are so very grateful for the scientific expertise you offer? On the inside there is still love and respect, yet mysteriously covered up on the outside by hatred and loathing.'

He tried to speak but could only emit a guttural, retching croak.

Part 2

Demoralise the Enemy from Within

Demoralise the enemy from within by surprise, terror, sabotage, assassination. This is the war of the future.
– Adolf Hitler.

Barak Obama has been boasting that he's killed more terrorist leaders than the previous four presidents combined...
– Gerard DeGroot, *The Sunday Telegraph Seven Supplement,* p27, 7 October 2012.

22

Teenage dirtbag
This must be fake
My lips start to shake

'*Vilhelm*? The future happiness of this poor student lies in your gift. Is it thumbs up or down?'

Professor Tullia D'Aragona looked over the top of her spectacles at the rear tier of seats where William was perched, isolated by yards of empty terraces from the group of academics that turned, following her gaze.

Thumbs down, he gesticulated. They were in the Institute's largest lecture theatre, but still the rest of the faculty appeared unhappy they hadn't managed to sidle yet further away from him.

She cleared her throat with a dry cough.

'But, Dr James, this is the fifth candidate in a row you have asked the committee to fail!'

He shrugged. Why did that matter? But William also was wary: whenever his head of department abandoned the affectionate Italian-accented "Vilhelm" or "Villy" for the more formal "Dr James", it normally meant an admonishment was on its way, often followed by extra departmental teaching duties, usually focused on the slower students.

His mobile vibrated. It was Gerrard. He pressed the busy button. Answering his phone in the middle of an examiners' meeting would be tantamount to *harakiri*. Also he had lost the will to live after explaining to the AC for the nth time that the fact David had made his co-conspirator wear a false face mask did *not* mean this was a case of the ultra-rare psychiatric syndrome *folie à deux*, where both patients share the same delusion.

In fact, it proved exactly the opposite, because the accomplice had not been keen to have his own face used as representing David's when the two of them had photographed it then dispatched it to the Foreign Secretary, masquerading that this was the stalker in the flesh. The collaborator clearly preferred they used the picture of him heavily disguised. He wasn't insane enough not to believe that sending a picture of your actual likeness as part of a stream of bizarre threats to the Foreign Office was anything other than buying a season ticket for the criminal justice system.

The key question was: what did this reveal about how crafty David Lewis was turning out to be? He was making Anders Breivik, the Norwegian mass killer, and the Unabomber look like rank amateurs. William couldn't confide in the AC, or even Philippa, but it was beginning to seem as though they were encountering a mind far more ingenious than any other in the history of Forensic Psychiatry. A mentality strangely driven to prove he was cannier than any psychiatrist.

Yet in the midst of this examiners' meeting, given the woeful standard of the current round of junior applicants to the profession, William thought that maybe David didn't have to go to such extraordinary lengths to prove himself.

The examinations committee was considering the merits of those candidates for the recent postgraduate exams who teetered precariously on the cusp of pass or fail. The standard of candidates endeavouring to become psychiatrists, even at the famous Institute of Mental Health, had fallen off the side of a cliff in recent years. They appointed junior doctors one day, then suspended them the next.

It was, literally, madness.

To William, the judgements he made were all about stopping doctors getting through who didn't give a damn about the patients. But for this committee it seemed to be a rubber-stamping exercise: pass them regardless. Psychiatry was suffering a deep recruitment crisis – half the posts in the regions were unfilled and shored up by locums.

'Could you explain to us in a little more detail why you believe she doesn't make the grade?' Tullia asked with formal politeness. 'I know you wrote the reason in the remarks section: *Inability to explain the difference between religion and psychosis.* But perhaps you could expand?'

William was distracted by the muffled wail of police sirens.

He nervously considered that the commotion was something to do with him – Philippa was a dangerous woman to annoy.

He hauled the patients to the front of his mind. He was, after all, fighting for them.

'Okaaay. So, in the pass-fail oral I gave her a clinical vignette. I described a case of a man who was brought to the clinic by his family. The patient maintained that he had been touched by the hand of the Divine. He believes he's a prophet and is here to save the world…'

Gerrard sent a text message: *Call me back – urgent – about DL.*

'Ah yes, this is the case that you shot a video of for the teaching tapes as well, isn't it?' Tullia interrupted.

'Yes. It's anonymous, of course, but this vignette is based on an actual patient.'

He hesitated for a moment as he glanced down at his phone again.

Urgent from AC. Call me re DL. Where are you?

'In order to differentiate a genuine mystic from someone with a clinical illness, I asked the candidate what questions she would ask of the patient, what tests she might order and what other information she would seek.'

Tullia leant forward, a tiny delicate clearing of the throat. Usually that was all she had to do: cough dryly in a committee meeting when William was off on one of his diatribes about the condition of the profession, or the state of the Institute, to bring him back into line.

'And what was it about her answer that rendered her unworthy of a pass?'

William shook his head, exasperated both with the student and the necessity to explain to people who were prepared to pass the unpassable.

'She couldn't answer the question. What she said, in the end, was that she would admit the patient to hospital for further assessment.'

'And what's wrong with that?' Tullia demanded. 'It's perfectly reasonable for a junior to admit where the situation isn't clear and await a more senior opinion.'

'Except that, say it was a Friday evening. That's three nights the poor man is going to be admitted to hospital against his will before Monday morning, when he's finally sprung by the consultant turning up to review what's washed up over the weekend.'

Our plan worked. We have him in custody. Call back, very urgent.

William's heart rubbed against his rib cage at the text message. He might soon be arriving back inside Philippa's circle of trust. One thing bothered him – *our?* It had been William's idea – not the AC's. But this wasn't the time to refer Gerrard to an academic committee, remonstrating about attribution. Not when the prize was Pip.

'But it would take an opinion from another doctor plus a social worker to sign the necessary commitment papers. The patient would not be admitted if these two other opinions disagreed with the admitting physician,' Tullia said. 'And we encourage our young doctors to ask for a senior opinion. If that was the candidate's answer, what on earth could be wrong with that?'

William read between the lines: let the system deal with it. Don't bring any clinical acumen to bear. Well, William *hated* the system. It ended up causing more distress than the mental illness it was supposed to treat.

'No,' he said firmly. 'The candidate didn't say they weren't sure – they said the patient was *definitely* psychotic. It was precisely that conviction which was so worrying to me. But the conclusion they came to isn't the point. I want them to show their reasoning process. *How* they think is more important than *what* they think.'

'Oh?' Tullia sat back. 'So now the actual answer they give is irrelevant – you were going to fail them anyway? But we train the doctors to follow National Institute for Clinical Excellence guidelines.'

'And I think we should educate them to think for themselves. I don't mind if they don't agree with me on the particular diagnosis in question. It's the *method* they deploy to argue their case. This candidate wasn't going to gather any more information from relatives or friends, or ask how the client had ended up in casualty. She decided purely on the patient's claims to be the next Messiah...'

'Perhaps' Tullia put the back of her hand to her forehead as if pained 'the candidate was playing the odds. After all, if there is to be just one Second Coming over 2,000 years, chances are you would have to be a very unlucky psychiatrist to call it wrong if you pragmatically assumed most Messiahs were psychologically troubled, rather than the actual deity.'

There was a titter from the audience, which relaxed the tension somewhat. Probably deliberate on her part.

Of course, he knew what this was really about.

She was infuriated with him because he wasn't helping keep the department's precarious finances afloat. In her view he was being his usual obsessive self in remaining aloof from the pop star's case. The diva's people were still circling like sharks, seeking a porthole. Abandon Philippa to gallivant across the world on a mindless rock tour? With a spoilt brat relishing annoying the God squad with a series of ridiculously juvenile pronouncements? The wheel might be spinning, but this hamster was dead.

William hadn't finished with this fight. He knew his head of department had the upper hand, but, if it came to it, he was going down all guns blazing.

'Surely the issue isn't whether the patient is God or not. It's whether we are *justified* in forcing treatment on them merely because they express a particular belief. It's got dramatic implications for their life, their employment prospects and their relationships if we admit them to hospital, even if just for a few days, given the stigma of a psychiatric admission – particularly one under the Mental Health Act.'

'But, Vilhelm,' Tullia's voice had taken on a steely edge, 'there are two possible errors here. One is that the patient isn't psychiatrically ill enough to warrant a detention against their will, so you admit them and discover you were wrong just a few days later. The second is that you let them go and discover too late that they were actively psychotic, and on top of that, dangerous. As a result they commit some harm to themselves or someone else, in which case you're going to end up in court. Plus you might be struck off. One is a career-ending error, while the other is a few days of discomfort for a patient. Which error would you prefer the candidate to make?'

He strained to contain his frustration. 'I thought, as an elite institution and a profession where we guard high standards fiercely, we were trying to admit candidates who aren't error prone as opposed to those who just make not such bad ones. Professor, colleagues – please! This is the last exam they are going to have to take, so it's downhill from here in terms of excellence. If they are intellectually sloppy now, what are they going to be like in a few years' time?'

'This is all about risk,' said Tullia. 'When we deal with the people we encounter on a daily basis – the suicidal, the angry – we juggle liability. That's why you should err on the side of caution – that's what we teach the juniors. Are you advocating they take the same dangerous gambles you do?' She shook her head. 'Your co-examiner passed the candidate, so we've decided that on this occasion it's a pass. Let's not forget this is a patient contending with absolute conviction they are God...sounding rather like a certain doctor not a million miles from here.'

'And I am sorry, but the Assistant Commissioner needs to speak to me,' William said, unable to control the tremble of resentment in his voice. He covered the earpiece with his hand. 'Gerrard? It's William. Look, I'm in the middle of an examiners' meeting – I can't talk.'

At first, police sirens gathering in the distance drowned the AC's voice. But not for long.

'We have him! You little ripper!' trumpeted the AC. 'He behaved just as predicted. He sent a stream of emails rebutting the false analysis of his personality that we published in the press this morning, enough to allow the boys in cyber forensics to match the anonymous threatening emails and notes he sent with other emails to Philippa Foot in her capacity as a trustee for St Martin-in-the-Fields. Turns out she was part of a committee that rebuffed his mad redesign plans for the church. We tracked the original emails that hadn't been encrypted back to the Internet café where he was using the wireless with his laptop, and we have him!'

'Great news, but...'

'My friend, no pointless questions! The problem now is that he refuses to talk properly to the docs at Belmarsh. He said he wants to see you. The Minister's orders are that you need to assess him, and she's insisting we send him to you at the Institute – under heavy guard, obviously. He's going to be with you in under an hour.'

'From the sound of things I think he's here already,' William said, the approaching sirens nearly drowning out the phone call. David Lewis was too dangerous to be anywhere outside maximum security, so this was a dicey game plan. What on earth was the imperious Philippa thinking now?

'No, that's the advance security party. Look, I think the Minister's got a bit obsessed with how he got into her bedroom. She wants to know what he did with that blessed photograph you said had disappeared.'

Then Gerrard was gone and William was wondering about Philippa's concern for the missing picture.

Tullia, adjusting her minuscule pillbox hat as if it was a crown that was too heavy, raised an elegant eyebrow. 'Perhaps you'd like to share what was so important, Vilhelm? Did you answer the Assistant Commissioner's prayers?'

Unable to stop himself, William grinned triumphantly. This might teach them that there was method in his madness.

'We've managed to snaffle the Foreign Secretary's stalker. That, er, personality profile we published in the papers today? His narcissistic personality couldn't allow some of the degrading theory on his background we put in there, so he sent in enough material via email for us to match his writing-style fingerprint with other emails he'd sent in when he wasn't stalking Philippa. I'd asked the cyber forensics team to screen all the emails and letters she'd ever had in a public capacity. I figured he'd have made some sort of contact before the stalking began, according to the official timeline.

'And as you know from Pennebaker's work, we can *all* be identified by recurrent patterns in our writing styles. Word usage, selection of special characters, the way we compose sentences, construct paragraphs – even the organisation of sentences into paragraphs, and paragraphs into documents. These are all a kind of personality signature.'

An impressed murmur was heard among the examiners.

Tullia examined William over the rim of her glasses. Doubtless she'd have words with him later on the ethics of planting a deliberately false profile.

'So why couldn't you do that before with the threatening notes he was sending?' one of the other professors asked.

'He was too clever. He obviously knew about stylometry and kept sending in communications that were too short for us to get a statistical purchase on his material. The high IQ psychotics like Anders Breivik think these things through to the nth degree, you know.'

'But Anders Breivik was found sane by the Norway Court!' sneered another examiner.

'I can't help it if the judiciary in Oslo had never heard of high IQ psychosis. Not all mental disturbance is biblical raving,' retorted William. 'The fact is that we needed something longer, so I concocted a bogus and demeaning personality profile. The point was to enrage him enough to set the record straight, to appeal to the narcissist in him who wants to demonstrate his superiority over us.'

'Very good, Vilhelm.' Tullia smiled like a mother proud of her brilliant but wayward son. 'And now we must get back to the examiners' meeting while we can.'

'Er...the only thing is that the police are bringing him here for me to assess him.'

'Which is my point entirely, Vilhelm. I think we are all very much aware of that, thank you.' Tullia's eyebrow rose again. By now it sounded as if a convoy of police cars was about to drive through the door.

'It is almost impossible for us to hear ourselves speak against the noise of the constabulary in full "bringing" mode. But let us try.' Her smile was sharp. 'We shall turn to clinical vignette number seven and eight on our sheets, two completely new case histories that Vilhelm himself just submitted. Indeed, they came in this morning. As you know, we're desperate for novel scenarios that the candidates won't have come across from past papers. So well done, Vilhelm.'

William stared.

He hadn't submitted a clinical vignette number seven or eight. He turned rapidly to that part of the new exam paper they were planning for next term. His chest struggled to support the crushing tons of lead that were being lowered on to it with every new sentence.

'The second one is a tad lurid even for Dr James, all about the Antichrist Delusion. This is too rare to be of use for exam purposes, but the first one…very interesting…'

William read with disbelief and horror.

…the father with chronic and severe alcoholism was convinced his wife was having an affair. The wife also drank heavily. They had frequent violent rows, which arose out of both developing similar paranoid delusions which also united them against the world. The police were called but didn't respond in time, or even at all on numerous occasions. This led to multiple visits to the local casualty departments. Eventually the father claimed to have definite evidence of her adultery, but his thirteen-year-old son refuted this piece of verification, resulting in the father serving a term in Broadmoor. On his release, even if they said they were reconciled, would you recommend this couple be allowed to re-engage in a relationship?

William's eyes battled to focus. The supposed vignette number seven was an unerringly accurate account of his childhood, a piece of ancient history he had managed to keep from his colleagues. Someone had found out and submitted the vignette to the examination committee in his name.

He now had his own stalker.

One of the front desk receptionists burst through the doors of the lecture theatre.

'I'm dreadfully sorry, Professor D'Aragona,' she began, flustered.

Behind the receptionist came a gaggle of armed police officers. Handcuffed in their midst was the hairy, twitching, dilapidated figure of David Lewis.

'The police said it was urgent – national security!' The receptionist wrung her hands.

Tullia considered David Lewis, who returned the look coolly, then looked behind her to the back-projected image of the clinical

135

vignette detailing William's past on the giant screen.

David squinted and studied it with a tilt of his head, shuffling back and forth on the spot.

'Obviously the dad is suffering from morbid jealousy,' his voice boomed out, confident but grating with scorn. Was there some kind of faded accent there? 'The couple have good-going *folie à deux* and the son has the Oedipus complex. I'm guessing the son's now got serious issues with authority figures. Do I pass?'

23

You got sirens for a welcome
There's bloodstain for your pain

'Level with me, Kwame. What's going on?'

Kwame briefly debated with himself. There was a flickering red and blue glow of police lights beyond the glass exit doors. These frosted panes were the last remaining barriers between Dread and the sanctuary of her hushed limousine. She wondered if she could take the question back and postpone this conversation for another day. She didn't want to remain another second in this lame-ass stadium.

'Okay, you know most crank mail is precisely that – from crazies who aren't ever going to be anyone to worry about. But this person is escalating and I think it's someone very close to you.'

Dread froze.

'I had already sent the mail to a man who is an expert on analysing crank mail. Han Fei's ex-FBI Behavioural Sciences Unit, and now works for his own security firm in LA.'

'Wait, I don't get it. If it's, like, someone in the band, what's the motivation?'

Kwame hesitated. In fact they both knew just how much everyone in the entourage hated her. Putting her sunny personality to one side, how many of the ex-boyfriends did he know about, or betrayed girlfriends of those boyfriends?

'That's why I want to bring another expert in. He's a psychiatrist based in London who also specialises in this area. But the American guy's threatened to pull out if we use anyone else, so we gotta play it carefully. I'm going to London tonight to check him out before we make a decision.'

'Why not try the LA dick-sneeze first? Then if he fails, switch to the English boffin.'

'Because I think we need every ounce of expertise working on this *now*. Also, this British geek has a completely different approach to the US consultant, and I think we need both techniques. One is statistical, mathematical, the other is psychological.'

'OK, I got an idea. We give them both boxing gloves and put them in a ring, and they fight for it. And the prize is me.'

'I don't think you understand. This Brit psych is so up himself he's ignoring my offer to fly him here on your private jet or first class travel and squillions in dosh for a meet, so now I've got to go all the way to London to drag him here.'

He opened the door to the warm night air, the conversation over as far as he was concerned. She was relieved – what on earth was he burbling on about? It sounded a bit like the time they had a problem choosing between two bass players. In the end they used both on stage until the two musicians couldn't stand it anymore and got into a vicious bar fight with each other, which resolved the problem once and for all.

Last man standing: it was simples.

Why couldn't they do the same with these two competing psycho-whatsits?

Kwame gestured at her to pause while he went outside to check the area. Through a crack in the door she could make out the rear end of a black stretch and, in the distance, some parked police cars with their roof lights flashing.

The row of limousines waiting to take her and the band away gleamed, shadowy and spectral, like a funeral cortege. She shivered. She mostly tried to forget that the band hated her guts. And after all she had done for them. Seriously?

So what. Screw 'em! she thought.

Kwame motioned for her to enter the car that was backing up towards her.

She dashed over, delighted to be seeing the last of the stadium. The door of the car was closing as Kwame banged on the roof, and the limousine sped away. She held the door open to shout at him for her phone, which he had confiscated just after the press conference, but the car was accelerating brutally and she fell back on to the leather seat. Loud music erupted out of the speakers and startled her.

You made a fool of me,
But them broken dreams have got to end.

Dread cursed, recollecting that Mean had said she'd put the CD of the final cuts for her next album into her limo. The driver seemed to have taken it upon himself to crank the volume up.

Hey woman you got the blues
'Cause you ain't got no one else to use.

'Yo! DJ!' She tried to shout above the din and reach for the open slammer at the same time.

There's an open road that leads nowhere,
So just make some miles between here and there.
Evil woman.

The privacy division between her and the driver remained resolutely up. The car was now speeding and careering from side to side, violently chucking her about. A loud clicking sound which paused then repeated puzzled her through the confusion of the parking lamps flashing past. Then she realised that the driver was trying to jam the central locking on. But the door on her side was still open. He must be trying to lock her in...

Wait, this didn't feel good.

There's a hole in my head where the rain comes in
You took my body and played to win.

A movement in the corner of her eye startled her. There was someone else on the back seat with her. She twisted, frightened, raising her hands instinctively to defend her face. Looming out of the murk was a ghostly flutter. Dread recoiled and brought her knees up ready to kick out with her boots.

'What the hell?'

Kristal's face swam into focus. 'What in tarnation is goin' on?' she said.

Kristal blearily considered her youngest sister. She had been asleep on the back seat.

'What's wrong? You're sweatin' heav'er than a hooker on nickel night.'

'You really scared me!' Dread shouted. 'What are you doing here?'

Kristal was taking her usual time to wake up.

'Why is the new album being played so loud?' Kristal asked,

putting her hands to her ears and groggily shaking her blonde locks like she was trying to flick the noise away.

Dread banged on the division.

'Yo, Mister. Fade the tunes and slow your shit down!'

No response.

Ha, ha, woman, it's a crying shame
But you ain't got nobody else to blame.

'Whoa!' Kristal grabbed a handhold as the limousine lurched wildly, throwing her against Dread.

Evil woman, evil woman.

'I'm a-gonna whup yuh like a red-headed stepchild!' Kristal bellowed at the division, one hand nursing her furrowed forehead.

The roaring automobile cantered and skidded, the door banging and smoulder ripping from the tyres as they pealed in a circle.

'What the Christ?' shouted Kristal. She kept trying to get up, but fell back as the limousine surged forward. The heels of her Manolos hit the ceiling.

Kwame was visible behind the swinging door at the centre of the circle, and Dread could see he had a gun gleaming in his hand.

'Get out of the car! Get out of the car right now!' he bellowed at her, voice fading as burning wheels put distance between them.

It was surely impossible to leap from the heaving vehicle. But the frantic desperation in his voice and the long muzzle of his revolver panicked her. She started to try clambering out, then lost her balance. The vehicle wrenched away as the bodyguard pointed the gun at the driver.

'Stop! I will shoot! Stop!'

The police cars had begun to hurtle towards them.

Dread grabbed for the seatbelt and pulled her way to the doorway. The car was now gathering speed in a straight line and the stench of burnt rubber filled the cabin. The police cars, sirens blaring, came racing up alongside them.

Evil woman how you done me wrong
But now you're to wail a different song.

Through the darkened glass Dread could see the driver was running out of options, because on both sides racing police cars were keeping him from turning. Ahead of them a concrete wall was coming up fast. Their car seemed to be accelerating towards it. Still the music bellowed at them.

I came runnin' every time you cried
I thought I saw love smilin' in your eyes.

'Kristal, focus! We're gonna bail,' Dread shouted at her dazed sister as she grabbed her.

Ha, ha, very nice to know
That you ain't got no place left to go.

Dread crouched by the door, preparing to leap out, but they'd smash into the police car alongside.

Evil woman, evil woman.

Dread's hand, gripping hold of the door, refused to let go. Fear had taken control, and the wall was coming up as fast as if they were falling down on to it.

Then the limo screeched to a shuddering halt, and the police posse raced by as tyres screamed and rubber burned in a billowing cloud of acrid smoke. Dread half fell, half jumped, so both girls hit the ground hard as the car catapulted forward.

Evil woman, evil woman was the last thing they heard of the CD.

Dread sat up, stunned. Her knees were covered in grit and burning scratches from the road. Kristal got to her feet, her balance unsteady, nursing a bruised elbow. A red patch bloomed in her glossy straw hair.

'Move! Move!' Kwame was bawling, running up from behind.

Dread looked up and realised that the limo had flown into reverse. She was staring at the fast-approaching rear end.

Kwame lunged forward, gathering both girls with his arms, rotating them out of the way like a matador twirling a cape from a rampaging bull.

Kristal rolled away, landing heavily. Dread clutched his sinewy shoulders as her legs swung up from the turning force. Kwame's other hand had his gun out again, pointed at the limo, which braked. Then, revving, it came straight back towards them.

Kwame's grip on Dread never loosened.

His gun barked.

Then the car exploded.

A wave of intense heat broke over them, and Dread thought her face had caught fire.

141

24

Your love is a mutt from hell
Your love is a mutt from hell I can do without
One of these days I'm going to get out

Professor Tullia d'Aragona moved across to a side table upon which was set an elegant glass-bowled pot, fine china and a Bugatti kettle.

'Tea, Vilhelm. We shall drink tea and talk.'

William always found it immensely comforting when Tullia made tea. It was not a pleasure he remembered from childhood. So was Tullia the idealised mother he had never had? He knew the impression amused those at the Institute who clung to it in error.

'I love those pictures...'

William nodded to the wall behind Tullia, which was decorated with photographs of her meeting eminent academics in the field.

'That's Aaron Beck, isn't it? He was at that presentation commemorating his founding of modern cognitive behavioural therapy approaches. And that's you with Anna Freud, isn't it? Oh my days, to be psychoanalysed by the very daughter of the great man who took forward Freud's work...'

Tullia poured hot water and cleared her throat. 'You know I treasure your idealism. The science first, last and always.'

'But all I'm doing is sticking to the ideals and principles you taught me when I arrived as a junior doctor. You confuse me. You've changed.'

Tullia brought a tray to her desk.

'Oh, Vilhelm, how poignant. Do I detect wisps of ragged-coated martyr clinging to the one true way in this awful storm of fickle self-servers?'

William accepted his cup of pale tea with a supplicant bow.

Tullia sat down and sipped.

'The clinic needs other income because we are going to lose the Home Office funding.'

It was a shock and William's voice came out unsteadily.

'Are you sure?'

Tullia didn't deign to repeat herself.

'You admire the great and the good on the wall of my office, Vilhelm. So then you must know that, at the moment, the great and good in this institution are scowling and waving their fists at you. The Dean is very upset. Not because David Lewis has escaped a *second* time, but because he did so from this institution.'

William sighed. 'Look, the Dean not getting me is an old story. He hasn't liked me since I press-released the Stalking Clinic and it generated so much media interest. Though, of course, the hacks thought it was all about celebs.'

'Perhaps the fact that the clinic didn't actually exist at the time of your press release…' Tullia gripped her cup with both hands, threatening to snap it.

'But the gamble worked!' William protested. 'The Government came under pressure to pledge funding because of all the publicity, so we got it up and running. It was a good thing.'

But it had been a close shave, William realised. If the money hadn't suddenly arrived from the Department of Health, and if Philippa hadn't seen the opportunity to jump on this bandwagon and gone public with her support, he would have been in deep doo-doo.

'And now we will lose it again. Gerrard will see to that,' Tullia said coldly.

'And funding, as always, is the heart of the matter,' William retorted.

She paused. 'What I love about you, Vilhelm, is you believe analysts are obsessed with the money: the fee for the session.'

William was upset. As he waved his pen he knocked over another of her pillbox hats lying on the desk. She followed with her eyes as he apologetically replaced it.

'Don't worry about interpreting that,' he said. 'It's a pen, not a knife…or a penis.'

For a long moment, Tullia sat wrapped in stillness. Then she straightened and spoke decisively.

'Vilhelm, we can't let David Lewis, Gerrard or Philippa split us. We must change direction. To begin with, you must accept some facts. By *their* conventions, Gerrard Winstanley is a very good policeman. A highly regarded officer, decorated and with a splendid record, and...'

'But...'

'No buts, Vilhelm! Gerrard appears to have become rather obsessed with you, and not in a good way.'

'But...'

'*No*, Vilhelm. You've been blind to the fact that officials don't listen to psychiatrists, *unless* the patient is naked and directing traffic in the streets.' For a moment something pained crossed her dark eyes. 'The Foreign Secretary has already agreed to Gerrard's demand to have you fired, so we can be sure the Department of Health won't continue its funding. The AC is determined to bury you – and the Dean is more than upset. He is perfectly capable of pulling the central funding on your clinic. You know how tight it is here – it's impossible to get money to fund psychiatric research. We're not Great Ormond Street.'

Tullia sat back. 'I blame myself. I missed the signs because it's so obvious you're a talented psychiatrist. You're the youngest ever winner of the Gaskell Medal, and because of your abilities you've been promoted way ahead of your years. But now the Dean is fearful that if the press get hold of the wrong side of this story, the Institute is going to suffer negative publicity. He's worried – very worried – about this complaint from Gerrard.'

'But it's because of *me* that David Lewis was caught in the first place.'

Tullia's hands lifted to the sides, palms up.

'And Gerrard is saying it's because of you that he then escaped!'

'What the?' William was incredulous. 'It was *me* who convinced the police to place a false psychological profile in the press after the mess in Maida Vale. *I'm* the one who got the fact that Lewis is a narcissist and used it against him.'

Tullia shook her head. 'Vilhelm, you've elevated Narcissistic Personality Disorder to something of a personal fetish. In their survey, Dietz and Martell found that only four per cent of their sample of stalkers of celebrities and politicians were suffering from Narcissistic Personality Disorder. The controversy in your field makes the Dean even more nervous.'

William sighed raggedly. 'At the heart of basic paranoia is narcissism. It's somehow better to be followed by the Government Intelligence Agencies than be ignored by them 'cos it means you must be a somebody. After his arrest for assassinating John Lennon, Mark Chapman said that he felt he was regarded as a nobody, and tried to explain why he'd done it by saying he had to put that right. The best way to show the world he was a somebody was to kill "the biggest somebody on earth". And let's not forget that the Exceptional Case Study Project by the US Secret Service found the second most common motive for attacking US public figures was the need for fame or notoriety.'

William had a disturbing thought.

The framed photographs across Tullia's office walls of her hanging out with the eminent in their field abruptly reminded William of the pictures of celebrities clinging to the Foreign Secretary in Philippa's bedroom. There remained the stubborn problem that one was inexplicably missing, and that both Philippa and David remained mysteriously silent on the issue.

There was a certain narcissistic urge to bask in reflected glory – the need to parade yourself in the presence of celebs intrigued him. This desire was reflected by the panorama of images surrounding them of Tullia being embraced by the famous in their field. He began to dwell on how Tullia and Philippa were psychologically connected.

But maybe the famous "triangulation" hypothesis was key here – the person most in danger from a jealous erotomaniac was often not the target of their affections. Instead it could be the other person in the victim's life – the third party in the relationship triangle – the husband or wife, or boyfriend or girlfriend of the target. These innocents often became the object of hatred from a paranoid or jealous assassin. A stalker might interpret being spurned, or perhaps discouragement from bodyguards, as down to the obstructive interference of a third party, and not a rejection from their desired.

He recalled the case of Peggy Lennon from the 1950s popular

singing group the Lennon Sisters, stalked for years by a fixated admirer, Chester Young. The fan was convinced that he and the singer were married and even had a child together. Despite judicial orders to stay away from the singer, Young held Peggy's father and manager, Bill Lennon, responsible for keeping the "couple" apart. Chester Young pursued Bill Lennon to a golf course where Bill worked as a golf pro, and shot him. After murdering the father, Chester Young then killed himself with the same gun.

William realised with a jolt of panic that it was ever more urgent to find out who was in that missing image. Their lives might be in grave jeopardy.

'But the fact is David Lewis is loose again.' Tullia had been talking, but William had been lost in his reverie. He looked up and blinked.

'Because the officers guarding him were idiots!'

'But he was only here in the first place because Philippa Foot was responding to your complaint that David Lewis wasn't going to receive the right treatment or assessment while remanded in prison. That, by the way, hasn't gone over well with the prison doctors.'

Oh God, more people in the profession he'd annoyed.

'But it's true! People like David need specialist assessment. But he is very dangerous – I've always said that. He should never have been sent here. That wasn't my idea. No one's listening. Not those bozos in…I mean, it's not the pinnacle of a medical career, is it, prison doctor…'

William stopped mid-protest, held by Tullia's unblinking gaze.

'Vilhelm! You need to give me your side of the story so I can deal with the Dean.'

William was startled by her injunction, but he began to respond, haltingly.

'Well, he supposedly went off under police escort to get his depot injection after my interview with him, so the rest I pieced together from the nurses. It's the long-acting injection he claimed he used to have once a week and which seemed to work.'

'How come you moved so fast in offering treatment? You could only have been assessing him for less than an hour.'

'I wanted to test just how much insight he had – he agreed to medication almost straightaway, but while he could talk the talk, could he walk the walk?'

'When you say walk the walk, what about that akathisia he has? A possible side-effect of the depot?'

'That's the thing, I'm beginning to wonder if that's all an act. We both know that most of the modern drugs don't inflict body movement side-effects as *de rigueur* in the Hollywood depiction of psychiatric medication.'

'So, on the one hand he seems to display a very sophisticated knowledge of psychiatry, on the other hand he's labouring under the old tired stereotypes still pedalled by the media that psychiatric patients twitch because of the tablets.'

'Can we now see that was all a set-up? He made up the stuff about accepting a depot injection to allow him to escape. He knows how psychiatry works and he's using it against us.'

Tullia laid her hands flat on the desk. 'So you allowed him to be taken for the injection, and you picked a long-acting depot to test his real willingness in assenting to actual treatment.'

'As the nurse was about to give it, he grabbed the syringe and stuck it into the neck of one of the officers, who panicked because he thought he was going to be zombified. As did his colleagues. I mean, how ridiculous! They were more concerned with getting the needle out rather than paying attention to Mr Lewis. In the melee that followed, David escaped through a window, apparently, and ran off down the back alley behind the hospital. Another not inconsiderable drop, by the way, to the ground from the window, so…anyway, he had grabbed a gun from the holster of the cop with the needle, then he threw it into a crowd of schoolkids who ran off with it, so the police got diverted retrieving it.'

Tullia shook her head. 'But Gerrard blames *you*. Apart from the huge fallout he has to deal with, he simply cannot afford to be responsible for David Lewis escaping twice. And it was your job to make sure he got injected…'

William exhaled explosively.

'It's a tiny space. The NHS is under-resourced. It's simply not physically possible to squeeze any more people in. So the policemen wanted the injection administered out in the corridor and the nurses refused. They said that it's not the way a nurse treats a patient. The nurses, Tullia! So how come I'm getting the blame for a nursing decision?'

'Maybe David was one step ahead of all of us. Getting himself moved – via Philippa, the only one with that kind of authority – out of Belmarsh Prison and to the less secure environment of the NHS was the beginning of this chain of events.'

Tullia made a thoughtful note.

'Like I've been saying all along, he seems to have got a lot of experience of how our system works,' William protested. Then he grasped that David was demonstrating an uncanny knowledge of his relationship with the Foreign Secretary. How it was just a little more than merely professional. David Lewis had calculated that Philippa would autocratically transfer him, playing fast and loose with the rules, if he himself gamed the prison doctors and the system from his end. Philippa trusted William to get what she wanted out of the stalker and keep it confidential, and somehow David knew this. There were wheels spinning within wheels, and William was struggling to keep up.

'Which is all academic as the escape is to be officially logged as all your responsibility. So, Vilhelm, stop chasing David. The health-focused approach of FTAC has been stretched past snapping point by him. He may have passed up his last chance at treatment, so you need a much bigger client.'

'Than the Foreign Secretary?'

'Yes. Which means you are going to have to sully your idealism with your knack of finding people's worst insecurities. You need to bring the little goddess to us.'

25

Used to dream of being a millionaire, without a care
But it doesn't mean anything

'Anyway, you know you're kinda too late. Doncha read the papers? Dread got run over by a parked car and the bad guy got blown up outside the Rose Bowl last night. It's all over, man.'

Dr Han Fei sighed. 'Look, I have an appointment. Am I going to get my case back?' His training from the FBI Behavioural Sciences Unit meant he made an immediate mental note of the disdain for their pop star her own bored security detail were radiating, even as they sullenly guarded her home.

'Sorry, we've gotta put it through some other scanners, and then we'll deliver it up to the main house.'

The uniform, with both fists closed over the top of the Tanner Krolle briefcase, kept his eyes on Han as he spoke.

The Chinese American stared back. There was a hardness to his features. Had they spotted his Smith & Wesson 500 Magnum in its lead-lined secret compartment? And if they did, would they work out why he'd brought the same weapon that Kwame used? It was the largest, most powerful production revolver in the world, boasting a satin steel muzzle more than 8 inches long; no wonder the limousine last night had exploded when Kwame fired just one round of 2,600 foot/pounds of muzzle energy into it.

'But it's got confidential documents inside! I can't let you do that.'

'You're just going to have to trust us on this one, Dr Fei.'

Han didn't budge.

'Dr Fei, relax, it's going to be returned to you up in the main house – it's policy.'

Han continued to meet the gaze of the man whose hands were on his case. His opponent began to blink nervously. If they wanted to play at the "mafia stare-down" it was fine with the psychologist.

As if he'd made his point, Han Fei turned on his heels. *You didn't beat me, I let you have this one*, his body language explained.

'Be very careful with those documents, tomorrow's headlines are in there,' was his parting shot.

Liberated from the gatehouse, Han sauntered up to the main complex where the protective scrutiny seemed to start all over again. This would be the third barricade. They were jumpy, all right. But if his gun got through, it was all rookie.

Dread's Malibu citadel sprawled across the edge of a cliff, at least seven large suburban homes stuck together. The bluff was not visible from where Han was standing, but he could hear the waves breaking on the beach more than 100 feet below.

Having negotiated his way past the sentries, he was wondering about the chinks, though miniscule so far, in their systems. Maybe it was the morning after the night before – everyone now relaxing because, as the guard had said, they assumed the stalker was chargrill on a mortician's slab.

Kwame had warned him that even after he'd made it this far through security, there was still the hurdle of Dread's most loyal "guard dog" – Flip, her longstanding Filipino housekeeper and general guardian. How easy he found it to get past this last fortification would reveal how safe Dread really was.

'I have an appointment with Mrs Anne Conway. And with Dread.'

A long pause from the intercom.

'Hello, hello?' Han Fei tried again, patiently. 'I have an *appointment*. My name is Dr Han Fei, I've a letter from Kwame Appiah...'

'Who? No one that name here. Dread not here. You go away. We have dogs. Big dogs.'

Bewilderingly for Han, the person at the other end of the intercom then proceeded to yelp a series of menacing canine growls. Yes, this sounded like Kwame's advice on how Flip would react.

Han exhaled and scrutinised the crisp white property which sprawled behind the second set of gates. The bigger the star, the flakier the entourage – it seemed to be a rule in Hollywood.

Han looked back. The guards at the gatehouse nearest the main road were deploying a mirror to check under the armour-plated stretch Bentley he had arrived in, and were trying to peer into the electrochromic privacy windows.

The heat-formed armour protected and aramid fabric passenger cabin could withstand ballistic attack, while the Kevlar and titanium body shrugged off magnetic mines. Gleaming chrome was fronted by a rotating bulletproof grille, all topped off with a sniper resistant roof. He chuckled to himself as they warily circled; they were right to, his vehicle could bite.

The door handles alone were programmed to administer electric shocks and then disappear. Kwame must have warned them about Han's guard dog on wheels and its special "modifications".

Beyond the outer gates a crowd of fans, bedecked in lurid fancy dress from her various hits, chanted choruses from Dread's songs. On the opposite pavement, kept apart by straining barricades, were the equally noisy religious groups, waving banners cautioning that Dread was the devil incarnate. The incantations between the two ragtag armies transformed this peaceful part of Malibu into a rumbling riot, waiting to erupt.

'You come in,' the voice on the intercom said suspiciously. 'I check. They say you okay. But you no flakeeeey! I keepee eye on you.'

No one came out to greet him when the mansion door opened, so Han strolled towards where he thought the main living area might be. There was no evidence of this supposed loyal guard dog, Flip – the "Thriller from Manila", as Kwame had referred to her. Indeed there was no one around at all, which began to make him uneasy.

He paused by Dread's Picasso and then a Rothko. In gloomy corners of the ceilings, miniature shadowy lenses blinked impassively as he ambled past. Infrared and motion detectors were scattered across the blind spots as well; grudgingly, his respect for the pop star's largesse on cutting-edge technology began to grow.

Was Flip monitoring him from some hidden central gallery where all the video feeds from the estate converged? Han could rule out the glowering presence of Kwame. The bodyguard had flown to London, scrutinising progress over security surrounding the upcoming Care for Congo concert and the construction of Dread's famed Ferris wheel in Hyde Park.

Han suspected Kwame's hasty departure had rushed the paperwork that had brought him on board. They must be worried now about leaving Dread on her own, even for 24 hours, without a forensic psychologist expert close to her.

Motorcycle tyre marks crossed the marble floor, meandered down a corridor and then seemed to career into a wall before winding away. Han found his way into the French-windowed living room, a black concert-sized piano hovering between him and the sapphire ocean. A pair of jarringly orange motorcycle helmets rolled gently on their sides across the gleaming ebony top of the Bösendorfer Grand. A berating Essex voice could be heard, with shrill childlike voices, indecipherable and responding.

Anne Conway breezed in, a hand held to her forehead, white tailored cigarette trousers and hourglass black tuxedo jacket top floating as she walked. Han recognised her from press photos and knew she was in her fifties, but she looked no more than forty.

'Oh, bloody 'ell, not them 'elmets again,' she swore at the shiny orbs on the piano. 'I *agreed* you could use the bike, no need to keep droppin' hints.' Then she turned sharply to him.

'Dr James, I'm dreadfully sorry. Kwame should be here but he's been called away.' Anne invited Han to take a seat on one of the sofas. His attaché was on the coffee table. Encountering Flip had led him to believe he'd seen the last of the Tanner Krolle.

'I'm not Dr James, I'm Dr Han Fei. Dr James – if that's Dr *William* James – I know him well, but he is a psychiatrist from London. And a bit of a voyeur, in my opinion.'

Uh-oh, was there another reason Kwame had gone to London? Was Han being played so they could lure the British psychiatrist on board? Han knew William would normally never take a case like this; he would see it as beneath him, but if he got competitive about Han, the way psychiatrists did with psychologists...

Anne stared at him, then shrugged. 'Okay, well, we gotta problem. Dread's having to do a last-minute reshoot on a cosmetics range, and immediately after that we gotta...' She leant forward conspiratorially over the onyx coffee table. 'Is it not possible that this whole thing is just crank mail?'

Han slowly shook his head.

'Statistically, crank mail very rarely threatens any real danger. The kind of criminal sending these particular notes, however, is likely to be a psychopath. Hervey Cleckley, a professor of psychiatry, wrote what remains the classic treatise on psychopathy. It was a book published in 1941 called *The Mask of Sanity.*'

Anne looked slightly happier. 'Well, if it's about make-up, Dread'll read it.'

'Psychopaths can evoke all the right emotional sounding noises and sentiments, but ultimately their complete lack of remorse and guilt makes them highly dangerous.'

'You're telling me this...'

'I am going to have to review everyone here in more psychological detail with you, but...'

'Okay, okay, just...do we have to go into all these details with Dread? Surely *we* worry about this stuff, leaving her to get on with focusing on performance and recording.'

Han snapped open his case and placed some papers on the onyx table. They had kept his gun – it was no longer in the attaché. Some personnel were pretty tight here – in which case, for the stalker to keep getting so close...

'We use a set of computer programs to analyse different aspects of the letters you sent us copies of. For example, handwriting changes with the ageing process and some letters may have been written a long time ago yet only posted recently. The software can give us a timeline over what was written when.'

'Well, we were getting crank mail from the start, when she broke through on *WLS.*'

'*WLS?*'

'Yeah, it's a British TV thingy – *The Weakest Lip-Sync.* Thank your lucky stars you don't have the equivalent of that lardass Roger Moirans over here.'

Han decided not to bother to enquire who Roger Moirans was. Anne seemed so distracted he had to suppress an urge to wave his hands in front of her eyes and shout 'Over here!'

'The analysis can even diagnose psychiatric problems remotely. For example, people suffering from Obsessive Compulsive Disorder have been shown to write differently from the rest of us. Our software can also examine vocabulary choice, sentence construction and make predictions about education, class and cultural background. Plus, we can analyse threatening words combined with variables such as length of time over which letters were sent and so build a surprisingly accurate picture of threat likelihood.'

Anne got up abruptly and disappeared without explanation. Han shrugged. Superstars were not known for their manners. He was used to it. But this crew were really out there.

She returned after a moment.

'Sorry, I was just checking on 'er 'ighness.'

He continued as if there had been no interruption. 'Our specialty is computerised algorithms. We like to remove the uncertainties introduced by the human element, keeping to the purity of the equations. We ascertain basic data points and feed them into our program. It then tells us whether or not you should employ our services, both in terms of monitoring the case and in providing physical security and specialised armed personnel. Each person when they speak, or more particularly when they write, produces a pattern which is peculiar to their personality.'

'Yeah, the critics are always saying that Dread's lyrics reveal what an air 'ead she is,' her mother said gloomily.

Han pressed on.

'The way you speak and write is like a fingerprint, a combination of features that invariably crop up – lexical, syntactical and structural. We use this to analyse messages from stalkers. When Oprah interviewed me on her show about my bestselling book, *Stalked: Celebrities I have Saved*, our system...'

Off-stage there was an indecipherable shout and Anne held up a dictatorial hand. She clenched her fist.

'Whassat?' she screamed.

Han was taken aback at the depth of the Essex accent, and by the sheer volume cranked out of such a petite frame. Then again, she had been a singer herself before a punch to the throat in a crowd riot at a concert had damaged her voice forever.

Another mangled cry in response.

'Oh!' She sighed loudly and got up, impatiently beckoning

154

Han. As she passed the piano she reached out, scooping up one of the helmets and tossing it without properly looking at him. He caught it, bewildered, then wondered what to do, deciding to embrace it under one arm.

They wafted down a corridor which was almost all glass on one side, allowing a spectacular view of the Pacific. Han was juggling the helmet and his papers, so he decided to abandon the lurid orb on a sideboard encrusted with MTV awards.

Over her shoulder, Anne waved at Han, indicating he was expected to keep talking.

'Another example of our work concerns the half-dozen letters that were sent to journalists and politicians about a week after the September 11 attacks of 2001 containing powdered anthrax spores and, on four occasions, notes.'

Anne checked her palms as if trying to recall which one she had used to shake Han's hand.

'Twenty-two people became infected and five died in the worst germ agent attack in US history. Most anthrax victims were postal workers known to have come into contact with contaminated mail. One letter was addressed to NBC TV news anchor Tom Brokaw, and another to the editor of the *New York Post* newspaper. Handwritten in block capitals were brief lines which included statements such as *death to America, death to Israel* and *Allah is great.*'

'Are those really pop music lyrics? That's all our stalker sends us.'

'Two other envelopes were addressed to Senator Tom Daschle and Senator Patrick Leahy and had similar content, but included *you cannot stop us* and *we have this anthrax*, among other lines.'

'Oh, I get it. Anthrax is the name of a heavy metal band.'

'We helped the FBI with a detailed psychological profile of the perpetrator.'

They entered a cavernous room the size of three tennis courts, punctuated with pillars. It was all white with no windows. Clustered at the far end were a photographer and several assistants flashing away at Dread, who flounced in an elegant backless ballgown.

Han's face revealed nothing of his shock. Whatever had happened in the Rose Bowl car park, it was clear the stalker had got much closer to her than had been spun to the media. The bruises rendered Dread even more startling than her publicity photographs. With the addition of careful make-up, she looked like she had just gone ten rounds in a boxing ring – hence the bulbous boxing gloves, raised and menacing.

Blood-red lipstick framed a mouth that was practising pouts. She was wearing her cinnamon hair up, leaving her face clear, but it made her look much more elegant than her usual raunchy poses, despite the blackened eye and Hollywood cuts. Assistants were arranging the glistening satin encompassing Dread, while chiffon was persuaded around one nearly exposed breast.

'This is going to get us into more trouble with the women's groups,' observed Anne with a frown. 'It looks like we're pedalling sex and violence. Again.'

The designer beaten-up look had somehow conspired to ensure Dread looked even more fascinatingly smutty than usual. Han couldn't take his eyes off her. A necklace in the form of several thick bands of fabulous diamonds choked her long throat, sparkling in the intense flare of the photographer's lights.

It was a well-documented gift from Wilfrid Sellars. The man was richer than God. Han wondered what his fiancée would think when she saw it in a magazine encircling her rival's neck.

Dread was looking away, and then in turn staring slyly into the camera lens, her head back against a whiteboard background. She looked as though she had been pushed against the wall and her arms had come up to protect herself. Every time she glanced back at the long lens, which was just inches from her face, the remote flash units would detonate.

Han shielded his eyes. She still looked in amazing shape given all that must have happened. It was dawning on him why they'd called him in right now. The Rose Bowl must have been a very close shave indeed. He mentally kicked himself: he could have asked for so much more money.

Anne hurried over to the group. 'Darling, the doctor was just sayin' 'ow we need to order some face masks to protect us from a new anfrax threat.'

Dread rolled her eyes at Han.

'Say hello, darling. This is Dr James.' Anne's voice was

restored to 1950s BBC pronunciation.

Dread smiled winningly at the psychologist. 'Dr James, you made it past our rude guards and our second and third line of defence, so congratulations. Few make it this far – most give up and go home. No wonder I'm so isolated up here.'

She shot her mother a glare.

'Ah, the thing is I'm not Dr...'

'Dr James, the question is: do I need you anymore? Isn't my stalker a bony piece of BBQ remains by now?'

'Actually, I'm Dr Han Fei. Dr James works in the British NHS.'

'What the? Mother, who are we talking to? Do we even know? Honestly, no wonder security is shot to pieces round here!'

'And as to whether you need me, I've discussed this at length with Mr Appiah and the local police and we are all agreed. Whoever went up in flames in that limo, there is still the problem of his collaborators, because this is far more than the work of an individual. Whoever they are, they will regroup and come at you again using different tactics, and at this time we can't even fathom what the point of the exercise was. The limo had been turned into a mobile bomb. It was packed with explosives. So was the driver on a suicide mission to take you out? Was the Tannerite and C-4 set off by Kwame's shot, or remotely detonated? And whether the police forensics are going to recover enough of the stalker to get a DNA match is a moot point.'

Han belatedly offered his hand, but the elegant head flounced back to the photographer.

'How much longer?'

The man behind the camera held up three fingers. The answer seemed to irritate Dread and her whole body squirmed with impatience.

'I have explained to Mr Appiah the way my company works when we are brought in to assist operations,' Han continued. 'And our contract categorically does not permit another psychology or psychiatry expert to be hired at the same time. Like Dr James. It just confuses things in our experience.'

'You see, Mother, you blew it! You weren't meant to divulge that Kwame was flying to London, were you!'

Dread stabbed a gesture and another flunkey came over with a tray bearing a large crystal ashtray on which a smouldering fat cigar was presented.

'The fans' forums have gone wild for the new husky element in Dread's voice,' Anne explained as a second attendant held the cigar to Dread's lips and she puffed it for a second. A third dutifully waved the smoke away with a fan. The photographer waited patiently for the cloud to clear before returning to snapping.

This was a predicament Han was familiar with in the celebrity universe. Conversations that were meant to be confidential were conducted on the run between appointments, and therefore in front of subordinates who were not to be trusted, but whom the celeb had long gone past caring about.

Han spoke crisply.

'I need you to understand that Dr James, no disrespect to him, works in an almost opposite way to our approach. And I very much doubt Dr James has ever picked a weapon up, far less fired a pistol. Exactly how he's meant to *practically* help a client who's being stalked feel safe eludes me.'

Just to show how impressed she was, Dread moved her boxing gloves up to her face in a mock fighting pose, peering at the photographer through the giant mitts.

'Oh lovely, really nice!' the shutterbug gushed.

Han pressed on.

'For example, on this work on a person's "write-print", we collaborated with Professor James Pennebaker who is a Professor of Psychology at the University of Texas. He is a world expert on how the words you use reveal your personality and identity.'

'If he's the world expert how come we haven't hired him?' Dread ignored Han, addressing the question to Anne, who dutifully took a note.

'What words you choose to use, their sequence, how a sentence is composed, plus how text is laid out on a page – these are all particular to a specific person, according to data analysis of large amounts of text by computer. We all make certain recurrent spelling and grammar mistakes – and another easy variable for a computer to measure is vocabulary richness. From that it calculates the IQ of the writer.'

'Well, let's not show it our lyrics from the latest album then,' Dread said through the corner of her mouth. 'And listen, that's all great, but there's just one problem – our stalker seems to know all about your little computer program, that's why he's sending us lyrics from songs we've covered. Geddit? Your analysis won't work 'cos these aren't his own words.'

Han was impressed. There was a brain encased within the high cheekbones after all.

'Sooner or later, he's going to crack and send you something more direct,' he said. 'They always do.'

'Can we step this up, dear?' Anne said anxiously. 'We've got an appointment in Southern California in a couple of hours.'

'Okay, where's me bone dome?' demanded Dread.

'Yeah, where's her helmet?' Anne turned to the psychologist.

Han frowned. 'Kwame said you were in all day. That's in the schedule he gave me. If we are going to help you run security we can't have changes to the timetable without being properly informed.'

'It's just a quickie down the road. We'll be back in no time. We've got guards coming with us, and your team can come as well, Mr Fei.'

'Where is it you want to go?' Han asked.

'Look, if we're going, let's do this,' Dread said from behind him.

Han turned and was startled to see she was now shouldering a full leather close-fitting motorcycle jacket and pants outfit, complete with boots up past her knees, multiple straps and gleaming buckles. Attendants were still zipping her in, so a lot of bare flesh remained on display, though it was rapidly disappearing. Han averted his gaze and Dread smirked.

'We'll talk on the way, so let's roll. There's a fleet of MPVs waiting. As Kwame will have told you, whenever we go out now, we get in one and another seven or so are decoys.'

Anne began hurrying him along a hallway. Dread followed. She had grabbed a proffered motorcycle helmet and was carrying it under the crook of her arm. Cantering past the sideboard laden with TV awards, Anne retrieved the helmet that Han had abandoned there, leading to a sort of tug-of-war between mother and daughter as they tussled for it along the corridor.

Han paused by an entrance to an extensive garage.

'I need to know where we are going, and why are you carrying a motorcycle helmet?'

The coven encircling Dread, led by her pushy mother, seemed a few cards short of a full deck.

'I agreed to go on one condition...' Dread tailed off. She seemed so irate it looked as if she was restraining herself from saying something she might regret later.

Anne stepped in.

'Okay, okay, it's my bad. We only had this one day off to get a chance to see a...surgeon. It has to be top secret, so we need your discretion. And in order to get Dread to agree, I said that she could ride her bike there.'

Dread pulled back the door and gestured at a line of six powerful looking two-wheeled machines.

She grinned.

'It's a very hush-hush cosmetic surgery clinic,' Anne said. 'Very remote because a lot of actresses go there. So we need to get there without the fans or the paparazzi knowing. It's in the middle of nowhere and that makes Kwame nervous. That's why you have to take us.'

'But,' Han argued, 'how am I meant to protect you if you are riding a motorbike and I'm following you in an MPV? What about taking the Bentley? Plus I need my gun back.'

Dread chuckled. 'Good point...' She reached on to a shelf and thrust another glossy helmet into his arms. 'I swore blind I would keep you as close as a lover for the whole day. And it was only because of that promise that Kwame took off to London.'

Han could make a last stand right now about how they got to the clinic, or whether to agree on the journey at all. But he would then be summarily axed by the coven. It would be the shortest contract of his career.

Then again, maybe, just maybe, bikes might be safer than a limousine after recent events.

Maybe the coven wasn't so crazy.

He was thinking about the case of Frank Mendoza who stalked his evading ex-girlfriend across the USA, attempting to disfigure her with acid-filled car bombs. Bottles filled with hydrochloric acid were designed to explode and spray caustic disfiguring fluid across the interior when she started her vehicle. The victim only escaped injury because the booby trap malfunctioned. Pleading guilty to interstate stalking, Mendoza was sentenced to ten years in 2014.

Han realised he had left the Bentley, with all its gadgets, in the unsupervised hands of the Dread posse for an extended period. If this stalking was an inside job, as Kwame suspected, then anyone could have tampered with his shield on wheels. The carriage might have been transformed into a lethal trap. He had to bear in mind that her attendants had managed to winkle out his concealed gun from inside a normally invulnerable case.

He returned from his reverie with a jolt, realising that Anne and Dread were considering him, waiting for a response.

'Sorry, what did you say? What did we decide?'

Dread's lips pouted a mocking kiss at him.

'You're riding with me.'

26

As she's spreading her wings she threw back the ring
When Smokey sings

'What about you befriending Gerrard's helicopters a bit more?'
Tullia's smile was implacable. 'Let's pack you off to Lippitts Hill.
We can say you are exploring how to deploy the technology on
the aircraft to pursue the stalker until you can work your way
back in.'

'But,' William spluttered, 'that'll mean having to go up and
down in the infernal machines!'

'Yes, yes, we all know about your fear of flying. Lippitts Hill
and making friends with the helicopters will be good for you, in
more ways than one. You know Gerrard will enjoy the idea. And
more to the point, I have another suitcase for you. Dread's head
of security is extremely efficient. He has supplied all his files on
her stalker, plus recordings of all her concerts and publicity events
and a lot of back stage stuff. It amounts to a picture of the diva's
life since this started.'

'Oh, I see. Very clever. I'm to be punished *twice* for something
I didn't do. I'm to be sidelined in the entourage of the pop star
with the Messiah complex.' William remembered trying to kick
a clitoral vibrator under a seat in the police car with Frances, and
blanched.

'In fact I was rather hoping you might take a leaf out of your
new follower Frances Wright's book. See how she has Gerrard
eating out of the palm of her hand? You need to use her to help
you with him. You might want to get a bit closer to her.'

'What? That journalist? Have you noticed how she specialises
in megalomaniac men of a certain age?'

'Calm down, William, you have a lot to learn from her.
Yes, she is famous because she has some warlords and a general

awaiting trial in The Hague after a recent stint of luring them.'

'Err, yes, I read she was using a kind of honey trap in the Congo, so how's she gonna help me convince Gerrard to accept psychiatric input more assiduously?'

Tullia leant forward, eyes gleaming.

'Unlike you, Frances is handling Gerrard. She has inveigled her way into command and control.'

'But…'

'I've told you, Vilhelm, no buts! Now, what was the key clinical nugget you wanted me to appraise?'

Gazing past his professor's chair and desk, he saw for the first time a couple of large pale-pink plastic buckets skulking in a corner. Gnarled walnut stippling on grey rubbery surfaces revealed the gleaming objects floating in the pails were brains.

William wasn't that taken aback. Tullia's office frequently sported containers of nerve tissue immersed in preservative, lying about, waiting for some neuropathology student to pick them up for various department research projects. He was surprised he hadn't detected over the Lapsang souchong tea the odour of formaldehyde, which he had hated with a passion since anatomy classes at medical school.

The brains made William feel like a specimen about to be dissected. Their incongruous appearance among the books, papers, sculptures, pictures, hanging diplomas and other accoutrements of an otherwise refined office would bother a lay person like Frances. Using her journalistic cod psychology, she would contend Tullia was hiding a more cold clinical side to her character, a bit like the almost furtive buckets of brains. She had suggested as much about his profession generally in the police car ride to the Institute that morning.

William detected the hidden hand of his professor, arranging a meeting on the backseat of the police car waiting for him at Paddington, and hopefully initiating the beginnings of a connection between the psychiatrist and the journalist. But Frances had disappeared once William arrived at the Institute, reappearing as if by magic only when law enforcement cordoned off Camberwell in a desperate attempt to close the net on David Lewis.

'What would your advice be to our boys in blue on where

to hunt for him now?' she had asked, pausing to wrestle out her boom microphone. 'They seem to think he's heading back to Maida Vale.'

'He now knows how Gerrard likes to spread the perimeter, so he's going to lurk nearby, because it's the last place anyone sane would anticipate,' William had responded before being dragged off to explain himself to Tullia. It was disappointing to glimpse Frances then choosing to ignore the psychiatrist's prediction, diving into a panda car that screeched away, heading for North London.

'Vilhelm, that light flashing on my phone is the Dean's office calling...we are out of time here.'

William's thoughts were immediately engaged with the patient.

'Okay, I'm not sure David Lewis is hearing voices. He was very distracted during the interview, in that way people who are hearing voices look – as if they're listening to something off stage. So I asked him directly what was going on and he explained that he's getting a buzzing and ringing in his ears.'

'But that could be his way of describing auditory hallucinations, Vilhelm. And the prison doctor in his report says that David *is* hearing voices. He was wearing ear-plugs, which as we both know is a well-known habit of those suffering from voices.'

William made a despairing, disparaging 'Kuh!' sound. 'What would *he* know? If you ask carefully, it's not actual voices he's hearing but a peculiar buzzing and ringing sound.'

'But that's not a classic symptom of psychosis,' Tullia protested.

'I'm beginning to wonder exactly how much of an erotomaniac he is if he's not hearing voices. To be fair, though, the prison doctors put great store on the fact he was wearing earplugs. But I think he's blocked his ears for another reason.'

27

He gets his fill oh constantly
Louie Louie

Kwame was irritated. This was meant to be an incognito low-profile visit to London, and now they had a bright orange Lamborghini tailing their limousine.

'He's right behind us! Kristal, for real, you girls need to discuss your plans instead of springing them on me all the time!'

Kwame switched off the screen. Rudolf Carnap, the organiser of the Care for Congo concert, had just come on the phone video link, a cheesed-off grimace flickering as he was cut off mid-sentence. Checking security and progress on the Ferris wheel in Hyde Park would have to wait while Kwame sorted this series of new predicaments the girls were throwing at him.

'Dern tootin', he's keen,' breathed Kristal. 'Yeah, I figured that while you were nipping in and out of that Institute for your appointment with whatsit…'

'Dr William James.'

'Yeah, whatever, we would be…discreet.'

'What? Here in the limo? With whoever's in the Lambo behind?'

'Listen, I would prefer The Ritz. That sports car is soooo uncomfortable.'

She fluttered her eyelashes at him outrageously, then grinned. He shook his head, amused despite himself.

'And I suppose this also explains that outfit. I mean, are you inside that dress trying to get out, or outside trying to get in?'

'Ha ha!' Kristal stretched her legs to tug on a garter halfway up her thigh, the stiletto heels of her thigh-high boots leaving a pockmark on the leather seat in front. 'D'ya like it?'

Kwame shook his head. 'All I can say is thank Christ we

came in the private jet.' Feathery wings sprouted from somewhere behind her, strands reaching up and also around to embrace her breasts, which were precariously cupped by glittering straps.

'You don't recognise it?'

'What I *do* recognise is the size of the goosebumps you're gonna get if you step outside in the cold.' It looked like something he recalled from a Victoria's Secret event Dread had guested at, but he thought better of remarking. Fashion was a minefield with these girls.

'You really don't recognise this outfit?' Kristal sounded disappointed. 'It's from that video we did – you know, *Angels, Demons and Zombies Too.*' Kristal contemplated him thoughtfully. 'I keep forgetting that 'cos of your job, you're too busy looking in the opposite direction to the rest of us.'

Kwame shook his head. 'Kristal, if that's a boyfriend in the Lambo, you're supposed to clear any meeting with me. I can't have people following us and not know what's going on. Especially now.'

'But whoever was sending Dread those awful notes was in the car that blew up, so it's all over, right, Kwame? What are you still worried about?'

'What I wanna find out is how they penetrated our security, and what precisely they were up to. And I want the DNA evidence of who was in the flaming car. And what if it's a conspiracy, so there are more of them? Aren't *you* curious?'

Kristal shrugged.

'Nutcases are two a dime. Anyway, I thought, since the crim is dead, it was okay to start living again.'

'What?'

'Aw, c'mon, you left Her Highness back in LA so even you must think it's now safer.'

She might have had a point were it not for the fact that he wasn't enthusiastic about separating from Dread, even for a few hours. He had been forced by the intransigence of Dr William James. The disdainful doctor wasn't just rejecting their offer of a private jet escort to Malibu, he had declined Kwame's calls, forcing the bodyguard to track the shrink down.

Kwame had only considered this scheme of leaving Dread

because they had just signed up Han Fei, who was turning out to be a lot more helpful than the British stuck-up douchebag. Handy in an altercation, the American forensic psychologist packed the same monstrous Smith & Wesson 500 Magnum as Kwame. The bodyguard had also issued strict instructions that Han Fei and Dread were to be no more than an arm's length apart throughout the time Kwame was in London.

Video screens accessing the remote cams in the gatehouse heartened the bodyguard. Glimmering on the screens embedded in the headrests of the front seats of their limousine negotiating London afternoon traffic were images of Han arriving at Dread's Malibu mansion bright and early in the morning, emerging from his specially outfitted armour-plated stretch Bentley.

Similarly reassuring was the fact Flip didn't let Han through until she'd got the personal phoned all clear from Kwame. After the Rose Bowl Stadium driver in the limousine incident…well, you couldn't be too careful now. There might be an eight-hour time difference between the bodyguard and the rest of the crew guarding Dread back in LA, but he was still in constant contact, and so far everyone had been obediently following his instructions.

And with all these extra stringent precautions, what could possibly go wrong? It was only a few hours until he got back, unless Kristal had more surprises up her…well, whatever.

'Dread got given that necklace worth four million dollars by Wilfrid Sellars!' Kristal folded her arms in a strop.

And Kwame instantly knew what this was all about. Wilfrid Sellars had given Dread an expensive item of jewellery, so inevitably this had to be followed by her sisters competing. Boyfriends anywhere in the world had better be braced for a run on their currency.

'But Wilfrid is in the top ten of the world's richest men. And he's got a thing for her.'

'So?' she flounced. 'The centre forward back there has a thing for *me*.'

'Look, Kristal, if you crave really, really expensive jewellery from men, then you gotta take a leaf outta Dread's book. Learn from the Jedi of Jewels.'

She sat forward, interested. 'Go on.' The wings sat up, looking attentive.

'If you hanker after the kind of gems and all that other shit that Dread gets, then you need to hang out with the people who *own* the clubs, not play for them.'

'But they're all old, fat, bald and ugly!' she protested. 'And anyway, Dread doesn't hang out with Wilfrid – quite the opposite. She doesn't return his calls, she avoids him.'

Kwame grinned. 'That's my point: she plays hard to get. This is why he bombards her with ever more stupid gifts.'

'You're saying I give out too easily? Well, thank you very much.' The wings began to flap as she shifted about.

'No! What I'm saying is that there's a game to be played here if *rocks* is what you're after.' He didn't for a moment think it was. 'It's precisely because Dread couldn't give two figs for Wilfrid that he's been stoked up to pursue her. You know about the wedding concert in the Caribbean on his private island?'

'Yeah.'

'Well, there you go. She ignores him until finally Wilfrid offers her so much money to appear at his wedding, it would be obscene to turn it down. The thing is, Kristal, it's an amusement to Dread – and the paradox is, only get involved if you're gonna play it for keeps, because it's a vicious, vicious game, and people get hurt. I don't think that's you, somehow.'

Kristal nodded, head bowed. 'Yeah, apparently Wilfrid's Charlotte didn't know about the last one, the Marie Antoinette necklace. And they're about to get married – it's not a great start, is it.'

'No. And Dread didn't send it back,' Kwame said.

'Okay, so basically you have to be a manipulative mistress to get the big rocks, yeah?'

In one of the rear-view mirrors, Kwame caught sight again of a black-helmeted motorcyclist who had been following them for a while.

'But how'd you explain the fact she's now having lots of sex with Robert Recorde? And she says it's cos she's in love with him.'

'Yeah, she's behaving like an amateur on that one,' Kwame murmured. He waved Kristal to be quiet so that he could concentrate. She turned to investigate what he was staring at. Her wings came round and Kwame had to flex to one side to keep the image in view.

'What's up?'

'Besides your boyfriend in the Lamborghini? We have more company – motorbike coming up on us fast.'

28

When your world is full of strange arrangements
The look of love

They emerged from a side door into a deserted alley half a mile from where the fans were demonstrating outside Dread's Malibu mansion. First they squeezed into an anonymous-looking compact, and a few deserted intersections later they skulked into an armoured military carrier, flanked by a pair of heavily modified Hummers. All the vehicles were riding on giant knobbly wheels, the riveted doors splattered with grab-handles.

In an emergency, a phalanx of guards could leap on to the wide step plates on either side, forming a human shield. That's if ten tonnes of ballistic hardened steel failed to keep Dread safe.

To the diva, Han still seemed unsettled that they weren't using the stretch Bentley with the titanium shock system that killed paparazzi, or whatever he kept babbling about. She didn't care how big Kwame explained his gun was, basically the man of steel had just been ambushed by two women tottering about in ridiculous heels.

'It was my idea to get this specialist opinion, Dr Fei,' Anne explained. 'We're just having a quick chat with a surgeon. I wouldn't want to go into the details, it's all very sensitive in terms of the press, so we couldn't take that limo you ever so kindly brought with you. It'll get rumbled as being Dread's straightaway, and we know the paps are out on scooters scouring the area.'

'Motherrrr! You have to tell the man. How can he do his job if you don't?' Dread didn't lift her eyes from the mobile she was texting from.

'All right, all right, so the procedure we're going to discuss involves…'

'Medial canthal tilt. Kuh!' Dread chanted.

'Yeah,' Anne agreed. 'But don't ask me what that means.'

'Medial refers to towards the midline of the body, canthal is the corner of the eye, where tears flow from, and tilt is an angle, so putting it together I would say that this refers to altering the angular tilt of the corner of the eye.'

Sitting very erect and still, Han looked like some kind of impassive Buddha. The question, Dread knew, wasn't: *Is he trying to impress me?* but *In his trying to showboat, how annoyed am I going to get?*

'Very good, Dr Fei! He *is* good, isn't he, darling?' said Anne.

'Yesss, Mother. He went to medical school, bravo for him.'

'No, I'm a psychologist,' Han said coldly.

Dread could see that he thought they were still trying to rile him with Dr James. She could sense him looking down his nose at them, just like the music press did.

'Psychiatrists do medical school, psychologists don't,' Han explained.

Dread realised that whoever this Dr James was, he seemed to threaten Han Fei. That meant the British shrink must be pretty good.

Anne blithely brushed by the comment. 'Yes, basically they tilt the angle of your eyes slightly downward so you develop a slightly more...what's the word that nice Dr Geist and Dr Bashour used, Dread, dear? *Feline* appearance. Oh dear me!'

'Yeah, "Oh dear me, Motherrr!" See, Dr Fei, when I start getting mad with people I do a thing the whole family calls...'

'"The Face".' Anne finished her daughter's sentence quickly, as if she was trying to divert a rampaging bull. 'Look! She's almost doing it now.'

'Oooh, Motherrr!'

Han stared at Dread who glared back, giving "The Face" her all. It should have been enough. He should have begun to look a bit perturbed at least. But he didn't. His features remained quite still.

'If you don't want to do what the surgeon suggests, that's fine. It's your decision,' Anne placated.

'Sure feels that way.'

'Yes, Dread is reluctant, Dr Fei. It's my idea. You see, Hannah, our beauty consultant, found some cosmetic experts who have shown that if you increase the inward angle of the eye by just a few degrees, this has a dramatic impact on how attractive a female face is rated by observers. These surgeons argue that it's this cat-like appearance to the eyes which explains why women such as Claire Forlani, Shalom Harlow, and...'

Anne seemed to have lost track.

'Jennifer Connelly, Motherrrr.'

'Yeah,' Anne said. 'It's why they are regarded as so stunningly attractive.'

Han interrupted. 'I think you are telling me all this for some reason?'

Dread was doing "The Face" again and she knew it should be disturbing him, which usually eased her fury with the world. But his indifference was riling. Maybe she should bring up Dr James again. Anne rubbed Dread's shoulder in consolation.

'The last message...'

'From the stalker?' Han queried.

Ah, now this was interesting. Dread could almost feel the prickle of arousal spread over Han's body. So the psychologist must regard the stalking as a real threat still.

'Yeah, before all that happened in the car park,' Anne said nervously.

'And you think there is a link between the note and our trip? Yet you only bring this up after we are on the road?'

'Dread thinks there's a link,' Anne said. 'I'm not convinced.'

'What did it say?'

Anne unfolded a sheet from a card file. Dread could see Han clocking the pile of cuttings in there. She read the words stiffly as if it was a letter from a bank manager, not a pop song.

...you gotta stand trial
Because all the while
I can see for miles and miles.
I can see for miles and miles.

There was a long silence. Dread inspected her reflection in the blacked-out windows, perfecting "The Face".

'I'm sorry, I don't get it,' said Han. 'What's the connection between those lines and our trip today?'

Dread flared. 'Doctor, it's a song with *seeing* in the title and *we* are going to a clinic, in what is supposed to be an ultra-secret appointment, to get an opinion on surgery around the *eyes*. There is a *major* leak somewhere in this organisation.'

'Calm down, darling,' Anne begged. 'You're reading way too much into it.'

On the outskirts of Malibu they connected with another pair of armoured trucks, and as they arrived at an abandoned petrol station, a team of overalls spilled out, pulling their rear doors open. It turned out the military style personnel carriers were not carrying fixed machine guns, as they seemed designed to, but were instead pregnant with motorcycles and biker gear.

As if they were dealing with a precious piece of kinetic sculpture, a team of mechanics tenderly worked a bike down a ramp.

Han walked around its gleaming black frame of chrome and carbon fibre. Gigantic brake callipers had BREMBO stencilled in big scarlet letters across them. The logo *MV Agusta* was low on the chassis.

'You prefer cars to bikes, Dr Fei?' Dread's voice was muffled because she'd been helped into her own motorcycle helmet, but she was calming down. Her machines had that effect on her. Also, wearing her hood and visor meant that no passing motorist or pedestrian was going to clock her for who she was.

'But this isn't a Suimizuki,' he said. 'I thought you had an advertising deal with them. Aren't they going to be upset if you are photographed riding a rival's bike?'

Oh, so he knew about the hush hush lawsuits.

Dread smiled pityingly at him.

'That's a *girl's trike*. I will only be seen on that Top Gun prop for a photo op. No, this isn't a Suimizuki and no one is going to photograph me on it. This is a limited edition MV Agusta F4-RR.'

'Dr Fei's just saying what I keep begging. Please don't get papped on this thing, darling, otherwise the Suimizuki people will sue us to kingdom come.' Anne had remained in the modified Hummer and was texting as she spoke to them. 'And I know you think that helmet means you won't be spotted by anyone – you're still not incognito.'

'Yeah, there's always a possibility I'll be made by someone recognising my ass.'

Anne looked up. 'Well, dear, it has featured in a series of ads for that Frenchy car company – I forget the name.'

Han hadn't forgotten. The TV commercials emphasised the pop star vigorously "shaking her ass".

Dread gave Anne "The Face" but then seemed torn about something as she glanced back at a bike still in the MPV.

'I had thought you could ride along on the Hayabusa there. But I had the MV modified to take a passenger. It's going to massively effect the balance and weight distribution, so be careful.'

She pointed at a plate of shining metal near the handlebars.

'This here is platinum, and see the number on it? Number one of 100. This is the very first one of just 100 built. It's arguably the fastest production bike in the world. And this...' she skipped round to the rear of the bike '...is the titanium exhaust, and this...' She was like a young girl showing off the features of a new toy, genuinely excited and enthusiastic. 'This is my favourite bit.' She gestured at the rear licence plate and flicked a switch on a remote in her palm. The plate flapped upwards and out of sight.

'Wireless remote control plate flipper – great, huh? We've got a ticket to ride, Dr Fei! Now change. You're holding us up.'

Lying on one of the back seats of a Hummer were a biker's helmet, leather jacket, gloves, boots, pants, and his revolver. Dread noted how he grabbed his weapon with alacrity. Identical to hers, the helmet was white with black zigzag motifs. He picked it up gingerly and found the label, Eley Kishimoto, plus a price tag still attached.

He blinked at the price and she knew he was looking at $1,350. She could read his frown as it shrieked *You paid that for a brain bucket?*

Dread kept an eye on him as he changed on the back seat. A burden was lifting from her – she always got a comforting sense of freedom from her bikes. As that sense rose, she considered Han Fei.

The jacket was a tight fit across his shoulder holster, and she frowned at the Smith & Wesson 500 Magnum disappearing inside. That was the personal weapon Kwame carried. Just as

Dread had calmed down as she got among her bikes, she detected Han seemed to relax with his gun returned.

Everything fitted, and she could see he was trying to figure out how they'd got his size. A couple of the mechanics came over to help him with the helmet.

'It's fitted with access to walkie-talkie which will keep you in contact with the MPVs here. And here is the rider-to-rider intercom so you can talk to her.' The mechanic motioned his head at Dread. 'There's also a cell phone connection, and an external mike if you need to hear what someone is saying outside – and here's a satnav pick-up. Basically you can switch between channels like this.'

'And before you ask…' Dread's voice came over in his helmet as soon as a grease monkey plugged a cable into the side of the bike '…the phones are encrypted, just like the ones on the MPVs.'

He flinched backwards as Dread high kicked her leathered leg over the superbike, nearly taking out his helmeted head. Crouching, she moved the bike beneath her, adjusting it expertly between her legs, and motioned impatiently for him to climb on the back.

Her back arched over the metal and her gloved hand danced across the dashboard, the engine roaring. A flock of birds, startled, leapt into the sky from the petrol station roof. She twisted the handle and the engine increased in intensity. She fluttered it a few times, and then allowed the motor to wind down.

Anne was almost immediately on the mobile pick-up inside both their helmets.

'Now, please drive carefully. And, Dread…'

'Yes, Mother?'

'Remember that we are gonna get sued for millions if you get snapped on this bike. So let's not attract the attention of the authorities.'

'Yessss, Motherrrrr!'

Han was fidgeting behind her.

'Put your hands on the rests behind your seat!'

He meekly reached behind to the rear handles on his kicked-up perch.

She circled the disused petrol station a few times, checking the grumbling bike beneath her. The mufflers growled, then spat as though the machine was irritated at having been cooped up and was raring to escape.

'You're a bit of a dead weight!' she grumbled through the intercom. Then she yanked the throttle. His neck jerked back, then they were out on the deserted street.

They rolled fairly docilely through the suburbs on their way to the freeway, so Han quickly got used to keeping his balance.

It was a warm Californian day, so Dread began to sweat inside her leathers. She was travelling within the speed limit, and in her mirrors she could discern Han's helmet twisting, so his eyes must be incessantly swivelling 360 degrees. The Hummers were directly behind, so at the moment she was safer than the President. Hell, she ached to cut loose from all the encumbrances that were her life!

Then she became distracted by something else in her rear-view mirrors, and as she leant in to examine the reflections, Han looked around.

'Oh, just bloody fabulous,' she breathed.

A group of motorcyclists had appeared, closing in on the Hummers, inspecting them. They were weaving fast and blipping accelerators. They buzzed aggressively past the chasing pack of blacked-out vehicles, causing them to brake sharply. Then they surged forward and were at once surrounding Han and Dread. Their machines were bulbous in comparison to Dread's sleek mount. The deep, lazy throb of their engines competed with the high-spirited whine of hers. They sat more upright and back, rounded stomachs protruding through leather jackets, while she was sprung, cat-like, over hers.

Because their goggles were closed over their helmets, their faces were menacingly expressionless.

Through her back, Dread felt Han's hands move to his holster.

'I think we should pull back to the Hummers,' he said.

But Dread instinctively sped up, and the trailing vans soon disappeared from view.

Part 3

An Act Of Love

My assassination attempt was an act of love...
I'm sorry love has to be so painful.
– John Hinkley's statement about his love for actress Jodie
Foster which led to his assassination attempt on Ronald Reagan.
Quoted from *The Insanity Defense and the Trial of John W
Hinckley Jr.* by Lincoln Caplan, p129–130,
published by New York: Dell, Caplan, L. 1987.

29

Diamonds are forever
Touch it, stroke it and undress it

The bike caught up with them and, as their limousine was now crawling in the South London traffic, the rider leant over and knocked on Kristal's blacked-out privacy glass.

'Any friend of yours,' Kwame paused, 'is a friend of yours.' His large meaty hand stopped her bringing the electric window down. 'We're gonna play this by the book.'

'Ah, if you will forgive meah, Kwame, that is not a bomb. It is, ah believe, an item of expensive jewellery.'

'How many boyfriends, Kristal?' Kwame stopped. He had to rein himself back at moments like these; keep reminding himself he was not the father of these three girls. Though if his developing attachment to Anne got much worse, things were going to get even more complicated.

She looked offended. 'Whaddya going on at me for? It's Mean who bangs like a dunny door in a hurricane!' Kristal craned round to peer through the dark of the rear window. Her wings nuzzled into Kwame's face again and he brushed them away.

'It's tha' sweet, sweet gentleman in the Lamborghini who is couriering meah a lil' ol' gift,' she pouted.

On his orders, the limo driver pulled over and Kwame beckoned the biker round to his side.

'If you're gonna wear that, can you please stay in the vehicle, at all times.'

'If you're going to wear *that*, can *you* please not get out of the car.' Kristal was nodding her head at Kwame's jacket, and he realised that he was still sporting his Smith & Wesson Magnum in a bulging shoulder holster underneath. He understood her point: they weren't exactly in Texas any more. He turned his back on the motorcyclist and carefully cradled the gun into the seat pocket in front of them.

Kristal, leaning out of the window, shook her head despairingly at the Lamborghini driver behind. Kwame suppressed a groan. Everyone was way too relaxed now they believed the stalker was dead, and this was dangerous.

'Get back inside,' he commanded, but the wings from her angel outfit floundered above her head when she tried to withdraw back into the limousine.

He hurried around to shield her from the agog pedestrians on her side. One had even started shuffling the pop star's infamous dance routine, "The Twitch". Dread fans were everywhere.

The suspect box was flat and square, and Kwame had seen enough of these gifts to recognise what it was.

'Okay, let's open it inside the car, not out here.'

The biker, shaking his head, roared away. The limo edged back to the middle of the road. Kwame kept a scrabbling Kristal at bay with one hand, while another expertly slit the packaging open with a hunting knife. He observed that Kristal was too obsessed with the gift to comment on how unusually tooled up he was.

'Ah do declare, y'all is no fun at all.'

When the familiar Tiffany blue box was revealed, she snatched it. Quivering, she lifted out a diamond necklace in a pattern of tiny twisting leaves. 'Oooh yeah!' She turned and presented her bare back to Kwame. 'C'mon, put it on.'

'That could be smeared with anthrax.'

'Would they go to so much effort and expense just to kill lil' ol' meah?'

'I've had tempting offers,' Kwame muttered, but he complied. 'So, he got what?'

'Get something that will go with this pretty lil' outfit, ah said, if yah want meah to wear this lil' old thing.'

'He requested that...that wound dressing you're wearing?'

She looked at him and laughed. 'All the boys've got their fantasies from our videos 'cos we're bad, bad girls – more wicked than even their minds.'

She pulled an illuminated vanity mirror from the ceiling of the limo and inspected her neckline.

'Bless my lil' soul, it definitely goes with this outfit, doesn't it.'

'If you're going to wear that, really, can you please *not* get out of the car? In this part of South London that would feed a whole family's drug habit for a year.'

'Relax!' Kristal turned to him, coquettishly displaying the necklace. 'So, waddya think?'

'It's...nice.'

She arched an eyebrow at him.

'You don't approve, do you. You're turning into our dad, d'you know that?'

Kwame slipped into his best Al Pacino impression.

'I always tell the truth. Even when I lie.'

Kristal resorted to puppy eyes. 'C'mon, check it, yeah?'

He sighed, and fingers better suited to forming a fist scampered over the on-board keyboard, bringing up the Tiffany website. Clicks later, they established that the necklace was designed by Dominique Schlumberger in eighteen carat gold with diamonds set in platinum. It was patterned to look like leaves growing on vines – £167,000 worth of leaves growing on vines.

'Damn!' Kristal's voice brought years of feeling to one exclamation. 'Lil' sister wins again.'

She tore at the leaves and vines, hurling them across the cabin. She pointedly turned away from Kwame, hands folded across her chest, knees brought into a foetal position.

Kwame shrugged. He could at these moments feel sorry for Kristal. She was put out because her necklace wasn't worth millions. What must it be like to be the sister of the most desired woman on the planet, barely noticed by her own mother?

Kristal began to stretch and yawn, and he knew in a few minutes she would be curled up asleep. She had no answers for herself, so sleep was her refuge. Kwame waited a bit, then reached forward and gathered the necklace, arranging it carefully by her side.

He hoped that she would change her mind about it.

The phone buzzed. As the traffic was gridlocked, Kwame rolled out and installed himself on the front passenger seat, lifting the electric privacy division so Kristal was soundproofed and centrally locking the vehicle. Caller ID told him it was Rudolf

Carnap on the phone. The organiser of Care for Congo was nothing if not persistent.

'Hi, Kwame.'

'Hey, Rudolf, great to hear from you – again! What were we talking about? Oh yeah – "I Don't Like Tuesdays", still one of my favourites. Are you going to be releasing any more singles? Or has being a UN Ambassador completely taken over?'

'Glad you liked the song. I didn't think much of Dread's dick-sneeze remix…'

'Okay, okay, what else can I do for you?'

'Yeah, er, so is she still gonna make it for the concert? She looks pretty beat up in the photos.'

He sounds almost hopeful that Dread is going to bow out, thought Kwame.

'Anne confirmed it's a go.'

'Oh, okay. Then are we hooking up later today and going over the Care for Congo site security? Seeing as how you seem to be over here.'

'Rudo, I'll be in London again in a couple of days. I could come over then? Something's come up.' Fighting through stop-start traffic along the Camberwell Road to reach Dr James was absorbing the time he would have used to check on the Ferris Wheel construction, but Dr James was too significant for Kwame to miss the appointment. They were going to have to let the Hyde Park inspection slide.

The number of police cars slipping past them meant some other more local security problem lay up ahead, and it was holding up the road. Kwame craned his head, attempting to make out what the snarl-up was.

'Sure it did, a car exploded at the Rose Bowl. And what if that happens in Central London on the Care for Congo day? Can you imagine the carnage? But, hey, the thing is, this concert does not belong to Dread! First there's the whole screw-up over her humping wheel, which meant the site had to be moved and turned so this carnival ride is where Dread wants, facing the way Dread specified. Now it's the final slot. Gaga, Bieber, McCartney, Jagger, Elton, Rhianna, Madonna, Rod and Kylie. Their people are giving me hell because everyone wants to be last on. It's a who's-the-biggest-star-in-the-world-right-now position, yeah?'

'Yesss, but that's for Anne to work out with you. I'm security, Rudo.'

'C'mon, you know how difficult she can be, but Anne and Dread listen to you. No one else. And you know all the other acts have accepted the strict no-encore policy. But the Internet and the press are wild with rumours that Dread is not only getting the last slot, she's going to do an encore regardless of our ruling.'

'Rudo, if you had left this without formalising it she wouldn't have noticed there'd be no encore. But now you've gone and said everyone plays just one song, guess what? She wants to demonstrate that only she can drive a crowd crazy enough to guarantee they won't let her off the stage.'

'That's exactly what I am calling you about. Kwame, there's a security as well as a health and safety dimension to this, so I need you to get through to Her Highness. We're gonna get ruthless and pull the plug on her. We're just gonna throw to the other stage and she'll have to suck it up.'

'So if you're going to do that, what d'you need to discuss with me?' Inwardly Kwame was wondering how long before Dread found out. She'd be fuming, and her response would be some crazy stunt.

'Well, security is going to be locked tight. But her fans are something else, man. We're getting wind that a group's planning to hack into our system, or break in physically and rig things so that we can't switch to the parallel stage. That they're gonna hijack the concert for her on the day.'

'Oh, c'mon – it's highly unlikely they're going to be able to do that!' Kwame laughed. A good example of Dread's fans had been the shambolic character doing "The Twitch" by the side of the road where the motorbike courier had stopped them. But he was also thinking, if her fans *could* achieve the sort of stunt Rudo was obsessing about on the big day, what about her enemies?

'Unlikely, yes, but…look, we started organising this concert forty-eight hours after they found the Congo death pits, and the point was we had to move fast to catch the anger and sympathy – you know how quickly they go when the next tragedy rolls along. And it's snowballed bigger than we ever imagined.

Listen, Kwame, maybe for the first time in her short spoiled life, Dread can do some good. If this concert goes well it's got the potential to raise the kind of money that will save, and turn around, the lives of hundreds of thousands. It will be a tragedy on a biblical scale if she passes up this chance by not playing by the rule book. We've got the best people building your dipshit Ferris whatever, and it's costing us. And what with recruiting sound engineers and lighting crew on the hoof, it's just not been possible to do the full security checks you wanted. Which were outrageous, by the way.'

'Yeah, yeah. I understand. But we take responsibility for our own protection, you know that. I've already loaned you a bunch of staff to protect the wheel – d'ya need more?'

Rudo snorted. 'I saw what happened at the Rose Bowl, man. The crowds that follow her are getting out of hand. This is becoming the suicide shift, man.'

Tell me about it, groaned Kwame inwardly.

'She's also informing us, through her people, that she's got the most spectacular end to a rock concert, or any live event ever, planned. So that's why she's absolutely got to go last. But she won't reveal what it is. Now what on earth is she talking about?'

Kwame mused over that himself. *Why has she not told me any of this?* Before he could respond, Rudolf continued.

'And another thing, she won't finalise the actual song she's gonna sing! We need to know. She's messing us about, refusing to confirm definitely. We, and the whole world, have been left guessing. Which explains all that graffiti on the sides of churches as her fans stoke the rumour mill. It's all part of her grandstanding.'

And that's precisely why she's the biggest star on the planet right now, you twat, Kwame bristled, *because she knows how to oil the publicity machine*. But he didn't interrupt the rant; he was used to everyone taking out their countless Dread frustrations on him.

'So can you please, please tell her to forget her voracious appetite always to be number one and let our concert pass without her messing with the plan?'

Rudolf Carnap's tone had changed: something scared was lurking in the back of his voice. 'There're serious crowd control issues here. Two million people squeezed into Central London. Many of them not the most stable people on the planet. I mean, just how far is she prepared to go? Even put lives on the line?'

30

Twenty-five was the speed limit
A motorcycle not allowed in it

The bikers were keeping pace. Dread examined them in her mirrors. They were waving, gloved hands pointing at the bike with thumbs up gestures.

As Dread slowed her MV Agusta to a crawl, approaching red traffic lights, the jockeys enveloping them kept pace. Two in front, two on either side and several behind: gleaming Harleys, Boss Hosses, a Kawasaki and a particularly loud highly-strung Suzuki.

Two of the bikers at the back began doing stunts: front wheelies followed by slap wheelies.

Dread loved the sound and petrol smell of these big beasts. They were like dinosaurs arriving at a watering hole, checking each other out.

'If it's tourist season, how come we ain't allowed to hunt 'em?' she asked her helmet intercom. Han's breathing was rasping in response. She was making the man of steel nervous.

Relax, Dread thought, *they can't hear us above the roar of their machines, and with us using our comms.*

She could also appreciate from the mirrors that her Hummers were now three vehicles behind. Narrow lanes and traffic meant it would be impossible for them to catch up suddenly.

The external mike was picking up traffic sounds. Dread pushed up the volume to check what the bikers might be saying to each other. Everyone stopped at the red signals.

The phone rang and another voice entered their helmets.

'Dread? It's KT. Where the hell are you?' Her sister's voice was cracking with anger. 'We need to finalise the remix cut on "Country Girl"! We're way over the deadline and Saul is giving us hell.'

'Yeah, well go with your edit, okay?' Dread said carelessly.

'No way! Last time you said that, you complained later and then the mix got completely redone. Wasted all our time.'

Bikes leant and boots scraped the ground. Eyewear lifted and heads craned to take the MV Agusta in. They were wearing retro World War II-styled headgear and old fashioned goggles, releasing stubbled faces to speak. They tried to engage Dread in conversation, but she kept her hands on the bars, shaking her helmet at them. Her visor was resolutely down. No way could they know who she was.

'Woweee, man, cool bike!'

'MV Agusta F4-RR...'

'One of the most expensive, most powerful production motorbikes in the world.' Broad Californian accents and appreciative lust for the metal, not the woman. 'One hundred built at $120,000 a pop.'

The riders seemed good natured enough. They appeared to be real petrol-heads and delighted to be witnessing an Agusta in the flesh.

'So what do you want me to do, Mean? If you think it's bumpin', you go with it.'

The bikers looked confused as to whom she was muttering to. It was difficult to hear anything clearly above the clatter of the engines.

'F4 power train...titanium con rods...peak rev limit 14,000 rpm...inertial platform lean angle sensor...8-level traction control...'

The riders were showing off who had most knowledge of Dread's bike.

KT was now furious. 'No, Dread, you listen to it now, confirm it's okay so there's no dispute afterwards. Do it! Do it!'

'Play it then, only make it fast, okay?'

One of the running commentators was leaning off his bike and stretching his neck to take in all the detailing on the petrol tank between Dread's legs. Dread could sense Han stirring, feeling for his gun beneath his jacket. But with their visors down, the riders surrounding them had no idea Han and Dread were talking with each other. To them, they were being blanked.

Dread came on the internal channel. 'These guys are ape

hangers and they're driving some real thumpers: V8 Boss Hosses with 445 bhp, and the guy over there is on a Kawasaki Ninja ZX-14.'

'I have no idea what that means,' Han said.

'It means zero to sixty in two point five seconds and a top speed of 186 miles per hour.'

The bikers weren't in full motorcycle gang garb, but they were all wearing the same outfit – black leather jackets with no motifs, black antique domes that resembled Nazi helmets, vintage aircraft goggles and faded blue jeans. A uniform whichever way you looked at it, and that definitely meant a gang or a club.

'I don't get it – most gangs don't mix up their bikes' marques and the brands like this. It's very strange,' Han said.

'You not talking to us? Your bike too good for us?'

Dread had switched channels to the outside to pick up what was being said. The biker's tone was skidding over to menacing.

'Do ya think $120,000 buys you something that can beat us?'

'You a waxer, or you wanna twist the wick?'

The opening bars of "Wild Boys" burst through the helmet speakers. Han's body flinched and the bikers turned to look at him. Dread brought the volume down. The longer she didn't respond, the more offended the petrol-heads became.

The wild boys are calling
On their way back from the fire

Reverberating rock music inside the bone dome wasn't helping her keep a grip on what was happening around them. She felt every movement as Han slowly unzipped his leather jacket then, gingerly reaching in, unbuttoned the holster cuddling the Smith & Wesson.

In august moon's surrender to
A dust cloud on the rise

Dread's body stiffened.

The bikers smacked their goggles back on and revved their engines, slowly bringing them to an agitated squeal. Leering at Dread, they let their machines jolt forward and then stop.

'The key advantage we have is...' Dread began.

The lights changed. Her hands on the handlebars twisted. The MV Agusta's engine ignited, spraying chainsaw revs.

'…the weight of your arse over the rear wheel!'

Wild boys fallen far from glory

Han nearly fell off the back with the jolt forwards. He clawed for her waist and held on. His neck cricked with the whiplash, or was that the sound of their helmets bumping? The front wheel lifted temporarily and the back scrabbled at the tarmac, spewing smoke. The engine note soared, like an animal in pain. Dread leant dramatically and the bike tilted at a crazy angle. Han, a quick learner, followed her body move. Quickly she zipped back in the other direction. Her machine bobbed and weaved between the bikes ahead of them, performing a wheelie, caning it.

Reckless and so hungered

On the razors edge you trail

The power train howled through the pitches, then snarled again as the gears changed. Dread could see in her mirrors that the bikers had been caught off guard and were moving after them as if in slow motion. One had similarly lifted his front wheel off the ground as his machine tore up the road to give chase.

Because there's murder by the roadside

In a sore afraid new world

The pursuer's bike began to wobble and then career from side to side. Flipping out from under him, it somersaulted into an oncoming car. The rider spun before being flung against the wreckage of the swerving vehicle. He ricocheted off, his helmet flopping back and forth.

Shards of metal cascaded in all directions.

'Aren't you going to stop?' Han shouted.

Dread shrugged. 'Tell 'em to keep blowin' their horns, we're reloading.'

Anne came on the phone.

'Are you all right? What happened? There's a biker back here in a terrible pile up. Have you gone from zero to bitchy in two seconds? Again?'

'Not now, for Chrissake!'

They could hear a muffled police siren in the distance. The bike catapulted on to the freeway at frenetic speed as she revelled in the sensation of freedom.

They tried to break us,

Looks like they'll try again

Han tried Kwame's phone but there was no answer. He contacted Anne – she knew the numbers and called in the decoys. They would be tracking Dread on their satnavs.

Minutes later, as Dread skated between cars in the fast lane, she picked out the black specks in her mirrors of what looked like buzzing insects.

Bikes.

Although the landscape was warping up on them and then whooshing by at a frenzied rate, she accelerated again.

From behind a corner a traffic jam veered – tailing back on all lanes. Dread dodged the rear-most vehicle as they began threading between lines of gridlock. She instinctively braced herself for impact. The bikers behind squealed under juddering brakes and followed, but their machines were squatter, so manoeuvring in the channels of metal became more precarious and they began to fall behind.

Wild boys never lose it
Wild boys never chose this way

Dread slipped between jutting chrome with millimetres separating mirrors and knees. Han furled his limbs in. The engine note, reflecting back at them from walls of car metal on either side, got much louder. Should a vehicle up ahead decide to swap queue, they would collide.

As the traffic thinned, they swaggered ahead again.

In the shuddering mirror, looking back, Dread could make out four bikes swaying through the melee. She swerved and tore down a slip road leading off the freeway.

A sprawling shopping mall trembled over the brow. She pivoted into the car park, and the bikers behind banked and followed. Cars thumped to a halt, shopping trolleys up-ended and shoppers ran as Dread zigzagged across the lined spaces. She smashed through some abandoned shopping bags which popped loudly, fluid inside spraying away. The bike's fuselage reflected and distorted the passing cars, the parking bay outlines looming and bending beneath her.

Chasing bikers slalomed past automobiles trying to park or emerge as well as shoppers dodging them. Packages and bags flew through the air. Braking bikes and cars squealed angrily at each other. One motorcycle tipped over and the rider slipped sideways across the road, hands still stretched out as if holding imaginary handlebars. His leg became trapped under the bike as it slid into a parked car. A crumping sound followed the flames springing up, then a whoosh as oxygen was sucked in.

Figures in the periphery of Dread's vision broke into a run towards the accident. She stood slightly as she lifted the bike over the parking humps and then slammed the kerb.

After describing a wide semi-circle, Dread leant sharply, leading the whining entourage back on itself. They were now heading for the mall. Large glass doors formed a barrier. Han braced himself for the crash as screaming pedestrians criss-crossed in front, pirouetting to evade them.

She braked brutally, wheels complaining as she slowed to an impatient hum. She looked back, every sense sharpened. Mayhem in the car park, but their pursuers were still hurtling towards them. Han's nose collided with the front of his helmet as the back of the bike tried to jackknife, Dread controlling it with sheer force from her hips.

The mall's revolving doors obediently swung round to squeeze them through. Just behind, the last two bikes still chasing caught up.

Wild boys never close your eyes
Wild boys always shine.

31

Fall in a long stray town
As the ice comes round

The bodyguard was startled to see that she was tapping the glass division with the muzzle of the Smith & Wesson. Anything to get his attention.

She was such a child. Maybe it was because Kristal was so used to constant movement as they bustled through the world on tour that the vehicle's idleness had woken her.

She rapped the division again. 'We're gonna be late if we don't do sommin',' she complained. Immobile cars hemming them in were shimmering with irritation.

And you won't get any nooky, reflected Kwame.

'Get off the phone to Her Highness and let's try another route!'

'It's not Dread, it's Rudolf Carnap, the organiser of Care for Congo. Will you put that away? Excuse me, Rudolf, I need to get back to you. I hear what you say, I'll have a word. I suspect if you give her the prime end slot we can negotiate...'

'You are not seriously telling me his name is Carnap,' Kristal said. 'Think I was born yesterday?'

'C'mon, he's famous. He's an ex-rock star, always doing those big charity events now.'

'Look, ask someone. There must be another way of getting there,' she commanded. She pointed at a man on the pavement. 'He looks local,' she decided, pulling her window down.

Kwame clambered hastily back to the seat beside her. 'Kristal, for Chrissake!'

Greying stubble turned to them and Kwame seemed to recollect he was one of the pedestrians staring at them when the courier dropped in. Was he stalking them?

'It'll be okay. Look, he's a fan.' Kristal tried to appease the agitated bodyguard. 'Aww, sweet – look, he's even doin' his version of "The Twitch".'

Kwame retrieved his gun and burrowed it back into the seat pocket facing them.

The stranger did have a fidget, and had responded to Kristal's imperative wave by lurching over. Kwame looked past his shoulder at the traffic in front of them as the sound of a police siren arrived. It was difficult to see, but twinkling red and blue illumination crowning the hump of the road indicated emergency vehicle involvement.

He pulled Kristal's window back up and waved the pedestrian round to his side of the car. The pedestrian's glistening head appeared and he craned in and stared about the vehicle, breathing hard. Kwame leant back and put a protective hand up by Kristal as the limousine filled with a sharp tang. The "local's" voluminous cloak seemed to billow up at them.

'Say, mistuh, can yah direct us to...where the hell is we goin' anyways, Kwame?'

Before the bodyguard could answer, the man stared at Kristal. 'So he's called in the angels now?' he growled.

'Yeah, this was on *Angels and Demons*.' Kristal brushed her wings behind her. 'The new album's out in a few weeks, but...'

The pedestrian's hand snaked out from under his cloak, and Kwame caught it just before it reached Kristal's feathers.

'Wings...' the man breathed, backing off as Kwame pushed him away from the vehicle.

'Aww c'mon, Kwame, don't overreact,' Kristal said, smiling.

The man stepped forward and checked up the road again. Kwame looked, and now several policemen could be seen dodging the gridlock up ahead, running towards them.

'You tell William: if he's called in the angels then we ain't got much time.' The man spat and turned, sprinting in the opposite direction.

'*William*? How the hell does a random stranger know who we're gonna see?' Kristal protested. 'Kwame, just how leaky is our ship?'

Kwame had opened the door to give chase, but was halted by

193

a shout from one of the running policemen.

'Armed police! Remain inside the vehicle! Armed police!'

Kwame ducked back as several uniforms pelted past.

'What was that all about?' Kristal asked as she strained to see what was going on out the back window. 'And where's my necklace?' she demanded, searching the car.

Kwame exclaimed, and she turned back sharply. 'What's up?'

Kwame was scrabbling at the seat pocket in front of him.

The gun was gone.

32

Bits and pieces
Now you're gone and I'm all alone
You're still way up there on your throne

Just approaching the giant Ferris wheel was making William edgy and irritable.

'It's not finished yet,' explained Tullia, wrapped in a jumble sale of pashminas.

'Even so, how could anyone sane contemplate balancing at the top, far less dancing?'

'That's the whole point: that she struts about without any safety railings,' Tullia instructed. 'It reveals her character.' This time when she cleared her throat it sounded gravelly, like she was going down with something, or the cold out here was getting to her.

Dread's chief bodyguard had unexpectedly cancelled their scheduled meeting at the Institute, and instead demanded their presence at the Hyde Park construction site. William didn't know if the sudden change in venue had something to do with the standstill roads created by the police lockdown of the area as they hunted for David, or whether there had been some crisis within Dread's camp requiring attention. He did know he would much prefer to be back in Camberwell, trying to make sure the manhunt didn't end in an assassination.

'Vilhelm, will you be terribly charming when we meet Dread?'

'How much has she promised the Institute for my services?'

Tullia's eyes sparked.

'We have a rival – Han Fei – so everything hangs in the balance.'

'So either I'm up on that Ferris wheel, or…'

Tullia smiled sweetly. 'Yes, how are the helicopter rides going? You're doing well, I hear.'

William scowled.

'A little bird tells me you persuaded the pilot to airlift you to the Royal London and the helipad on their roof. You've been checking the trauma unit is ready for a VIP casualty. William, really!'

At the main gate, near Hyde Park Corner, when Tullia had asked for Mr Kwame Appiah, the officers had pointed up Park Lane towards Marble Arch. Almost opposite the Dorchester Hotel they could discern a tall black man surrounded by a gesticulating crowd waving placards. He was bantering with the army of fans camped along the side of the park.

The Dread disciples were sporting the infamous skull and crossed microphones insignia on the backs of their leather jackets, while the bodyguard had *Dread Security* stencilled across the shoulders of a bomber coat.

'He's making friends with them, trying to turn them all into informants, hoping that being in regular contact means they'll come to him with information on the stalker,' William remarked, shielding his eyes against the spotlights gazing up at the huge stage.

'So, he's not just a rather friendly chap?' smiled Tullia. William returned a withering glance. 'Seriously, Vilhelm, be careful with him. He has a reputation for...'

'People are living in tents out here already?' William was unbelieving of the transformation that had been wrought on Central London, and he remained unconcerned about entourage trivia.

'...savagery. Don't you watch the news, Vilhelm? They started arriving a week ago. Everyone wants to be ahead of the two million who are coming.'

Muzzles of Heckler & Koch machine guns examined the two psychiatrists attempting to gain entry.

'In contrast to the pop festival feel the newspaper pictures convey, the atmosphere is very tense,' Tullia observed.

'It's keeping the two sides apart that's the real battle,' offered one of the officers, satisfied Tullia and William were who they said they were. 'They hate each another.'

The sentry indicated another large throng massed outside

The Hilton, brandishing their banners with equal devotion. *On the Cross He Bled – Not Dread!* was one that caught William's eye. They were singing hymns.

'These are the devout folk upset by the "more famous than God" thing?' he asked the officer. The guard scowled a quizzical look which said, *You need to get out more.*

'Yeah. Once in a while one or two will run at the other camp and jump the central reservation. Then there's a fight and Park Lane grinds to a halt. I'll be glad when this is over. It's a miracle no one's been badly hurt.'

'You remember that paper, Vilhelm? John Maltby and Lynn McCutcheon found that those who followed and worshipped celebrities tended *not* to be religious?'

'Yeah, it was, *Thou shalt worship no other gods, unless they are celebrities: the relationship between celebrity worship and religious orientation* by Maltby, Houran, Lange, Ashe and McCutcheon, in the journal *Personality and Individual Differences* back in 2002,' William said. 'While the devout tend not to revere the famous, it looks as if everyone here is after someone to worship.'

Tullia was visibly wrestling with exasperation over his autistic need to fill in the full reference, while the police officer looked slightly stunned.

'Love has filled the space religion did in the old days. Now it's romance and attachment that gives life meaning,' Tullia considered.

'There's something possessive about worship,' William said. 'Basically, your followers would never allow you to be an indifferent God. And yet any true deity, by definition, is. Killing your deity was always the best way to get their attention.'

'You're referring to our tendency to crucify?' Tullia asked.

William waved at the Ferris wheel and the stage being constructed as it began to loom over them.

'Is that an altar or a stage?'

He became aware of one of Gerrard's infernal helicopters hovering in the sky. 'I swear to God those helicopters are following me.'

'Given all that time you've endured up at Lippitts Hill, I'm surprised just looking at a whirlybird makes you airsick.'

'Ah well, you know me. I could never learn to be just a passenger.'

She raised a querying eyebrow, but he did not expand.

'Mr Kwame Appiah wants to meet us in a temporary office by the main stage.' She flourished more security passes, and the entrance to the site was opened for them as a roaring chant sprang up from the Dread supporters.

Their new companion, another security guard, visibly shrank a few inches.

'This will go on for at least half an hour, and then the other side will crank up the volume as well,' he said.

The mantra turned into a football terrace tribal shout, words stabbed out and punctuated by synchronised clapping on a grand scale.

'It's not bad,' mused William, impressed at the coordination involved in getting thousands to be so immaculately in time.

'Wait till you gotta put up with it day in, day out. See how you feel then.'

'The stalker may now be dead – in that exploding car,' Tullia said to William as the man moved forward out of listening range. 'But Mr Appiah is still interested in getting your take on the motivation, and how the notes got past security. In fact, he thinks there must have been more than one stalker.'

'Yes, yes,' said William impatiently, 'but what about David Lewis?'

Tullia's lips pursed.

'Don't chase Philippa. With her it's the wrong approach. Wait for her to come after you. Just as Dread is now.'

'Tullia, when we're working with the Cabinet Office, we're concerned about the threat to Philippa because it interferes with Affairs of State. That guy who attacked Berlusconi in Italy after a speech he delivered? That assault from a total stranger put the head of the Italian State out of action for a significant period and potentially altered the course of history. This is an important area where mental illness and politics intersect.'

'Vilhelm, do have a care. Your pompous rear end is showing.'

She lowered her voice. 'Please remember Philippa brought you in because the police kept tasering the usual suspects rather publicly at any event she attended, which just made her look terrible to the electorate. She's awfully grateful all that nonsense stopped once you came on board. Now with Dread...'

'Not that pop star again? She's not going to follow our advice anyway, and she's going to be completely untrustworthy!'

'If she's completely untrustworthy, then she's trustworthy.'

But something inside William snapped.

'I'm not interested in looking after a narcissistic bimbo who's encouraged the problem in the first place!' he boomed just as they rounded a corner. Towering over them was the black man they had seen in Park Lane.

He had been chatting to construction workers outside a Portakabin, dwarfing the group of hard hats and Hi Vis waistcoats, but he stopped and frowned the instant he heard William's pronouncement. The hulking presence seemed to squeeze essential air from their space as he turned towards them.

The psychiatrist gulped.

33

Nowhere to run to baby
Nowhere to hide

The phone line down which Mean had been feeding "Country Girl" went dead, maybe because Dread and Han had just entered the galleria. One of the last two riders pursuing them dismounted outside and rushed at them, his bike writhing on the ground, the engine still howling. Dread could only make him out as filmy as he was moving swiftly between panes of glass in the revolving entrance. He looked as if he had a weapon in his hand. In her mirrors Dread saw Han expertly release the gun into his gloves. He held the enormous revolver up, muzzle pointing at the roof.

On foot, the biker crashed through a smaller gateway and charged at them. Han flinched out of the man's first lunge, while Dread swivelled her handlebars and pulled away as the assailant grabbed air.

Front wheels lifted as she gunned the engine, so the assailant fell over with the momentum of his lunge. His companion was fighting through the rotating door on his muttering machine, his feet on the ground, powerfully forcing his two wheels forward.

The engine note was louder now, reflecting back at them from glass shop fronts. The commune of shoppers was staring, confused and frightened – was this a retail promotion for bikes in poor taste? Mall security began running towards them, yelling into their walkie-talkies, hands pointing to where people needed to take cover.

They were down to their last pursuer from the posse, both bikes racing together while patrons scrambled for safety. They jockeyed with each other, chrome to chrome, handlebar to handlebar.

A nail concessionary stand slewed into their path. Dread

swerved too hastily and they careered into the cardboard structure sideways, a kaleidoscope of polish bottles showering them.

The biker was right on top of them. Up ahead, on either side of the escalators, Hi Vis vests, guns unsheathed, daisy chained across the width of the atrium.

Shouted warnings clashed with wails from the terrified shoppers.

Dread was banking and sliding the heavy machine to avoid hitting people, but the rider behind struck someone full on. The body was thrown, rolling with a thudding slap.

And staying down.

They had run out of places to go. The security men had all sides ahead of them covered.

'From my police experience, if there's no pedestrians in the line of fire, they could take a shot at you!' Han bellowed.

Particularly given that you still have your gun in your hand and are waving it around stupidly, she thought.

So he wanted her to turn herself in. Didn't he know the principal concert of her career beckoned?

She brought the machine round in a tight circle. Behind her was the other biker, and in his wake, a further gang of yellow vests blocked any hope of a passage back.

Dread gunned the engine. The bike bounded for the escalators. Han flinched as the wheels grappled with the serrated edge of the moving steps. Acrid burning rubber penetrated the helmet. The extra weight of Han on the back of the bike meant she found it easier to perform a wheelie on to the incline of the escalator.

They surged skywards, sparks showering on either side as her footrests scraped the steel banking. The rider behind tried to follow. Outstretched boot assisting, he listed. Then he tried a wheelie, but his front tyre partially embedded in the saw-toothed edges of the steps. The bike tipped forward, hurling its passenger off with a clonking thud. The rider desperately grappled and leant on to the side of the escalator. Pulled away from his grip by the moving stairs, the spitting machine paused, then toppled back down on him. They both clanged to the bottom of the stairwell.

Dread soared into air at the top, her engine bitching about it.

No guards in sight here. As consumers cowered in doorways, Gucci, Tommy Hilfiger, Prada and Ralph Lauren smeared past.

'Can you believe how badly made this shit is? Who'd pay for this tat?' Dread remarked through the helmet microphone, pointing with her Trussardi boot.

Then, skidding another corner, they came upon an additional ring of security guards, closing in quickly. Dread evaded them by slithering down new wide corridors, embroidered with glittering shops and scampering pedestrians, as she desperately searched for a way out.

All she could see ahead was a cul-de-sac, yet she accelerated, feeling her bodyguard stir as Han realised where she was heading.

The elevator.

Translucent and suspended over the main atrium, it beckoned. She screeched up alongside and pressed the button to summon it. The mall guards paused, then crouched forward more warily. She twirled the bike to confront their creeping adversaries. They believed she was about to shunt them, so they backed up. The spitting engine menaced growls as she twisted her grip.

Then the lift doors arrived and Dread backed the sneering machine in, reaching out a gloved hand, stabbing the close-doors button.

Han's agitated fidgeting suggested he had decided with absolute conviction that she was crazy. They were backing themselves into the tightest corner possible.

The doors sealed.

Lift music played.

'Is that Coldplay?' Dread jeered, looking for the speakers.

'How are we going to get out?' Han asked. Dread guessed that right at this moment, Han was praying that Dr James would take her case.

'Coldplay performed in the closing ceremony for the Paralympics. Now I know there are worse things than losing your legs...'

The platform was rising up and she stabbed the down button impatiently. The glass cage resolutely stayed on course: upwards.

Dread hummed in tune with the lift music. 'Para, para, paralysed...'

Carbon monoxide from the bike's mufflers wafted into her

nose. They were going to be asphyxiated in here if she didn't halt the beating pistons soon.

The lift reached the top floor. Dread kicked at the door with her booted foot and jammed at the switch again.

Grudgingly the lift descended.

'What the hell is happening?' she asked. 'Why didn't the doors open?'

'I don't know!' Han sounded mystified, like he could not believe how perfectly cool she was. 'But if we don't get them open soon we're going to suffocate.'

I don't ruffle, unlike you, she reflected on the consternation in his voice.

Han peered out of the glass. People were bolting for the exits and the sprinkler system had switched on. A blue and white flashing light, and an automated tannoy voice bansheed outside, and inside the lift.

'Attention! Attention! Attention! There is a fire alert! Evacuate the building! Go to your nearest exit! Fire alert! Evacuate the building! This is not a drill! Do not use the elevators!'

'No, wait,' said Dread. 'Now it's U2 they're playing – which is worse in your opinion, Dr Fei? U2 or Coldplay?' Dread was ignoring the mayhem outside, continuing to search for the speakers. 'Maybe U2 have the edge?'

'Oh Hell!' exclaimed Han, looking up at the smoke detector in the lift ceiling.

'What?'

'The exhaust fumes in here must have set the automated fire suppression system off.'

'Is that why the lift won't open the doors?'

'Yes! It'll be programmed to descend to a designated floor and only then will the electronics release us.'

The lift approached the ground floor. Musak returned in the form of a muted version of "The Girl From Ipanema", creating a surreal calm inside the lift, a stark contrast to the chaos outside.

What was the preassigned level where the computer would command the doors to open? If it was ground, they were finished. Security had them completely surrounded down there. The parade pressed against the glass, staring up at them impotently as they slowly neared and then passed. Crowding in from behind was a newly arrived group of police officers. Flushed faces on the outside, ice cool anonymous gleaming helmets on the inside. Separated by just a few inches of glass. Guards' hands jammed at the open-doors button, but the lift sailed past and down.

In the basement the doors opened the instant the lift halted.

No welcoming committee here. Dread delicately nosed the bike out into the vaulted car park. Cars were streaming out. The barriers had lifted automatically to permit an emergency fire evacuation. Shoppers were flooding in via the stairs and flowing to their vehicles. Dread negotiated the torrent of human traffic and then eased the bike into the exit lane. She tacked between cars as panicked drivers flattened horns.

Weaving past the barrier, they accelerated away.

'I don't get the whole mall thing. That was, like, so ratchet. My personal shopper has every possible option delivered, thank God.'

The psychologist turned to look back at the shopping centre, which was rapidly disappearing over the horizon. An anthill of insects, fleeing their broken hive, scuttled from all the exits, drenched from the sprinkler system. Security staff also emerged sprinting, but then pulled up short as they scanned for Dread's bike through the chaos. Police cars blared towards them, but passed and kept going towards the mall. Three fire trucks were pulling in next to the raging fire between the crashed bike and crumpled car. Other bikers, who might have been part of the original gang, were roaring away in all directions as law enforcement arrived then gave chase.

The phone line returned and electric guitars scraped their ears again.

You got sirens for a welcome
There's bloodstain for your pain

Siren moaning and roof rack flashing, a patrol car was arriving from another entrance.

They tried to tame you
Looks like they'll try again

The music echoed away as Mean came back on. 'Well? You were quiet through the whole thing – amazing! Finally we got you to listen to it properly. C'mon – it's not that bad, is it?'

'I geddit, really.' Han's voice was cracking dry in the tinny helmet speaker. 'You're in a negative space right now, Dread. You're furious with Kwame for deserting you today, but…'

She silenced him with a wave of a glove, forefinger extended.

'If you're still in control, then you ain't goin' fast enough,' Dread snapped. 'It's still way too slow,' and the line clicked as she dismissed her sister.

34

Ninety-nine red balloons
The war machine springs to life
Opens up one eager eye

Kwame waved the other men away and extended a gigantic palm. William scowled. Tullia smiled professionally.

'Remember, Vilhelm, we've been dealing with Mr Appiah via email. It was he who sent you the packages of Dread's material.'

William grumbled a greeting as Kwame shook his hand firmly.

'Good to meet you, Dr James. I found your writings on stalking fascinating.'

William was surprised by the well-modulated voice, with just a hint of a West Indian accent. Could it be that this man *had* read his papers? Even Philippa had lied about that.

'Sorry, Dr James, Professor d'Aragona, but with anyone who might end up working closely with Dread, we have a comprehensive screening procedure.' He held out his hand again, and this time Tullia meekly handed her mobile phone over. Kwame looked at William, obviously expecting him to deposit his as well, but the psychiatrist now seemed to be lost in a world of his own and was muttering to himself.

Tullia hastily intervened. 'They need our mobiles to add encryption software so the line to Kwame is secure when we discuss this case.'

William snorted. 'You've got to be joking. They're just gonna be stalking us with our phones!'

'But Dr Han Fei agreed to let us put the same software on his phone,' Kwame protested.

Tullia turned to Kwame. 'Dr James is finding the proposal we are putting to him – that he represents our department in assisting you with your stalker – a bit of a surprise, Mr Appiah.

He is used to working here in London with the Foreign Office.'

'Sure, no problem. We understand it's a bit of a stretch, but we now believe these notes show signs of being linked in some way to an insider with the Dread team. So we need an expert like yourself, Dr James, to help us identify who this might be, and also to assess how problematic a threat this is, or was.'

William pointedly looked around the site. The unfinished girders jutting up from each platform of the Ferris wheel seemed to resemble gleaming teeth, laughing at him. Kwame appeared perplexed by his non-response. The psychiatrist figured that the bodyguard was mystified because everyone else on the planet would be tearing off one of his limbs to get the chance to work with the diva.

'What's going on over there?' William pointed at some workmen beavering over a large searchlight.

'That's one of the iconic parts of the Dread set. It's called The Dominator and it's the most powerful spotlight on the planet. We use it to illuminate Dread when she's on the wheel.'

'You've got more than one?'

'Yeah, we use 'em to sweep the crowd as well, and for other effects. One of them is able to project her image into the sky. We do this twenty-four hours before a concert begins – like the Batman symbol hovering over Gotham City.'

'So why are they dismantling it?'

William's direct questioning offered no concession to conversational etiquette, but Kwame accepted it.

'They're not – they're taking some of the light filaments out.'

'Why?'

'Basically those are special UV filaments which are used to project what we in the industry call black light, because you can't normally see it. But it interacts with special paints to cause fluorescence in the dark. Dread and the other dancers use these make-up materials on stage, and it delivers some spectacular special effects. Another advantage of the black light is that it doesn't blind out people's night vision.'

'So why are they taking the filaments out?'

'There's a lot of ego involved as to who gets the top spot of last performer on stage. So they're trying to make sure Dread doesn't get her way by insisting we take out the UV elements. This way she won't be able to exploit that part of her set, which would only come alive as a special effect as darkness comes down.'

'So, in an industry of the self-obsessed, she's seen as a bit of a unique ego-maniac?'

'Pretty much.' Kwame shrugged.

William disappeared into himself for more long moments. Tullia let a benign smile spread across her face. The psychiatrist understood that her scheme was for his intellectual curiosity to be so pricked by the case he'd get lured in.

William spoke abruptly. 'It has implications for your security arrangements as well, doesn't it? The UV light?'

Kwame was startled at William's insight.

'Yes, it does. As forgeries are in such wide circulation, we use the same technology to check the veracity of the tickets and backstage passes for her shows. UV black lights are carried by all our security personnel – it's similar to the equipment stores use to check on counterfeit currency. Most legal tender has fluorescent markings on it that only show up under a black light – the kind of fluorescent ink which it's not easy to use in counterfeiting.'

'And most Dread fans have taken the whole black light thing to their hearts, haven't they,' William responded. 'They now have fluorescent tattoos which only show up once a black light is shone on them. So it's a way for Dread-heads to distinguish true fans, and to avoid problems at work or places where signalling you are a follower could get you into trouble.'

Kwame nodded. The psychiatrist had done an impressive amount of homework for a man who wasn't interested in 'looking after a narcissistic bimbo'. The fluorescent tattoo epidemic hadn't yet reached the mainstream media.

'So it's going to be less easy for you without using your massive black light to keep an eye on those who may not be fans in the front row getting near Dread.'

'Right, though most don't know we sweep the audience with the black light for that purpose, so please keep that to yourself.'

William shrugged. 'You probably don't need us at all. There are loads of US experts, like Dr Han Fei, cashing in on celebs. Stick with him.'

William turned on his heel, but Kwame reached out and a hunk of meaty palm held his shoulder.

'You know we lost a band member a few months ago? It was in an incident that was put down to suicide. But it could have been more than that. Then we had a serious failure of the crash barriers and Dread nearly died in the stampede. We now suspect that the fencing had been tampered with. When she fell into the crowd, she says a group tried to kill her. And then after the concert there was a car suicide in which she could have died. We do think the stalker, or someone involved with all of this, might have been trapped in that exploded vehicle, but whoever it was also left notes backstage where only those with the highest security clearance would have access, no matter where in the world we are. We're almost in the middle of a sell-out tour – 150 venues in total, and we're on our thirty-eighth. There has to be more than one person involved. There's an obvious element of organisation, so maybe this guy had inside help. We also need to find out who the mole was – is! We know you have a different approach, more psychological. We want your opinion.'

'Also, Vilhelm,' Tullia's voice was honey, 'I know your particular interest is infamy seekers, and this may be one.'

Kwame looked blankly at her, and for once, in William's company, it was Tullia doing the lecturing.

'For instance, John Wilkes Booth was an actor desiring fame. On the evening he shot Abraham Lincoln in the Ford Theatre in Washington, he distributed tickets for that evening's "performance" to his friends and claimed "there would be great acting". This could be a case just like that.'

'And then,' Kwame persisted, 'there's the fact that the lyrics in the messages are predictive. "I can see for miles" arrives…anyway, let's just say they're predictive.'

'So you've come to check me out, to see whether we could work together?' William asked Kwame.

'And Han Fei,' added the chief of security.

'Ah, yeah, he did important work on WHCs. Yep, he's good.' William allowed himself to mellow. 'He's a showman and celebrities are wowed by the superficial glitz. Go with him, it'll be fine. He's ideal for your pop star.'

'WHCs?'

'The White House in Washington gets so many deranged visitors seeking an audience with the President, or attempting to contact him in order to harm him, that they have their own name now: "White House Cases". And Han Fei did some pioneering work collating all the WHCs over the last few years and classifying them. WHCs are somewhat different to the kind of interactions we would be dealing with in the case of a pop star, of course.'

'Let's discuss how you and Han could work together,' Tullia said eagerly.

For the first time, William almost smiled. Psychologists had done most of the decent research in the field, but some, like Han, couldn't abide psychiatrists. Often with good reason.

Kwame seemed to have read his thoughts. 'Look, I know this isn't going to be easy – while we've been talking, my phone's been buzzing with Han Fei trying to reach me repeatedly. Doubtless he's less than keen that I'm talking to you and he's trying to pull out, which is why I'm ignoring his calls right now until you and I have had a chance to talk. Let's work something out between the two of you.'

'Mr Appiah, I study people, Han Fei number crunches them. Han's approach is severely mathematical. For example, he codes all the letters that stalkers send into a computer for text analysis. From that he can tell whether the writer is a woman or a man, and what age, if English is their first language, and so on. It's a statistical model which he claims can mathematically predict who is dangerous and who isn't, and even when the next attack is due.'

'If you insist on a mathematical approach, Mr Appiah, we also have a large biometrics department at the Institute of Mental Health,' Tullia added encouragingly. 'On the other hand, Vilhelm gets inside the mind of the letter writer.'

'Han Fei's view is that people are more like automatons than reflective sentient beings,' William added gloomily. 'It's the way modern psychiatry is heading.'

'I don't get it.' Kwame looked flummoxed.

'Are you born a narcissist?' William mused. 'Our view is that we're all on a personal journey – we are all moulded and shaped by things that happen to us. So the letters from an individual over a period of time need to be deconstructed to understand if the individual is crossing over to the dark side. How are they changing? Are they becoming dangerous? Han lumps them all together into a statistical mess...sorry, mass.'

'In fact,' Tullia said, 'William's developing a special theory that the stalker and the star are, in fact, more similar than is commonly appreciated in one key aspect – narcissism.'

William was thrilled they had finally got on to his specialist subject.

'Sufferers from Narcissistic Personality Disorder are likely to fly into a rage when the world doesn't recognise them for the special, talented person they believe themselves to be. Stalking is basically a disorder of entitlement. This links the star with the follower. This is referred to as Narcissistic Rage because it's such a common feature of the condition. It's what I think stalkers are suffering from when they become dangerous.'

'But I don't get the star and the stalker *both* being narcissists,' Kwame said.

'Anger arises when others are not being obedient to the narcissist's sense of entitlement. For Dread, it will be with the audience and her staff and the press. For the stalker, it will be anger with the star they are pursuing or the security people tasked with keeping them out. The narcissist expects and demands total control. They need absolute dominion over their target, for example.'

'So they're control freaks – but surely all successful people are.' Kwame was rubbing his chin.

'But the pathologically narcissistic individual is imbued with such a sense of self-importance, omnipotence and uniqueness that they have little interest in recognising the existence of others.'

'Whoa, you're talking about half the music industry. We're never going to track down...'

'Narcissists need constant validation of their special status, and require this with the intensity of addicts: the presence of a public or audience. The person they are stalking reflects back to them the self-perceived greatness, power and superior status to which they are rightfully entitled in their own eyes.

'So…it's clever to use only song lyrics – very adroit. I think you'll find that the person who is sending these messages is not the same person in the car that detonated.'

'Wow!' exclaimed Kwame. 'You can tell that from these lyrics?'

'Whoever this is knows about computerised text analysis like the kind Han Fei uses. By sending other people's words they evade scrutiny by most of the mathematical techniques. It takes Han's methodology out of the picture. Anyone this astute isn't going to be found driving a car with a bomb in it. They're risk averse, cautious, calculating.'

'Hmmm. Okay, I'm waiting on a phone call which should confirm if DNA analysis of human tissue found in the car matches anyone on the databases.' Kwame shrugged. 'Guess we're gonna find out shortly how clever they were.'

'Is there anyone else who gets up on the wheel?'

'Sometimes all the dancers are on it, but none of them rides it right to the summit, not for any length of time. Dread is always, er, on top – a comment about her bossy style and sex position that's been doing the rounds for years. Alonzo Church, our former lead guitarist, died falling off the wheel six months ago. It was months after he'd left the band, so it's a mystery what he was doing up there in the first place during a technical rehearsal.'

'The Ferris wheel's an ultimate testament to her narcissism, isn't it. It can be seen for miles, just like The Who lyric which you sent us hints. It puts her up on a pedestal, separating her from the other performers, and no other rival act has anything to compare. The wheel is a brilliant manoeuvre because now it makes this supposed mass compilation event all about her. Throughout everyone else's performance, this thing will be there, glowering in the background, reminding everyone just who the main act is.'

'Hmmm.'

'Okay, my best guess, but it is a *preliminary* guess, is that you've got a disgruntled ex-employee here. Someone who got the sack or was demoted, or isn't getting what they want from the organisation if they still work there. Or even perhaps someone who feels they're about to be axed.'

'And how dangerous does that make them?' asked Kwame.

'It's the Resentful Stalkers that keep me awake at night. They're the ones who are driven by a grievance. They frighten or intimidate as part of a quest for justice or revenge, which takes over their lives. It's the sense of absolute righteousness that is so worrying. Worst of all are those driven by divine purpose. If it's God's will, all forms of social restraint fall by the wayside. It's the stuff that drives wars and crusades and rationalises massacres in the name of salvation.'

Kwame brandished sheets of paper with various images of Dread being mutilated or pulled apart.

'There's something else you should know,' he said. 'At that last concert in Pasadena, Dread fell into the audience, so someone got close enough to touch her, repeating these song lyrics: *There's magic in my eyes, I know you've deceived me, now here's a surprise, I can see for miles and miles and miles and miles.* We think therefore it's a fan.'

'It's the constant retention of anonymity which is so unusual. Usually stalkers, because of their pathology, want you to know who they are,' William said flatly. 'The fact you use black light as such a central part of her act kind of proves this is an inside job, given that the fence failing with spectators breaking through was part of another attempt on Dread's life.'

'Come again?'

'If you want to find areas of weakness in metal, it's common in metallurgy to spray fluorescing dyes on the suspect surface then deploy UV light to detect the fissures.'

Just then Kwame's phone rang.

'Sorry, I need to take this.'

Tullia clapped William on his shoulders with a perfectly straight face.

'You're so good at this,' she said admiringly.

Then her phone chirped as well.

'Are you sure?' Kwame's pitch had gone up in a mixture of frustration and shock. 'But that can't be right!'

Tullia looked up with a ghost of a smile.

'Vilhelm, it's Philippa's office. They want you to go to Surrey right away.'

William's heart leapt. He was back to tracking down David

213

Lewis before anything untoward happened to Pip. Tullia snapped the receiver shut.

'They need you to help with a press conference on soldiers suffering from Post-traumatic Stress Disorder. You'll be briefed on the way. They're sending a ministerial car right now. There's a soldier – a sniper – who needs your urgent help. He's developed PTSD, name of Tom Nagel. He's your ticket back in.'

They stared at each other. William could sense the reproach in Tullia's gaze. *You should not have doubted our plan.*

Kwame bawled into his receiver, 'Run the test again!'

William squinted up at the Ferris wheel. He was suddenly much more relaxed now he was back in Philippa's team.

'The organisers are constructing that wheel as an open invitation to her. Dread's making all sorts of demands, so they're building her wheel for all the world to see. If she doesn't come, it's obvious who didn't turn up, and why.'

Something caught William's eye. He pointed.

'What's that?'

Tullia shaded her eyes against the sky.

'The tiny balloon?'

'Yes, tied to the top of the wheel.'

Kwame's voice reflected his rising tension.

'Get your superior to call me and tell me in person this ridiculous result!' He stabbed his phone off. 'Sorry about that. The lab has the result for the DNA found in the car that exploded outside the Rose Bowl, but the analysis is just stupid.'

'Why is there a balloon tied to the top of the wheel?' William asked, but Kwame's phone had erupted again. The combination of William's incessant quizzing and the source of the call seemed to ignite an explosion within the hulking bodyguard.

'I've no idea! For Chrissake, ask construction!'

Kwame turned away to deal with his phone. Tullia tugged on William's sleeve, glaring at him to cease fire on the questions front.

'Okay, sorry. But look, when she fell off the stage... When anything happens, even chance accidents, those who've gone over to the dark side – malignant narcissism – they've basically gone psychotic...'

214

'Yes, I know of course, William,' she agreed, 'they interpret the fortuitous as having special meaning. They imbue flukes with huge personal significance, but not now – okay?'

She swivelled her eyes over to Kwame emphatically, but William couldn't let it go.

'...as meant to be, confirming some warped destiny – that's why small details...'

Kwame came off the receiver. He looked at them both very strangely.

'The DNA from the limo...' Kwame turned to William. 'You said your number one guess was a disgruntled ex-employee. Well, you were spot on. It was from someone who fell out with Dread big time, and was kicked out of the group nine months ago. But they're going to rerun the tests, because the result is ridiculous. I still can't believe it – it was Alonzo Church. But he's six foot under. I was a pall-bearer, and I saw him disappear into the ground.'

35

Close to me
But if I had your face
I could make it safe and clean

Han had the extraordinary impression of not being sure whether his eyes were open or not. He tried to shift his hands to his face, but found them impossible to move. Panic began. Maybe there had been an accident and he had been badly injured or paralysed.

He recalled the motorcycle chase. Had he been in a crash?

Then, beyond the surging emotional turmoil, he became aware of rustling sounds entering the room.

'Oh, there he is,' he heard someone shout with a mixture of relief and surprise. 'We've found him. Dr Han Fei is in here.'

There was the clattering echo of people running, and then he had a definite sense of the chamber filling up with bodies.

'Oh my God! What's wrong with his face?' someone exclaimed.

Han reached a new plateau of alarm.

'Okay, okay. Calm down. Look at his eyeballs moving under his lids. Okay, Han is waking up and he's hearing us – all this is going to frighten him.' The calm assurance of what sounded like a doctor blanketed the squirming room. 'Mr Fei, can you hear me? I'm one of the surgeons here at the clinic, everything is going to be okay.'

In the background there was whispering that was meant to be inaudible. 'He's a doctor, so...'

'No he's not, he's a psychologist.'

'Wh...what happened? Why can't I see anything?' At least Han could speak, and his hearing was intact.

'Okay – there is a problem with your eyes, but we can fix it. Just stay calm. Nurse, can you get me those over there?'

It was clear to Han that the surgeon was not specifying the

particular instrument so as not to distress him, which just added to his consternation.

'What the hell is going on? What are you doing?' he shouted. Maybe if he yelled loudly enough the darkness would go away.

'Shouldn't we anaesthetise him?' someone from further back asked.

'No, I think he has had quite enough anaesthetic for one day.'

'Wh...what are you talking about?' Han exclaimed.

'Mr Fei, we believe that you have had a sedative – we are not sure who gave it to you, and we just need to do this one thing...'

Han was aware of something brushing his eyelid, and something else was gripping his head, preventing any movement. The brushing sensation was accompanied by a clipping sound, and soon light began to creep under his eyelids. Blinded by the brightness, he blinked a lot, inducing tears.

He sat up abruptly, hands automatically reaching for his face.

'Whoa there, slow down, take it easy...'

He blurrily searched the crowded room. At the front there seemed to be various white-coated clinicians, while towards the rear he could just make out a hazy Anne Conway and Dread. Right at the back, four of his own staff appeared fuzzily, but then converged into a focal point.

Everyone was staring at him.

'Will someone explain what the hell is going on?'

Was that his voice? It sounded so croaky.

The surgeon, blotchy-looking through a film covering Han's eyes, stepped forward, calm and confident. Blinking just seemed to make his eyes water more, and the white coat looked like it smudged.

'Brace yourself for a bit of a shock, Mr Fei. Basically, it seems that while you were waiting in the recovery suite by the room where Dread was getting a surgical opinion...you're looking disorientated. It's okay – you're at the clinic that you were escorting Dread and her mother to. Well, while you were waiting, you appear to have been drugged. We think someone put something in the coffee you ordered. Obviously there's going to be a full investigation...'

'No there isn't.' Han recognised Anne's voice coming from

the back of the group. 'We don't want no police involved. This was all meant to be on the QT.'

'Er, anyway, someone appears to have given you a fast acting anaesthetic on top of that. And then sutured your eyes shut with a couple of stitches through your eyelids. It's a bizarre and, well, macabre…but see…'

The surgeon reached behind him and a flashing oblong appeared, reflecting the bright lights.

'The lids should heal up fine.'

Through the tears and blood in his eyes, Han didn't recognise the likeness in the mirror. His lids were swollen and pockmarked, like a clown who had gone overboard with the mascara.

36

What I feel when I hesitate
The man with the child in his eyes

'He *is* going to hit the target, isn't he?'

Philippa, sporting army camouflage fatigues, two wide belts embroidered with long bullet cartridges embracing her from shoulder to hip, an empty gun holster and a businesslike ponytail, had fallen back from the crowd of journalists surrounding the sniper as he emerged from the ramshackle wooden hut.

Tom Nagel had just finished a session of treatment with William.

Resembling an abandoned back lot Hollywood set from an old-fashioned cowboy movie, the sprawling army shooting complex at Bisley felt eerie in the middle of the Surrey countryside. Ordinarily deserted except for firearms enthusiasts and soldiers sent to hone their shooting skills, it was currently overrun with a herd of press corps like cattle being run through town in a western. They were now so used to the rat-a-tat of machine gun fire penetrating the heavy wood surrounding them, punctuated by booms from high-velocity rifles, that none startled any more. At first they had been much more skittish. Embracing the rodeo-style setting, which had been the Foreign Secretary's scheme all along, camera crews dotted the landscape, busy framing it as the perfect back-drop for their correspondents' pieces to camera.

Disconcertingly, Philippa was looking into the psychiatrist's eyes.

'You don't do this in the management of PTSD. It's too hard on Mr Nagel – he's traumatised by staring down a scope. You know his wife is leaving him because of all this?'

Despite the constraints, William thought he had made just enough progress with Tom that the nervy squaddie might make it through the press junket element of the afternoon. Perhaps this was long enough to allow William the chance to offer more treatment later, away from the glare of the press when the Foreign Secretary's public relations exercise was all over.

Then again, maybe William was being too cocky and the sniper was going to resume falling apart, only this time in the full glare of the nation's media. In which case the psychiatrist had just made the patient's predicament a whole lot worse.

'No, that can't be right. I am about to give them VIP tickets for the Hyde Park concert. Right here. In front of all the press.' Philippa glanced over at the reporters, who were gratefully receiving ear plugs being distributed by the Foreign Secretary's assistant. Tom was expected to shoot stuff up any moment now. 'He told me his wife's a big Dread fan. I've got spare tickets because none of the pro-war lobby in my party is going to go to an anti-war gig.'

'But Tom told me he and his wife were splitting up!'

Philippa looked at William sharply.

'He confided that? He's not going to say that in front of the press, is he?'

'His wife, like many spouses, has had enough of his untreated PTSD and she's thrown in the towel. Tom regards it as the ultimate betrayal and has become even more welded to his spotter. See that guy over there, Carl.'

'But you've cured him, right?' Philippa threw a sideways glance at the sniper, who was being mobbed by the fourth estate. 'I mean, you were in there with him for *hours*.'

In fact, William had been allowed less than an hour to assess and "cure" the sniper, which was completely ridiculous. But then again, he had agreed to the whole hair-brained publicity stunt in order to get back in with Philippa.

'He was avoiding the scope because of what he saw the last time he looked down it on the battlefield...'

She turned back to him and smiled. In the distance a ripple of firearms discharged and William flinched.

'Atta boy, I knew you wouldn't let me down.' Philippa gripped him on the elbow, the force betraying how tense she was. 'You can get anyone to do anything, right?'

William felt exasperation and anxiety rise. 'Pip, you shouldn't be here. It's too dangerous with David loose. There are loads of people with guns. If I were him, this is where I'd take you out...'

'Don't be ridiculous, we are standing at the epicentre of the British army on mainland UK. This is absolutely the last place terrorists would strike – Gerrard was firm about that. We needed to do this press event, and now. You seem to forget there is a war on.'

'Maybe Gerrard's using you as bait to flush David Lewis out – ever thought of that?'

'Not all that again, William! I can't let your paranoia about our security forces and your madman ruin my career.' Philippa was looking at the press pack. She seemed torn over whether to continue talking to the shrink or go over there and schmooze. William was trying to divine what her real agenda was behind this masquerade when nodding boom microphones reminded him of Frances. He scanned the rat pack, but she wasn't lurking there.

'Pip, why'd you let Gerrard run with Frances?'

'Because if I allow him his indulgence, he's less tense about allowing me mine,' she said, stroking his arm, an eye checking that the press contingent hadn't clocked the gesture. His stomach wobbled.

'Pip!' At his tone she turned to face him full on. 'You can't ignore the cost of all this to *you*. Despite all the physical security and the personal protection officers, you're bound to find being on the end of inappropriate unwanted attention much more unsettling than you ever anticipated.'

'Yeah,' her tone had softened, 'it's partly the intrusiveness of the messages...'

'But it's the uncertainty which gets to you?

'Yes, you're absolutely right, William.' Her voice was thoughtful, warm. 'You know, you seem to be the only one who understands. Who *is* this man? What harm does he mean me? Are his motives personal, political or simply insane?'

She looked down at her polished army boots, blinking.

William nodded, feeling a heady sense of being at one with her.

She lowered her voice further.

'I, ah, I avoid opening any letters myself. And the apprehension at returning home, the protection officers checking out the house before I enter it. In bed, I literally jump at the noises of the night. Most times I just lie awake, staring at the green glow of the panic alarm.'

'Of course you do! It's the natural reaction, Pip. Stalking's described by those who've experienced it as psychological terrorism or psychological rape. And Pip, if you're going to do this, then wear the right protection.'

'A vest? Again with the bullet-proof vest? They're not exactly slimming...' Her voice was hardening again and he knew he'd lost her. She tugged her army jacket down over her camouflage pants, but something about the heavy macho attire made her look more feminine and vulnerable than ever. Even the scrunchie gripping her ponytail was a matching camouflage print.

The Minister sped up to catch the main posse who were shuffling over to the open-air range. In a rising hubbub, the press pack converged on her, and she closed in on William's patient.

'He gonna be okay, Doc?' Carl, the spotter, had hung back.

Would he admit to what he was hiding? Even tacitly?

'Listen,' William turned to confide in Carl, 'when you're out on operations, he might see things down his scope which no one is meant to observe, right? Because he's so far away, he might not be spotted.'

'What are you getting at?' Carl's eyes narrowed.

'There's a thing called a flashback, when you vividly relive an experience as if it was happening again. Suppose he saw something earlier, a few days before, then had a flashback, but didn't realise it, when he was targeting that village.'

'Did he say?' Carl was being called away by the marshal as William shook his head in the negative.

Photographers were going right up to Tom and snapping away. William could see the immense control the sniper was exerting. Philippa kept skirting the sergeant, ensuring she was in the pictures.

The marshal raised his voice.

'Sergeant Nagel will be deploying an L115A3 long-range rifle. The target is not really discernible to you, but I will be confirming his score using binoculars, and you, gentlemen of the press, will see everything on this screen we've set up here. There's a video camera pointing at the target, projecting the image back to us here.'

Heads turned to watch the video screen.

'Right, Sergeant Nagel, if you please.' The marshal kept flicking his eyes up at the cloud-heavy sky.

Tom strode up the steps to the small grassy mound and turned to wave at the press. A salvo of flashes splattered him.

An airport-style windsock was nuzzling the breeze in the distance. William remembered the precise mathematical adjustments that Tom would be making.

During the consultation, Tom had explained, through a quivering voice, 'After gravity, there's drag. The slowing effect the atmosphere has on the bullet. This pulls back on the speed of the shot according to the air density. The more dense – like the nearer sea level you are – the more the drag, and vice versa. Drag and density are influenced by temperature, altitude, barometric pressure, humidity, efficiency of the bullet and wind. Carl does all the calculations and feeds the numbers to me. At these distances, with these kinds of long range targets, a slight movement in a leaf behind the target means the wind has changed, and you've got to start over with the calculations.'

William detected that anxiety had stolen the sniper's normal decisiveness, which was crucial in his line of work. Such methodical detail in his answers betrayed a possible lurking Obsessive Compulsive personality, but the strain betrayed something else – ambivalence about the target? Were his secret orders on the front-line in the Congo the hidden problem here?

The sniper and his spotter seemed to spend an eternity conferring before both got down on their fronts. Carl brought a high-powered monocular scope to his eye and the breeze flung some mumbled numbers back to the crowd.

The wait dragged into minutes. Philippa shuffled back to William. The press fell deadly quiet and the only sound was the wind rustling the trees in the distance.

'What the hell is going on?' Philippa whispered tersely at him. She gestured up at the gathering clouds. 'They've got to get a move on before it starts to rain.'

'It's treatable, Pip, just not under these conditions.'

Her impatience flared. 'William, let's live in the real world! We've got reporters waiting. If this goes pear-shaped it would have been better to have the Defence Secretary here to absorb some of the stench of failure.'

She was jiggling a pen as if it was a cigarette.

'You haven't taken up smoking again, have you?' he asked suspiciously.

'No, of course not – and you're not my mother.'

'Um, Pip, one thing: Gerrard has never come clean about what database they got the DNA match with David Lewis off. And how come there's so little info about him?'

'Oh, for God's sake, William! Try and fit in – stop kicking against the system! It's always going to win in the end.'

Philippa turned and made for the hillock.

Carl and Tom appeared to be arguing. The marshal went over to the sniper and spotter, then went down on one knee to talk to them. He leant in and listened, said a single word and then listened again. He stood up and went back to address the crowd.

'Ladies and Gentlemen, we have a problem. We've got a rapidly dropping barometer which is making the calculation difficult at this range – please bear with us.'

Heads craned up and fingers pointed at the menacing black clouds racing in. Another interminable age, and then drops began to fall.

The marshal walked over to William and said quietly, 'He wants a word with you.'

William followed the marshal up the mound and hunkered down next to Tom.

'What's up?' he whispered.

Carl looked up over Tom's shoulder. 'He can't pull the trigger again – his finger is locked. I keep talking to him, but he won't execute,' he breathed.

'Okay, okay.' William leant in close to the sniper's ears. 'I want you to imagine that story you told me – about the target that was eating lunch? You waited until he'd finished before firing? Okay, I want you to visualise that's what's happening. The target is out there, he's finishing his meal, and once he's done, you pull the trigger. See every detail.'

William backed into a crouch and then retreated, almost tiptoeing down the mound. The marshal mouthed an 'Are we a go?' at him as he passed.

Then a report. Birds on the trees behind them flew up and the marshal swung round, startled.

Philippa raced up the mound. The marshal had his binoculars up to his face. He made a signal and then the image came up on the screen.

'Ladies and gentlemen, a bullseye!'

The next few minutes were a blur. There was applause as the rain fell. Tom and Carl stood up and had their photos taken by the video capture of the target. Carl had one hand looping Tom's shoulders and was repeatedly gripping him. The other hand described a thumbs up in William's direction.

Philippa, cowed under the ever-increasing deluge, said a few words standing next to Tom and Carl. She brandished an envelope and passed it over to Tom, who grinned and waved it at the gathering. Flash photography mingled with lightning, and then the sky opened up. The crowd rushed for their waiting cars.

'You're still giving me a lift back to London, right?' William shouted at Philippa as she disappeared into her limousine. She waved at him.

One by one the various transports swerved by, mud spattering William's trousers as vehicles splashed through the swamp, disappearing down the single track back to civilisation. William stared dumbstruck as Philippa's limousine roared past. She was just visible on the phone through gobbets of water bouncing off her window. She didn't look up as her car flew by.

He tried to remind himself that he needed to stay to check what was happening to his patient. Both Carl and Tom were oblivious to the rain. Tom's hands were describing an arc, Carl was disagreeing.

The soldiers shook their heads at William.

'Why did that work? The thing you told him,' Carl asked.

'It removed the decision point from himself. The trigger pull became reliant on something out there not something internal, and that sometimes helps,' William shouted back above the torrent. The soldiers turned away and headed into the trees.

225

The deluge felt like an ice cold bucket of water tipping down his neck.

'Where are you going?' William shrieked. He didn't fancy being left alone out there, especially with David Lewis loose.

'We're walking back to Aldershot – it's about an hour through the woods,' Carl bellowed back.

William nodded and feebly turned his collar up. He knew now that Philippa would always use him to suit herself, and felt himself tearing up.

'Why don't you use the coat?' Carl shouted.

'What coat?'

'The one she's offering you!' Carl pointed.

William whirled. Had Philippa come back for him?

In the middle of the meadow, rain splintering down on her and forming a kind of halo effect, was a sepulchral figure holding out a tarpaulin-like garment.

'Jesus,' William exclaimed. 'Who the hell is that?'

'Don't you know?' Carl and Tom had walked back to him. 'She organised all this.'

The ethereal figure moved towards them, trudging through the mud. The meadow had become a quagmire under the monsoon downpour.

'Thanks for everything, Frances,' Carl shouted.

'Frances?' William said blankly.

'Yeah, Frances Wright. She said she knew you – that's how come we managed to get Tom treated so quickly. She was the one who suggested we contact the local MP, who then called the Minister.'

As she neared, she started to whisper what seemed like a strange incantation.

Alas, the storm is come again! My best way is to creep under his gabardine. There is no other shelter hereabout: misery acquaints a man with strange bedfellows. I will here shroud till the dregs of the storm be past.

He tried to work that out. It sounded like Shakespeare.

'Look, Frances, you're trying to tell me something. What was it I was meant to see in Philippa's bedroom? You hinted at it in the police car.'

'William, I didn't want to have to be the one to break it to you, but Philippa…she never told you, did she.'

'Told me what?' Gathering trepidation furled up in his chest.

'She should have. Especially given this…'

'Will you get on with it?'

'Gerrard has formally, finally and completely axed you from FTAC – it's all over. Philippa must have been keeping it back from you until you helped her with this fiasco.'

'How do you know all this? What was in her bedroom?'

'I'm a journalist, William, please. I get invited to all those press briefings at her place where she cosies up to the journos. Only unlike the other hacks eating out of her hand, I take the opportunity to slink away and investigate. Like I did just now. By the way, who in fact hit that target?'

She glanced over at the sniper and his spotter disappearing into the forest.

'You don't trust Philippa at all, do you.'

Grabbing the sodden lapels of his coat, she continued.

'Those two were out on some special covert operation in the Congo…'

'I…I can't say anything to you. I can't break patient confidentiality.'

'Or the Official Secrets Act.'

'Look, Frances, if you arranged all this so I could glean some info about what's happing on the frontline in the Congo and then reveal it to you, sorry, but you're wasting your time.'

'There's war crimes being perpetrated out there.'

'Maybe, but my duty to my patient comes first.'

His answer enraged her.

'Listen, I can get you back into her circle of trust, but…'

Her breathing was getting laboured.

'Sorry, no deals. Not when it comes to the patients.'

She stepped back, and William flinched because he thought she was about to slap him.

'And I've been over her place. I've seen it, so you must have. And if you can't scope it when it was right in front of you up there in her boudoir, then as a psychiatrist you need to go back to the drawing board. She was rubbing it in your face, man.'

His knees wobbled. Frances's eyes seemed very close, very big, very...

So he had been set up, like a sitting target.

37

And if I only could, I'd make a deal with god
And I'd get him to swap our places

Kwame sensed her sneaking up on him. He didn't turn, but kept surveying the heaving Pacific. This perimeter tour of the Malibu mansion would be his last for quite a while.

'What d'you want?' He was still furious with her. He'd only just got off the phone with the local police, who were suspicious that Dread was implicated in the recent motorcycle carnage. Too many of the modified Hummers in the traffic had been registered to her security arm. And the man on the back of the bike had been caught on camera brandishing a Smith & Wesson 500 Magnum – the enormous revolver Kwame was famous in police circles for favouring.

The fact he could prove he was in London at the time was definitely working in his, and her, favour. There were advantages to two members of the security detail carrying the same iconic weapon: they were easily confused for each other.

'It's slammin' out here, isn't it.'

Uh-oh, she wanted something. She was only this smooth, this appealing, when she did. And she clearly wasn't going to apologise about the shopping mall incident.

'We're not going to be back here for a while.'

'A long while,' agreed Kwame. All the more reason to relish their last moments here, with the Pacific swelling in response to a whipping from a fresh breeze.

'Tomorrow it's the Coliseum, then we come back to San Fran, then Rio, then the band goes on to Florida. I go to Wilfrid's thing, then Miami, Switzerland, Munich…'

She was hanging back behind him. Fuzzy in his peripheral vision, he could just detect her darting about, limbering up for her run. As her bodyguard he was expected to lumber along beside her during these cliff-edge excursions, and this explained his tracksuit, flapping in the breeze. Whenever Dread went for a canter along the cliff top, her exercise schedule seemed to coincide mysteriously with the arrival of a paparazzi bearing helicopter which shadowed her, photographing her as she dodged the scrub. Kwame reflected on all these little rituals that peppered their day. There was no time to relax – from behind every corner lunged a new possible threat.

He couldn't bear to turn to inspect properly what she was wearing this time for the jog, but whatever it was, it wouldn't be practical for exercise. He could just make out that her hazel hair was bunched upwards so it looked like her head was shaking an angry fist at the sky.

'Yeah, then Tibet, but before Miami it's the big one – the concert in Hyde Park. That's going to be the worst security nightmare yet.'

He sighed.

'So, we're not going to be around here for long, and sooo…'

'You want some refresher highway code lessons?'

'Oh, you're still busted about the shopping mall thing.'

Try hopping mad.

'Hello? Hello? Your lame-arse hiring sat on his arse while I was nearly rammed, avoided several collisions, and had to work out my own escape when surrounded. But hey! How was your day?'

He knew she was still convinced she'd killed someone back at the Rose Bowl, or at least seriously injured them. But that no body, nor law suit, had turned up was a stubbornly inconvenient fact. No matter which way you looked at it, she was becoming unglued.

Kwame took some deep breaths. He began to turn to her, finally calmer.

'I was wondering if you could teach me to shoot,' she said.

She was cradling a leviathan Smith & Wesson 500 Magnum in her hands. And the press were due to arrive at any second to photograph her run.

'Whisky. Tango. Foxtrot! Where'd you get that?'

'It's Dr Han Fei's. I thought you'd recognise it.'

'What on earth are you doing taking his gun from him? He ain't gonna appreciate that. And the paps are gonna be here, like, now!'

'He was getting his eyes fixed. He was in no condition to notice. Remember we then flew him out to London on the private jet to get his lids seen to by the top eye surgeons...'

'Well...it was to butter him up so he didn't sue us or anything, and it got him out of the way of any local police investigation about the private clinic and the shopping mall stuff...'

'So now the muff-diver is in London, what happened to that plan to protect me?'

Kwame had himself begun to wonder how safe the ritual helicopter jogging photo shoot remained, given all the recent events. Might Dread loose off a few rounds at the photographers should they annoy her again? He considered the gun pensively.

'Yeah, anyhow, relax. We'll hear the helicopter coming. Show me how to use it.' One hand was on her hip now. She dangled the revolver with the other, but the heft of it looked like it might topple her over.

'Have you checked it isn't loaded?'

'Dunno how to. That's the kind of thing I want you to teach me.'

'Jeezus!' He relieved her of it and flipped out the chamber, then he tilted it up and collected the shells.

'This isn't the right gun for you. With all five .50-cal shells in the cylinder, this cannon weighs five pounds.'

Since he'd lost his own cannon in Camberwell just a short while ago, and hadn't had time to get a proper replacement, it almost seemed fate had dealt him a mightily convenient way of retrieving his favourite weapon. Luckily Kristal had been too distracted by her vanished necklace to remember his Smith & Wesson had disappeared too. If she had alerted Dread, then he might have faced yet more diatribe from the princess, but all Kristal had done since was bitch about her missing jewellery.

The fact the forensic psychologist used the same giant revolver as Dread's bodyguard had been one of the reasons Kwame had warmed to him. Here was a practical man of action, unlike Dr James, plus Dr Fei grasped the need to intimidate. But now the weapon had found its way into Dread's own palms, he felt things were swerving out of control faster than even he realised.

'You do know we're getting a replacement shrink for Han. His name's Dr William James.'

Given William's reluctance to join them, this was something of a falsehood. But Kwame knew that dealing with prima donnas like Dread required the ability to lie brazenly.

'Yeah, but no matter what bitchtit precautions you take, it seems the bottom line is I may have to look after *numero uno*. I would feel a whole lot safer if I knew I could defend myself.'

She stared at the gun pointedly.

'Okay, but…before you take the law into your own hands…'

'I only have to do this because you're letting me down. You've taken your eye off the ball. Something's distracting you.'

Kwame took some deep breaths. If Dread was getting suspicious about Anne's relationship with him, this would not be good.

'Okay, I'll teach you to shoot. Maybe you should give this British shrink a chance.'

'Maybe? You sound hesitant.'

There was a distant beat in the air. The helicopter must be coming. They needed to get ready for the long lenses photographing Dread running along the cliff side in skin-tight shorts and a top that clawed vainly for her belly button.

He stuffed her weapon into the back of his tracksuit.

Dread looked up at him with reproachful eyes.

'You're basically trying to get me psychological help from the two top psyches in the world, using the subterfuge of the stalker.'

Kwame laughed. Too loudly. 'Well, it turns out keeping an eye on you is not without its hazards. You've already taken out one.'

And the other one – well, it looked like he would argue with a signpost, he thought.

A long pause.

'I understand that your current favourite nerd has never heard of me,' Dread replied.

Kwame stopped smiling. He had believed he was home and dry.

He changed the subject. 'How come the paps are snapping us today? I thought this cliff top run was boring to them now.'

'They want to see how the legs are healing after my dive on to the stadium floor, followed by the roll on the Rose Bowl's tarmac. Everyone wants to know if I'm going to be ready for Hyde Park. But don't change the subject – he's really never heard of me?'

'Yeah, well, whaddya want? Another fan, or someone too busy being an expert to know much about pop?'

'So if he's never heard of me, he's never heard of God either?'

She was entirely serious.

38

She says she's going to jail, for going through my mail
Stalker

William lurked in the housing estate just around the corner from David Lewis's council flat. The graffiti song lyrics emblazoned across the walls were as he had remembered them, and more appeared to have been added.

The surveillance detail of two police officers was changed every four hours, and William's only plan was to exploit the stalker's friend: their boredom. An inevitable hazard for all guards, it explained the high alcoholism rate in the security professions.

A young sergeant the psychiatrist recognised was ambling up to the block. His colleague was joking and chatting, but he remained aloof. The psychiatrist made a mental note on exploiting this hint of status anxiety in the senior. It might open the security sealed door into David's flat.

William's ruminations about how to catch the stalker and get himself back inside Philippa's circle of trust had returned him to here. He was convinced that there must be something in that hovel that would give him a fresh direction. In particular, where Philippa's missing picture had vanished to had become an obsession. He remained convinced the photograph was a significant clue.

It must have been David who sent in the humiliating clinical vignette of the psychiatrist's own secret past. It was so obviously passive aggressive. So you want to publish my personality profile – well, Doctor, what about yours? And let's examine your reaction if your own colleagues get to read it.

But how did the stalker get hold of such confidential information? Even given it was the kind of digging that these hunters excelled at.

William took a deep breath, whipped round the corner, and

gaily gestured at the officers. The police duo looked up, but then his phone rang. It was Frances. He pulled up short and took the call.

'Frances, I can't talk now. I'm just about to...'

'...get into David's place. Yeah, I could work out that would be your last roll of the dice, the final deal of the cards. Hell, you soooo need me! You're going there to retrieve something. What is it?'

He frowned. 'What do you think I'm looking for?' The enigmatic hint Frances had dropped that he was meant to have divined Philippa's secret from her bedroom was driving him mad.

'Yes, so typical psychobabble – answer a question with a question. Why is it, by the way, that you manipulate everyone rather than having a proper relationship? Gerrard's just taken us up in the chopper for a tour of the Hyde Park site for the concert, so I've now figured out why Helicopter Pilot Number One has become such a big fan of yours. You took the flak when he was gonna get a disciplinary for flying too close to the tarpaulin which ripped off that building, covering David's escape.'

'Why does that make me manipulative?'

Frances didn't do small talk, which he found beguiling. But she also always seemed to be in an almighty rush, harrying him, and anyone else, to get to the point or get out of her way. What deadline was she working to? Whatever her real target was meant she seemed to have put aside her fury with him. He was being used by her; he had to keep reminding himself of that.

'Because in return you got him to...'

'It's an occupational hazard,' William agreed, 'being over-analysed by armchair experts, but honestly, this is not the time.'

The police were examining him curiously. He didn't need this now; he had to shake her off.

'Look, the real reason I'm ringing is much more immediately important, William. All the political correspondents have been told to be on standby. So we think that Philippa is planning a big public announcement, and I suspect it's about the war.'

'Oh my days! Where?'

'Oh...you don't know? Anyway, it's still secret, you bozo. They're going to tell the press at the last moment. If you want, I'll...'

But he killed the call before she could finish. She had managed to work him into revealing, from his reaction just now, that he still wasn't back in with FTAC.

William was running out of time. He had warned Philippa not to do any public appearances unless he had cleared them. But now he was out of the fold, she was violating all the conditions he had imposed on her. Damn! This was exceedingly dangerous. His sense was that David was planning something big, terrible and soon.

The officers stared at the psychiatrist as he approached. His plan had been to cultivate them slowly, but now he had to get into the flat – pronto.

'Hi ya!' he said cheerfully and waved his security clearance ID. In the chaos Gerrard had forgotten to take back his pass. 'I'm Dr William James, and...'

'I know who you are,' interrupted the sergeant.

He had to play this just right. He was gambling on them not knowing he was off the case.

'Okay, right. Well, we need to search the premises for Mr Lewis's Dosette box.'

'Dosette box?'

'Yeah, it's a plastic container used to dispense medication. It's divided up into days to help patients not forget. It'll assist us calculating how much treatment he has on board, or not. Might be crucial. So we're double checking it wasn't missed first time round.'

'No one told us anything,' the sergeant said, dubious.

'Damn! I tell you, HQ is so clunky it's a miracle Philippa Foot is still alive!'

He'd hit the right note: the sergeant rolled his eyes in recognition. William pressed on.

'Wait a minute. How long have you been on this duty?'

'We just got here.' The sergeant was unhooking his walkie-talkie.

No, no. Not good, thought William.

'Ah, that explains it – must've been the last watch who got the message from Gerrard and forgot to pass it on. Look, if you want to reach the Assistant Commissioner, you'll take forever if you go via the radios. I've got him on speed dial. Here.'

William depressed a button and handed the officer his mobile phone.

Ever since Frances had broken the news that he'd been sacked from FTAC, the AC had diverted every single one of the psychiatrist's calls to voicemail. William prayed that Gerrard didn't decide, at this very moment, to accept his ring. The sergeant took the phone and hesitantly put it to his ear. William's heart was burrowing its way out.

C'mon, c'mon...

An extended wait later, the sergeant thoughtfully looked at the phone.

'All I got was his voicemail.'

'Oh damn, yeah, I forgot. He's probably still in the meeting with the Cabinet Secretary that I've just come from. Look, we haven't got time to wait. Pip – sorry – Philip – sorry – the Foreign Secretary's wife – sorry, *life* – is at stake...'

William had been banking on the sergeant not appreciating what a Dosette box was, putting him at a disadvantage. What else did he not know? Like perhaps he'd missed out on this instruction from on high? Being reminded of ignorance helped subconsciously link to the impression there might be other things he was uninformed of.

William grabbed his phone back. The handing over had been a symbolic tactic to cement trust between them.

'Oh wait, a call coming in...oh my days, it's the Foreign Sec!' William glanced briefly at the receiver before putting it to his ear. 'Uh-uh, uh-huh, no, no, still out here. Yes, I know it's urgent,' he said to silence. 'Nah, Pip, you're being a bit harsh. They're just doing their job,' he offered, making eye contact with the sergeant. Then he surreptitiously pressed the button to retrieve his voicemail messages, and handed the phone back to the startled badge. 'She wants to speak to you,' he said regretfully.

'Is this Bozo Number One or Bozo Number Two?' Philippa's voice was just as cold as the first time he'd heard the voicemail message in the police car with Frances staring at him.

'S...sorry?' The officer looked stunned.

The gamble relied on the listener not realising they were the victim of a scolding from William's voicemail. He would have to time getting the phone back exactly right before it offered the recorded menu of options.

'Is this the idiot who blocks all attempts to get on with the job and catch this madman? Is this the dipshit who is making my life a misery and who is now stopping me doing my job as a Cabinet Minister? Both you *and* Gerrard! I simply cannot believe it! I've only just been briefed on what went wrong in the raid on David Lewis's flat. From now on, you let your betters make the decisions. If you continue to obstruct this investigation I'm going to have you terminated!'

William grabbed back the phone and shrugged at an ashen sergeant.

'Don't worry, I understand. I'll wait until someone more senior and in the loop gets here.' William held up an emollient hand. He wondered if they'd notice it was shaking.

The sergeant made a motion to his colleague to open the door, and the psychiatrist scrambled in. There seemed to be a stronger tang than William remembered the first time round, elevating his disquiet.

And hadn't forensics replaced the lights?

The place had been screened and the lighting had been re-rigged so everyone could see properly. William flicked the switch on and off, but nothing happened. David Lewis had extracted the bulbs. Again.

He had been back in here since the police cordoned off the flat.

William's handset began to buzz. Heart thumping, he checked it. It would just be his luck that Gerrard decided to return his call now.

It was Kwame. That bloody pop star and her entourage were chasing him. Good. He ignored the phone. He'd given Kwame enough for now; he'd take one more call later to close the snare.

Something was wrong. The officers unsheathed their torches and beams of light criss-crossed the gloom.

'Jesus Christ!' exclaimed William.

Everywhere, their shadows thrown at crazy angles from floor to ceiling, were crucifixes.

39

I don't hardly know her
But I think I could love her

'There's one last thing before the chopper gets here...' Kwame reached into his hoodie and pulled out some sheets of A4 paper. They fluttered and clapped in the Pacific breeze.

'I spoke to our good doctor in the UK. He says he's spotted a pattern in the lyrics the stalker is sending us and wants us to take a look. He asked me to print out all the lyrics in date order from the start. Here they are.'

The lines reminded him of a disjointed mash-up song, the type the band was favouring at the moment.

Remember just who you are
Like the circles that you find in the windmills of your mind
Swing low
All for freedom and for pleasure, nothing lasts forever
Flowers every day
Fire in the sky
Nothing is more dangerous than desire when it's wrong
Lipstick cherry all over the lens as she's falling
The hunter gets captured by the game
She's got all the friends that money can buy
If you believe it
If you look closely it's easy to trace
Everything you know is wrong
Come on baby let's start anew
You come and you go, leaving just your picture behind
And fiery demons all dance when you walk through that door
Ain't no mountain high enough
And you keep it just for fun, for a laugh, ha-ha-ha

Hungry like the wolf
You'll be dead before your time is due
Although she may be cute
Teenage dirtbag
You got sirens for a welcome
Your love is a mutt from hell
Used to dream of being a millionaire, without a care
As she's spreading her wings she threw back the ring
He gets his fill oh constantly
When your world is full of strange arrangements
Diamonds are forever
Twenty-five was the speed limit
Fall in a long stray town
Bits and pieces
Nowhere to run to baby nowhere to hide
Ninety-nine red balloons
Close to me
What I feel when I hesitate
And if I only could, I'd make a deal with god
She says she's going to jail, for going through my mail
I don't hardly know her
We move in line
Gonna make you, make you, make you notice me
Is there something I should know?
I have danced inside your eyes, how can I be real?
I can't get any rest, people say I am obsessed
When I met you in the restaurant, you could tell I was no
      debutante
They tried to break us, looks like they'll try again
The man who invented plastic, saved my soul
Can the people on tv see me or am I paranoid?
She drives me crazy, and I can't help myself
I sometimes lose myself in me
It's a habit of mine
I could make you an offer you can't refuse
My, my, the sky will cry
This is my only escape from it all
I hear your face start to call

Losing my way
We move in line
There's not a problem that I can't fix
They're gonna call me sir
And if you think that I don't make sense
Can't get you out of my head
I'm a glossy magazine, an advert on the tube
And destruction lay around me from a fight I could not win
The things we do for love
I can see for miles and miles.

Dread inclined her head while she inspected the list. Absent mindedly she undid her hair bun and started doing it up again. Then changed her mind. The sea breeze gusting over the cliff edge whipped her locks across her face. She pulled them back impatiently.

Most women going on a run might just tie their braids back and be done with it, mused Kwame. But not Dread. She always had the picture editor's decision to consider. Everything she did was designed to assist them choosing her countenance for the front page over some rival, like Charlotte Perkins.

'So? The experts, including your Han Fei, have been over these a hundred times – and they've come up with zilch.'

'Yeah, but Dr James says that the pattern emerges when you consider the lyrics in the date order in which they were sent. He said that proved one of his theories on how stalkers change over time.'

'Well, what is it?' Dread continued to stare, but after a pause shook her head. 'They are all lyrics from songs we've covered over the years. Kwame, we've been through this a billion times.'

'Dr James asked me to show them to you, your family and the band to see if anyone else notices an underlying structure – particularly anyone close to you. He claims that because of the pattern he can reveal who the scumbag is, but he needs the stalker's next lyrics.'

Dread's eyes widened. 'He thinks the wanksta is alive? So who was in the exploding car at the Rose Bowl?'

Kwame shrugged. 'He says that was just a minion – he says there's going to be another note.'

'If he knows who it is, then why doesn't he just tell us? Is he grandstandin' or something?' She was becoming more agitated. Kwame knew she hated mind games being played on her, and that was exactly what the psychiatrist was doing.

'Probably. But he also says the next note's coming soon.'

'I thought he was supposed to be helping us 5–0 the krunk, not toying with us.' She bent over, folding nimbly like a pocket-knife, allowing her hair to drape down, unnervingly close to the cliff edge, before gathering it in yet another attempt to tie it against the whipping breeze.

'Mind games with the stalker. If it's someone in the inner circle, this is what may be needed to smoke them out. He said to call him directly when the next threat is found, but not to tell him its contents – that he'd make the revelation there and then about the perpetrator. He also wants one of the people in the inner circle, someone closest to you, to be with him when he makes his pronouncement, so I'm gonna send Kristal back to London in the G650.'

'Why don't we just fly him over to us?'

'He's made it clear that he doesn't want to join the team – just act as an adviser. He's even waived the retainer.'

'We're throwing money at him and he's still not joining us? What gives?'

Kwame inwardly grimaced. The diva reviled anyone who was immune to her charms.

'I don't think he's motivated by money, hard though that is for you to understand.'

Dread sneered. 'Of course he's motivated by green! Boo that! He's just aggressively negotiating a fatter fee. Screw him, Kwame!'

Something about the way she looked away and held herself meant that an aspect of their conversation had thoroughly whacked her. He quickly realised that the list included lyrics they had never showed her in the past. They had been trying to protect the diva from being disturbed by them. Anne's orders.

'Listen, Kwame, I don't know what you and your shrink friends are playing at,' her breathing was coming in starts, 'but you need to get a grip on this, 'cos I am teetering on the brink now.'

40

We move in line
But never reach an end

These crucifixes hadn't been there when William and Gerrard had checked out the flat, so David had somehow managed to get back in. Possibly he'd even been staying here, guarded by the unsuspecting police outside.

Cunning, very cunning, William thought. They might be turning London over to find him, but they certainly weren't checking his lair.

William tried to hold his face still, to look as if the crucifixes had been here all along. Otherwise the sergeant would close the place down and treat it as a new crime scene. And that wouldn't allow William to search.

'Yeah, absolutely,' the senior officer grinned. He hadn't realised that William's exclamation had been from gobsmacked surprise at seeing the crucifixes for the first time.

The crosses varied in size, from small pocket ones to much more imposing sculpted bloody versions several feet along.

William went searching. What was David trying to tell them?

Something else wasn't right. The classic stalker's space had been covered from ceiling to floor with mouthless pictures of Philippa Foot. Now the gaping images were gone, replaced by religious icons.

This didn't feel good. Was it possible that he'd been completely wrong in his diagnosis of David?

The police had taken up the floorboards and tiles where David had fashioned a cramped hiding space, and where he must have been skulking when they first searched the place. The fact William had deduced this and predicted it reassured him a little that he wasn't completely hopeless. But then again, David remained one step ahead, and William was still playing catch up.

'Notice there's always a crucified figure, never just a simple cross,' commented William to himself.

He found a shelf of DVDs and videos, opening each packet to check the film inside. He flicked through the paperback books interspersed with piles of crucifixes on each shelf. The gumshoes began to gather around William, basking him in an intersection of torchlight. Why hadn't he noticed all the religious texts before? Many were about devil worship. Occult symbols loomed up at him out of the pages.

'What does it matter what films he watches or books he reads?' the sergeant asked, intrigued.

'Do you know about Mark Chapman – the twenty-five-year-old who shot John Lennon dead in December 1980? Well, the police found him because, after the slaying, he immediately sat down on the pavement outside the Dakota Building reading *The Catcher in the Rye* by JD Salinger. He made no attempt to escape. Three months later, John Hinckley Jr, also twenty-five, tried to shoot President Ronald Reagan. That same novel, *Catcher in the Rye,* was later discovered in his hotel room. Robert Bardo killed actress Rebecca Schaeffer eight years later – and he was reported to have been carrying the same novel.'

'What's it about?' asked the sergeant.

'It's about hatred for phoniness. But it's not just that the book is a link between them, it's also that they identified with each other. Frances Bremer had tried to assassinate Governor George Wallace of Alabama a few years earlier, but ended up crippling him instead. He'd written in his diaries that he needed to do something bold to prove his manhood, and to do so in a way the whole world would witness.'

William was talking apparently confidently, but inside he was despairing. Were his lecturing words just to reassure himself he knew something about stalkers? Because at this moment he had no idea what David was up to, or even what exactly he was obsessed with.

If anything.

'Paul Shafer, the screenwriter for the film *Taxi Driver*, partly constructed his script on the diaries of Bremer. John Hinckley

Jr is reported to have become obsessed with *Taxi Driver* too. It's supposed to have partly inspired his attack on the President as a warped way of proving his love for, and gaining the attention of, Jodie Foster, who he stalked for years beforehand. And Hinckley is said to have also been fixated on Holden Caufield, the hero of *Catcher in the Rye*. So I'm checking for some of the films and books we know are linked with an unhealthy stalking interest.'

But there was no sign of the missing picture from Philippa's bedroom. Maybe her exasperation, that this was a wild-goose chase of his, had been justified all along.

William was beginning to feel ever more hopeless. He flicked open the blinds and stared at a portable radio, now revealed on the windowsill.

'Come on,' the sergeant urged, 'what's so interesting about the window?'

'Don't you notice something odd?' William asked, crouching down and examining the shelf.

'Not really. It's a radio.'

William tried not to sigh. 'Look, I specialise in people who become obsessed with surveillance. Means you have to know all the different ways there are to keep tabs on a target. Most people think that in order to bug a room you have to penetrate the building and leave a listening device there. But you don't. Look at this – it's angled towards the window. If you listen to a radio, you turn it so the speaker faces the room. This one is facing the glass.'

The officer shrugged.

'So what?'

'It's very close to the pane – almost touching. See?'

'Will you get to the point?'

'Okay, here's a basic physics lesson. Sound is transmitted by vibration. So when we talk to each other we are doing no more than vibrating air between us. Unfortunately for those who want to keep their conversations secret, the resonating atmosphere reverberates *everything* it's in contact with. And in a room like this, the object that is most easily going to pick up the pulsations of our conversation is the window.'

William was now circumventing the room, gesticulating.

'Now in a microphone, acoustic waves, or vibrating air, cause a thin, sensitive diaphragm to quiver back and forth in time with the noise pulses entering the microphone. The diaphragm is rigged to electricity, so as it moves it produces a signal that can then be reinterpreted by speakers, or any recording device, as a version of the original sound.'

William pounced on David's filthy windowsill.

'This pane of glass is the same as the beginning stage of that microphone. It's the diaphragm that is vibrating to our conversation. Question is, could someone measure those vibrations outside the flat then reinterpret the signal? Could they decode the oscillating window and therefore pick up our conversation in here without even having to bug the room?'

The sergeant whistled in admiration. He was beginning to see where William was heading.

'Now if we shone a laser light from outside the flat so that it bounced off the glass surface, catching the reflection of the beam, we could electronically process that signal and, under controlled conditions, using audio laboratory processing equipment and software, recover high quality sound.'

'Is that really possible?'

William snorted. 'Not only is it possible, but the Internet is awash with kits and advice on how. Using everyday objects, like a lecturer's laser pointer, a laptop computer, photocells available from any gadget store and headphones, you can build your own audio surveillance device to record conversations going on in a room you are outside of.'

The officers inspected the radio, the window and William with new respect.

'Now, here's the thing. If you are aware of that technology, you're also conscious that one of the best ways of *avoiding* being recorded is to play a radio close to the window you're worried about. Interference from the radio drowns out all conversational sound.'

The sergeant stared.

'You think he was ensuring no one was recording his conversations via a laser bounced off the pane?'

'Not only that. I think we need to go over to Philippa Foot's house and check the windows there and the line of sight. The psychological mechanism in play here is projection. He knows he's monitoring her, so he projects his paranoia outwards and imagines others might be doing it to him.'

William was terrified that David had been covertly listening to Pip in her home, had found out her undisclosed schedule and was planning an ambush. As the psychiatrist ran out of the flat, the sergeant dashed after him, radioing for a panda car to race them to the Minister's home.

William kicked himself that he hadn't spotted the radio turned to the window before. But, he then recalled, the first time he had entered the flat, days ago with Gerrard, it hadn't been.

The police officers at Maida Vale were confused by the shouted explanation the sergeant gave them as he charged into the house. But they didn't stand in the way as William burst through the doors of Philippa's office.

Philippa's constituency secretary looked up, startled, from behind the oversized lid of a large red briefcase sporting the insignia of the Houses of Parliament as the office filled up with uniforms. They inspected the windows carefully. No sign of any laser lights beaming in.

William started yanking the drawers out of Philippa's desk. Right in the deepest reach of the bottom drawer was her secret stash of cigarettes. William distributed them to a dumbfounded group and invited them to light up. Given his discovery of the radio, they played along. William, puffing vigorously, coughed and retched.

'Look, HQ wants to know why the risk has now gone up,' the sergeant insisted through the fog.

William rolled his eyes skywards in exasperation.

'What do you mean "risk"? Risk of what? Risk isn't a unitary concept. There are different domains of risk. Each type of risk is associated with different hazard factors. And the risk in each domain is influenced by the underlying motivational type.'

'But all we want…'

With the smoke filling the office, William pointed.

Revealed by the mist, through the window of Philippa's office shimmered a thin line of red light, lined up precisely with Philippa's chair. William went back to the window, retraced the line of sight, and saw it disappear into the scaffolded block opposite.

'We're gonna get shit-canned!' the sergeant exclaimed, stubbing out his cigarette and dashing after William, who was disappearing out the door.

Part 4

Killing is Climax

Every instance of an attack on a public figure by a lone stranger in the United States for which adequate information has been made publically available has been the work of a mentally disordered person who issued one or more pre-attack signals in the form of inappropriate letters, visits or statements...
– Dietz, P and Martell, DA (2012) "Commentary: Approaching and Stalking Public Figures – A Prerequisite to Attack", *Journal of the American Academy of Psychiatry and the Law*, 38: 341–8.

41

Gonna make you, make you, make you notice me
I got brass in pocket

Followed by his sergeant and a flurry of constables, William raced across the road to the renovation site. He dodged past dust-covered builders and clattered up the stairs, searching for the right floor.

Workmen shouted in broken English that they weren't allowed in without permission from the foreman. The sergeant breathlessly radioed their discovery into the central operations room, while an officer behind him explained to the builders what was going on. They couldn't make much sense of it, but the Eastern Europeans did recognise uniforms and the words 'Police business' so they sullenly quietened down.

Because the site was a church with the houses on either side being knocked through to create a long mansion with floor-to-ceiling arched windows, there was ample opportunity for David to spy on Philippa's place. Each floor appeared to be just a typical building site, until the penthouse level. There the door wouldn't budge. A set of overalls was on a mobile, protesting to the Russian oligarch who owned the place as they crashed through.

At first William thought they had burst into a sniper's nest with banks of rifles on stands trained down on Philippa's office below. But then he realised the jungle of three-legged tripods was supporting an array of telescopes and binoculars.

By the window overlooking Philippa's office, astride some battered chairs, lay a pair of old headphones, an ancient laptop, a pack of Cadmium Sulfide Photocells, soldering equipment, a laser pointer, a large old reel-to-reel tape recorder and a pair of tripods.

'Don't touch!' William yelped as one of the workers who'd come in with them reached out to the computer. It was set up to collect and convert the laser energy bouncing back from Philippa's windowpane into audio waves.

He turned to the sergeant. 'The impressive thing about this technology is that it wouldn't be picked up by a standard sweep for electronics devices in the Minister's office.'

William unsheathed his battered fountain pen and delicately touched a computer key with it. The dusty screen confirmed that the program had been running continuously for several days, so David must have set this up immediately after the tarpaulin had blown off the scaffolding outside.

'So he's aware of her *actual* schedule as opposed to the fake one put out to throw him off her scent,' William confirmed.

'Shouldn't we leave the room to forensics?' the sergeant worried.

'No time – the priority is to check the Foreign Sec isn't about to be hit.'

'What you talking about?' the foreman interrupted. William had to remind himself that he might be in on it with David.

While the sergeant demanded the names of everyone who had access, William had a flash of inspiration and fished out a crumpled picture of David Lewis. He waved this at the workers. From their body language, William saw straightaway that they all recognised the man in the photograph. However, they shrugged ambiguously.

William frowned. 'We're going to have to take you all in for questioning. Where's the site office? We need to check your paperwork.'

You have to put yourself in their shoes, he quickly thought. They were used to police back home bullying them. William had to exploit this. They would be thinking that he was a plainclothes officer – he must be the senior person.

Nothing but sullen eyes.

'Right!' barked William. 'We're going to search the place.' He pushed past the builders and began clattering down the stairs. But he knew the site was too big and they had too little time.

He scrambled from floor to floor, looking briefly through doorways.

'Isn't this Sergei Bulgakov's place?' asked the sergeant, following. 'So what about that famous safe the size of a room?'

'Nothing of any use will be there,' William said emphatically. He paused on the ground floor. At the back was a Portakabin – the site office. Something caught his eye. He cupped his hands to block out reflections across the glazed door.

'What are you looking for exactly?' asked the sergeant. He would be getting concerned about the legality of their intrusion as time went on, and, if nothing turned up right now, he'd begin to pull the search team out. The psychiatrist had just seconds left.

'There – a black and white picture, see?'

'So?'

William gestured at the door and the foreman shrugged. William stood back and kicked the lock. The door splintered and William bounded into the Portakabin. The monochrome picture he had seen became less opaque.

The sergeant was inspecting the damage to the door. He seemed to be in shock. 'Sir, I'm going to have to ask you to…we have no warrant, so…'

William pointed.

'Isn't that the Foreign Secretary?' the sergeant asked, puzzled.

'Yes, it is.' The missing portrait from Philippa's bedroom: the same ebony frame; the same black and white finish.

'Official, isn't it? She's opening a building…but, sir, that still doesn't…'

'What building is that and who is that cutting the tape with her?' demanded William.

'That's Robert Recorde,' the sergeant supplied. 'The TV presenter. Used to host *Big Bother* and *The Weakest Lip-Sync*. But he's covering the war out in the Congo right now.' There was a tone of incredulity that William hadn't recognised the famous TV personality.

And in the background of the image, amidst a gaggle of officials, was David Lewis. He was shaven, groomed hair, in a suit and tie, but it was still David Lewis. All the other officials were staring up at something on the building being opened. But David was glaring at Philippa, who was glancing at Robert, who was staring down the barrel of the lens. Actually no, the TV presenter was looking just above the lens at the photographer, and he sported a shifty, guilty smile. William turned to indicate Lewis for the benefit of the foreman. This was the nail in the coffin for him.

'But he one of architects working on building!' the foreman spluttered.

William began to feel queasy. It was one of the basic rules of stalking – get a job which allows you access to the person you're targeting. He checked the back of the frame. There was a scrawled note: *Remember the first time?*

And now that H9 code she had kept texting him on the evening of the Mansion House ball became clearer. William had subsequently found out from a sex-addict patient that this was mobile phone text code for *Husband in room*. She was warning him that her new "husband" was keeping her under surveillance. The night before, as she had paraded provocatively in front of the mirror discussing different shoes, he'd wondered if there was someone else in the house. Now he knew there had been – Robert Recorde.

All those press briefings at her home were just a ruse to get this broadcaster in, evading all the extra security that William had helped Gerrard install to keep potential suitors at bay. When she had been stroking his arm, explaining that she allowed Gerrard to consort with Frances as his press muse, he had assumed the AC was reciprocally allowing her to indulge herself with William.

'I let him have his so he lets me have mine,' she'd purred.

She had been referring to Robert all this time. Gerrard had allowed the TV presenter to venture in and out of her place, assuming it was all strictly professional.

Well, it wasn't. And that bloody David Lewis had removed the precise photo which would have at once given Philippa's game away to the psychiatrist.

It walloped him hard, winding him.

'Is that St Martin-in-the-Fields?' he asked, trying to keep the quiver of emotion from his voice.

'Yeah, but all that scaffolding in the picture has come down now – it's nearly finished,' the sergeant confirmed.

'Right, we need to find the rest of David's stuff that's bound to be here,' William commanded. The last thing Philippa needed right now, knowing the danger she was facing, was hurt pride getting in the way of him doing his job.

A desk was covered in plans and architectural drawings. William pored over them, gripping the picture of Robert Recorde, Philippa and David.

'But where are these for?' demanded William, pulling a group of drawings together. His tone had become hectoring, and the foreman began to get scared.

'I no idea...some kind church? Not this one.'

News filtered back from the search party delegated to the massive safe that there was nothing of any use there.

'How did David manage to get hired? Did he mention an important project? Claim to be associated with it?' William held up the photograph. 'Did he use this? Was he involved in the St Martin's project?'

'Hang on second, it here... He brought it at beginning.' The foreman gestured at an alcove where a framed poster hung. 'That project he worked on.'

The poster was of a towering ribbed very modern glass structure. The Bell Tower in Perth, Western Australia, so the lettering alongside it proudly indicated. At its base were large sail-like structures resembling the Sydney Opera House.

'He very proud of that.'

'But how did he get them to believe it was his work? Anyone can buy a poster!' The sergeant was shocked.

'No, no! He had press cuttings, they mention his name as part of architect team.'

'You don't think it's true, do you,' the sergeant demanded of William, 'that this raving lunatic had something to do with that?'

William sighed. 'There's a thing called the social drift hypothesis of schizophrenia. The question is: why is it that major psychoses like this are found much more in the lower social classes? The theory is that once you are in the grip of the illness then you start to drift downwards because your function becomes impaired.'

'Drift? Try falling off the side of a cliff if he used to be capable of *that*,' said the sergeant.

William shook his head. 'You start to say strange things and your work colleagues edge away from you. Bit by bit you lose jobs, friends, and end up isolated and on the streets. It's one of the crippling aspects of what has been described as the most serious non-fatal illness you can get.'

'So he once helped build this iconic tower and now he's sending rambling notes to the Foreign Secretary?'

'People can end up stalking for very different reasons, and stalkers can have a wide variety of mental illnesses – or none at all. People stalk ex-partners, acquaintances or even complete strangers. They can stalk them out of love, out of hate, out of resentment, out of an exaggerated sense of entitlement, or as part of a grievance or a righteous quest for justice. They can stalk them for completely crazy psychotic reasons – real "signals from Mars" stuff.'

'And this villain is from Mars?'

'If you don't explore the motivation, you won't have a hope in hell of identifying the risks or working out scenarios as to what might happen next,' William said patiently. 'Don't you see that the dangers are going to be different from someone who is spurred on by hatred compared with someone who is inspired by adoration?'

'And the pictures reveal his motivation?'

'Yes, yes!' William contemplated the poster and Philippa's photograph. 'These were his calling cards. He showed this one to prospective clients in order to get work, and he used it because relying on references was more difficult. But why did he take this one of Robert and Philippa?' William was thinking out loud. 'He stored it here because he knew we would be searching his flat, which means he keeps other things he doesn't want us to find here.'

William grasped the large framed poster and asked for assistance in removing it from the wall. Once down, they carefully turned it over on the desk. Pinned to its back were photocopied press cuttings. William scanned them feverishly, reading out bits of relevant information.

'The Bell Tower was finished as part of Australia's millennium celebrations. It was built to house a set of eighteen ancient bells gifted from the UK as part of the Bicentennial celebrations. The bells weigh about nine tonnes, and when rung exert extraordinary forces on the foundations which required deft engineering and architecture. The team…oh, my days!'

'What is it?'

'He *was* some kind of engineer. There's his name in the team that helped build this thing. This explains why we found it so difficult to find out anything about him here. And it's also why he refused to talk most of the time. He was hiding his Australian accent.

'Look, the tower has bells taken from St Martin-in-the-Fields. That's how he first connected with Philippa – she was on one of the charity committees of the church!'

Among the cuttings was correspondence. David had been writing to a committee at St Martin-in-the-Fields in Trafalgar Square, negotiating the moving of the bells to Australia. Philippa, before she was Foreign Secretary, had been in charge of one of the committees overseeing the work and it was how they had first met: via formal letters. He had later scribbled all over the printed sheets ramblings about God and the Devil.

William wondered whether the fact the Australian Government had secured the bells had been misinterpreted by David. The gift of the bells could, if his mind had become unstable, have been seen as a sign of something more going on in their relationship. He may also have thought that Philippa had that picture in her bedroom because she fancied *him*, not Robert Recorde.

Then they found a letter.

There were several photocopies, so David must be carrying the original on his person. It was from Philippa to David, regretfully explaining that the part of the project involving him was now being wound down. It did thank him. For exactly what remained a mystery, as it was clear he had by this stage become a real pain. The letter complained that, among other problems, he'd got the specifications on the load-bearing hanging areas of St Martin-in-the-Fields completely wrong.

That bit was a tad concerning, as it was for his expertise in engineering, given what he'd achieved with the huge bells in Australia, that the oligarch Bulgakov must have hired the architect. He was supposed to construct the chamber housing the billionaire's gold.

The letter was signed by Philippa, but William understood she saw it for a nanosecond as it was swept past her among a torrent of paperwork for her signature. The letter would have been dictated by someone else, and this explained why the name had meant nothing to her now.

David's letters to the project and Philippa after this became handwritten incoherence. A lot had been sent back to him with post office notes *return to sender* because the addressee was no longer there – exactly as advised by William to victims of stalking.

David had then begun to send letters to all and sundry, suggesting a variety of increasingly bizarre alterations to St Martin-in-the-Fields. He also seemed to have become unhappy with the final design and construction of the Bell Tower in Western Australia. Then a fire had broken out in the tower, and David had been sacked shortly afterwards. Intriguingly his final threats to Philippa explained that if they didn't change the design as he had outlined, some catastrophic biblical event was going to destroy their architectural plan anyway. So they might as well go with his.

'So the bells in the tower in Australia came from St Martin's. So what?' asked the sergeant.

'These aren't any old bells,' William said. 'These are ancient bells that date back to before the fourteenth century. Hmmm... I wonder...'

He scrabbled through the papers and came upon a map of London. It had circles drawn on it, and each one seemed to be over a church.

Another insight. The churches that had been victims of arson attacks formed an arc from Philippa's street across London, ending just west of St Martin's, as if whoever was doing this was drawing a giant arrow pointing from opposite the Foreign Secretary's home to St Martin's. David's handiwork. It was all coming together, and a religious delusional syndrome was getting more likely.

Hadn't the second vignette, one of the two new scenarios sent in to the exam board attributed to him, been about a religious delusion? That reminded William about the first case history sent to the examiners' committee which revealed his own troubled childhood. But how had Lewis got hold of all that information? William scrabbled through the papers some more and unearthed a document that made his chest heave. It was a Foreign Office high level security clearance background check on himself. It was all there – his parents being admitted to Broadmoor and the terrible tragedy that happened afterwards in the Friern Barnet Asylum. Gerrard must have commissioned it and passed it to Philippa in an attempt to get him off the case.

There was a scribbled note over the top from the AC which read: *Can we get someone else who hasn't got such a personal stake in stalking? Now we understand why he's so obsessed with tracking down and treating mental illness.*

Philippa had scrawled back: *He's the best in the business. All those academic papers the professor sent us confirm that. All this shows is that he's got a special insight from first-hand experience. You leave him alone.*

The psychiatrist gathered the cuttings together and the floor plans. His knees faltered. David must have pinched this document from the Minister's bedroom along with the picture of Robert Recorde. He had left the other papers on her sideboard, and no one had noticed which specific sheet he had filched. Now the psychiatrist finally understood why Philippa Foot never asked him about himself – she was doing him a favour.

Had she not realised that this particular document had been taken because she was too distracted with her picture of Robert Recorde disappearing? Stealing her underwear had been a diversion intended to put them all on the wrong trail.

'I wonder if he had some kind of religious conversion, some experience of a quasi-psychotic kind that's somehow linked to him getting involved in this project.'

William was disappearing out the door. The psychiatrist recalled that Philippa had invited Bulgakov's architect over to advise on her own place. Probably a ruse to get closer to the oligarch while circumventing official channels. She was also in the process of transforming her ground floor into a branch of the constituency office. Had she inadvertently welcomed her disguised stalker into her home? No wonder the flower arrangement on her bed suggested someone who had been there before.

'Where are you going?' the sergeant queried anxiously, following him.

William dashed back to the surveillance room. Breathing heavily, he pressed the rewind button on the tape machine and then pressed play. Squeaky helium-like voices stretched and then stopped.

There was a long pause of grinding and rasping and then a lot of what sounded like howling wind. Then suddenly the room was filled with Philippa's voice.

'Look, Tullia, your shrink was turning into a real pain. First thing I know about his latest madcap scheme is two resignations from the Cabinet – both completely out of the blue. The PM asked me to investigate, and blow me if I only then uncover that Gerrard's gone round asking the whole Cabinet for salivary swabs for DNA testing. This led to two with murky pasts taking fright and assuming we knew about their misdemeanours...'

'So it was a good thing you got rid of them!' Tullia sounded like she was struggling to hide her exasperation from Philippa.

'But Gerrard then explains that it was William's idea to get hold of the whole Cabinet's DNA, telling the AC it was on my authority.'

'But if you got rid of two senior colleagues who were going to turn out to be a future embarrassment, then...'

'Ah, Tullia, it's much more than that. His banning us from activities was getting in the way of the business of Government!'

'Dr James is convinced that looking after the mentally ill is the most important thing in the world,' replied Tullia. 'We at the Institute appreciate you have other considerations to think of. From now on, why don't you check with me what events you want to attend. Perhaps I have a greater sympathy for the needs the Government has to meet its obligations.'

'There's an event to do with opening a new homeless centre at St Martin-in-the-Fields in two days' time,' said Philippa.

At the mention of the church, William began scrabbling through the floor plans.

'William told me not to attend *any* public events for the time being,' she continued. 'He said this period was particularly dangerous because David was accelerating in his head, feeling he

260

was running out of time having been caught once. Something about when the authorities make contact with a stalker they can escalate. But it's a key Government initiative – I need to be there!'

She's still scared that I'm right! William could hear it plainly in her voice. But why was the homeless centre opening at the church suddenly so important to Philippa? Something else was going on here – there was more to this event than met the eye. She had some kind of covert agenda, and Tullia, because she didn't know Philippa as well as William, wasn't factoring this in.

But what was the Minister's real motive?

'Absolutely.' Tullia spoke warmly. 'Look, as far as I'm concerned, if you feel you need to be there and that your Government obligations are more important than any other consideration, then that's your choice. I've also discussed this with Gerrard. He explained the church will be packed with extra security. He believes Dr James is stopping the police doing their job, but there should not be an issue here with William no longer being on FTAC. I'm taking over the day-to-day management of your case while we've deployed Dr James on another, and this is highly confidential – his new client is Dread.'

'But our stalker is more serious!' Philippa said, sounding put out.

The sergeant looked sharply at William.

'You're doing the Dread stalker?'

The room seemed to have gathered instant respect for him and awestruck muttering broke out at the back. This was despite the fact they'd also heard he'd been sacked from FTAC.

'Listen, Prof, don't get me wrong. I like the guy, I really do. Unlike Gerrard's helicopters, that FTAC thing of William's actually saves money – it economises on all the cash that would need to be spent on police, court time and imprisonment when a stalker reoffends. I honestly get what he's trying to do.'

Tullia's voice surged with pride. 'Absolutely. We've seen enough stalking cases to have come across that all too familiar scenario – the stalker who's released from prison and takes a taxi straight to the victim's house. Treat them while we've got them and they stand a chance of breaking free of their stalking behaviour, getting on with their lives and giving their victims some peace.'

'But, Tullia, treatment rather than punishment isn't good politics right now.'

William could bear no more and put a trembling finger out to switch off the tape recorder.

The sergeant looked puzzled.

'Which case are we on right now, sir?'

William was staring with blank fury out the window at the street several floors below. The obstructions to him doing his job felt complete and final. Now seemed like a good time to jump.

Something came into focus.

Frances was down there.

'For God's sake!' he exclaimed. 'Everyone's joining the party!'

Astride a motorbike down on the street, dressed in black leather, the journalist was gazing up at them. Cradling her helmet, she grinned and waved, then pulled out a mobile.

'Motorbikes!' William moaned.

'Come again?' the sergeant asked.

'The favourite transportation of stalkers, 'cos they can follow a car more easily.'

His mobile rang. It was Frances. He'd felt a definite connection to her from their first meeting. But this was no time for personal explorations.

'We're in the middle of a crisis,' he began.

'Yeah? Why do you think I'm ringing you?' Her voice rippled with amusement.

William turned to beseech the sergeant. 'Anyone know Philippa's schedule for today? The real one, not the decoy.'

The sergeant shook his head.

'Sorry, only her protection detail has that information.'

Frances made a loud noise in William's ear.

'It's the event at St Martin-in-the-Fields for the homeless. It's happening right now,' Frances said. 'She's going to make her big announcement there. Remember I said all correspondents were told to stand by?'

William hit his forehead with the palm of his hand.

'We need to get to St Martin-in-the-Fields right now!'

'Why?' asked the sergeant.

'Because these plans here are a map of the interior of that

church. It's the kind of floor plan you'd need if you were planning an attack!'

'But the place will be drowning in police, and there's nowhere to hide!' The sergeant had to shout because William was already heading down the stairs.

The psychiatrist bellowed back over his shoulder. 'Yes, there *is* somewhere to hide, somewhere no one would bother to look. Because they'd figure if you hid there, you'd lose your hearing.'

'Where?' The sergeant was leaping down the steps after William.

'The bells in the Bell Tower in Perth, Australia – twelve of them originally came from St Martin-in-the-Fields. So David would have every reason to know the architectural layout of that part of the church well. And he had ringing in his ears!'

They burst out the front of the site. Frances had already re-donned her helmet and her bike was describing high-revving circles in the street. She craned her neck to one side, examining the picture of Philippa which William was brandishing.

'You'll get there quicker with me!' she shouted through her open visor and patted the back of her bike. But the sergeant had already bundled William through the open doors of the waiting police BMW. With a squeal of tyres and siren howling they catapulted away.

42

Is there something I should know?
Don't say you're easy on me,
you're about as easy as a nuclear war

He looked on patiently while she bent over and took some deep breaths. Dread was trying to disguise her anxiety by stretching. She turned to look over, her hands on the ground, her pert behind up in the air.

'I'm guessing by the silence that there's more.'

Kwame knew that there would be little point holding back on the final bombshell as the diva would insist on knowing everything. He took a deep breath. The ocean crashing on to the beach below had never looked more inviting – anywhere was better than here right now.

'Er, one other thing then. He wants a list of everyone you've ever hooked up with.'

She was astonished. It seemed to cure her agitation.

'Apparently the research on stalking shows that if you've had sex with someone, the chances of them getting violent when stalking you goes up dramatically.'

'Compared to who?'

'Compared to people you've not slept with. There *are* people you've not slept with, right?' Kwame was deliberately winding Dread up. Sometimes it was the only way to reach her. And he needed to get through to her fast given she'd taken Han Fei's Smith & Wesson Magnum in readiness for her own personal vendettas. Han must have been very badly perturbed by having his eyes sewn up – Kwame was surprised he hadn't yet taken a phone call from the Forensic Psychologist demanding to know where his revolver had got to. Then again, they had managed to dispatch him to London precisely to keep him quiet, and out of the way, until his eyes recovered. If only Dr James knew that his competition had been neutralised temporarily, making the Dread security team even more desperate to get the British psychiatrist on board.

'So Dr James says he needs a list of everyone you've got jiggy with.'

'And you expect me to email that to the pecker-head? Have you any idea what the press would do if they got hold of that?'

'So that means this has to be face to face, but he won't...'

Dread was trembling with rage.

'So basically we sit tight and wait for the next note? Great!' Dread stomped off. 'He knows that if he messes with us we mobilise the army, right?'

'They are not an army!' Kwame despaired. They had had this argument so often – she seemed to think she was some kind of general. 'They are a ragtag mob known as your fans. There may be legions of them, millions of them, but it's a very blunt instrument. You have to know that, Dread.'

Right now he felt the shrink's douchebag behaviour was the most counterproductive courting of a new client he had ever encountered. And now he had to get in Dread's face. She came stomping back with "The Face" pinned on worse than a gun to his head.

'He is so ratchet. No, listen, Kwame, he's cheesed me off now, so I'm gonna have to show him just who I am.'

43

I have danced inside your eyes, how can I be real?
Do you really want to hurt me?

'So you're seriously trying to tell me it was the bells that drove him mad?' The sergeant turned in the front seat of the weaving police car to address William.

'He was wearing earplugs and had buzzing in his ears, but the bozo prison doctors thought he was hearing voices,' William tried to explain. 'I think he's been hiding in the bell tower of St Martin's.'

First the construction site opposite Philippa's place in Maida Vale, and now St Martin-in-the-Fields. The engineering required to hold the enormously heavy bells sent from St Martin's to Australia was how David had wheedled his way into Sergei Bulgakov's project because the bullion magnate wanted somewhere to store gold.

But was that the only connection?

Bulgakov was remodelling a disused church. Was there some religious delusion in play here?

Thinking about it just made William more frightened. And there was something about Philippa's picture. He re-examined the framed photograph he had been cradling in his lap, now noticing a small indistinct blur at the top edge of the shot. He had seen something similar somewhere before, but where?

Then it came to him.

Frances's documentaries apparently always had the boom mike bouncing into shot; it was one of her signature ways of filming.

The tiny fuzz at the top edge of the photograph, easy to miss on a casual glance, meant that the reporter had taken the picture herself. So that was what she had been referring to all along. It was this portrait which William was supposed to have seen in Philippa's bedroom. Only of course Frances wasn't to know that David Lewis had appropriated the image.

The journalist was right: one glance at the depiction, to anyone who could decipher body language, did indeed reveal their relationship. He'd deduced instantaneously that the Foreign Sec had hooked up with Robert Recorde. Had Frances even given Philippa the picture as a message – I know what you're up to? Had the Minister, in her pouting arrogance, put it up to admire herself and her boyfriend?

And had Frances kept the secret to use as a weapon? No wonder she managed to get Tom Nagel treated so quickly.

Cars in front scuttled to the side and William's police car zipped past as gaps emerged. When William turned to check their rear, Frances gestured at him from her bike. He followed her hand movements. Pouring out of a side street was a stream of motorbikes, undulating like a snake behind the police car as it wove through the traffic.

'Dread-heads!' the sergeant exclaimed.

'Dread who?' asked William, dumbfounded. Their driver was so amazed that the psychiatrist didn't know, he briefly turned back to stare.

'They're fans of Dread who all wear Dreadlock hairpieces and T-shirts with clown faces.'

'Look, your officers need to stop a reporter who's going to try and get in, Frances Wright.' William thumbed towards her bike. Frances wouldn't thank him, but he was trying to save her life from the carnage he was certain was about to be unleashed at the church.

A message had come through that William was to be brought immediately to the church where Philippa was speaking at the ceremony. But the police hadn't agreed to pull the Minister out, as the psychiatrist had pleaded.

'We need some ambulances on stand-by at the church,' William demanded.

His hands drummed on the glass covering the photograph. He came to a conclusion and flipped the frame over, removing the picture and folding it so it would fit in his breast pocket.

'The emergency crews can't get through, but they're sending some paramedics on motorcycles,' the sergeant explained.

'He's known her moments of vulnerability in terms of police presence, so why not make one of his harassing approaches then?' William thought aloud. 'Why target her when the police protection's at its maximum, like Mansion House dinners? And now at St Martin-in-the-Fields?'

'But she's the key Minister in terms of terrorist threat – she's *always* surrounded by protection, and it's been tripled ever since he was assessed as a threat.'

'That's exactly my point. Because David Lewis was so cack-handed in his threats, security was tripled around his target. Why do that? He's an intelligent man, it doesn't stack up.'

'I thought that was the whole point about craziness – that it doesn't make sense.'

Brilliant, fumed William, *everyone's an armchair expert.*

The radio crackled again. Tullia was trying to get hold of William.

'Vilhelm? I'm so pleased you are back in the protection team again. The situation might be critical. A picture has arrived in the public email inbox of every member of the Cabinet from that email address David Lewis used. But the cryptographers can't make head nor tail of it, so we were wondering if you could assess it. I'm at Paddington Police Station and the security service people have acknowledged they're stumped.'

'I'll try in the time I have, but we're on the way to St Martin-in-the-Fields. We now have evidence that he's planning a strike on her there. Can you make sure there are paramedics on the scene.'

'But this picture reveals why we haven't found more info on him on our national databases.'

'I know why. It's because he's Australian. And let me take a wild guess – the picture is of the Bell Tower in Perth, Western Australia.'

There was nothing but crackling ether from the radio.

'How did you *know* that? There's no way that could have leaked out.' Tullia's voice was quieter than William could ever recall.

'It's a long story. Is the picture a standard one, like the local tourist authority might use on a poster?'

'Yes, yes, so?'

'If it's just a picture and no message...'

'That's right!'

'Then you're wasting your time bringing in the cryptographers.'

'Jeezus!' exclaimed the sergeant. He pointed behind them. 'There's more and more of these Dread-heads joining all the time. Why are they following us?'

William looked. From the side streets, rivers of bikes were pouring forth.

'Vilhelm, explain,' said Tullia from the police radio.

'This is an example of another kind of secret message sending. You need steganography, which is the science of hiding a message so that no one knows it's there. Once you find it, the communication leaps out at you.'

'So there's a directive hidden in this picture?'

'Of course there is! Has it got a white border?'

'Yes, it has.'

'Oh, Jeezus, there's a welcoming committee!' the sergeant exclaimed.

They had pulled into Trafalgar Square, and surrounding the church was an enormous crush of brawling Dread-heads. William now understood why no ambulance was going to penetrate anywhere near the building. The police were fighting with the mob to create a temporary corridor down which William could enter. The sergeant threw himself out of the car before it screeched to a stop. Flickering blue and red from the armada of police vehicles surrounding the building shimmered off the church's grey brickwork.

'What the hell is going on? What do these people want?' the sergeant bellowed above the roar of the crowd at an officer who swam through to them.

'Call me back on my mobile, we're getting out of the car!' William had to shout at the radio handset as it was yanked from his grip. He was bundled out and manhandled through the screaming multitude. Hands reached out from the wall of faces on both sides, grabbing at him.

'Now you know how a rock star feels!' a bobby growled next to his ear.

Angry expressions flowed by William as bystanders were shoved aside. His phone trilled insistently. It was Tullia.

'Have you got the picture up on a computer now?' William could barely hear her above the roar of the skirmish.

'Yes.'

'Okay, open it in Photoshop. Go to the top left hand menu and go to image...'

The sergeant pushed ahead, clearing a path for him. The photographers sensed he must be important so flash bombs exploded, blinding him.

'Who are you?' one shouted. 'Why do all these Dread-heads want you?'

'Prof, please hurry up!' William yelled at his phone.

'Hang on a sec! Yes, got it.'

'Okay, within that menu go to adjustments and then levels.'

They moved up the broad stairs and into the atrium. Inside was a blur of uniforms, milling in different directions. Security passes were brandished and checked. Then they were through.

'Yes, yes...'

'So now what you should have is a histogram diagram of the distribution of brightness levels in the picture.'

'Er...okay...yes, yes.'

'Okay, so now put your pointer over the bottom of the histogram where there's a slider. Move it from the far left of the graph to the far right. Any letters written in an almost completely white font over a completely white background will now stand out, whereas before the two whites would be too close together in brightness for the human eye to spot the difference.'

'Okay, yes, everything is getting very dark.'

The sergeant leant in. 'You want to go up to the bell chamber? That's where you think he is?'

William nodded impatiently.

They began scaling the spiral staircase. Gerrard had appeared and was coming up behind. He didn't look pleased. William pulled his phone from his ear.

'Gerrard, I told you to pull Pip out! David is going to strike here! She's in real danger,' he yelled down the staircase. His voice echoed back, amplifying his desperation.

'And now practically everything is black.'

William returned to his phone call.

'Yes, and?'

Tullia started to sound very far away.

Gerrard puffed up alongside.

'What the hell is going on, Dr James?'

William shook his phone at him. 'I've got Professor D'Aragona on the line – we're checking the message David just sent to the Cabinet. It might give us a clue as to what he's planning.'

Gerrard shook his head and moved past William.

'You seriously think he's in the bell tower?'

They reached a landing, and further, narrower stairs beckoned, lined with a body armoured tactical squad. Surely no one could get away with anything here?

'Yes, yes, a message has come up. You were right, of course.' Tullia's voice sounded strange. 'It reads: *got some splinters, didn't you, Books of Moses brought me right here back to you.*'

44

I can't get any rest, people say I'm obsessed
She drives me crazy

'Dr James said that something else happened at the Rose Bowl concert which it's vital you know about because we may need to take action before the next event.' Kwame leant closer into her ear. They were alone on the cliff top, but it was as if he didn't even want the Pacific swelling below to hear these immortal words.

'He says you had a panic attack on stage.'

Dread's eyes widened.

'He said *what*? Why are you listening to someone nuttier than squirrel shit?'

'I know, I know. After that I put in a call to that private eye clinic in London to get Dr Han Fei back with us faster and he's coming back right now in one of our private jets. But...'

'But if Han Fei is back on board...'

She was spinning. First she didn't want this shrink, nor the other, and then they were back on a merry-go-round where she changed her mind.

'Yeah, until then...Dr James admits it doesn't make sense given what a seasoned performer you are. But he's very confident you had a panic attack – it explains, he argues, why you had to get off the stage, and get off fast. Hence your leap into the crowd, which if you recall started the riot.

'That again...always with the riot thing,' muttered Dread.

'Dr James says the nature of panic is the need to get away urgently from the thing that's causing the fear. He explains that something must have happened up there on the wheel, some new event, and that was what caused the panic. He says he needs to speak to you to find out what it was, that it's all linked – your panic and us finding Alonzo's DNA in the limousine that exploded...'

'Huh?'

'Well, let's not forget that you mentioned you had stabbed someone in the eye socket with your microphone as we evaded the chasing pack, and yet no one came forward with such an injury, or tried to sue us – no nothing.'

He had indeed probed the psychiatrist as to whether it was possible that Dread had hallucinated the last incident, an enquiry which the bodyguard was not going to reveal to the diva right now. But surprisingly, given how flaky Kwame was worried that Dread was getting, William had appeared very dubious as to the straight "she's mad enough to argue with a signpost" possibility.

Instead, he had indicated that the assailant not appearing in any local hospital casualty department (Kwame had checked), nor complaining to anyone, nor seeking publicity, nor legal redress, more indicated they were part of the hostile conspiracy with whoever was in the limousine. The psychiatrist did seem to consider they had a very real threat on their hands; it was just that he couldn't, or wouldn't, get involved in their case right now.

Kwame almost got the impression that the shrink might be sceptical about how assiduously Dread was taking her stalking problem. It was true that ever since the pursuer had arrived, Dread was rarely out of the headlines, and sales, which had been faltering, had revived. Reading between the lines, the psychiatrist's cynical view might be that a stalker could be a rather convenient problem for some celebrities, and maybe he didn't hanker after becoming part of the circus.

'Look, Dr James doesn't want to be hired. He just wants a chat with you in private. What can the harm be? And you can use your womanly wiles to lure him in.'

'He doesn't have an explanation for the supposed panic?' Kwame realised that Dread hadn't come straight out and denied the anxiety attack theory. She might have clocked this recognition by him. Why did it feel like they were poised to open a can of worms with the potential to alter their relationship permanently? Dr James had a nasty habit of disturbing the equilibrium between people.

Kwame grasped that the shrink was part of the rest of the planet who believed she'd started out a nervous performer. In which case, as Dr James had queried, why was she so tense about anyone discussing the return of the panics? There was some aspect about all of that background which just didn't ring true, the doctor hinted. Kwame sensed Dr James's growing suspicions from the grilling he'd endured from the psychiatrist over *The Weakest Lip-Sync*.

Plus, the shrink asked, if this was simple stage fright, why did the Rose Bowl terror crash upon her in waves? She'd been panicky one moment and calm the next. Then the fright had rebounded back with a vengeance, Dr James explained, from his analysis of the video.

The pop star and bodyguard were glaring at each other, spiralling the tension.

'He's got theories. One is that it has something to do with the song you were singing. He said the phrase "Tears for Fears", which is also the name of the original group who wrote and performed the piece, was derived from a kind of psychotherapy referred to as Primal Therapy. The treatment became famous for John Lennon being a patient.'

'So?'

'So the song "Everybody Wants to Rule the World" came from a multiple platinum-selling album entitled *Songs from the Big Chair*. The big chair was a line from a bestselling book entitled *Sybil* which was based on a true story about a woman suffering from multiple personality disorder. Sybil only feels safe and complete in her psychoanalyst's big chair or couch. Dr James thinks the idea that the song is jinxed could be playing on your mind.'

'Jinxed?'

45

When I met you in the restaurant,
you could tell I was no debutante
Dreaming

'But why send it? He thinks we'll be interested in the meaning of the words? That they come from a song by – who was it?' William was chasing Gerrard up winding stairs.

'We're Googling it right now.' Tullia sounded as if she was reading from a menu of dubious dishes in a foreign restaurant she wanted to leave.

William smacked his head. A light bulb went on as if David's brooding flat was suddenly properly illuminated for the first time.

'Oh my days!' he exclaimed. 'In 1980, Arthur Jackson saw Theresa Saldana starring in the film *Raging Bull*. He seems to have fallen instantly and delusionally in love with her, but at some level he also appears to have understood they could never have a relationship. So he left his home in Scotland and went all the way to Los Angeles to kill her, get arrested, receive the death penalty, and then be united with her for eternity in the afterlife.'

'But Jackson doesn't fit Lewis's profile in any sense!' Tullia objected.

William set the handset on speaker phone and said, 'Jackson went to Saldana's home and waited for her. He stabbed her ten times when she left the house.'

'I know the case, Vilhelm. Saldana was lucky, she survived. But how can this possibly have anything to do with Philippa Foot and David Lewis?'

'Saldana was lucky twice over, Tullia. Jackson kept sending her threatening letters while in gaol,' William continued as they pounded up the narrow stairs towards the bell tower. 'But at the end of his sentence he was extradited back to the UK and found guilty of a murder committed years before the Saldana incident.

He died in a secure hospital over here.'

'So?' Gerrard asked.

'Don't you see? Lewis *wants* to be killed just as Philippa is executed so they're united in the afterlife, just like Jackson! We've got to alert everyone in the church that this is suicide by cop.'

'What?' Gerrard had paused at the foot of the final metal ladder to the bell tower.

'He's come here because it's where he's going to make his final confrontation of Philippa!' the psychiatrist almost screamed. 'He kept provoking you by trying to get closer to her when she was surrounded by armed officers, ensuring that this final time he gets taken out once and for all.'

'Vilhelm, you're getting hysterical,' Tullia said, but he could hear the alarm in her voice. 'You think David Lewis is in full control of his faculties – a psychopath rather than a psychotic?'

'He's pulled me out the congregation!' Gerrard's irritability was now directed at Tullia. 'That's counterproductive if Philippa is about to buy it.'

William was struggling to speak, so the sergeant stepped in.

'We went over to Ms Foot's office and there's a laser beam pointed at her window from the development opposite. David Lewis has been monitoring her conversations. It was Dr James who found it. He seems to be on to something.' The sergeant faltered over the words of support as Gerrard glared at him.

William regained control of himself.

'David Lewis was complaining of ringing in his ears. It's because he was hiding in the bell tower of the church. Security sweeps would've missed him because naturally they assumed no one could tolerate the sound of the bells.'

Gerrard peered up the ladder.

'OK, but down here she's surrounded by officers five-deep, so there's no way he's going to succeed.'

William almost wobbled with frustration.

'He doesn't want to actually get to her, to form a relationship like a classic erotomaniac. Listen to me! He wants to die with her!'

Another clue clicked into place inside William's spinning head. Lewis had left contaminated urine evidence he was taking the anti-psychotic drug chlorpromazine in the loo bowl back in his flat, which had been designed to show up on William's dipstick testing. Now it was becoming clear this was a ruse designed to lead to the conclusion he was psychotic, unpredictable, so the police would view him as too unstable to do anything other than pull the trigger should he get near the Foreign Sec.

William had always found the evidence over the chlorpromazine a curious slip up, given how meticulous Lewis had been in all his planning. Lewis had wanted them to believe he had been under care for years: a resistant, hopeless case. How could William explain all this to the people who should be protecting Philippa right now, but who weren't listening? He wanted to shriek at the top of his lungs so the reverb would bounce off the vaulted ceilings and finally enter Gerrard's brain.

'He thought only I would decode the message,' continued William. 'Because in a sense, the special relationship is with me, not just Philippa.'

'All right then, what do the lyrics mean? What's this message for?'

William was still working on this. 'Aaaah,' was all he could muster. Then he recovered.

'How assassins operate can influence each other. Robert Bardo read in the press how Arthur Jackson, who almost murdered Theresa Saldana, had used a detective agency to get the actress's address, so Bardo copied this and murdered Rebecca Schaeffer at the doorway of her flat in 1989. I think whoever Dread's stalker is has influenced David Lewis.'

After all, that wasn't important right now. How could they waste time debating here and not be pulling Philippa from this event?

'If they can't be united in life, he believes they will finally be joined in death,' he spluttered.

'Come again? Only this time use English!' pleaded Gerrard.

'There's a group of people, often very psychiatrically disturbed, usually severely depressed, who want to get killed by the police. It's a much better known phenomenon in the States, and it's called Suicide by Cop. David Lewis is endeavouring to be shot by your men.'

Gerrard and the sergeant swapped a look.

'This has been a suicide act all along. He *knew* that targeting someone like a Foreign Office Minister as a high-profile stalker would get armed officers on his case.'

'Like Anders Breivik,' said Gerrard. 'Have the one delusion, the one obsession, but be otherwise sane away from the borders of the central disturbance – a high IQ, a planner, methodical, and so very dangerous. So Breivik planned to be shot after his massacre?'

Gerrard must have been paying attention after all. He was also beginning to understand William's deduction.

'Prof, the most useful thing you can do is get over to the trauma unit at The London Hospital, right now,' William pleaded.

'Because Philippa's going to end up there?' Tullia was horrified.

'Yes, and you need to warn them that if she comes in having taken a hit, her serum potassium levels will be in her boots. And we need some paramedics here now.'

'Yes, and how to get them in through the riot of Dread fans out there in Trafalgar Square?'

Did Gerrard realise what he was saying? They were effectively marooned, cut off from outside help.

'Gerrard, I'm going to research the lines on the emailed picture, see what we can find out.' And with that, Tullia was gone.

One less thing to worry about.

'I know what you're doing – you're getting her to anticipate future regret. You did it to me in the chopper,' Gerrard snarled.

'And you never explained what database you got his DNA from.'

Gerrard seemed to be burning with rage. He gripped the rungs as they moved upwards through another floor as if practising for William's neck.

'Okay, okay, he made a false confession months ago when the Dread stalker thing was at its height. He came into a station and made a full confession that he was Dread's prowler. But he couldn't have been – he was on the wrong side of the earth when her notes were planted. He was rambling and chaotic, so he got dismissed as a crazy and sent on his way. I mean, *hundreds* of nutters were coming into stations all over the country and confessing. Because the case was a celeb the lads got carried away and took his blood, so we had his DNA on the database, but it wasn't legitimately obtained.'

William could have told them that the kind of person who stalked a politician usually had a different psychological profile to the type who pursued entertainers, if they had bothered to ask.

'Gerrard, all the details he gave you when he was arrested were false – all except his address. David *led* you to his flat – it was a set up. Even if he wasn't Dread's stalker, he caught on to the idea. That's why he's sent us this lyric now. He's copycatting her stalker.'

'We're going up to this bell tower! We're gonna clear this up once and for all,' the AC snapped.

The ladder vibrated alarmingly as they reached the bell chamber. Louvered windows sheathed dim light, but the bell-ringers were oblivious to the bubbling up of officers beneath them. They were clustered by their bell ropes, looking upwards. Being lowered gingerly by a cord, that must have been on some pulley far above where the bells were, was a black package, like a cocoon.

William was filled with trepidation.

'I thought you said you hadn't found anything.' Gerrard directed this accusingly at the ringers.

One of them explained, 'We began to look more closely when your men shouted up that we had to check again. We spotted this thing tied right up there among the bells.'

The pullers lowered the sack to the floor gently and uniforms sprang to the cloth and clawed it open.

A man's body spilled out on to the ground. The wrists and hands took up impossible angles.

'Jeezus,' Gerrard breathed.

William checked the body for injuries but couldn't find any. And the flesh was warm.

'This is not David Lewis!'

'I know *that*!' snapped Gerrard.

William checked the body's neck, then wrist.

'He's alive, just unconscious.'

'It's lucky we spotted it before we caught hold – he'd 'ave been crushed once the bells got going,' commented one of the ringers.

'People don't realise how heavy they are – it took twelve tonnes of copper to cast them,' another added.

The bell-ringers were clearly protective of their chimes.

William checked the body's eyes. 'I think he's been drugged. Now at least we know what David Lewis was using the medication for. He may never have been suffering from a treated psychosis, just using it as a ploy.'

'So you got it wrong,' accused Gerrard.

A great time to start point scoring, thought William.

'These are the clothes David was wearing when he escaped,' William pointed out.

'I know what's happened!' Gerrard snapped his fingers. 'This is one of the homeless people who are meant to take part in the service. David's replaced one. So we've gotta get back and stop the homeless bit.' Gerrard began issuing orders and the room emptied of uniforms. Then Gerrard was clattering back down the ladder.

'Hey, wait up! Are we meant to peal the bells as planned or not?' the chief bell-ringer yelled after them as they headed back down to the main chancel. 'And what are we meant to do with this body?'

'Gerrard!' William shouted as he followed. 'The hidden message in the emailed picture he sent. It's obviously a threat and we're meant to interpret it as such and be prepared to defend her, killing him as a result.' William missed the last few steps and just made it, stumbling to the bottom of the staircase without pitching into a gaggle of uniforms.

The sergeant had waited there. 'You mean you don't know where the line comes from?' He seemed surprised, but then embarrassed that he knew. 'Professor d'Aragona just messaged it in as well,' he said defensively. 'She also told me to tell you she was leaving immediately for The London Hospital's Trauma Unit.'

He paused, then added, 'It's a line from a song by Skip Spence, covered by Tom Waits. It's called "The Books of Moses".'

46

They tried to break us, looks like they'll try again
Wild Boys

'Okay, the jinx shit goes something like this. On the morning of 13 July 1985 Tears for Fears were scheduled to sing at the Live Aid concert. They didn't appear – a decision that apparently had been made right at the last second. There was even a rumour the band had splintered irrevocably on that day, over that concert and because of that song.'

Kwame was praying that Wikipedia had got all this dead-on as he had briefed William on this somewhat dubious basis. He appreciated that the psychiatrist had been disdainful about the veracity of some of these claims, given their source.

'Well, for Chrissake, thanks a bunch for that,' Dread said. 'If I wasn't worrying about it before, I sure am going to now.'

He ignored her. In the distance, hovering over the beat of the Pacific waves, he could detect the drone of the approaching press helicopter, which would be bristling with paparazzi. They didn't have much time to sort this out.

'Dr James said he had a theory which he could only discuss with you. Something about the wheel going round and round. Taking you back to somewhere. Look, I told him that now you didn't know the meaning of the word fear.'

'And what did clitface say to that?' asked Dread. She had to raise her voice to be heard over the rising flapping sound of rotor blades from the aircraft, still somewhere out of sight.

'Er, he said you didn't seem to know the meaning of most words.'

'What!'

The helicopter could now be seen storming towards them along the cliff edge from behind Kwame's shoulder.

'Something about your lyrics recently not being as good as…' Kwame shrugged. He pulled down his tracksuit hood as it flapped in the turbulence.

'What else did he say?' Dread's smile over her yelp had become that of a hangman inspecting a neck. 'I'm sure the insults didn't stop there.'

'He said your most recent lyrics were as thoughtful as the dialogue from a porno flick,' he bellowed back.

Kwame was perplexed as to why William had been quite so rude about Dread. He must have known his criticism was all getting back to the pop star and would seal his fate in terms of being hired by her.

But Dread looked like she was rapidly calculating the next bet in a high-stakes poker game. The chopper was hovering a few hundred yards away, facing them, the downdraught nearly pushing Dread's slight frame back into the grounds of the mansion.

Kwame felt the crew must be wondering what they were going on about, and why they weren't starting to run as per the schedule. As these aircraft were expensive and hired by the hour, Kwame could feel the photographers' impatience for them to get a move on and stop mucking about on the cliff top.

'We absolutely have to do a face to face,' she demanded, screaming at him now. 'Which means he *has* to fly here.' Her hair had unravelled in the whirlwind, so she looked a bit raving as it thrashed about her head.

Kwame struggled to hide his astonishment. She had never expressed such aggressive desire for any man before. She had never had to.

'But a talk on the phone is all he's offering,' he protested. Then he yelled it out again, as she seemed to turn away as if she hadn't heard him above the roar of the helicopter blades. The chopper retreated as the pilot anticipated she was finally beginning her run, and the reverberation lessened for a moment as the breeze off the crags fought back against the racket from the rotors.

But then she swung and lunged in close, her words bawling back at him like pummelling fists as she moved up to his face. The downdraught seized her shout and threw it echoing off the side of the cliff.

'In which case you're gonna have to snatch him. You think he's on to something and we need him, so he's got to come. Send Kristal in the jet – she can get any man to do anything. And… well…we've got an army of millions – they aren't called legions of fans for nothing. Either you or they are going to bring him to me.'

47

The man who invented plastic, saved my soul
Plastic Jesus

They scampered down the spiral staircase, boots tap dancing a riot of clanging on the metal steps. Then they squeezed through basement rooms, past ranks of TV cameras. An empty podium rebuked them – Philippa must have delivered her speech from there.

As they pushed through the press room, most of the crews were packing away equipment. But someone was playing back the recording of the press conference that had just ended on a screen.

'As a result of meeting those traumatised by the war I am announcing my intention to work much harder for peace in the Congo…'

Gerrard caught sight of William stopping to stare at the profound about-face in her attitude to the war.

'Yeah, came as a complete shock to her colleagues as well,' Gerrard said. 'She's renounced the war effort and resolved to work for peace.' He looked around warily and then leant in. 'The gossip is that this is her big play for the leadership of the party, 'cos it's put her in direct conflict with the PM.'

William figured Gerrard was warning him that he was beginning to meddle in affairs way above his pay grade. Instead, he was wondering, had the snipers and their trauma had a real impact on her?

It wasn't important now. Philippa would be up in the main church above them for the service of thanksgiving for the refurbishment of the church. The AC and his lieutenants were moving up the stairs, and all round them the stacked crowd was being squeezed into diversionary routes out of the building. There was no room to breathe.

The service had already started as they fought their way into the atrium alongside the main cavernous chamber. Gerrard's orders dropped to a whisper. The back rows were extracted with gestures from the AC's minions. The flock followed instructions, eyes wide with curiosity.

William was restrained by Gerrard.

'Keep back! If Lewis sees you he'll know the game is up.'

So the AC now agreed David was about to strike. *That's a lurch in the right direction*, William thought, nerves at full stretch.

'Doctor, Doctor, I keep thinking I'm invisible,' a familiar voice whispered.

William whirled.

'Who said that?'

'It's a joke, geddit?' Tom, the sniper from Bisley, waved his hand in front of William.

William was startled. He tried to grab Gerrard's sleeve to explain this new development, but the AC was shepherding officers ringing the edges of the main auditorium.

'What are you doing here?' William asked.

Tom turned to Carl.

'He doesn't geddit.' He turned back to William. 'A man goes to a psychiatrist and he says: "Doctor, Doctor, I think I'm invisible", and the psychiatrist says, "Oo said that?"'

Carl smirked, and William could now see that the sniper was cradling a long rifle in the folds of his civilian coat.

'You got taken on by Philippa?' The psychiatrist was swimming against a tidal wave of new information.

'Yeah, she wanted some specialist snipers on the protection team, and *voila*!' Tom gave a little bow.

Carl leant in conspiratorially.

'It didn't go down too well with these boys.' He nodded at the firearms officers on either side.

Tom shrugged. 'They think we're going to steal their thunder.'

Carl winked at William.

'And we are.'

Philippa found it reassuring to bring the military on board? Tom thought he was completely cured just because William managed to get him to hit one target?

Tom was being pulled away by Carl and officers were disappearing up some stairs.

'Wait a minute,' William called, 'where's Frances?' He suddenly realised that the sniper and the journalist were probably not far apart.

'Oh, don't worry – we said we ain't performing if they don't let 'er in.' Tom and Carl disappeared up the steps to the balcony encircling the upper levels of the main chamber. William searched for the journalist.

A phalanx of police wearing plain clothes sidled into the emptied back rows, some hiding Heckler and Koch semi-automatic carbines under their mufti. A special choir made up of the homeless was going to sing. Another complication was that the interfaith aspect of the service meant several choristers were wearing burkas and other national dress which covered their faces. They couldn't be asked to take them off. The psychiatrist and the cop both could anticipate the Foreign Secretary's reaction to that demand.

William, Gerrard and the sergeant crouched down the side aisle, crawling past the astonished parishioners. Officers following them, bent double, were gesturing for silence. Up on the gallery, creeping over the banister, were the dark thin shadows of sniper rifles.

48

Can the people on TV see me or am I just paranoid?
Somebody's watching me

'You do know your lips look like they're trying to eat your face?'

Mean's voice flew out of the gloom like a spear.

Inside, the limousine remained coffin black, the privacy glass resisting all efforts of the barrage of flashes to force entry. Hannah's brushes moved in a shadowy hustle across Dread's face. Dodging and batting at the make-up artist's hands with her mobile phone, Dread was looking preoccupied.

'Miffed, pay attention. Time to bail.'

Kristal waved dismissively at Mean. She was checking her BlackBerry.

'Come on! Time to roll! We're already late.' KT Mean cupped her hands to check on their progress through the darkened window, impatient to escape her sisters, but in the queue leading to the red carpet, the procession of limousines maintained a glacial creep.

'It doesn't matter. These film premieres always start way behind schedule,' Dread mused. 'And Kristal, you might wanna pay more attention to how you do the emerge.'

'Yeah, flashing your knickers as you get out the car and then doing the dress tug thing once you're out looks really *rookie*,' Mean chimed in.

'It's called the limo shimmy,' Dread intoned.

'Yeah, watch the pro. To what do we owe your silence throughout the ride? Meditating on Wilfrid Sellars's playlist for the wedding of the century?'

'I'm not gonna pick a fight with you, KT. All I'm sayin' is, why spend hours on the dress and make-up, and then roll out of the stretch like trailer trash on hen night?'

'Not going to pick a fight... Oh dear, what's up?' Mean enquired.

Dread debated for a second, but then confided.

'It's Robert. He's going to be out there doing the red carpet interviews for the BBC. So I'm cheesed. He took the opportunity of us flying him out here to be with me to lever himself into another gig. The jagoff's just using me to advance his career.'

Hannah disappeared towards the privacy glass division, rearming herself with more war paint.

'Well, you had fun last night, didn't you?' Kristal offered.

'Yes, but he got a free ride and then sharked the red carpet.'

'Celebrity stuff is not meant to be his bag anymore. He's meant to be a news journalist now,' Mean argued.

Dread was wary, waiting for the cutting remark. But it didn't come.

'What can you do? It was a freebie for the Beeb – and there's a kind of link. He's their foreign correspondent now, and the proceeds from this evening do go to the Care for Congo campaign.' Mean seemed sympathetic, but Dread remained wary. Whichever of the sisterhood secured the most desirable boyfriend automatically became the mark. KT Mean and Kristal Miffed were being unnaturally restrained, so they must be jockeying with each other, frantic for her summons to join the Wilfrid Sellars wedding gig.

'After tonight, when are you going to see him again?' asked Kristal, appearing to join the compassion convoy.

'Dunno, probably when we make the video for Care for Congo. We're flying into Africa in a few days, and he's going to be there to help with it.'

'The reason you allow him into your bed is because you think he's above the whole celebrity thing. But actually his teeth are brighter than he is.'

'KT, the reason you don't understand their relationship is because he doesn't always whisper your favourite words – "I'll buy it for you",' Kristal sniped.

'Kristal? Is that you? Sorry, in the dark I got confused with that fake tan. Anyway, it's such a pity to ruin such gorgeous blonde hair by dyeing your roots black.'

'KT, leave her alone.' Dread's tone warned them her last nerve was shredded, yet they were still trampling on it.

'Why don't you tell us the real reason you're upset with him?' Mean asked.

'Okay, Kwame flew Robert in, and as usual Kwame had his own agenda. That was the reason he did it, although it looked like our head of security was doing me a favour. He scanned Robert's mobile while he was dozing on our jet, and printed out some incriminating text messages. The dick-sneeze is such a player!'

'How many others?' asked Kristal.

'Philippa Foot. I Googled her. She's some MP always posing with guns. The hoe bloody stole that look from me.'

'So you told him he had to dump her.' Mean knew the form so well she was now bored and checking her lashes in a mirror. She motioned to Hannah for help.

'With you listening in, like you got him to dump that other woman?' Kristal asked.

'Yeah, some hack. Franny somethin' or other.'

'Frances Wright, actually. She's famous for her reportage on the war. Be careful if Robert's filming from the Congo. It could be a ruse, 'cos that journo is always out there sending dispatches back.' Mean liked to show off her role as the "Posh Spice" of the three sisters.

'Nah. Pretty unlikely. That's why you two should take a leaf. Getting your boyfriend to dump on the phone while you listen in is very effective. When Robert did it to this journo, it was ugly. She didn't take it at all well. She kept asking who the other woman was. She named me mostly, but she did mention the MP whore as well. She started to beg and plead and I had to hold back from shouting down the line, "Show some respect for yo'self, girl".'

'But you don't take any chances. You just get any man you're with to scatter dump all and sundry, even if he wasn't seeing them.' Mean said this as if she was explaining it to Kristal.

'Robert later told me that after she was axed, this journo turned up outside his flat in all the motorcycle gear on a bike. Looks like she thought it was my leather outfits and the bike stunts in the music videos which revved him up. He got worried she was going to start stalking him.'

'Did she?'

'No idea. No, I don't think so. Anyways that's not important now. I told him to axe Philippa, and he begged to be allowed to wait for a good moment 'cos she's 'aving a lot of stress with a stalker. He denied anything was going on between 'em now. Said it was historical...'

'Bet that didn't go down well.' Mean puzzled at Robert's naivety – that was the worst possible thing to have said to her sister. Philippa's fate was now sealed.

'"Stalker? Stalker? Hello? Hello?" I said. Trouble with a stalker – who the 'ell is she? I've 'ad *real* trouble with a stalker!'

'Philippa Foot? She's really famous, you 'tard!' Mean couldn't believe Dread's ignorance. 'She's the Minister for the Foreign Office. In the UK.'

'I don't care who she is, he's ditchin' her live on air with me listening in on his line.'

'Usin' one of Kwame's famous techno tricks?' Kristal asked.

'Is that the one where he fixes it so the mute button at the other end fails and you hear whatever they think is private?'

Leaving your mobile unsupervised in Kwame's vicinity meant stealth software covertly installed, his furtive gift to you.

'If she's a Minister he may not get through on the phone so easily,' Mean pointed out.

'Oh, he'll get through all right. Kwame found out from Robert's phone that she'd just sent him some texts and voicemails trying to track down a missing picture of him with her. It had sentimental value to the whore. Like it was the day they did it for the first time. Or something.'

'Oh Christ – and he's interviewing you on the red carpet now?' Kristal looked newly reluctant to leave the safety of the limousine.

The car swayed to a halt. The shadows of pulsing light from the cameras reached a crescendo.

'Get Kwame to disappear him,' suggested Mean.

Kristal reached for the handle, signalling the end of the group therapy session.

'Wait, let them do the entry,' Dread commanded. Hannah curled up in the back, her work done. Dread noticed she had sullenly flung her brushes across the back seat.

The door now opened a smidge and paused. *So it's Kwame himself*, noted Dread. Wails from the multitude pressing the crash barriers swirled around them. She looked up at him. In his dark glasses she could pick out the curved reflection of the firestorm of popping flash from the paparazzi and the crowds. He grinned. It was all she needed before going out over the top into the salvo of shouted questions and retina-searing blazes from the lights.

Intimate moments in the midst of the whirlwind.

That was what relationships in the eye of a media storm came down to. And she didn't have that with Robert Recorde, while Hannah seemed distant recently. Her beautician must be surly because of the severely limited places on the Dread entourage invited to the billionaire's private island.

Then the door was dramatically pulled back and Mean was on and liberated. She succumbed to the reflex and yanked her outfit down.

'I think she needs some fries to go with that shake,' Dread commented.

Smiling, Mean slowly turned and waved to the crowd who were now going hysterical. Her pirouette right in front of the door stopped the other two sisters making their entrance.

'Ah do decleah…' Kristal was looking up at her, waiting to be allowed out '…that she looks like somethin' the dawg's been hidin' under the porch.'

'Hold Kwame's hand,' Dread whispered tersely to Kristal, 'it looks much better.'

Kristal stepped out, head coming up. She stood regally – but then her hands flitted instinctively downwards to the folds created from sitting, shaking her body at the same time. Dread sighed. Kwame grinned at her again. She scowled.

A crescendo of calls from the mob pursued the two sisters prancing on the red carpet, turning, waving, grinning.

'Kristal! Mean! Over here!' bellowed the photographers.

Dread let the strobe pandemic abate, then settled an elegant gloved hand on Kwame's, levitating in one graceful shimmer.

He leant in to whisper in her ear.

'Please tell me you didn't mobilise the fans in the UK to get

291

to Dr James. I'm reeling him in, and we're all meant to be on the same side. Let me do it my way.'

Sunglasses shielding her from the stabbing pain of assaults by incandescent explosions, she rotated imperiously on Louboutin heels, waving at the crowds.

He tried again. 'If you're still upset about me liposucking Robert's phone, please, please don't take it out on him, or, ah, me, now. This is live before millions of people. And the Care for Congo Concert organisers are watching.'

49

She drives me crazy, and I can't help myself
She drives me crazy

Philippa Foot was either feeling the cold of the echoing chamber, or her pale make-up made her appear tired and drawn. Clenched back tight against her scalp, her copper hair seemed tinged with blood red, but that could have been the stained glass windows, which were blinding if you stared at them.

The church was crawling, literally, with security. William couldn't make out the faces of the choir. Several of the twelve figures were in monks' habits with hoods covering their heads.

The Minister for the Foreign Office contemplated the altar with an unfocused dreamy gaze, a ghost of a smile brushing her lips.

As he squinted around St Martin-in-the-Fields, cupping his hands to shield his eyes from the window glare, it suddenly came to William, with a conviction he rarely experienced, that Philippa and Robert had been inside the shrine the day that photo was taken. And somehow they had stolen a moment of what they believed was privacy – and used it like two teenagers in heat. This cavern had witnessed their foreplay. Tormenting mental images of Robert and Philippa entwined distracted the psychiatrist. Had David, stalking the Foreign Secretary, been a secret witness to some sex act here in the chancel?

Obsessed fan Robert Bardo had fatally shot Rebecca Schaeffer in the chest at close range on the doorstep of her apartment in 1989. He had become furious with the actress, because the 'goddess...too sweet, clean, and pure for (sex) fantasies' had moved on in her career from playing innocent roles to film a bedroom scene in a movie.

'Dr James says we need to pull the Foreign Secretary out,

now!' Gerrard appeared apologetic, and accusing, as he spoke to the Minister's people.

'And how is this going to look to the press?'

While her chief civil servant was arguing, Philippa turned and frowned at William. The psychiatrist was now behind her and her entourage in the second pew, crouching low so that no one up on the dais would see him.

'What on earth is going on?' she asked him. Her frown was in shadow. Through the enormous tinted windows behind, streaming sunlight threw a shadow play on the altar.

'We need to get you out of here, stat!' He leant in, his sweating hands trying to gain a purchase on the wood behind her.

'This is ridiculous!' she snapped. 'If there's a threat then let us know about it *before* public events, not during.' She shook her head at him. A glittering necklace embracing her neck quivered, setting her face ablaze.

An official turned to berate William in a tense whisper.

'You're preventing the Minister doing her job. Is Mr Lewis here now?'

'We don't know,' Gerrard said.

'Yes, definitely,' said William.

Philippa exchanged looks with her advisers.

The civil servant next to her pointed at the robed choristers.

'We can't hold someone down by gunpoint in the middle of a service and on an altar. Think of the headlines if we've got this wrong.'

'Listen,' William warned Philippa, 'we found out that you wrote to him, thanking him several years ago. He was involved in the transfer of the bells from here to Australia, remember?'

Philippa gave him a look that suggested he was raving. She began to play with her gold necklace, diamonds glittering among an interweaving leaf pattern, and from the gesture William knew she was getting so exasperated she was close to her limit.

'I've thanked thousands of people over the years in letters, how on earth would I remember that?'

'This is very, very important. *You* thanked him, which means if the Government gave Australia the bells, then you got something in return – what was it?'

'How the hell am I supposed to remember that?' Philippa asked helplessly of her staff. 'There were various gifts to this church: new windows, all sorts of stuff...oh, wait, yes I do remember! A lot of the trappings they sent to us just weren't suitable – they were too modern. The altar sculptures, that table, the pulpit and the stairs up to it, and even the crucifix, for example, needed altering. We had to ask them to send over some people to...'

At her gesture the group looked up at the large items of chancel furniture. Writhing figures fought all over the Lord's table, a gory war between good and evil. The pulpit and crucifix were extremely vivid.

William's mind was racing. So David had been part of the process by which new, large objects had been placed in the church. Was there a bomb hidden in one of them? Some kind of booby trap?

He turned to the AC.

'Ah, Gerrard, can we have a word?'

But the AC motioned at a choir who were surrounding the altar. The service was beginning, so he dragged the psychiatrist into a seat.

50

I sometimes lose myself in me
Things can only get better

Dread glided backwards along the red carpet, unhurriedly beaming at the screeching clamour, the diamonds clasping her neck scintillating in the night sky. Long lenses followed her like snipers on a target. On one side, hovering in the periphery of her vision she could also make out the inevitable small but vocal group of demonstrators holding up banners about her degradation of religion. Fashion journalists, clustered on the other edge of the red carpet, swirled, barking into the cameras.

Dread is wearing a long gold dress by designer Oscar de la Renta, and I can see dazzling sequins and small metallic ribbons all over it. This gorgeous champagne tulle gown bears gold paillette embroidery, and she is accessorised with a Hilde Palladino haute couture sesame clutch, gold satin Wagner pumps by Valentino and white gold jewellery by Graff. The Hollywood gossip might be that the movie is yet another example of her terrible taste in films to star in, but no one could ever fault Dread's appearance. From her look alone on the red carpet of this premiere, she deserves best picture from the Academy tonight.

Kwame shuffled out of shot, but kept close, scanning the throng.

'You look absolutely stunning!' he whispered. Her sisters gracefully drew alongside in a choreographed posing routine. Kristal Miffed and KT Mean twinkled on either side of Dread, both arms draped casually around the youngest sister's neck and hips.

'Thank you, girls, now can we have one just with Dread?' the cameramen shouted. The girls dutifully peeled away, swishing over to a line of admirers to sign autographs.

Dread paused for the barrage of flash explosions, then was striding to follow her sisters when Kwame's hand gently but firmly pulled her back.

'I don't want you up close and personal with a crowd of fans for the time being,' he said. 'I took a phone call from Dr James a short while ago, and we need to alter our plans a little. He went through the file we left him and he's found something else.'

'Neither Dominique nor Mum are gonna like it if I don't press flesh with the fans.'

'Forget them. I've dispatched both to Dom's favourite occupation – inserting the latest press release into all the goody bags in the auditorium. Look, we need to talk about the stalker.'

'And why are we discussing it here?'

'Because it's urgent. Firstly, Dr James says that after scrutinising the video of the last concert at the Rose Bowl, he noticed a couple of significant things happened that we missed.'

'You mean *you* missed, and Han Fei your super psych?'

'Yes.'

They both smiled at the welcoming line of video cameras from the major networks. But while beaming and nodding, she and Kwame continued their whispered tense conversation.

'See, he thinks that when you fell into the audience, someone tried to take a blood sample from you.'

'*What?*'

'He says that sometimes stalkers, who are toppling off the side of a cliff in terms of psychosis, develop very strange beliefs, and someone wanted your blood. So they tried to stick a syringe in your arm when you were out there in the middle of the swarm. Remember? When you fell into the crowd? If you look at the video of you on top of the wheel afterwards – I went over the frame numbers with him – there's a scratch running down your arm, and a puncture point, but we don't think they actually got anything out of you. So I don't want you anywhere near this kind of free-for-all. They tried once, for whatever sick reason, and this means they may try again.'

51

It's a habit of mine
To watch the sun go down

The bishop came forward to the main lectern and welcomed the assembly. The amplification system was particularly finely tuned, and something about the edginess of the sound made William shiver.

The sermon became difficult to hear because the beat of a distant police helicopter gradually got louder. Philippa grimaced in exasperation at this intrusion as the bishop began explaining that the choristers behind him had all been helped by the projects at St Martin's.

Tullia was furiously texting information on the lyrics David Lewis had sent. The song was by a musician, Skip Spence, who'd had a nervous breakdown in 1968. He'd been admitted to Bellevue Psychiatric Hospital following an attempted axe attack on various people, including chopping down the hotel door of a band member in an apparent attempt to kill. It looked like his psychosis had been sparked by an overdose of LSD.

The story sounded like one of many about a talented career blighted by mental illness and poor treatment. On discharge from the hospital, apparently still wearing the institution's nightclothes, Skip Spence seems to have ridden his motorbike all the way to Nashville to cut the solo album on which this song had appeared. Did that mean the lyrics had been written in the midst of a breakdown?

A pulpit supported by some curved wooden stairs was off to the bishop's left. He turned and climbed up them as he addressed the congregation. Now he stood above them. Behind was a towering crucifix which threw a shadow over him as he moved around, making it difficult to see his face.

William fought to keep his concentration on the fragments of the puzzle.

The bishop half turned and gestured at the crucifix, explaining that its installation was made possible by various charitable donations directly facilitated by Philippa Foot. She had assisted in a project, begun many years ago but only just finished, whereby gifts from Western Australia had finally been integrated into the church, including twelve tonnes of Australian copper to forge new bells.

This just made William ever more convinced they had inadvertently stepped into a giant elaborate trap constructed by the deranged architect. In time, pews became obstacles to the security squad surrounding the Foreign Secretary, while the constrained exits now seemed impeccably planned to ensnare a panicking congregation and transform this meditative service into murderous anarchy.

The bishop's amplified voice echoed down the church hall and rebounded. Even William, who wasn't religious, had to acknowledge that the figurines across the altar and pulpit and the cross with the body of Christ were magnificent in their intricate depictions. There was something almost intimate about the detailing.

The congregation burst into spontaneous applause which sounded like gun-fire.

William jumped.

Philippa turned, acknowledging the church with a curt nod and a smile. William again noticed the dramatic necklace gracing her slender neck. He leant in to examine it, but she pulled away from him. He could make out a pattern of leaves intertwined with gold, possibly platinum and diamonds. He raced back mentally to the clip of the press conference Philippa had given just before the service, where she announced her change of heart over the war, filmed while Gerrard and he had been galloping up the stairs to check the bell tower.

But she wasn't wearing this ribbon of jewels then.

'Where'd you get the necklace?' He leant forward, reaching for it.

'Mind your own business,' she snapped back.

'Someone gave it to you just now, right?'

'It's a gift from an unimpeachable source, and no, it's not got a bomb hidden inside it.' But the fact she was bothering to answer his apparently inane questions meant the jewellery was significant somehow. Her hand reached up to stroke it.

'We screened it comprehensively and it comes from someone we both know and have cleared.' Gerrard bristled. 'It's negative for anthrax so...'

'Listen to me! Take it off, now! You might as well be hanging a target around your neck.' As William reached for the clasp behind Philippa's neck, Gerrard grabbed his hand.

'We checked it out, top and bottom, and besides, it's simply too expensive to be part of any plot. It's platinum, gold and diamonds.'

William wasn't sure precisely what it was that drew his attention to one of the choir. But there was something about the way his hood was fitting, and for William a religious delusional syndrome was getting more likely. Was it the psychiatrist's imagination or was this obscured face throwing sidelong glances at Philippa?

She leant back. 'Look, William, forget the necklace, it's a red herring. I know who it came from with absolute certainty because the note with it thanked me for a very special gift I gave them. Only one person in the world knows about that.'

People grumbled as William squeezed by them. Philippa turned, aggravated at the disturbance.

'William, for Chrissake be still!' she hissed.

William was hauling her out of the pew into the aisle. He had to get her out, but she yanked back.

The stalker had blamed her because she had exercised a sexual preference – it was one of the dumb things obsessionals did. If only he could get the professors at the Institute to realise why stalking had risen to such dramatic proportions in recent years. As modern societies advanced, and women became ever freer to exercise choices, it left an unselected group of resentful men unable to connect using normal means. These became stalkers. In the more distant past, others – their parents, guardians, brothers – had made choices for women. Society had condemned the spinster, and lauded the woman who was a wife. This was why many men, no matter how unpalatable, got dates and spouses.

It was what Jane Austen was all about, really.

Out of the corner of William's eye, he noted with horror that the bishop had invited one of the choir to give a reading. It was the man who had been glancing at Philippa. And at the lectern, he was just five metres from her, staring directly at her, ignoring the book in front of him.

'This reading is from Numbers 31:13–18: *And Moses, and Eleazar the priest, and all the princes of the congregation, went forth to meet them without the camp.*'

His voice was rising.

'*And Moses was wroth with the officers of the host, with the captains over thousands, and captains over hundreds, who came from the battle.*'

With each quote, he appeared to be shouting, and then screaming at Philippa.

'*And Moses said unto them, "Have ye saved all the women alive?"*'

Gerrard held a protective arm around Philippa and was trying to back her away, but she was still resisting.

'*Behold, these caused the children of Israel, through the counsel of Balaam, to commit trespass against the Lord in the matter of Peor, and there was a plague among the congregation of the Lord.*'

'It's just a reading!' William heard her protest.

'*Now therefore kill every male among the little ones, and kill every woman that hath known man by lying with him.*'

The hooded figure at the podium began gesticulating at Philippa and the folds of his monk's habit flapped in agitation. From brief glints of exposed corneas, William decided the man was in fact staring at Philippa's decorated neck.

'*But all the women children, who have not known a man by lying with him, keep alive for yourselves.*'

Then William saw it.

The bishop and churchwardens were swapping weary glances. They had seen this before. They were used to this person's tendency to go off message. If they knew him so well as to exchange this exhausted look, it couldn't be David – just someone who was a bit chaotic.

'*Now therefore kill every male among the little ones, and kill every woman who hath known a man by lying with him.*'

Another member of the choir moved towards the reader, hands outstretched in a calming gesture. He rested a hand on his shoulder, but the reader lurched towards Philippa. He did have a kind of twitch – was it the akathisia that David seemed to suffer from? Or, come to think of it, had that been an act the stalker put on to distract the psychiatrist? Had he been setting up this fall guy to be the target to play his role in the moment of maximum distraction?

William had indeed been feverishly scanning the congregation specifically for involuntary body movements – mentally skipping over anyone or anything that was perfectly tranquil. If that had been a diversion strategy by a devious mind, then maybe he should be doing the very opposite – focusing on anything that became hidden by remaining absolutely motionless.

What in life was immobile? Nothing.

The dead – the dead were still.

Very still.

'That Bible reading seems to have something to do with David's message. The song "The Books of Moses". Is there a link?' whispered the sergeant to William.

'What?'

Coiling figures were surrounding Philippa. The drill of an anticipated attack on the Minister had been triggered.

Flecks of spit glistened on the reader's chin. The police were un-holstering their Glocks. Someone barked 'Halt!' The clicks of safeties being withdrawn echoed about the gilt-edged high chamber.

Unexpectedly the organ emitted a strange sound like a needle being ripped across a vinyl record. William jumped. The noise swelled up in volume and began to blare; hands instinctively blocked ears. The sergeant was mouthing something at William and pointing up at the glistening silver pipes above the nave. The blast turned into the opening bars of the famous Bach Toccata, menacing and grand, as if heralding a fateful event.

The psychiatrist got the gesture. Was that David up in the organ loft? Then the church bells began to peal.

The policeman next to William shouted something incomprehensible into his walkie-talkie while freeing his weapon from his jacket. He pointed his strapped machine gun at the drunken movements of the reader, who kept staggering like a puppet towards Philippa. She should have found herself surrounded by officers hustling her away, but the flock was shifting.

Uniforms were shouting at the choristers by the altar. The congregation, disorientated, surged backwards and forwards, looking for a way out. But they were trapped, encircled by armed officers. No clear voice could be discerned above the swelling cacophony of the organ. The bishop on the top of the pulpit was waving frantically across the cavernous chamber to where the organ player would normally sit.

William realised that if the organ had also been a gift from Australia, then it could have been rigged to detonate in sound. Then he grasped that if the enormous bells were booby-trapped to fail their supports, abruptly falling, their immense weight would plunge through the cathedral, destroying it, crushing anyone below.

Officers clambered through the uproar to get to Philippa. There was a thunderclap as pews fell over.

Philippa's eyes rotated wildly until they locked with William's.

The reader was confronted by officers mounting the stairs to the altar. Screeching organ music and resounding chimes smothered their demands. William was stunned at the disorientation rebounding off the walls. The skirmishing mob were screaming at each other, terror in their stretched faces.

A new voice towered even higher above them.

William wheeled, searching desperately for the origin. It was an echoing, booming utterance from the heavens, as if God was speaking to them at last in His house, amplified above the music but too distorted for the words to come through.

The puppet who'd been reciting biblical verses ceased. He cowered on his knees, hands up before a semicircle of snub-nosed semi-automatics.

The group of officers surrounding Philippa was battling her away. She seemed to glint in the melee. The wooden sculpture adorning the crucifix right at the back of the altar, halfway up the wall, shifted. The Christ figure was writhing. One wood-brown arm had detached itself from the cross, waving something admonishingly at Philippa.

It was a gun.

William froze with shock.

The life-sized wooden Christ on the crucifix was shouting, bellowing, but his words were lost in the huge grinding music. The reader panicked. He thrust to his feet and careered off the steps, colliding with Philippa. In his pulpit, the bishop had turned and was transfixed by the man twitching on the crucifix.

The Christ figure was David Lewis.

Flashing detonations blinded William while deafening thwacks pummelled his ears. The candles on the altar exploded in the hail of bullets, and the flames fled on to the white cloth. Something invisible clawed violently at Philippa and spun her. She pirouetted before falling into Gerrard's arms, crashing down as he dropped her. Banging her head on the stone floor, she went still.

Shimmering red dots from laser rifle sights peppered the writhing Jesus while the chatter of firing weapons shook the church. The stained glass in the windows behind the altar shattered into shards of gleaming rainbow light. The downdraught from the police helicopter hovering outside flung the slivers at the congregation, who buckled in front of the wave. Fittings swayed and fell. David jerked. His hand convulsed, the gun spilled from his limbs, and he collapsed, slumping on his harness.

William wanted to bawl: 'Cease fire!'

What he did shout was, 'It's the antichrist delusion. He thinks he's the antichrist – he believes he should be killed to save others from himself.'

William saw it now. David had witnessed Philippa and Robert perform some sexual act in the church, and this had sparked, or consolidated, the delusion.

Slowly the cross, and David, twisted forward and crashed on to the pulpit. The bishop was scrabbling into the air, extending himself far out as if to help the figure. The force of the falling structure and man cracked the pulpit apart, so the bishop was catapulted over the side, rolling down the curved staircase while the banister shredded and splintered. An avalanche came down on the altar as a consequence, and a jagged stake, jutting from the shattered bannister, speared through the bishop's neck. A fountain of arterial spray blotched the white draping across the altar.

As a pool of crimson spread beneath the bishop, it reached out to ripple down, joining the flow from David's bullet-torn body.

The sweet reek of gunpowder assaulted William's nostrils and woke him up like smelling salts. As the upturned candles flung blazes across the shrine, the tang of burning arrived.

'Let me through, I'm a doctor!' William shouted.

From being frozen, he now heaved pews and people away. He helped Gerrard rest Philippa on the cold church marble, tore off her jacket to get a better look and pressed hard, scrunching it up on the side of her stomach to staunch the blood. He applied all the pressure he could muster, but his hands were trembling. She was in shock, not truly comprehending that the top of her head looked like it had been ripped open by a bullet. Conscious and breathing, she was no longer aware of her surroundings.

Gerrard looked at William, pale with fear.

'She's got a scalp laceration from the fall,' William announced, examining her, 'and it looks like she took a hit in the abdomen somewhere.'

He pulled off his tie with his other hand and whipped it around her head, fashioning a bandage. There was blood everywhere, and he tried to check through the mess and matted hair whether there was another wound.

'We need some oxygen,' he demanded, and looked up. The police, mysteriously, had their guns trained on them both.

William motioned to the sergeant to keep the pressure on Philippa's wound and pulled Gerrard away.

'She needs to get to hospital, quickly – she might have a head wound as well. It's difficult to see properly with all that muck in her hair.'

'But all those Dread fans rioting out there mean no ambulance is going to get through,' Gerrard barked back, 'not even the motorcycle paramedics.'

William was yanked away by officers who wanted his help elsewhere.

The reader was spreadeagled, back arched off the steps joining the altar to the nave. Gurgling noises were coming from his neck. His hands were reaching for his throat, but he couldn't seem to use them. The fingers shook. And then he lay still. A loud sigh followed the end of the horrible wet breathing.

Bullets had lacerated his throat. The blood loss was massive – there was no pulse.

Others were calling William; he had to move.

The bishop's lifeless eyes appeared to be turned to where the cross had been. His last thought must have been an encounter with his saviour.

William crunched through broken glass and crouched next to David's body.

A hand on his neck couldn't locate a beat.

William realised dimly that he must be in shock, given that he was still searching for signs of life while the evidence of death from multiple fatal bullet wounds was unmistakeable.

David's still eyes met William's. They seemed disappointed and his skin was moist and warm to the touch. Brown paint came away on William's fingers and the organ was suddenly stilled.

Silence arrived, deafening and disorientating in its own way.

Gerrard stepped up and kicked a mammoth revolver away from where it had toppled from David's hand.

'Smith & Wesson Magnum 500 – the most powerful production handgun. Exactly the kind of weapon a professional would use…'

Every word sounded like a curse as William was dragged away by the sergeant.

'The antichrist delusion,' William mumbled, too quietly for anyone to hear, though he found it comforting listening to himself. 'A rare delusional-misidentification syndrome where the patient comes to believe they're the antichrist. Often lasts for decades undetected. Best description is in a paper by Arturo Silva, Robert Weinstock and colleagues entitled "Violent Behaviors Associated with the Antichrist Delusion" published in the *Journal of Forensic Sciences*. Some become hostile and threaten to kill, believing they're fated to perpetrate evil. Others believe governments fear their power as the antichrist and have implanted electronic devices in their heads to monitor them, while others have kidnapped and raped.'

William went back over to Philippa. Her eyes were closed and she was breathing more shallowly. Paramedics were working on her, and an oxygen canister had been found.

'These lads were already on the scene – we still aren't going to get a vehicle in, and the air ambulance is deployed down to the south and can't get back,' Gerrard explained before turning away to bellow into his phone.

Then William remembered. The clinical vignette after his own life story had been about the antichrist delusion. David had even done William the courtesy of sending him his own diagnosis – a kind of double narcissism. But, of course, William had been too self-obsessed to get past the vignette concerning himself and look properly at the second one, which had in fact been all about David.

He went back to Philippa and helped keep the oxygen mask on her face while paramedics worked to deal with the abdominal wound properly. Clenched in her fist was the necklace, and she released it into his hands when he tried to hold her fingers.

More movement at the back caught his eye. By the main rear door Frances was watching William cradling Philippa's head. His eyes locked with Frances's. She turned and ran out.

'Gerrard!' William shouted. The AC elbowed his way through the crowd of officers surrounding him. 'Gerrard, if you can't use the air ambulance, and nothing will get through on the road, then let's use the police chopper!'

'What?'

'It's very unorthodox, sir.' One of the paramedics stood up to complain.

'But you have good cervical spine control, and if it's the only way to get her to The London – and she's losing a lot of blood,' William pressed as Gerrard stood torn between the ambulance workers shaking their heads.

'Get it to land in Trafalgar Square,' William panted. He turned to the paramedics. 'I need some bottles of Isoflurane,' he demanded. 'You know, the anaesthetic.'

William's phone buzzed so he turned away from their

complaining that they didn't understand what he was going on about, and why Philippa would need that. The request had the desired effect: Gerrard seemed to make a decision, ordering them to do what William asked. The AC needed to re-establish a sense of control.

William looked at his buzzing phone absent-mindedly, still dazed. His fingers were covered in blood and soiled the handset. Had he been hit and not realised it? Reaching up to his forehead, his hands came away with grit. His brow must have been lacerated by flying glass from the shattered windows.

He wiped the blood off the phone with his sleeve, trying to make the screen readable.

Glowing through the crimson smear was a text from Tullia. *Might be useful to know, Skip Spence when he attacked a band member with an axe is thought to have believed he was the antichrist.*

The broken windows vibrated and tinkled, announcing that the chopper was coming in.

52

I could make you an offer you can't refuse
Whatever you want

Kwame disappeared back down the red carpet after motioning to another clump of his security staff to move over and stand by Dread.

But steaming up the aisle towards her was the one person he couldn't protect her from right now in front of all the lenses at a movie premiere – it was Robert Recorde, with his camera crew tailing him. He waved his microphone at her, grinning inanely.

Oh, this is all I need, she thought.

'Hello, Dread! This is Robert Recorde from the BBC. Would you say a few words to us?'

'Why yes, of course!' Dread glared at the audience. Their excited voices had fallen into a hush. Her long gloved hand reached out to straighten the black tie Robert wore with his tuxedo.

I even bought you that for tonight. You fell off my jet not realising it's black tie – I've got to do everything for everybody, Dread fumed.

'So, Dread, tell us – what is the movie about?'

You're meant to comment first on how lovely I look, you prat, she thought.

'Robert, I enjoy these little chats. But let's not forget the important thing tonight is that we're raising money for the Care for Congo campaign – have you given anything?'

Robert nervously laughed.

'Well, Dread, I'm covering the story of the war. The minute I finish here I'm going back to the Congo.'

'Oh dear, haven't they suffered enough already?'

'So listen, Dread, thank you so much for talking to us...'

'I think you should donate this!' she said as she grabbed his Chopard watch. She had always wondered how he could afford it, and now she had her suspicions. Its glinting in the spotlights seemed to be mocking her. She deftly undid the crocodile strap, despite his attempt to wrestle away, and triumphantly held it up to the crowds.

'I'm going to donate it for the charity auction later tonight. That's okay, isn't it?'

Encouraging applause percolated from the barriers.

'Errr' was all he could muster, 'could I donate…something… else?'

She turned it over. 'Wow, it's so heavy, is that all real gold? It must be worth a fortune.' The cameras converged on the twinkling orb as she juggled it with her white silk gloves.

Robert's grin had frozen.

The transparent back of the case revealed a finely jewelled beating movement, decorated in glittering italic with the inscribed words: *All My Love, P.*

Dread then reached for his trouser crotch.

'What about donating this lovely tuxedo as well? What is it, buttons or zip?' Robert backed away again, warily. 'Oh, it's buttons! Is that because sheep can hear a zip at 100 yards?'

She turned on her Louboutins and marched away.

There was a silence, but then some of the crowd drunkenly cheered, a splatter of clapping.

Kwame fell into step beside her, fending off other camera crews that had been hovering like fireflies. Dread flung Robert's watch at him in fury and the bodyguard only just caught it.

She irately brushed aside a camera crew from Fox News trying to secure an interview. Kwame and she continued angrily whispering at each other in the midst of a press melee, marching up the red carpet to the cinema entrance. As they made it into the auditorium, illuminated only with dimmed lights, she was flustered and breathing heavily.

'Look, I'm sorry about back there. It was my bad idea to bring him in on the jet,' Kwame began apologetically. 'It's my fault.'

She held up her hand.

'No, he's just a lameass pillock. This is ridiculous. I'm *so* hot, and what do I get? The useless piece of skin on a penis called a boyfriend.'

A gawping usher showed her to her seat laden with the usual goodies. The auditorium darkened and Dread offered the bag disdainfully to her neighbour, who was more interested in its contents than the donor. The gloom hid the most famous face on the planet from everyone adjacent.

The person sitting next to Dread excitedly leafed through the chocolates, advertising cards and bottled water in the goody bag she had contemptuously passed on.

'Hey, you've got something we haven't!' the neighbour announced and produced a letter.

Kwame moved to place himself between Dread and the neighbour, who was agitatedly waving a thick envelope. It was glowing eerily, the paper inside it fluorescing.

Kwame put away his portable black light and swooped on the envelope. 'I'll take that.' He grabbed Dread and yanked her up, then slit the wrapping and scanned it as he pushed her back past the seating. His head came in close to her, eyes inside the dark glasses probing the pitch black theatre, aware that all ears were invisibly straining to hear.

How come the star of the show was leaving early?

He whispered to her, 'This is another one of those douchebag notes! We need that shrink, like, yesterday.'

53

My, my, the sky will cry
Senses workin' overtime

'The line's not good. Are you patched through from the radio somewhere?' Tullia demanded.

'Yeah, we're in an ASU on our way to The Royal London. Our other chopper took Philippa there with William on board. They think she has a scalp laceration from when she fell. Her abdomen took a ricochet, but they've stabilised the blood loss.' The AC's voice was tense. 'We couldn't wait for the air ambulance, it was busy out to the south – the roads over there are utter pandemonium and there's been several pileups. We've got traffic chaos all the way out to the southern stretch of the M25 because there are rumours that Dread is flying in, so her fans are wreaking havoc. As they did besieging the church. Tullia, we need to find William before the press do.'

'Don't worry about William,' she said coolly. 'He'll see no good in anyone starting the blame game.'

'She took a hit from a high-velocity weapon, the kind only a professional assassin would use. Like I've been complaining about all along, a terrorist.'

'Gerrard, what are you saying?'

'But the chopper's been on the roof at The Royal London for fifteen minutes, so where is Dr James?'

'You mean he's missing?'

'He's not missing.' Gerrard sounded irritated at the implication. 'We know where he is – he helped the crew bring Philippa down to the trauma unit, and then I have reports of him donning a white coat, and then…well, I put several officers on to keeping tabs on him, but now I can't raise them either. But they're four of my best men – even William can't overpower four officers.

I divided the protection squad in two – half to guard the Foreign Secretary and the other half to keep an eye on William.'

Tullia was worried William was doing something impulsive and silly. But what? It seemed that Gerrard's plan was now focused on keeping William and Philippa apart. Was the fact the pop star was flying in a mere coincidence, or was William up to something in that department? But he couldn't stand her. Should she, Tullia, try to set up a meeting with Kwame so they didn't lose that contract?

'We have the hospital surrounded and a total security lockdown around Philippa, so he can't get out. He's there, Tullia. And *you* need to find him. Immediately. He's a loose cannon. What if he talks to the press?'

'I think he's going to want to be close to Philippa now. I'm going up to the trauma unit.'

'Okay, I'll tell her security to let you in.'

Tullia found the neurosurgical team hovering near the doors to Philippa's room. They had been bantering with the armed police who seemed to fill the corridor, and who carefully checked the professor's ID, called a superior, and then let her through. All this was partly to keep William out?

'Tullia!' The consultant surgeon greeted her warmly. 'Good news – the head wound is an uncomplicated laceration from the fall, and she's now semi-conscious.'

'Can I go in?' the professor asked.

'Yes, but not for long. She's a bit incoherent – must be the shock and the anaesthetic. Um, listen, she went a bit crazy when she discovered we had to shave all her hair off to repair the scalp wound. Um…could you explain to her it was a surgical thing, we needed a clear field to do the suturing…'

'Only William could calm her down,' Tullia muttered to herself.

'Oh yes, by the way, that colleague of yours, Dr William James. He warned the paramedics in the helicopter that her serum potassium levels would be in her boots, and indeed they were! The levels came back from the initial blood gases. But how did he know? The officers back there were saying he's some kind of clairvoyant. It meant we got some potassium into her drip straight away, which was life-saving.'

'I'm not sure how he knew,' she replied, having wondered herself when he'd told her. Cautiously she entered the private room. Philippa's head was almost entirely bandaged. All that could be made out was the blink of her eyelids, staring upwards.

'Philippa, it's Tullia. How are you doing?'

The blinking accelerated.

'You're searching for William? He's missing?' The Minister's voice was different, weaker.

'Yes, as a matter of fact... We – ah – we're looking for him. How did you know?'

Philippa turned her head slowly, painfully, towards Tullia. The surgical team had begun to crowd in.

'I know he's gone into hiding and you're looking for him. Seen him? Me? Yes, no. Sort of,' Philippa rambled.

'He's definitely not here,' one of the doctors said.

'Yes, he is,' Philippa mumbled.

Nobody listened.

Tullia had to consider that Philippa was in shock and might say anything, her brain scrambled by the carnage she'd been a part of, plus losing her crimson mane.

'Should we talk about this now?' Tullia said soothingly. 'You need to rest, you've had a close shave.'

Philippa laughed bitterly.

'Ha! Yeah, well they have indeed shaved my hair off, so no public appearances for a while. I'm going to have to pull out of the party leadership contest.'

'But you're alive and the stalker is dead,' Tullia protested. 'Things will go back to how they were.'

Even now, she's obsessed with her career, Tullia pondered. Philippa believed her flowing locks were her greatest electoral asset.

'Gerrard is going to try and close FTAC. He was looking for an excuse. That bloody newshound, Frances Wright, will be pleased. She always believed it was just a way of locking up undesirables.'

Tullia bridled. 'People present themselves through their communications or actions, and most of the fixated are mentally

314

ill. William's convinced that if he gets them treatment they will get better and cease the fixated threat. The interests of protection and public health overlap completely.'

Philippa just laughed bitterly. 'For all William's loopy spaniel eyes as he follows you about the place, it's when this happens to you' she gestured at her shaved head 'and no one's going to want you anymore, you realise he still would.'

'I suppose...' Tullia sounded doubtful. Was this hallucinatory rambling from the concussion or the anaesthetic from Philippa's operation?

Philippa was breathing deeply, trying to regain composure. 'All your resources couldn't keep him out. It was what William said all along: the lone individual obsessed. You've got to understand them, get them treatment rather than just trying to stop them.'

'Those papers and books on stalking that William sent you right back at the beginning...' Tullia tried to sound casual. 'Did you show them to anyone else?'

Philippa seemed distracted by Tullia's questions, which made it more likely she was going to tell the truth.

'Of course, they were fascinating! The team showed them to colleagues. And some of the people working on remodelling St Martin's found some of William's stuff in our papers on the church and asked for copies. It was going to help them understand the church's needs when helping the homeless and mentally ill. And...'

'And?' Tullia leant forward.

'...there was Bulgakov's architect. He wanted help with the security systems they were putting in across the road from my place – state of the art. They were going to share some of the technology with us, so I helped him by getting my people to pass over William's stuff on stalking. Apparently the oligarch had a lot of problems back in Russia...y'know...along these lines.'

So that explained how David knew more than a little about stalking, and ended up even sounding a bit like William: Philippa had been trying to get close to Bulgakov.

But there had also been something competitive about David's incessant attempts to demonstrate his superior knowledge of stalking and psychiatry. Tullia mused on the stalker's surveillance of Philippa, which probably extended back for quite a period. He would have observed her attachment to William gradually develop. The psychiatrist had, after all, been lobbying the Member of Parliament for years to change the legislation on stalking – long before he joined FTAC.

It had been the case of Rana Faruqui, stabbed to death by her former partner Stephen Griffiths, that had in fact brought them together.

'Do you remember how you first met William?' Tullia asked.

'What? Oh, you mean the case with that poor woman? The one who kept reporting being harassed by her ex, but the cops did nothing. On her final visit to the local police station, she complained her ex-turned-stalker had cut the brake pipes on her car, but even then the police failed to follow up her report.'

'Yes, that's the one. The case affected you, and as a result you sought to change the law.'

'Yeah, William drew my attention to her tragedy. Somehow he knew I would find it profoundly disturbing that despite her repeated complaints to the police, she was not better safeguarded from him.'

David Lewis would have witnessed the fact that Dr William James was the only outsider of her well-heeled circle to penetrate Philippa's guard successfully. Consumed with envy, he had then endeavoured to out-shrink the doctor, just as John Hinkley's obsession with impressing Jodie Foster had culminated in an assassination attempt on Ronald Reagan.

'But you don't understand, Tullia! William even managed to get a message to me. Here. Despite the fact I'm surrounded by extra security. Please listen!' Philippa didn't normally do pleading, and the unexpected wheedle in her voice snapped Tullia back into the room.

'Just because he's an expert doesn't mean he's going to be able to penetrate Gerrard's security better than...'

Tullia trailed off and looked around nervously. It's the Resentful Stalkers who are possibly most dangerous, driven by a grievance and a sense of absolute righteousness.

'If Gerrard is chasing him down, the hunter and the hunted have swapped places.' Philippa rested her head back dreamily.

'William's going to see it as a personal affront if the police catch him. He'll see it as inelegant and intellectually embarrassing'.

'What are you talking about?'

'I know he's dodging you all now because he sent me a message – a dispatch that would get through no matter how much anyone tried to prevent it. You know he predicted I would end up here with a bullet in my head. He got them to practise landing the police helicopter on the helipad here, when he was over at Lippitts Hill.'

'A message? To you? From William? What message?'

'An epistle just for me, from him. It means he could come and see me, but he's got other things to do right now.'

Philippa's blinking squeezed a tear. Tullia wondered what other things William had to do.

Tullia looked up and followed Philippa's eye line. On the ceiling above the bed something was scrawled. Tullia stared up until the small letters came into focus. They were only visible if you were lying on the bed and staring up, as any patient might be.

The words, blotchy and smudged in William's unmistakeable drunk spider script, with even half a thumbprint, read: *Can't Get You Out of My Head.*

54

This is my only escape from it all
Watching a film or a face on the wall

The three policemen who had been meant to keep an eye on William were slumped against the insides of the helicopter cockpit. They had assumed it would be a harmless place to sit and wait.

How wrong could they be?

William gingerly felt for the bandage that had been hastily wrapped around the cuts on his forehead, a legacy from the slivers off the church windows. His fingers came back red, so the grazes were weeping again.

The tarmac behind the waste disposal bins, seventeen floors below the heliport on the hospital roof, was unusually fascinating. It certainly guaranteed a swift alternative exit. The leap would definitely kill him, William knew, because various London hospitals, in their wisdom, had put the psychiatric unit on the top floor and lost several patients that way.

He took a deep breath and turned away. He was feeling very odd. It was as if he was watching himself, considering his own pain from a cold height with a slight taste of hysteria. Shock, he supposed, could have strange effects.

He had lost this one. He had failed. The patient was dead, Pip was wounded and other innocents had been killed because he had not thought quickly enough, nor clearly enough, nor got his relationships right with the Minister and the police.

Tullia would be so disappointed in him. He should have done much better.

He wandered across the roof towards the other side of the building, watching the crouched helicopter as if it might lurch up and bite him. It was presumably wise to open the doors now and drag the unconscious bodies out. He couldn't leave the police officers breathing the Isoflurane forever. He had surreptitiously cracked open the bottles of the vaporising anaesthetic under the seats as the paramedics were preoccupied with levering Philippa out of the cockpit on her stretcher. He had also warmed up the bottles using his hands to make sure the liquid would vaporise fast into the atmosphere, quickly knocking out the constabulary who were meant to be guarding him.

He felt utterly self-destructive, bitter, angry, incompetent, and beyond that a dreadful numbness. Yet it was odd, he still had no wish to leave evidence in his wake, like his OCD refused to let him go.

Tears burned the back of his eyes. Pip was seriously injured and might not make it. Bulimics, because they threw up a lot after meals, had low blood potassium levels. Luckily the paramedics in the chopper had allowed for that when he'd advised them to.

It was after he had found the classic bulimia paraphernalia in the handbags in Philippa's bedroom that he'd realised she was suffering from the eating disorder almost endemic among women in the public eye. Bathing cap to keep vomit out of her hair, mints to freshen breath, and spray air freshener to remove the smell from any loo she was visiting after an official meal, plus short fingernails and copious amounts of water – it all added up.

The *coup de grace* had been the piles of tomatoes in Philippa's kitchen. This signature red food, once it turned up in your vomit if you had eaten it first, meant you had got everything out. The tomatoes, added together with all the other evidence, indicated that the Foreign Secretary was a hardcore case. Well, she was a perfectionist.

By now Gerrard should have worked out that William must be on the roof, so they would be coming to get him very soon.

William drew in a shuddering breath. He had lost everything, and his work had come to nothing. And Gerrard would be banking on him conforming and playing the system, accepting whatever the AC had to offer in return for his silence.

Let's draw a veil over this, he thought. Nothing would now change in the longer term treatment of the seriously mentally ill.

But William had news for Gerrard Winstanley. He, blunderer

though he was, had a lot of dirt on the whole creaking system of looking after the mentally ill. Their cavalier disregard for psychiatric advice when dealing with the disordered – William could use it to get them to...to what?

William peered over the rim of the building again. Is this what leapers did just before taking the plunge?

Thumping pop music assailed his ears, the whoops of a crowd. If anything could make William jump, it would be this cacophony.

I can see for miles and miles and miles.

The lyric and voice were familiar.

Was it possible? Could Kwame and Dread know he was up here?

How?

Builders on the construction site next to the main hospital building were shouting and dancing on the scaffolding. Metal pipes and girders clanged in time with their cavorting. An audience was clustered in the street, pointing up at the construction dance team. The street was thronging with police cars and Dread fans, flags billowing with the skull and crossed microphones insignia. Everyone was pointing at each other in the rather inane way the psychiatrist had observed was rampant at Dread's concerts. They were doing a kind of twitching dance which looked to him like a medication side effect.

An impossibly long stretch limousine with blacked out windows was parked at the side of the road, just beyond a police road block. Emblazoned across its roof was an image of Dread, and the car was apparently the source of the music.

Dread would want William. He had worked very hard to ensure that. If there was one thing he had learnt about the stalking mindset, it was what drove obsession.

Sending anonymous messages was incredibly rare in the world of stalking. Stalkers' pathology meant they wanted to be known, to be identified. William had gleaned more experience of what anonymous threats could signify now, thanks to David, than anyone else in the field. Dread was getting unidentified threats, which he was in a better position to unravel than anyone else.

If he could get Dread to fly him out of the country, and then if he could start sending anonymous messages to the media, the Institute and the Government about what really happened...

He could harry the system into changing.

He didn't have to accept their terms.

Dread's smirk from the roof of the vehicle seemed to be inviting him over. Her mouth was strategically placed so that anyone emerging from the sunroof made it look as if she was sticking her tongue out. And someone was jutting out, scanning the hospital roof with binoculars. So they were indeed stalking him.

So, how to get to the car without falling into Gerrard's clutches? And following the shooting at the church, damage control would be the name of the game. With everyone hiding incriminating evidence, William would be the perfect scapegoat for the headlines of shame.

That was not going to happen. With Care for Congo coming up on them fast, he had little enough time to save Dread and the Hyde Park horde from some deranged loner, or a cult, or herself. If something spectacular happened to Dread in front of millions on stage, like a public assassination JFK-style, it would spark a riot of gargantuan proportions which could kill hundreds.

He had to prove psychiatry could work, if left unfettered.

William took off the white coat he had donned while in the trauma unit and waved it madly like a flag at the limousine. He couldn't be sure they saw him.

He was going to have to fly solo for the first time.

The air crew had been part of the team bundling Philippa down to neurosurgery and were guarding her. No one was here to remind him of all the pre-flight checks he'd learnt so religiously at Lippitts Hill from the pilot he'd saved from suspension.

The thought of what he was about to do terrified him. He was going to have to confront his fear of heights, but...but...he'd seen the pilots in action up close and personal quite a lot now thanks to being banished to Lippitts Hill. They had even insisted he have a go, gleefully tormenting him and radioing the results back to Gerrard, seeing how far they could push the fear envelope inside. But now that bullying might in fact prove useful.

How hard could it be?

William walked over to the helicopter with an almost sublime sense of dissociation and opened the door. The policemen were heavier than he'd anticipated, but he managed to lever them out. It was only as he strapped himself into the pilot's seat in the now deserted cockpit that his heart seemed to wake up to what he was doing and declared that it wanted to stay on the ground by crowbarring through his ribs.

He switched the battery on, performed fuel and clutch checks, then hit the engine starter button. It fired up. He saw the engine rpms climb to 1500, remembering to check that the area surrounding the chopper was clear as he lifted the collective control stick down to his left.

He was just about to change his mind and abandon the flight when the other police helicopter hovered into view over the horizon. It was making a beeline for the helipad on the roof of the hospital.

Uh-oh.

Gingerly William's helicopter pushed the roof away.

For some reason his bird began to drift towards the building's roof stair housing. He tugged back on the cyclic control stick, at the same time stamping on the tail rotor rudder pedals at his feet.

The helicopter swung away – but rotated.

This wasn't going well.

Calm down!

The other police chopper skirted him warily, then set down carefully on the roof behind him. They must be in a tearing hurry to get to the hospital for some reason.

William tried to recall what the pilot at Lippitts Hill had said. *The key thing about these infernal machines is that they're statically and dynamically unstable.* William was bobbing about, hanging in the air at awkward angles.

The builders had stopped dancing and were staring up at him, open-mouthed. Then, as he drifted towards them, they scrambled for the ladders down the side of the scaffolding. The world swung past William, going round and round. If he didn't master forward motion, this was going to make him dizzy quite soon, the analytical part of his mind told him.

His aircraft shuddered back to the hospital roof and wavered over the sister bird, but then, as he approached much too close, his downdraught pushed it over, blowing it on to its side, mangling its rotors.

'That's going to leave a mark,' William breathed.

The door opened and officers clambered out, including one, with decorations on his uniform, bearing an uncanny resemblance to Gerrard Winstanley.

William fought with the joystick and slowly the bird moved over the main road, though he was still much closer to the ground than he would have liked. Cars coming down Whitechapel Road screeched to a halt. Rotating too far one way, and then another, he tacked over towards the river. Whenever the rear-view came around, he could see that the limousine had taken up the chase and was barrelling along the dual carriageway.

The helicopter was like a toy boat in the middle of a fierce storm. A vague sideways drift factor to the whole sorry equation superimposed a general scudding in the wrong direction.

'C'mon! Keep up, keep up! Keep calm and get over yourself!' he shouted. He only had a short while before the police sent cars after him. Then the bandage on his forehead began to droop down, half covering one eye. In truth, it was a race between his pursuers and whether he hit something, including the ground.

How hard could it be? Very hard.

55

I hear your face start to call
Long year in a hostile place

The mobile phone on Philippa's bedside cabinet vibrated. The bandaged Minister waved her hand.

'Check who it is – can't talk to the press now,' she whispered hoarsely.

The handset display had a curious text: *H9*.

'Er, not sure who this is.' Tullia brandished the phone at Philippa, who looked away from the ceiling then grabbed the handset with a sudden burst of energy.

'Hello, Robert? Robert? No, let me speak. No, this is important too... No, Robert, listen – did you send me a Dominique Schlumberger necklace?... No, it's eighteen carat gold with diamonds set in platinum... What do you mean no? It had a note...at the church...oh, let me speak!... Oh, for Chrissake, okay, okay, you go ahead if it can't wait.'

Philippa's head fell back in exasperation as she listened. Her eyes grew wide.

'Are you dumping me? Now?... Of course it's not a good time, d'you know what's just happened? Of course you don't know, you're just a journalist!'

Tullia was surprised by the irate explosion from Philippa.

'I'm sorry my timetable doesn't fit in with your dumping schedule! Oh, screw you!' She flung her mobile phone in fury and it exploded against the ceiling. She had hit William's *Can't Get You Out of My Head* with a bullseye. The professor flinched.

'What the...are you all right?' Tullia asked, shuffling away from the Foreign Secretary in alarm.

'Oh just some arsehole taking the opportunity of terminating...' Philippa struggled to regain her composure. Tullia was startled to see a spreading damp patch under her eyes on the bandage wrapping her head.

The Cabinet Minister sank back into her pillows, staring up at William's words. She tilted her head, considering them, lost in thought, then gestured impatiently to some staff behind the glass door that she needed another phone.

While she waited for them, she turned back to Tullia conspiratorially. 'Listen, Prof, there's a dark secret I need to tell you about William. No one but me knows it, and so…anyway, the thing is…'

After a long pause, Tullia cleared her throat. 'Ahh, Philippa, the thing is, about FTAC and the stalking clinic…'

'No, it's not about that, it's…well, you know he keeps quoting these case histories of notorious stalking incidents involving celebrities? He bandies names about – Madonna, Gwyneth Paltrow, Bjork, David Letterman, Brad Pitt, Stephen Spielberg, Olivia Newton-John…'

'He's not name dropping, you know, he's just…'

'Yes, yes, I know *that*. That's just the thing: he doesn't actually *know* who any of them are. It's strange, and a bit, well, mad. To him, they're just people who got stalked and victimised. He has no idea that one is an actor, and the other a pop star, or the third is a film director. He's completely oblivious to the world of celebrity. He's vaguely aware that these names have an impact in conversation, which is why he weaves them into his attempts to persuade you of his case. He doesn't watch TV, or read the papers other than foreign news…'

Tullia raised an eyebrow. 'But what does that matter? Vilhelm is a Greek.'

'A Greek? Really?'

'No, not a Greek like in Athens – a *geek*. He lives in the library or in the clinic. The academic world is his universe, so when he's dealing with these superstars…'

'Er, you don't think there's something a bit darker going on here? A level of self-loathing lurking beneath the surface to dedicate your life to self-obsessed impossible people you positively despise – both stalkers and their targets?'

'Everyone speculates about the motive behind becoming

a psychiatrist and undertaking this difficult work. Freud referred to us as the impossible profession. Why is it not possible William is simply moved by the suffering of victims? Most are not famous, they are not self-obsessed, they are just ordinary people, and when it comes to the celebrities, he does them the biggest favour of all – he ignores the fact they are…'

'That's genius!' Philippa almost leapt up in excitement, turning to the professor. She seemed to have got past being discarded by phone call surprisingly quickly.

'Wha…what do you mean?' Tullia asked, leaning back.

'Don't you see? He's trying to tell me something. He won't even know those are the lyrics from a pop song. He's saying it's not all over – I can flip this!'

Philippa reached for the mobile the staff had brought in.

'I…I don't understand.'

'Of course you do. You shrinks, honestly!' Philippa waved at the scrawl on her ceiling again. 'The way I look now, it's the perfect opportunity. I'm going to turn this to my advantage. I'll finally get the female vote. They all hated me before 'cos of my hair and my looks, but now – well, the public will see me looking like this. We blame the pro-war lobby, explain it was a politically motivated assassination attempt and I ride on a tide of sympathy. The PM doesn't…'

Philippa halted herself and stared at Tullia. 'I need William and I need him now.'

'But even Gerrard can't find him,' protested Tullia.

The Foreign Secretary dismissed the professor with a shrug. 'Ah c'mon, of course Gerrard would be no match for William, but I've got much more resources at my disposal. Don't forget this is national security we're talking about…remember, I've got the ultimate stalkers at my disposal. All these insane bozos that William deals with are just amateur hour in comparison.'

'So, he's still got a chance, he just mustn't do anything silly?'

'Absolutely, like go to the press in a fit of pique – or self-importance – defending himself against Gerrard's accusations over the assassination attempt. Once he does that, it's over between us. There's no way back. He may have to suck up some of the fallout, that's just tough. It's also key he doesn't do anything the Met can pin on him like bending any laws, no matter how trivial. But if I want him, I'll get him. Don't you worry. It's time to unleash my dogs of war!'

Tullia realised she had been dismissed as Philippa vigorously beckoned her advisers into the room. As Tullia was backing out the door, she heard Philippa bark into her receiver, 'Get me MI5! We need them to track down someone right now.'

56

Losing my way
And if you think that I've been losing my way
That's because I'm slightly blinded

'You need bucket?' The middle-aged Filipino woman peered at William from the door of the limousine.

'The bucket? What bucket?'

William felt spaced out, but try as he might he couldn't work out who this woman was or why he would need a pail on the rugby playing fields of Dulwich College. The limousine had churned up the hallowed turf as it careered towards his downed helicopter. He looked round and almost fell to the ground as he waved apologetically to the cowering excited schoolboys whose game he'd interrupted.

He surveyed the damage. A reek of gasoline rose up from metal fragments ornamenting the cratered grass. One of the rotor blades had broken, the badly scratched and dented fuselage of the aircraft lay on its side, twisted, while one set of rugby goalposts was mangled.

Strange. He thought he'd managed to avoid them on the way down.

Clearly not.

'You want to wait for police or you come now?' said the woman. It was a redundant question. Two huge minders squeezed out of the rear of the limousine, grabbed William and frog-marched him back to the car. In the distance, the police car sirens wailed, coming ever closer.

Was this how it felt to be kidnapped?

'You very broken-up, hurt bad, covered in blood.'

William tried to speak, but how could he explain that in fact he was okay? The blood on him was not his, but the result of an assassination gone wrong earlier in the day.

328

'He need bucket?' The woman addressed her question to the two lumbering minders who were pushing William into the rear of the car.

'He need cross match?'

They shoved him in.

'Relax, Flip. He ain't been drinking or bleeding.'

William, disorientated, wasn't entirely convinced that this wasn't some dream. A nightmare, in fact, in which he found himself confronting the witch from Hansel and Gretel.

The bodyguards plonked themselves down in the rear seats, flicking on the TV. The broadcast news headlines were confused about the catastrophe that had occurred at St Martin-in-the-Fields. There was clearly some kind of security clampdown on reporting, which had come from on high.

'Hmmm,' Flip said disbelievingly and slapped a pale blue plastic canister into William's chest.

'I'm not sure about the bucket, but I do need another bandage.' He gestured to his forehead. The bandage that had been applied at St Martin's was now damply falling over his eyes.

On the screen, Gerrard was giving some kind of press conference outside The Royal London Hospital. Frances appeared to be getting special privileges in asking the questions at the front of the press pack. She had successfully stalked her prey.

The car swerved off the field and bumped on to the road.

Flip opened a cupboard box, revealing a medical kit as extensive as any William had seen outside a hospital. With a fresh bandage gripping his forehead, he peered up from under it as his eyes were almost covered, checking himself in the cocktail cabinet mirror while she packed the equipment away. He looked like a kamikaze pilot, and in a sense he had become one.

As they zigzagged across South London, William kept straining to find out what was being said about the incident and whether Philippa was okay. His mobile phone was somewhere in the wreckage of the helicopter. That meant if the police were trying to get a triangulation fix on him from it, they weren't going to be in luck.

The woman, Flip, stared at him.

'I don't geddit. Did she sleep with you? I mean, you don't look her type! This a kiss an' tell?' The woman felt William's biceps thoughtfully. 'No, she didn't sleep with you.'

Inspiration struck.

'Of course! She didn't sleep with you cons…whass the word? Cons…consensually.'

She held up her hands to silence William before he could raise his voice in protest.

'I don't wanna hear it, I've heard it all before. You were drunk and she led you on, blah, blah, blah. Yeah…listen, don't feel bad, you gettin' a payday. They won't want this going to court or in the papers, obviously. Now I look at you – you *do* look the type…'

The car came to a halt as William lifted his hands in the air in remonstration.

'I did not sleep with Dread!'

The woman gave him an old-fashioned look.

'Hmmm. Maybe your thing little boys? Could it be Nish?'

'We're off!' Another bodyguard was at the door, motioning William to rise.

'Listen, it was nice to meet you.' William offered his hand, but the woman simply grabbed her bucket back and shooed him out. She produced a portable vacuum cleaner and started hoovering his former seat noisily. He could hear the tinkle as glass disappeared inside the cleaner. He was still shedding bits of church window.

The bodyguards bundled him into yet another limousine parked in what seemed to be the yard of a farmhouse, and they were moving as the doors closed.

Not only did he have no passport, he also had no clothes. He was certainly travelling light. The only thing he was really taking to his next destination was the photograph of Philippa and Robert taken by Frances.

And, of course, how could he forget?

Philippa's necklace, still soaked in her blood.

Suddenly he needed the bucket.

57

We move in line
But never reach an end

Roger Moirans was becoming the most important controller in TV, and Frances had only the seconds it would take to reach the top of the tallest building in Europe to clear her head.

It was the first limousine she had experienced with its own "stewardess" who raided the drinks cabinet and mixed cocktails for her. Normally she wouldn't touch anything Roger might send for her, and knocking back the never-ending Cosmopolitans, served up by the feline apparition in the taut uniform behind her own bar, had been a mistake. It was obvious what Roger got from watching the quivering art-deco cocktail shaker: it was like a lap-dance on the back seat.

So this is how he softens you up before a meeting.

Padding like a cheetah between the crystal decanters, the hostess seemed to be appraising just how sloshed Frances was with raked kitten eyes. The stewardess had expertly separated her from the herd that was galloping across Trafalgar Square like hunting cats did when hungry for a gazelle.

But after the debacle in the church and realising William's continued feelings for Philippa, Frances had needed a stiff drink. Only now, as London folded away through the glass wall of Roger's private lift in The Shard, the acceleration upwards began to make her feel most peculiar.

Frances glanced up. There was a plasma screen in the lift to Roger's office. Roger insisted his visitors suffered television so dumb it took his presenters two hours to grasp *60 Minutes.* The title of this particular show was *The Weakest Lip-Sync.* Frances shuddered as that shrill banshee known the world over as "Dread" stared out of the screen at her, an enticing combination of knowing and innocence.

The video in the lift swooped on Dread and her spectacular finale. Seven-inch heels strutted the stage as she belted out a melodrama about the strain of a childhood spent between Romford and Hollywood with a white pop star mother and a black producer father. Emotion-proof mascara framed cat-like green eyes.

Frances knew she needed to be wary. Once she got angry she was quite capable of stabbing Roger in the chest with her detachable boom microphone, as she had at the documentary festival. She had to retain her composure no matter the provocation. After all, she had exclusive shocking footage of the Foreign Secretary caught in cross-fire: a scoop of the decade, the kind of material that transformed a journalist's career. This was her Woodward and Bernstein moment, her Watergate. But would Roger be willing to trade it for what Frances wanted?

And what was wrong with her anyhow? Most journalists would be content to live off the glory of such an achievement, for a while at least, but already she had moved on. Craving something that only Roger could deliver right now.

It was an itch that could never be scratched.

Like a boxer groping for the ropes, she groggily reached for the cool metal wall of the lift. She had to clear her head. Otherwise, in her current state she'd stagger right past Roger's outstretched hand, searching for a ledge to heave the cocktails back to earth.

58

There's not a problem that I can't fix
'Cause I can do it in the mix

Flip dragged him across the Surrey countryside and into a series of different cars which were waiting for them in various remote locations, like a deserted barn or an abandoned farm house. While William was impressed with how Dread and Kwame covered their tracks, he did begin to wonder where they were heading. He had a horrible feeling that from time to time they merely orbited a giant circle, as if someone up above hadn't made their mind up what to do with him. Every time a car appeared behind them, he began fretting Gerrard's or Philippa's forces had finally found them.

His new limousine, accelerating, began to swing from side to side.

William grabbed the handholds and checked his seat belt. He wasn't sure what had been going on for Dread on top of that Ferris wheel back at the Rose Bowl. She was having a panic attack of some kind. He had reviewed the tapes Kwame had sent, and on most occasions she looked positively bored up there.

Despite inspecting the video again and again, reversing and forwarding the feed, nothing untoward showed up. So what had transpired? Had she seen a ghost? William counted her respiratory tempo in the filming and calculated she had been hyperventilating at a scary rate. That alone would change her body's biochemistry to induce some strange physical sensations. It was part of the terror circle whereby fright produced more – well – dread, hence perhaps her stage name.

But what had kick-started the whole process? She had been utterly alone.

The wheel had kept turning, and when she was taken away

from the apex, she calmed down. But as it creaked to the top again, she began to alarm. Yet, historically, she had no fear of heights. Why had she suddenly been agitated by this place?

Panics had many causes – trauma was one – and the interesting thing about trauma related terror was that time got distorted and reshuffled. You could suddenly feel you were reliving some horror from the past, or the present could flip into the future or swap with the historical, creating a vivid sense of unreality.

Had Dread been afflicted with a sudden unexpected flashback? Tom had experienced one looking down the scope of his rifle, and from the look in Frances's face at the church, she might be vulnerable to them now. So would Philippa be, but at least she was surrounded by doctors.

And he had left a helpful warning on her ceiling for her to beware the inevitable intrusive memories.

If William wasn't mistaken, he could sense the same thing creeping up on himself now.

Being swallowed by his own panic.

The remedy was to slow his breathing and focus on something outside of himself. Try to keep time in the right order.

It didn't surprise William that someone in the crowd had tried to take the pop star's blood, or perhaps taken a stab at injecting her with something. Obsessed fans and stalkers were into this kind of craziness.

Would it make her feel better to know that a biography of Sachin Tendulkar, the Indian cricketer celebrated as a deity by the sub-continent, had recently been published with pages made from paper pulp that included his blood? The signature page was mixed with Tendulkar's haemoglobin – folded in so that it became a red resin. The book cost almost £50,000.

Tendulkar was revered as a God, Dread behaved like one – was there a link?

Having strained once to get Dread's essence, for whatever reason, the stalker was bound to try again.

And then there was the puzzle of finding Alonzo Church's DNA in the car used to bash her, or blow her up. William had recommended that they disinter Alonzo's body. They certainly needed to check if he really was still below ground, or whether some macabre plot lay behind his tissue turning up at the crime scene despite him being buried months earlier.

William also couldn't fathom why, given the pop star had so publicly panicked on the talent TV show *The Weakest Lip-Sync,* she was now being secretive about the Rose Bowl fright. What had added to her stress enormously was wrestling with the inner turmoil and trying desperately to keep it hidden, yet she hadn't done that in the early days of her broadcast career. Instead she had poignantly bared her soul, generating enormous audience sympathy. But having re-checked the tapes of her distress back then, William wasn't overly impressed. She was always being mobbed by sympathetic sobbing contestants obscuring camera angles, but with each episode Dread's tears looked ever more histrionic.

After she'd conquered her "stage fright", or whatever the hell was transpiring, and then gone on to perform so relentlessly, why should the terrors return? Unless, of course, the Rose Bowl was in fact her *first* panic, catching her off-guard. In which case she'd *faked* the first set.

As he began to unravel Dread's secret, something came back to William. It was a study published by Lionel and Katie Page in the *Journal of Economic Behavior & Organization* in 2010. They'd analysed music talent shows which involved public voting, such as *Pop Idol* and *X Factor,* from eight countries, and performed a statistical analysis of over 1,500 performances, concluding that various psychological processes combined to ensure the final performer was more likely to get a higher score. It was true even for contestants in classical music competitions, subjected to more expert judgements than the pop music farces on TV, and was something to do with the tendency to remember more the last to perform, and also that every performance was compared with previous ones.

So, like at Hyde Park coming up, on *The Weakest Lip-Sync* Dread always sang last – but that was because she began each live show with a trepidation attack and had to delay and delay until right at the end, when she plucked up the courage to stage a return.

It must have been high drama indeed, adding unbearable tension to each show.

So she's smart and she's aware of the effect from classical music competitions, thought William. *She was at the Royal Academy, wasn't she? Page and Page even quote a previous study from a Queen Elizabeth Violin and Piano Competition where the same effect was found.*

Dread had faked her frights, William concluded.

She intuitively knew going last gave her a psychological edge over the other participants. According to the research, moving one position closer to the end of the show provided a contestant an additional five percentage point chance of being safe.

'It's a powerful effect,' William announced to the limousine.

'You sounding funny, voice strangle-like, you develop American accent? You okay?' Flip demanded.

No one seemed to be listening.

If Dread had faked the panics which launched her career and now unexpectedly real ones had arrived, did her entourage know? Were they all in on it? Frances had spoken about someone called Roger who had built his career on being a sarcastic biting judge. He had torn strips off Dread and continued trying to get her ejected, but the British public kept voting her back in.

William also recalled that Frances had explained "Friggin' in the Riggin'" was the star's very first chart hit after the competition – which, if she'd rigged things, was flaunting it somewhat. But to whom?

If her very first hit concealed a secret communication, why not all the others since? Did that mean all her songs afterwards embodied coded messages? Could that explain why the stalker was sending *her* song lyric communications? And if she was being made a victim of extortion, by whom?

Of course, if he revealed his surmises to her, his rumbling of the secret to her success, he might be sacked instantly. That was the unique thing about psychiatry. Conveying the truth often delivered an outraged client who then summarily abandoned you, even on the side of the road.

Yet at the moment, Flip, Dread's trusty housekeeper, was directing a platoon of limousines, moving them like a gigantic chess game across the countryside, trying to protect this precious piece from capture. He watched her hunched over the phone, an array of passports on her lap. Could he persuade her to place a call to Kwame or even Dread?

William appreciated that he had become a pawn in a larger scheme being played out by unseen hands. But he must at all costs not lose his head now; not panic and run ahead of himself. He must confine time to its correct order.

The problem was, pawns got sacrificed.

59

They're gonna call me sir
God is a bullet

The man inside the limousine handed over a passport to the officer and complained he was a psychologist being flown out of the country by Dread the "Pop Star". He was going to miss his private jet if they didn't get a move on with this roadside check. He demanded they call her bodyguard to confirm the story.

Recovering from the jolt of surprise as to how much of the passenger's head was bound with surgical dressing, the MI5 agent wasn't fazed. This classic 'Do you know who I am?' ploy just got everyone's back up. Didn't celebs realise this? And more so for those clinging on to their coat tails.

Also, he'd been advised their target might still be wearing a bandage from the incident in the church. So he'd hit the bullseye with this roadblock.

Admittedly it hadn't been that difficult once the double-cross had been implemented and the hidden location software on the target's mobile phone had been activated. Plus, wasn't it Dread's chief bodyguard, a Mr Kwame Appiah, who'd given up this fractious passenger in the first place to the agency? It had been made clear to him that Dread's security surrounding the Hyde Park concert hinged on the pop star's team first handing over this shrink. They, so the gossip went, had given up this small cog in their various wheels in order to gain extra special intensive protection.

'I think you will find I'm their top priority right now, she needs me.' The bandaged head in the back seat continued to fulminate, hands folded in a mega-strop.

It made sense that her safety would take precedence right now over the muffled jerk fidgeting in the limousine. There had been a very large carrot dangled at Kwame Appiah to give up this whingeing know-it-all.

You had to take your hat off to them. No other performer had levered this exceptional treatment out of the UK authorities – to secure armour-plated guarding in advance of the performance – in return for a mere pawn. Dread was a master negotiator, no matter what they said about her being all volume and no content.

So, this was the prize: the particular therapist the Foreign Secretary was after. Curious, because he didn't look like much. He must be part of some scheme being played out way above his pay grade; maybe he was now just surplus to requirements. Didn't these stars boast an army of shrinks?

The MI5 agent perused the deserted rural road. Luckily they had managed to stop the limousine before it got nearer the private aerodrome it must have been rushing for. The raving Dread fans charging the countryside were congregating there. It would have kicked off if they'd witnessed a vehicle belonging to her entourage being stopped. Neither they nor the agitated passenger would appreciate it was the intelligence service *posing* as the Metropolitan Police. The uniforms would have been a red rag to the rioters, and they had the constabulary tied in knots right across Surrey this nightmare afternoon.

The double agent began to skim the passport. Inside were some extra stapled papers with official hospital stamps, and a signature from a doctor explaining that the bandaged man could not be un-bandaged for border security checks because he was receiving treatment. Something to do with his eyes. But he was who he said he was. Honest.

The officer triumphantly radioed in that he had located the trophy everyone was searching for. The police would be pissed off that it was MI5 who had done the business. Now the undercover operative had entered their game, he mulled over how to lever himself into Dread's inner circle of bodyguards while she was in transit for Hyde Park. His kids would be so impressed, even if all he got out of this was her autograph.

He was turning back to the stretched car to break the bad news the fugitive was going to be detained when he was distracted by a buzzing engine coming from far away, growing louder by the instant.

The other MI5 operatives posing as police motorcyclists had been bitten by curiosity as to whom this person close to Dread in the limousine was. They had commanded the driver and other grumpy members of the support act out of the car and were questioning them on the side of the road, as well as inspecting the boot. The group stopped remonstrating with each other and turned to check what was happening down the road.

A hush fell over them.

The bandaged head inside the limousine leant out the window and craned backwards. He pushed the gauze up to peer into the gathering evening. Whoever was responsible for the amplifying chainsaw hum was travelling with ferocious velocity down the hillside. Yet they were still approximately two miles away.

The road was obscured by hedgerows and trees. A couple of white flashes punctuated the gloom.

'What's that?' the man in the limo asked in a strangled way. It sounded like an accent – of course, the shrink could be a Yankee. Everyone had one over there, right? This chap seemed particularly unnerved about being followed.

'Speed cameras,' breathed the policeman. He had one hand poised over the passport, but his head craned to see the mysterious rapid projectile. 'They're moving illegally fast.'

Across the brow of the rise, a dark shape was hunched over a roaring motorcycle and leaning into a wide corner. The MI5 agent cursed internally. This was always how an undercover mission got fouled up. Someone had to go and break the law right in front of you, just when you're pretending to be a member of the constabulary.

The bike disappeared into a long dip in the road momentarily, then bounded aloft, both wheels off the ground before landing, bouncing then leaping towards them.

Feeling for the gun under his uniform, the policeman wavered, but then stepped out into the road. He raised the hand holding the detained man's passport, authoritatively signalling the bike to stop like a referee red-carding a dangerous tackle.

60

And if you think that I don't make too much sense
That's because I'm broken minded

Dread's disciples began to appear. First a few stragglers, then they clumped, and finally there was one long queue along the roadside. They flourished wigs of exaggerated Dreadlocks and flapped banners. Costumes that highlighted characters from her albums swayed drunkenly across the road, meandering to the side like a herd of lazy elephants as the limousine sped past them.

Clowns, a hooded grim reaper, hosts of angels in gear too skimpy for the weather, and a myriad of elves, goblins and firemen all blurred across the privacy glass. The largest contingent appeared to be made up of marching drummers. Batons waved at them as they hustled by. Did they think Dread was in the car? Were they all going to converge on the same destination?

As the rhythm sections beat out hit after hit, the crowds encircling them would clap back in unison. Her face was everywhere: on their T-shirts, bags, flags, stickers, shoes and balloons.

William gazed in wonder. This ragtag army had assembled in just a few hours. He lowered the window a crack and the chanting penetrated the limousine.

I can see for miles and miles!

A bodyguard reached over and patiently pressed the window button, returning the soundproofing.

The police had tried to set up roadblocks to control the traffic, pulling vehicles over. Fed up with waiting in protracted queues, passengers had abandoned their rides on the verge, and were now marching. The barriers were beleaguered by the massed never-ending stream of Dread's troops.

Enveloped by a gang of bikers who came out of nowhere, shielding them as escorting outriders, William began to feel like the Foreign Secretary defended in official transportation.

Flip kept barking at the driver, 'Go, go, go!' so the limousine swerved gridlocks, careering over into oncoming traffic then weaving back at the last moment. Assembling into an arrow formation, the motorcycles edged up front, zipping through the blockades which had been overrun anyway by fans on foot.

But sooner or later, reinforcements must arrive, then these officers would rally and impose order on the chaos. The limousine would be stopped, and then it would be over.

No, don't panic, keep breathing. Everything in its right time, don't lose track.

William stared through the back window at the upturned barricades and skirmishing. Wherever Dread went, trouble seemed to follow. And he was heading straight for it.

61

Can't get you out of my head
Nah-nah-na, na-na-na-nah-nah, nah-nah-na

The officer became more uncertain as the motorcyclist hunched and their engine roared in defiance. The bike wasn't slowing despite the fact he was standing resolutely in the middle of the road, holding his hand out. Did no one respect the uniform anymore? As it hurtled towards them, the bandaged head pulled back inside the limousine, and the two other agents leapt into the verge. The other passengers from the vehicle took the opportunity to dart away through the fields.

Drawing up to them, the helmeted figure took one hand off the handlebars and seemed to be delivering a Hitler salute to the group. The officer whirled, clutching his hand as he fell against the car door. The operatives gingerly raised themselves to check the silhouette roaring into the distance.

'What the hell?' the officer panted, realising he'd just had a scrape with death and nursing the palm that had been clutching the limousine passenger's passport.

'Am I free to go now?' the man asked impatiently from inside the limousine. 'Where are my travel documents?'

Frances looked down at the fluttering pages of the passport gripped in her motorbike gloves, nearly falling off the bike. She swerved, wobbled, but then regained control and roared on.

62

I'm a glossy magazine, an advert on the tube
Urban Spaceman

William was intrigued that the pop star's jet appeared to sport even more bulges than Gerrard's choppers. He counted the various scopes and cameras. Besides the FLIR system, they also had a black light.

Of course! Dread had made sure the wheel in Hyde Park was orientated in a particular direction because they were not allowed to fly over Buckingham Palace. So her plan must be for this plane to zoom in low while she was on stage and use the black light to deliver a spectacular final effect.

They might be taking the UV filaments out of her searchlight, but the diva was not going to take no for an answer.

You really had to hand it to her.

William had no idea where they were, but this was obviously an ultra-discreet private airfield. One other aircraft stood in the distance, wing lights blinking. The fans clogging the roads had disappeared several miles back when the limousine had turned off on to the quiet B roads.

Climbing into the jet, William felt as if he had walked into an exclusive boutique brimming with expensive ornaments. Gleaming walnut alternated with leather. The seats were three enormous slabs of pristine soft luxurious hide, resembling outsized cushions of buffalo mozzarella. Everything was so perfect he didn't dare to sit down, aware that his coat remained extravagantly splattered in blood.

He peered out of the windows. Would the police be arriving at any moment to arrest him for the theft of a helicopter? Gerrard would have an all-ports alert out on him, so how were Dread and Kwame going to get him through passport control? He appreciated that when you were as big a VIP as Dread, with your own jet gracing a private aerodrome like this, passport control came to you, so he was bracing himself for an inspection of papers he didn't have.

Inside the hushed cabin there was room for twelve people to sprawl in comfort, while a gigantic plasma TV was embedded in the wall at the back, towards which the huge chairs could swivel. Four antique seats accompanied a polished gleaming dining table curving against a row of wider windows. It had been prepared for a champagne supper, and a bottle leant inside a glistening bucket dripping gently on to a silver platter.

William realised he was ravenous. He hadn't eaten all day.

On another wall was a bank of smaller TV screens, and still images had been punched up on them. The pictures had all been taken with the benefit of black light illumination. There was an image of a spectacular concert at the Rose Bowl, the sun setting in the distance, with the garish make-up on Dread and her dancers on stage spookily lighting up. Then a depiction of a press conference: rows of silhouettes of press with only their security passes glowing in their shirt pockets or tacked to their lapels. They were all turning as if some commotion had attracted their attention behind them.

So Kwame had followed William's advice and rechecked any black light pictures.

'How come their shirts light up as well?'

A young blonde woman, hidden because she was reclining deep in one of the seats, was lazily straightening out her tight skirt as she asked the question. Her breasts, fascinatingly, appeared to be cupped for presentation to the outside world by her strained blouse. William accepted the vision as just another part of this surreal day and stammered an answer.

'Er, anything white will fluoresce under a black light because washing powder manufacturers add fluorescing agents to give that whiter than white look.'

'Gosh, dang! Wuhd ya *believe* it? You're a fan of *Angels, Demons and Zombies Too!*' She was staring at his bandaged head and his blood-spattered coat. 'Welcome aboard, Dr...' she glanced down at some papers on the table '...James.'

She seemed to be aware he was gawping at her and straightened her skirt, which did nothing at all to conceal her long streamlined legs. Shining hair, draped across her face, obscured everything but glossy pink lips.

'Wealcome aboahd this, ah, Gulfstream G650, which is one of the world's ultimate business aircraft. We'll be cruisin' at a speed of nine-tenths the speed of sound and achieving altitudes of up to 51,000 feet,' she said, imitating the perfect air hostess.

She paused and appeared to be looking for something on the table. She scooped up a passport and waved it triumphantly at William.

'Who is your strange bedfellow?'

'I beg your pardon?'

'Actually, she looked a bit sinister – like a stalker. She dropped this off for you to help you get past the security checks here. When we asked her who she was, she just said she was a "strange bedfellow". So who is that?'

William stared. Was it possible that Frances was helping him get out?

'...believed we'd owe her something? Anyhows...forget her. When you start climbing into the stratosphere, it's always the crazies sky high on something who get closest to you.'

'Yes, but did she ask you for anything? In return for the passport?' When William caught sight of Han Fei's photo, he twigged. Some additional papers fell out on to the table. There was a stamped official photo attached of the forensic psychologist in dressings swaddling the upper half of his head because of some operation he was due to have here in the UK.

William had seen documents like these before: they advised national border officials that the holder of the passport was receiving essential treatment necessitating bandages, or whatever medical equipment, which prevented a proper full face or body check.

Unconsciously William felt for the bandage gripping his head again.

'She left without any trouble, so relax. *We've* a range of more than 7,000 nautical miles, so she can't follow us. This leetle trip to LA of 4,700 nautical miles is routine for us.' The twang to her melodious voice from the baking South already made the cabin feel much warmer than the English summer.

Had Frances made the ultimate sacrifice in terms of landing her story? No strings attached?

Kristal seemed to sense that William was distracted so she extended herself from the recliner and offered him her hand. How was it possible that this displayed even more of her legs? From the look of her, it was possible there were a few kangaroos loose in the top paddock.

'N...n...nice to meet you,' he stammered, reaching out. She was tall, probably six feet, and ridiculously symmetrical. She looked like she'd stepped from a technical drawing, curvy and very striking. A natural blonde with skin the colour of creamy coffee.

She grinned at him. 'I'm not as dumb as you look, Dr James. There's a reason Kwame wanted you to see these.'

'Er...' William turned again to look at the bank of images. He peered at the post Rose Bowl press conference. The main lights had gone down so everyone was sitting in pitch blackness except for the fluorescing passes. A few also had Dread tattoos that were glowing eerily. This must have been a nanosecond before the cannonade of pap flash had bombarded Dread. He'd seen the video before, but in this split second the fluorescence from the black light wouldn't have been apparent to anyone.

Then, as he looked more closely, he made out the cluster of figures at the back – Dread and her party. He moved in closer. Fluorescing on Dread's forehead was a symbol of an eye.

'Yup, we saw that as well. Hannah, the make-up artist, denies all knowledge. But whoever did it, did it right under the noses of the rest of the group who all surrounded Dread in the dressing room. I, of course, am beyond suspicion because I was – well, anyway, let's just say it cain't be meah.'

'And what does Dread say?'

'Turns out Kwame had the room rigged with CCTV. Anyhows, the images don't show much – everyone in the peckerhead group was mobbing Dread in her chair so it coulda been anyone. Kwame wants to ditch our make-up artist, but Dread won't. My lil' sis says it's all our attempt to get rid of the last person she truly trusts. Plus if we keep axing people who fall under suspicion, very soon this tour is gonna wind up with Dread on stage alone with a single microphone. An acoustic set. Thass why we need to find these stalkahs fast.'

Kristal beckoned him over to a seat by the dining table. She lowered herself into a chair opposite him and unwrapped her napkin. Her long tanned legs stretched out into the aisle.

'We're leavin' soon. Right now there's an argument with the tower as to who's takin' off first,' she explained airily, indicating the general direction of the other private jet William had seen lurking in the distance.

At any moment he expected a phalanx of blue flashing lights to arrive at the periphery of the airfield and buzz angrily towards them. He imagined Gerrard brandishing handcuffs and smiling at the flash photography.

'Wanna aperitif and sumpin' t' eat?' Kristal gestured at the champagne bucket. A uniformed waiter emerged from another cabin at the rear and served piping hot salmon blinis with cool cream and caviar.

The waiter liberated the fizzing champagne and she toasted him.

'*Budem Zdorovy!*'

The sudden move to excellent Russian was disconcerting.

Before he could ask what that meant, the plane shrugged and began to move. Kristal's golden mane bent to stare out the window. Enormous diamond earrings dangled into view for the first time.

'They don't know the first dang thing about bob war fences round here, do they.'

William struggled, but then realised she was referring to barbed wire. Out of the porthole it was becoming apparent in the gathering gloom that devotees were arriving on the periphery of the fenced airfield. And they were scaling the barriers.

'Arnold'll git us up before the fans git to us.'

A waiter brought some food – a risotto with a medley of fish. Even the steaming vegetables in this glitzy cabin appeared polished.

'We also got some great corn bread and taters and peaaacan pie!'

The uniform expertly opened white wine while the plane appeared to be jockeying for position with the other aircraft in the falling dusk.

'So, it's good to see that you're now over the eating disorder,' William commented, attempting to make conversation as his fork chased some reluctant rice across his plate.

Kristal choked and did a double take.

'Ah beg your purdon?' she exclaimed.

'You know, the bulimia – the throwing-up after meals? You had it badly at one point but now you're much better.'

Why was she so upset? He'd waited until the waiter disappeared. And he'd lowered his voice. He was being discreet. He had noticed, paid attention to her.

Kristal collapsed on the side of the table and put her head in her hands. Through a fistful of straw curls, she asked weakly, 'Howevah did yah know? Not even my mother or my sisters have any idea, but you're right. I had a purdy bad episode of 'limia for a lil' while. 'Bout a year ago, and now it's much better. But who told you?'

'Oh, no one,' William said airily. 'When we shook hands back there, I couldn't help noticing and feeling the slightly roughened skin over your knuckles. It's old scarring that's now healing nicely. It's caused by a reflex when you stick your fingers down your throat to induce vomiting which stimulates a gag reflex, causing the front teeth to clamp down on your hand. This then scars the knuckles with the corresponding bite. People with bulimia tend to have these marks across the knuckles.'

William lapsed into silence and returned his focus to the fish. What it was, he thought, to be an incompetent suitor.

'My ambition is to have some medical sign like that named after me.' He gave the corpse of the conversation a final stab. 'Or perhaps, even better, a whole disease. You know, James's Syndrome?'

'Er, listen. Ah don't mind you telling me this stuff, but be purdy careful with ma sis. She's quick to git riled up an' bring the axe down on anyone who steps outta line.'

William raised his head and smiled. After his confiding in her, Kristal had begun to reciprocate.

349

'Yeah, I understand she's constantly auditioning new dancers and musicians, and the current ones have to watch while their possible replacements are put through their paces. She likes you to meet your competition.'

Kristal shook her head sadly. 'Ah believe she was auditioning that Japanese-American policeman guy – the dishy one – to take your place.'

'*Chinese*-American,' William corrected her.

'Dat too. That whole stunt of having him on the back of her bike? She was checking to see if he could keep up with her and how he would respond under pressure. We call that takin' a newbie out on a road test.'

She drained her glass then waved it in the air. Somehow the waiter saw through the wooden door and shimmered in to top her up from the bottle on the table.

'Actually, I was surprised that Han hadn't worked out what was really going on.'

'Whaddya mean?'

'Well, Kwame didn't say – he's too discreet for that – but I'm taking a wild guess she went to visit a cosmetic surgery clinic.'

Kristal gave him a look that said she wondered if they had hired the devil.

'It's not that difficult. There are very few other places out there she could have been heading for. And my patients who suffer from Body Dysmorphic Disorder or Imagined Ugliness Syndrome – they take up riding a motorbike in order to keep their faces hidden with a helmet. So if you're visiting a clinic – and normally if you have something done, your face looks pretty horrendous for a short while afterwards – what better way to arrive and leave than by bike? Allowing you to wear a helmet to cover your features up more completely and secretly than any other method.'

This time she didn't wait for the attendant to appear. She poured wine for herself. 'So yuh is gonna ketch him? Right? Ya knows who he is? Sorry – 'oo 'e *was*? No wait...'

Kristal looked befuddled.

'The stalker? He must have sent some more lyrics in otherwise I wouldn't be here. Can't we, ah, get on with it? This audition? Is Han Fei going to be joining us or not?'

The pilot's voice filled the room as the plane bumped along on the tarmac. 'We got a problem – the other jet is as keen to go as we are. They're demanding the first slot out.'

William followed Kristal's gaze out of the elongated porthole into the festering dusk. Fans had cut through the fencing and were storming towards them. A battered Land Rover careered over the bumpy outer field, a banner waving from the window declaring *We Fled On A Dread Sled*.

The pilot's voice came over the intercom. 'I know you don't like doing this, Kristal, but on this occasion I would buckle up. It looks like this take-off is going to be hairier than usual. That other jet isn't waiting for permission from the tower – it's trying to elbow us off the runway. He's in a tearing hurry to leave.'

Just as we are, prayed William.

Uh-oh, was it possible that Frances was on board the other jet? After coming so far, coming so close, he'd been dealt the wrong ticket out?

On the horizon a police car with siren wailing had joined the chase. The plane juddered and began barrelling down the airstrip. William puzzled over when dinner was going to be put away. They did strap in for take-off, didn't they?

Kristal cantered over to the wall and flattened some buttons. The lights dimmed, then new floor lighting appeared emulating a mini dance floor. A strobe effect began to flicker, while globes with rotating lights and other shimmering effects sprang out from the ceiling and walls. A brief spurt of smoky carbon dioxide drifted upwards.

'What are you doing? I thought the captain said to buckle up.' William wrestled with the seat straps.

'It's a kinda family tradition. Given we're on our own jet, we don't have to pay no mind with rules. So we always dance as we lift off – first person to fall over has to buy the drinks!'

She began to gyrate as music detonated from the speakers. The melody swelled and drowned out the growing insistence of the jet engines.

You got me runnin' goin' out of my mind,
You got me thinkin' that I'm wastin' my time.

Don't bring me down, no no no no no,
I'll tell you once more before I get off the floor
Don't bring me down.

'And you always play this?' William looked blankly at her.

You wanna stay out with your fancy friends.
I'm tellin' you it's got to be the end.

'From ELO, but we remixed it!' she shouted above the jingle, and pranced over to William holding out both hands. 'C'mon!' she demanded. 'Dance!'

Don't bring me down, no-no no-no no-no no-no no.
I'll tell you once more before I get off the floor
Don't bring me down.

William was reluctantly pulled to his feet. He continued to stare out the windows. Some of the pop star's supporters embroidering the runway scampered alongside as the plane passed them, buffeting from the jet thrusters ripping at their hair, flags and banners. The sunset in the background sparkled as if it had been ignited by their flaming torches. Other vehicles bobbing over from hangars joined the chase. A veritable cavalcade penetrated the barriers guarding the airfield.

Don't bring me down, grrooss.
Don't bring me down, grrooss.
Don't bring me down, grrooss.
Don't bring me down.

The psychiatrist clung on to the table. A phone buzzed and Kristal danced over to it. Kwame's voice came on the line, audible to William just a few feet away. Abandoning all caution in the jet's slipstream as she twisted to the beat, Kristal was too inebriated to protect the receiver, so he heard every confiding word of Kwame's.

'So did you manage to find out what he knows? Can we dump him at the airfield, or do we need him?'

'Yeah, we dumped one of his entourage here already. Like you said.'

Kwame's voice sounded strangled, like he was fighting himself. 'No, Kristal, pay attention. Something's made you deviate from the flight-path. You were meant to extract from the shrink who the stalker is and then cut him loose. Remember?'

'Kwame, you'll have to deal with the package because it's wound too tight for me,' she said gaily.

Kwame seemed taken aback.

'Is this the first time you didn't manage to flip this? Can you put him on?'

Kristal lowered her voice as she motioned to William.

'And by the way, Kwame, he looks just terrible – like somethin' the dog's been keepin' under the porch. Han Fei is *way* better lookin'!'

William took the phone from Kristal, who returned to the dance floor. His fingers shook with trepidation as he grasped the receiver. He realised, from the conversation he had overheard, that his flight had just nosedived.

If he revealed who Dread's stalker was, then they were going to abandon him here. From talking to Kristal, and viewing the video images she had just shown him, he had finally identified for himself the person pursuing and threatening the pop star. But he needed to be able to use this valuable information so Dread would snatch him from the clutches of Gerrard.

On the other hand, if he stalled and played for time, Kwame would assume he hadn't cracked the case and was just holding them to ransom, using them for his own ends. Then he would still get ejected here and now. If he merely hinted, then they were liable to misinterpret the clue and pursue the wrong target. Wasn't that what Gerrard had done at every opportunity? On the other hand, if he didn't explain he'd unravelled the mystery, then Dread's life would continue to be in imminent danger.

He flapped at the carbon dioxide fog effect from the dance floor, trying to clear his mind.

'William? Kwame here. We got another message from the stalker. It was in Dread's goody bag at the premiere of her latest movie. You said you were going to expose who it is before we revealed what the lyrics were.'

William looked over at Kristal. The bopping blonde didn't exactly represent clinically controlled conditions, but it would have to do.

'The stalker's last message will have a personal pronoun in it – a word like me, we, our, my, mine, I or myself.'

'What? You said you were gonna tell us who it is, not critique their grammar!'

'I never said that. I explained I would divulge something about the message which exposes a crucial clue as to who it is.'

'Nooo, you promised...'

'Look, we can debate all night, but it's psychology. You needed to hear me say something, so that's what you heard. But it's definitely not my prediction. Check your tapes – you record everything, don't you?'

There was a pause while Kwame was reading the line. 'Bloody hell! You're spot on. Amazing – the line is *Don't Bring Me Down*. You were right! But how did you know?'

'Isn't that the song Kristal is dancing to right now?'

'It's a tune Kristal likes to boogie to whenever the jet is taking off – it's a bit of a family tradition.'

'So the stalker could be warning Dread about her next flight?' It occurred to William that he was on the very journey the pursuer was cautioning Dread about.

'Okay, but how did you guess the lyric would have "me" in it?'

'Basically there is a clear pattern, with the lines before Alonzo's death and afterwards being very different. The message the stalker left after Alonzo's death was *Close to me*. If you divide the stanzas into two halves, those before that lyric and those after, a striking pattern emerges.'

There was a pause while Kwame perused the list.

'No, sorry, I don't see it,' he said.

'A psychologist called Mark Schaller at the University of British Columbia in 1997 published a paper in the *Journal of Personality* where he showed that use of first-person singular pronouns increased in the song lyrics penned by Kurt Cobain and Cole Porter as they became more famous. He argued it was a symptom of increased self-consciousness, self-reference or self-obsession as they became better known. The study was entitled "The psychological consequences of fame: Three tests of the self-consciousness hypothesis" and argued that first-person singular pronouns are a measure of increased self-reference, perhaps a sign of the self-obsession that is the price of fame. If you list the stalker's messages and divide the list in two, in the sequence before his death there are no first-person singular pronouns – yet after Alonzo's demise, every single lyric has a first-person singular or plural pronoun of some description.'

'So what does all that *mean*?'

'It means that something happened coinciding with Alonzo's death. Perhaps the stalker changed. Maybe he fed off his increased fame – after all, there was a massive spike in his notoriety from that moment onwards. Or maybe the identity of the stalker changed. Self-reference goes up dramatically. The stalker thought he was being clever by using lyrics because it defeated all the analytic software. But a pattern emerges if you compare the lyrics over time, which means…well, I think the stalker may have changed psychologically. Perhaps Alonzo is the key. Always examine the pattern.'

'What about that eye thing on Dread's forehead?'

'The eye is a target painted on her forehead. And it means she absolutely cannot appear on stage. She must pull out of the Hyde Park concert.'

'*What?*'

'The pictures tell me this was done after the Rose Bowl concert. It's the back-up plan if she makes it alive to Hyde Park. I think the lyrics she is being sent are all about a group of snipers deciding on what line she'll be singing when they hit her. It's a communication, Kwame. The intention is to shoot her on the platform at Hyde Park. The daubed eye on her brow, fluorescing only when a black light shines on it, turns her head into a glowing bullseye.'

'*What?*'

'There was a small balloon tied to the top of the Ferris wheel on the platform she's going to sing from. It's the kind of wind marker a sniper needs for a long shot to allow for the wind deviation of the bullet. She's playing an anti-war benefit – so the pro-war paramilitary groups are out to get her.'

'You're building a crazy theory on very little.'

'Perhaps. But a sniper I treated and his estranged wife have tickets for the VIP area. If Dread gets hit there'll be pandemonium and a massive crush. People close to the stage will be squashed in the chaos and the media will be distracted by the assassination. The fact that non-celebs get killed as well will slide under the radar. A perfect opportunity, if you know it's coming, to put anyone you don't like in the VIP area. Until we have a clearer view, this is a scenario we need to take very, very seriously. I think it's possible that somebody has been trying to recruit a sniper, that the word is out and that there's even a kind of sick competition as to whose bullet is going to be found in her head. The cue for the shot is a lyric. The debate is which one.'

'And how do you expect to persuade her not to do the concert on this flimsy argument?'

'There's all the rumours about potential trouble at the event. The Foreign Secretary joked with me that if there was a mass riot at the concert it could wipe out anti-war protest in this country for a generation.'

'So the stalking is really about the Congo thing?'

'Look, Kwame, anyone in this field that pretends certainty is a snake oil salesman. Human behaviour does not permit absolutes. But it goes down well in the US, particularly in the courts. Not that the experts don't occasionally get a career-threatening comeuppance.'

'Dr James…'

'The expert who testified for the prosecution that the accused had been following the modus operandi of a TV show, only for it to be later revealed that the episode had never been broadcast. The expert who testified that the drawings were diagnostic of a sex attacker, only for it years after conviction to be shown through DNA evidence that the defendant was innocent. But you get what you pay for. The certainty merchants are the whores of the system. They will give you the absolute opinion that you desire, and they will be happy to moralise with it.'

'Is this about Han Fei? Because…'

'In the UK, we view mentally ill offenders as being as much the victims of their illness as their victims are of their offending. We admit them to hospital and treat them. In the US, they lock them up for life in solitary confinement or fry them. It's a difference of attitude, and I think you'd be happier with the certainty-mongers. Or at least, I don't think you'd be happy with the uncertainties that I'd have to offer.'

William paused for breath, mouth parched, heart thudding.

Screw it – if Kwame was going to have him thrown off the jet, then he was going to go down swinging.

'Dr James, frankly I was kind of hoping for a bit more than this. I was hoping for a big reveal. We've all come a long way – and for what?'

'You're just not *getting* him, are you. Your stalker. Look, stalking is all about control, and he's got you hanging on every word. He's controlled you this far, hasn't he? You can no more let go than he can.'

'You know what Han Fei said about you? That secretly you're a voyeur. He predicted you were going to ask for a list of everyone Dread had ever slept with. Said you did it with every female client sooner or later.'

William snorted. 'Yeah? Let me take a wild guess about Han. Did he by any chance do anything that was likely to make you feel closer to him? Convince you that you were both on the same wavelength? Wear an item of clothing that you do? Turn up in the same car? Mention staying at the same hotel? Cos...'

'You mean he doesn't normally carry a Smith & Wesson Magnum?' Kwame asked. 'The 500 Magnum? 'Cos that's my gun.'

'Bingo!' snapped William. 'He would research you closely, believe me, then knowing you used that weapon he'd get the same one to help you feel bonded.'

'Douchebag!' Kwame was insulted that he'd fallen for Fei's mind games and William laughed. But at the back of his mind he also recalled that this particular weapon was the same one David Lewis had used, which was an odd coincidence. Maybe there were more loose ends than could be tied up right now. He deliberated over Philippa's necklace, still rattling in his pocket and soaked in her blood. Later, if he was still on board the jet, he might get Kristal's opinion on it. Bedecked in similar jewellery, she looked like the sort of person who'd know more than him about that kind of thing.

'Okay, okay, Dr James, but who is our stalker?'

'Since we're doing show and tell – your pop star has managed to annoy just about every religious person on the planet, so it's entirely possible we're not dealing only with a stalker. Maybe, just maybe, half the world is after her. Everyone who gets a chance decides to stick the boot in. She's taking hits from all sides. In which case, you don't need me, you need an army.'

'You are not answering my question, Doctor. You're giving me just enough to keep me hanging on. To keep me wanting to know more. To stop it ending here and now.'

'Whatever you decide, be aware that your stalker, or stalkers maybe aren't even ready for proper contact yet,' said William. 'This, in their eyes, could be the slow build, the curtain raiser.'

Several thousand miles away Kwame came to a conclusion. He asked for Kristal again, so William carefully stepped over to hand the whirling dervish the phone.

'Okay, Kristal,' he heard Kwame say, 'tell Arnold it's a go.'

Dread's laughing sister replaced the receiver and returned even more energetically to the dance floor.

What happened to the girl I used to know,
You let your mind out somewhere down the road,
Don't bring me down, no no no no no,
I'll tell you once more before I get off the floor
Don't bring me down.

The jet engines screamed louder and the plane heaved forward. The rumble from the wheels on the tarmac smoothed out.

Don't bring me down, no no no no no.

The other jet also began to move and seemed to chase after them, but was on converging tarmac. If Frances had commandeered that aircraft, she was crazy enough to play some kind of private plane chicken to challenge him to blink first, divert and be left behind for arrest by Gerrard. She might have been the police pawn all along.

I'll tell you once more before I get off the floor
Don't bring me down.

Lights and buildings streamed past the window and William was flung back, colliding with a swivel armchair that caught him and spun. Kristal Miffed deftly retained her balance.

'I think y'all is buyin' the drinks!' she shouted at him. Cutlery started to slide off the table and chase after William. Crockery smashed on walls.

A blue flashing light seemed to come at them from the side and William ducked instinctively.

63

And destruction lay around me from a fight I could not win
Lady in Black

It wasn't William's passport she had levered away from the entourage at the limousine, as she had expected. It was someone called Han Fei's.

She smiled grimly to herself: the plot thickened. William wasn't as easy to stop as everyone thought he would be. He was hurtling like a missile now, evading all the counter-measures everyone was throwing at him.

Think, Frances, think.

So maybe Dread's people had a back-up plan if they couldn't get William out. People were so easily befuddled about the difference between a psychologist and a psychiatrist. Maybe the pop star wouldn't notice, or even care. Given Han Fei had now been stopped by the fuzz, mistaking him for William, their scheme wasn't going to work, but another one was forming in her mind.

She yanked the handlebars and the bike accelerated in the opposite direction to where everyone would think she should be heading. Well, William, Dread, Gerrard, Roger, Philippa, whoever – none of them would be reckoning that she, Frances, was still very much in the game. She just had to remember exactly what Roger Moirans had revealed in his office.

She began to replay the video-tape of their argument in her head.

Had the deck just been reshuffled? Had she been dealt some unexpected aces to play?

The Bluetooth headset on the inside of her helmet buzzed – it was Moirans, again. Before he had never wanted anything to do with her, would never commission any work from her, but now it felt like he was stalking her.

'Are you delivering Dread? A deal is a deal.'

'Roger, relax. I'm getting someone embedded in the Dread inner circle who's going to let us know everything right from the inside.'

'What? But no one's been able to penetrate the family. Kwame, the girls and the mother – they're tighter than a drum.'

'I thought you hired me because I am the best.'

'And I thought you were always after the Foreign Secretary. Seems like someone got to her before you. Maybe she's not so interesting now. Are you okay, Frances? Your voice sounds funny. How close were you when it all kicked off in the church?'

'Roger, this isn't a TV show anymore. It's all about what's going on behind the scenes. I can get inside Dread's inner circle.'

'But even so, how'd you wrangle this? To be honest, I wasn't sure your heart was in it. I thought it was Philippa you wanted.'

'I can't give you the details now – just fire up your private plane and get me on it. You promised me, remember? And I'm nearly at the airfield now.'

'Y'know, I never thought I'd see the day, but you've turned into a version of Dread.'

'What?'

'All this commandeering jets…'

'Are you lending me your ride? Yes or no? D'you want this Britney Brat or not? 'Cos I can deliver. Make a decision. I need it if I am going to keep track of her on this World Tour before Hyde Park.'

'Can't you give me something from your source now?' he asked. 'I mean, I already gave you me bike, and now you want me plane.'

'No, I can't give you anything yet. My source is getting embedded – I'll have something for you very soon.'

'Okay, okay. I gotta say, not much surprises me, but if you've managed to get someone in…'

'Roger, as we speak everyone is getting out following the debacle in the church with the Foreign Sec. I need that jet so I can still be in this game. There's someone who's gonna need secret transport. So are you in or are you out?'

'Okay, Frances. You're talking in riddles. I get that you

can't be frank because you're on the phone, and you always were paranoid about the Foreign Secretary, but who are you following really? Now? This pop star stuff isn't you, surely.'

'Whatever people say about Dread, she always gets her man.'

'Yeah, the Black Widow. She always gets her man *killed*, you mean. Remember Alonzo Church?'

64

The things we do for love
And you feel like a part of you is dying

'Kristal!' The pilot's voice filled the cabin. 'Sergei Bulgakov, that Russian billionaire – his plane is taking off too. I think they're as scared of the fuzz as we are for some reason, and if neither of us gives there's gonna be a collision.'

As the pilot was begging Kristal to tell him what to do, William deduced she was more than mere decoration.

William and Kristal bent to look out of the portholes. Sergei Bulgakov? The name came back to him with a start. That was the Russian oligarch who was reconstructing the house opposite Philippa's home in Maida Vale. David Lewis had helped build the safe room for his gold.

The other private jet was careering along asphalt, running at right angles to theirs. In the closing dusk, the gleam of the fuselage reflecting aerodrome lights was the only blur they could make out.

'Kwame ordered us to go, so any moment now we're gonna pass the point of no return – what do we do?'

Kristal looked askance at William. The aviators in Dread's own cockpit continued arguing with each other.

'The pilots in Bulgakov's jet are crazy – they're trying to take off from a service road. Our paths are going to intersect.'

'Go for it!' William shouted at the ceiling, desperate to get them to focus.

'But if we both take off, one has to go high, a steep climb, and the other low. 'Cos we both can't take the same flight path.'

'If you wanna know what the guy on the other plane is gonna do, ask William – he reads minds!' Kristal shouted at the intercom.

No matter what doubts the pilots were expressing, their engine note continued to rise.

'And we've got to allow for wake turbulence.' The pilots' frantic argument over the decision continued through the intercom.

'C'mon, William, what's Sergei going to do – go high or low?' asked Kristal, grinning.

She's as drunk as a skunk, realised William, *and no use at all.*

'Er, it's not just Sergei's mind I have to read – it's the shrinking violets'! Sorry, blinking pilots',' William complained, ducking back to check the other plane.

Both jets were clamouring towards a converging point half a mile away. William recalled that every time Dread had received the stalker's lyrics, she had narrowly avoided death shortly afterwards. They had been remarkably prescient. The latest lyrics were about this very take-off because the stalker had expected the pop star herself to be on board.

'Okay then, if you read minds, high or low? C'mon, make a decision!' the chief pilot snapped through the intercom.

'You do know what the lyrics mean, dontcha?' Kristal asked with great gravity.

This sister knew the answer all along? William tried not to sound too dumbfounded. 'Everyone's been trying to work out the meaning behind these lines being sent to Dread,' he said flatly.

'Yeah? Cos KT Mean and I know what they really mean.'

William was distracted, ruminating the billionaire wouldn't like any other jet to be more powerful than his. He would try to prove a point. Why was Kristal bringing this up now? She had to work on her timing.

'When Don MacLean was asked what the words to "American Pie" meant, he replied, "They mean I never have to work again".' Kristal started giggling.

'Seven, six, five – we've got seconds! Climb high or low? Come on!'

The co-pilot flung the door open to the cockpit and glared at the psychiatrist.

'F...f...fly!' William stammered. He abruptly recalled that Sergei had hired David because he specialised in construction-bearing great loads. And all that gold of Bulgakov's would weigh an enormous amount. But the police crawling all over his property after William's forced entry earlier today would have spooked the Russian. After all, he wouldn't know what they'd been looking for.

'So g...g...low?' His voice continued to falter.

Whatever, Bulgakov's gold would now be on his private jet heading to some tax haven. The plane would be carrying the extra weight of all that bullion. That meant it couldn't climb steeply even if the pilot wanted to.

'Climb high!' he shouted.

The plane accelerated, but so did Bulgakov's, a glow of orange bursting from its thrusters.

Suddenly that feeling of weightlessness William hated so much arrived as the aircraft kicked away from the ground. The engines ripped the air with a whine of agony, and then flung them into the night sky.

65

I can see for miles and miles
There's magic in my eyes

It was vital to piece together exactly what had been said in their meeting at the top of The Shard, just after the church tragedy. It would explain why Roger Moirans couldn't let go. And much else.

In his office, in Roger's actual presence, Frances recalled that she had felt less sure of her plan, but she also remembered that she mustn't doubt herself. Wouldn't that be what William would have advised?

Across a marble desk you could have landed a plane on, he had been on his headset and had spun away from her.

'You tell 'em that if they don't let my OB van into the space I've paid for an' reserved outside Dread's safe house, I'm coming down there to kill 'em wiv a bent coat 'anger!'

He'd whirled back and his tone changed.

'Frances Wright! We are in the presence of greatness.' He had screamed past her shoulder, 'Hey, all of yer, relax! We've gotta proper reporter here now!' He had rubbed his chest. Was he unconsciously remembering the documentary festival stabbing?

At last he had considered her properly.

Embedded screens on the wall behind him displayed Roger's networks from all over the world. Dread pirouetted across them all.

Frances relived that she couldn't believe Roger had his own accent light illuminating him at his desk. And every screen behind him sported Dread's face. Her lithe limbs bestrode the globe, and beneath that lustrous coffee countenance was there a hint of a leer – challenging Frances? Think you can seduce them like I can?

'So you know we can't use any of your footage from St Martin-in-the-Fields, right?'

'What?' She had felt nauseous, and somewhere in her stomach the cocktails had flipped. Dread seemed to mock her from the screens behind Roger.

'Ah, c'mon, you knew they would invoke national security and clamp down on this kind of thing.'

Frances had fought with herself to remain impervious and appear as if she had been expecting this news. Betraying any emotion would be game over with an adversary like Roger Moirans.

But if her scoop was being shelved, how come Roger had still been so keen to meet – sending his limousine for her? She just shrugged and smirked at him as if having the best work of her career summarily canned was an everyday occurrence.

'However, seeing as how you managed to get the footage in the first place, against all odds, and ahead of the rest of the press pack who'd been invited to the press conference just moments before but then were escorted off the premises, so you were the only hack in the congregation…well, seeing all that made me think. Since Dread's being stalked, and Philippa was, I joined up the dots – why not commission you to get inside the Dread stalker story?'

Frances had blinked.

Roger seemed to interpret this as her playing hard to get. He had leant forward and begun to look anxious that she might not take the assignment. Because he was so used to getting his way, he did what he always did in this situation – he became menacing.

'Deadline's changed, we need to bring this whole thing forward. It's because you make documentaries about, ah…'

'Yes?'

'Your last picture. It's on the tip of my tongue…'

'Wars, famines…'

'Yeah. *Foreigners.* Anyway, we thought you'd be ideal.'

'Mr Moirans, why d'you want me? It's not my bag, you know that. And no one close to Dread has ever talked properly to the press. She has the best publicists in the business, complete spin control. Why am *I* going to get anywhere with this story?'

'Because you're not part of the usual rat pack that chases her down. There's no history between anyone in her band or their entourage and yourself. You were always too busy making films about *coups d'état*...'

'Things that really matter, which you won't commission.'

'From the other side of the world. The fact you've been in Togo...'

'The Congo.'

'...throughout this period means you're gonna ask the kind of blindingly obvious questions those *Hello!* and *OK!* hacks wouldn't think to bother with. You start with no assumptions. We want you to kick-off from the beginning of her career and get under her skin, then explain what is happening *now*. Why is she being stalked? Who is it? You've got to track down these rumours about Hyde Park. Is it backlash? Is it 'cos her fans are burning down all those churches? Is this gonna be Dread's crucifixion by all those in the music industry who can't stand her? Care for Congo is the biggest charity concert in history, and just two weeks away at Hyde Park. Two million people in the Park and a global TV audience of five billion, and the buzz is somebody in the army lobby wants to turn this anti-war rally into a bloodbath. Or is it the religious nutters who are against Dread's blaspheming? Who's saying it? Who wants it? That's what you do, isn't it? You're crack at finding all those little, leetle people that were crushed on the way up, but who've got the real back story. I mean, that's how you slam dunk all those dictators, isn't it?'

Frances shuddered.

Metal clinked and Frances was presented with a gleaming chrome espresso cup by some graceful slender arms which sneaked up behind her.

The cups match the furniture, she thought.

'Ah, thanks, Cheryl. Cheryl's a massive fan. Of Dread, that is,' said Roger.

Jeezus, which model agency did you come from? thought Frances, swivelling to take in a statuesque personal assistant.

'She actually met Dread when she filmed that notorious episode of *The XXX Factor*. Even has some of the outfits. Phwoah! Oh sorry, Cheryl, this is the legendary Frances Wright – hard to tell under all that camouflage because she was just undercover in…Botswana?'

'Trafalgar Square. Remember, you sent your car for me?' Frances glanced at her watch. She was running out of time if her sources were to glean where MI5 and the Met had been deployed to hunt down the psychiatrist. Pursuing Philippa and Gerrard would lead her to William, but she had to get to him before they did. Otherwise his career was over, or he would be forever Philippa's poodle. Roger was hopefully on the cusp of handing over to her all the considerable resources at his disposal.

They needed to save FTAC.

Philippa and Gerrard would discover Frances a worthy challenger in the race to catch the shrink. But was it all too late? How to get this pompous twat opposite her to get a move on without blowing her real agenda?

'Anyway, she's the Kate Adie, Bob Woodward and Carl Bernstein of her day. Whassat nickname of yours? Oh yeah, the GC. Yeah, she's the human Geiger Counter 'cos she starts to click when there's just one suspicious particle in a million to pick up, which everyone else has missed. Way-hay! That's great, yeah, close down the phones. I'm not to be disturbed.'

'Fairtrade?' Frances queried.

'Cheryl? She's a bit of all right, isn't she. When she wears those thigh-length Dominatrix boots Dread made famous – Jeezus! I tell you, I could do with a bit of "discipline" myself.'

'No, Roger, the *coffee*. Is it Fairtrade?'

'It's an espresso. Way-hay!'

Roger thumbed at the images of the pop star behind him.

'You ain't gonna believe this, but she refused to ride in me lift. Said the lighting was too harsh.'

Frances let his show reel whip before her mind's eye. Roger had started out as a music producer, but it was as a viciously sarcastic judge on a talent show that he had made his name. Much thinner then – without the enormous arse he kept hidden – rolling eyeballs at yet another hapless performer he'd divined would produce laughter and embarrassment. Dread had been a flustered contestant on the series, so round after round he'd torn strips off her, lecturing the novice that she couldn't sing.

But he didn't have his own private lift back then, thought Frances.

So his throwaway remark about Dread riding in his lift, as they were sworn enemies, was a bit strange.

No. Roger, up this close, was looking more like an abandoned lover. Surely not. No. Not him and her?

Click!

Her nose hadn't lost its ability to pick up that one particle of plutonium in a million. First the "flight attendant" in Roger's limousine, then Cheryl – they were all of a type. A mould into which Dread fitted perfectly. Petite, beautiful, long dark hair, feline eyes that slanted just slightly, perfectly, inwards.

Now it came back to Frances: one of Dread's first hits had been "Friggin in the Rigging". Had everyone missed the real meaning of the words? Yes, yes, yes! Because no one would have dreamt that the vote for her talent show final could've been rigged by Roger.

'I know you and I, we've 'ad our differences, but facts is facts, Frances…' his sly grin was still there '…that quote was a complete fabrication. I never, ever would say about you "The antenna's up, but it's not pickin' up all the channels".'

Dread and Roger had been on-camera enemies. Who'd have believed that anything between them was possible? The public loathing between them now began to make a lot more sense. They were covering their tracks.

Frances wondered who'd dumped who.

So that's what had catapulted Dread to fame – the vote that ignited her career had been rigged. And this was just the tip of the iceberg. Frances had only been on this case for a few minutes and already she had a world-class exclusive.

Then she remembered what William had said. Maybe he was somewhat biased by his area of expertise – stalking – after all.

If you love someone – truly love them – then set them free.

66

Don't bring me down
You let your mind out somewhere down the road

The wing lights from Roger Moirans's private plane blinked a welcome to Frances through the gloom as it emerged from the hangar. She should be running over, commandeering it to follow the story.

But the "story" was accelerating and thundering down the runway while another jet came at it from across a service road.

She stood by the clicks and cracks of the cooling motorbike, transfixed, watching two aircraft sprint and scream at each other. Chasing after them was a procession of police cars, vans and various vehicles of the Dread fans. The heat trail from the jets wobbled the sun, which was setting behind woods and fields, quivering in the haze.

She realised that surrendering the passport to that skanky cow, Kristal Miffed, on board Dread's jet had allowed the bimbo to spirit William out of the country, despite the aerodrome and port checks that Gerrard and Philippa would have established. It seemed to be what William wanted, so Frances had released him into the sky.

Her phone buzzed, but she could barely take her eyes off the impending collision. Something inside her told her she should be filming this.

She glanced down. It was Gerrard.

He wouldn't understand.

She had let go. Now maybe all she could do was wait for the experiment to deliver its result, as William would have put it.

But she had also inadvertently set him up for this final collision...

*

370

Kristal crashed on to William, who collapsed on to the dance floor. The dinner service spewed across the walls and floor, splintering and tinkling. They clung together, bracing for impact. The floor shuddered violently and the blast from the protesting turbines grumbled into a shrieking pitch. She squirmed in his arms, burrowing her body closer into his. She smelt of alcohol, perfume and dissolution.

'Yeehaw! Ride 'em, cowboy!' she squealed, raising her head up.

What did an exploding plane feel like? At any second they were going to hit the other jet and become a fireball.

The plane banked steeply and they rolled together across the floor until they bumped into a curving sidewall. He saw it coming and put out his hand to protect her head. Her flowing hair fell all over his face. It was gossamer soft.

Through the porthole, the other jet filled the view. So he braced for another impact.

But Bulgakov's jet disappeared beneath.

Seconds went by, and the heaving, howling cabin began to calm down. They pulled themselves up, surfing the steep incline of the floor. William's hands circled the air as he tried to keep his balance. Kristal resumed dancing.

She looked straight into his eyes.

'So what is the cure for stalking anyhow?' she asked.

William more shakily regained the arm of a chair, brushing glass and broken china from his hair and arms.

'Somebody once said: if you truly love someone, set them free.'

Kristal shrugged, peering down at the aerodrome below. 'Oh yeah? Seems a recipe to be left standing beside the runway of life.'

'No, everyone forgets the second half of the quote. The first half is – *if you love someone, set them free*, but the second bit is – *if you let them go and they come back, they're yours. If they don't, they never were.*'

William wondered what she was looking at so intently and tried to peer over her shoulder. She boogied over to another window and waved cheerily at the crowd below, who were gesticulating up at the departing jet. Another battalion of police cars were converging on the ground, too late to block the take off.

'Wow, look at that!' She pointed out the porthole at the disappearing runway. Spreading flames flickered beneath black smoke in the tree tops just beyond where the runways ended. 'What gives with the forest fire?' Kristal hollered up at the intercom to her pilots.

'I think that Bulgakov's engines got too close to the topmost branches. Boy, he didn't just go low, he went *very* low. He only just made it off the ground.'

'Listen, Kristal,' William pleaded, 'I need to make an urgent call. Can I borrow your line?' It might be too late. Frances would be well within her rights to shun him now for taking her gift of freedom for granted.

'Sorry, Kwame insists all phone stuff goes through him now. I'll get him.'

Kristal bent over the receiver, then the phone went again and she gestured at William to get it.

'Er, William James here.' His heart was hammering. He wasn't sure how to fully thank Frances, but he did know he had a habit of blowing it with women. He should have called her before to express his gratitude, but take-off had proved somewhat touch and go.

'Hi ya, Will, Kwame here. I've got your party on the line. Play nice, otherwise I'm going to be in big trouble – and we can't have that. I need all the cooperation I can get over the Hyde Park concert. The Assistant Commissioner himself insisted I put her through.'

How come everybody thought Frances was so influential?

A click, a dry cough, and then Tullia seemed to join them in the cabin.

'Vilhelm? Vilhelm, I've been so worried about you. Listen, Gerrard has a block on you at every port and border. And…'

Uh-oh, this he didn't need. There was no time to regroup and come up with a plan on how to handle it all. He wanted Frances, she would know what to do. The one thing he mustn't do now, as she had nagged him, was revert to his tendency of jabbering defiantly.

'It's too late for him – I'm already airborne.'

'What? But that's not possible…Philippa…Gerrard…'

'If they'd known the difference between a psychologist and a psychiatrist then maybe they could have stopped me!'

'Philippa has loosed her MI5 dogs on to you. I know you're calling for my help, and I can reassure you I'm on your side. You mustn't worry about that. But Gerrard will want to pin the blame for the church debacle on you.'

'What I learnt from this case, what it means to me,' William interrupted, 'is to be always hanging on to a parachute, because the rules of engagement can get shuffled on you.'

'Quite right. So think of me as your back-up chute,' Tullia replied. 'Vilhelm, you're bound to be a bit emotional about Philippa, but don't let all this cloud your judgement right now. Don't do anything you're going to regret...'

'We dancin' or not?' Kristal interrupted, bopping over. 'These people giving you trouble?' she asked, her face clouding as she indicated the phone still in William's grasp.

'Listen, William, before you go anywhere, you need to think about how you are going to get back,' Tullia insisted. 'Maybe I can help, and get you out of the blame for the shooting in St Martin's. But they certainly will target you for stealing a police helicopter that cost £3.2 million – and breaking it! So think about extradition, think about getting arrested the moment you set foot in the UK again.'

So Tullia didn't yet know about his damaging the other of Winstanley's choppers on the roof of the hospital. Wait till she got the bill for that one as well, she might be a lot less mellow.

'Ahh, ahh!' William flapped his hands about. 'The helicopter was just a pawn. And pawns get sacrificed. Even Lewis has managed to get the church remodelled as he itched for all along – it'll have to be gutted and rebuilt. Maybe we were all pieces in his game. Wait – why are you telling me any of this now?

'Vilhelm, you are sounding like them. Don't go over to their side, stay true to your principles. People are not pieces of chess to be used for your own ends...'

'It's the only game in town. I learnt that the hard way.'

'Okay, you want to be a player. Now is the time to make the right move. Because now is when the AC needs you to save his career, and now is when Philippa thinks she can go onwards and upwards and is begging for you at the top of her voice. Now is the time to do a deal, unless you have £3.2 million to spare. Or you fancy being – what was it? – a prison doctor bozo.'

'Ahh, ahh!' William found he was repeating himself. 'That's not funny, Tullia.'

'No, but it got your attention. And, as it happens, you do have £3 million – £12 million, in fact.'

'What?'

The professor's breathing down the phone line sounded as if she was torn on whether to continue.

'A few moments ago I took a phone call from Wilfrid Sellars's people.'

'Who's that?'

'The Wilfrid Sellars? The billionaire you Dodo! Ninth richest person on the planet.'

'Yes, so?'

'Dread is doing a wedding night personal concert for him on his private island. C'mon, William, it's all over the press. She's being paid twelve million…'

'Does he need a psychiatrist?'

'No, there've been developments. Sellars's people told me, and this is hush-hush, that she's now waived the fee. Instead of paying her, he's to make a confidential donation to a charity of her choice – and she told him to back our department's research. She doesn't want any publicity over the donation and no link to her. Clever girl.'

William felt giddy.

'Okay, the thing is she's funding *you, Vilhelm, you and your* research. Not the Institute. It's designated funding. You choose what you want to back – you can fund all that psychology you're such a fan of, rather than the supposedly overly simplistic disease model of psychiatry you so despise. If you leave now then the money travels with you, but the clinic you started will close. And your patients – what happens to them, Vilhelm?'

The plane bucked and William rocked back on his heels.

The megastar had surprised him – spectacularly so. Had she decided to support rigorous enquiry into the psychology behind stalking because she was being afflicted with it?

Was it possible he had *misjudged* her? That being a bimbo was just her act?

'Money like this will fund a lifetime's research and treatment for innumerable patients. A team of skilled psychologists and psychiatrists where before there was nothing, only arrest after the attack. What will you do, Vilhelm? Will you fund the clinic or fly away and leave your patients without care? Shall I see what deal can be done, or just wave goodbye?'

'But you said the money follows me wherever I go,' William protested.

Kristal weaved over. Oddly her inebriated and wobbling body surfed the bucking of the plane better than William, who kept banging off walls.

'D'you want me to handle this? Is she a fan who won't let go? Is this another one of your strange bedfellows?' She snatched the phone from him, a new menacing tone entering her voice. 'The show always goes on. Don't let a few of the smitten get in the way. So yuh stop your nonsense right there. Yuh will perform and yuh will not disappoint us.'

Kristal cupped her hands over the mouthpiece and her tone softened.

'Listen, we understand how it is, dealing with the besotted. They can get clingy, but you've always gotta be able to move on. Don't explain, just get the hell off the stage. Leave them wanting more – the next big thing. It's our family motto.'

'What if the next big thing is death?' William asked. The plane lurched and he grabbed a ledge to stop himself falling. What had he been thinking? His fear of heights was back. The runway corkscrewed far, far below them.

Kristal stared for an instant, then seemed to make up her mind about him.

'Look, I'll show you how it's done. You'll get into the groove as you hang out with us, but until then I'll help. I know it can seem heartless, brutal even, but it's for the best.'

She put the phone to her lips.

'Ahh! No!' William yelped. After all, she was totally trollied. And Professor d'Aragona was one of the most senior figures in British psychiatry. His relationship, or at least what was left of it, with the whole profession swayed in the balance.

Tullia's voice wafted over from the buzzing line. 'Vilhelm? Please think very carefully, the next few moments are a turning point in your life.'

Kristal leant towards him confidentially. 'I used to do this back in the day. I had the deepest voice,' she said proudly. She held a finger up and undulated her body. Her lips touched the receiver in a kiss, and William hunched his hands in his armpits as if he was waiting to be punched.

'Kristal, tell the Prof that if she really understood me it would be obvious what I'm going to do,' he said.

'Ladiessssh and Gentlemennnn,' Kristal said into the phone, 'can ah have your attention, please?'

Bending down to check the sunset, she waved at the crowds and police vehicles, who all seemed to be waving back. The forest fire spread, fanning the night sky.

'The experiment requires that you continue,' William breathed.

'Ladies and Gentlemen.' She straightened her body, patted her hair and addressed the handset. As she met William's eyes, she gave him a lascivious wink. 'Elvis has now left the building!'

THE END

TO BE FOLLOWED

Hit Me, Baby, One More Time

The sequel to *Can't Get You Out of My Head* takes up the story. Does William crash-land into Dread's bickering and hostile entourage?

Should Kwame teach her how to use that Smith & Wesson magnum revolver, especially if the pop star is becoming unhinged?

A pulsating dash across continents visiting vast amphitheatres provides a dramatic backdrop to evermore bizarre events, many live on stage, during the rest of the world tour.

Acronyms

AC – Assistant Commissioner for the Metropolitan Police.

ASU – Air Support Unit, police helicopter.

BAFTA – British Academy of Film and Television Arts.

CIA – Central Intelligence Agency, United States Government intelligence service.

FBI – Federal Bureau of Investigation, Federal or cross-state police organisation in the United States of America.

JFK – John F Kennedy, former President of the United States who was assassinated under mysterious or controversial circumstances.

LSD – Lysergic Acid Diethylamide, an hallucinogenic drug.

The MET – the Metropolitan Police.

NFDD – Noise Flash Diversionary Devices.

NHS – United Kingdom National Health Service, a national state provider.

MI5 – Military Intelligence.

MO – Modus Operandi, the way a criminal has of acting.

MP – Member of Parliament, elected representative usually of the House of Commons.

NATO – North Atlantic Treaty Organisation

OB – Outside Broadcast unit or van, vehicle which holds video equipment and often editing suite equipment and satellite uplink.

OCD – Obsessive Compulsive Disorder, an anxiety disorder characterised by rituals and compulsions such as excessive checking and washing hands.

QT – Abbreviation of quiet. Used in the expression 'On the QT', meaning secretly or in confidence.

SECO – Security Coordinator for the police. Role is *to provide a clear focus for all aspects of operational security for any particular event or location, and for active planning, co-ordination and initiation of counter-measures to deliver it effectively.*

SOCO – A Scene of Crime Officer, an officer who gathers forensic evidence for the British police.

Acknowledgements

These people helped more than they will ever know – thanks to them all. I start with heartfelt appreciation for my long-suffering family – my gorgeous wife, Francesca Cordeiro, and two delightful children, Asha and Sachin. I have dedicated the book to my parents, and I should also like to thank Francesca's mother and father, Lira and Rufino Cordeiro.

Then, of course, I recognise everyone else who helped. There are so many I must have inevitably but inadvertently missed some people out – to them, apologies.

Special thanks in the list below go to Peter Lawlor for allowing me to use the lyrics from the Stiltskin song "Inside" so liberally in the chapter headings, and to Leah Webb from Sony/ATV Music Publishing for permission to use many of the other lyrics in the book, all of which come from real songs.

Juno Baker, Lindsay Bamfield, Helen Barbour, Gema Belmonte, Marius Brill, Joan and Peter Bruggen, Rosie Canning, David Canter, Bettina von Cossel, Carol Decker, Judy Finnigan, Christine Freeman, Adrian and Alison Furnham, Elizabeth Goes, Helen Holmes, Robert Howard, Jacqueline Hopson, David James, Matthew Kneale, Raj Kohil, Peter Lawlor, Richard Madeley, Gary McConnell, Troy McEwan, Roger Mills, Kati Nicholl, Maggie Pearlstine, Stephen Potts, Esther Rantzen, Sara Sjolund, Polly Tamplin, Maya Twersky, Leah Webb and Kyle Wallace.

I have endeavoured to be accurate in the accounts given of real life stalking cases, and in particular should like to acknowledge as an essential academic source the book *Stalking, Threatening, and Attacking Public Figures: A Psychological and Behavioral Analysis* by J. Reid Meloy, Lorraine Sheridan and Jens Hoffmann, published by Oxford University Press. References to the stalking incidents mentioned in the novel that affected cases including David Letterman, John Lennon, Peggy Lennon, Madonna, Olivia Newton-John, Gwyneth Paltrow, Monica Seles, Theresa Saldana and Rebecca Schaeffer are detailed in *Stalking, Threatening, and Attacking Public Figures: A Psychological and Behavioral Analysis.*

References

Bashour, M. and Geist, C. (2007) "Is medial canthal tilt a powerful cue for facial attractiveness?", *Ophthal Plast Reconstr Surg*, 23, 1, 52–6.

Meloy, J.R., James, D.V., Farnham, F.R., Mullen, P.E., Pathé, M., Darnley, B. and Preston, L. (2004) "A Research Review of Public Figure Threats, Approaches, Attacks, and Assassinations in the United States", *Journal of Forensic Sciences*, 49, 5, 1086–1093.

James, D.V., Mullen, P.E., Meloy, J.R., Pathé, M.T., Farnham, F.R., Preston, L. and Darnley, B. (2007) "The Role of Mental Disorder in Attacks on European Politicians 1990-2004", *Acta Psychiatrica Scandinavica*, 116, 334–344.

James, D.V., Mullen, P.E., Pathé, M.T., Meloy, J.R., Farnham, F.R., Preston, L. and Darnley, B. (2008) "Attacks on the British Royal Family: the Role of Psychotic Illness", *Journal of the American Academy of Psychiatry and the Law*, 36, 59–67.

Maltby, J., Houranb, J., Langec, R., Ashed, D. and McCutcheone, L.E. (2002) "Thou shalt worship no other gods – unless they are celebrities: the relationship between celebrity worship and religious orientation", *Personality and Individual Differences*, 32, 7, 1157–1172.

Mullen, P.E., James, D.V., Meloy, J.R., Pathé, M.T., Farnham, F.R., Preston, L., Darnley, B. and Berman, J. (2009) "The Fixated And The Pursuit Of Public Figures", *Journal of Forensic Psychiatry and Psychology*, 20, 33–47.

James, D.V., Mullen, P.E., Pathé, M.T., Meloy, J.R., Preston, L.F., Darnley, B., Farnham, F. (2009) "Stalkers and Harassers of Royalty: The Role of Mental Illness and Motivation", *Psychological Medicine*, 39, 9, 1479–90.

Schaller, M. (1997) "The psychological consequences of fame: Three tests of the self-consciousness hypothesis", *Journal of Personality*, 65, 291–310.

James, D.V., Mullen, P.E., Pathé, M.T., Meloy, J.R., Farnham, F.R., Preston, L. and Darnley, B. (2011) "Stalkers and Harassers of Royalty: an exploration of proxy behaviours for violence", *Behavioural Sciences and the Law*, 29, 1, 64–80.

James, D.V. (2010) "Protecting the prominent? A research journey with Paul Mullen", *Criminal Behaviour and Mental Health*, 20, 3, 242–250.

Page, L and Page, K. (2010) "Last shall be first: A field study of biases in sequential performance evaluation on the *Idol* series", *Journal of Economic Behavior & Organization*, 73, 2, 186–198.

James, D.V., Meloy, J.R., Mullen, P.E., Pathé, M.T., Preston, L.F., Darnley, B. and Farnham, F. (2010) "Abnormal attentions towards the British Royal Family: factors associated with approach and escalation", *Journal of the American Academy of Psychiatry and the Law*, 38, 329–40.

Music Credits

"I Can See For Miles" (Pete Townsend) (c) 1967 Fabulous Music Ltd.

"Inside" (Peter Lawlor) Stiltskin.

"Evil Woman" words and music by Jeff Lynne © 1975, reproduced by permission of EMI Blackwood Music/EMI Music Publishing UK Ltd, London W1F 9LD.

"Don't Bring Me Down" words and music by Jeff Lynne © 1979, reproduced by permission of EMI Blackwood Music/EMI Music Publishing UK Ltd, London W1F 9LD.

"Stalker" words and music by John Feldmann © 2004, reproduced by permission of EMI April Music INC/EMI Music Publishing UK Ltd, London W1F 9LD.

"Smoke on the Water" words and music by Ian Gillan, Ian Paice, Jon Lord, Ritchie Blackmore and Roger Glover © 1972, reproduced by permission of B Feldman & Co Ltd/EMI Music Publishing UK Ltd, London W1F 9LD.

"Girls on Film" words and music by Andy Taylor, John Taylor, Nick Rhodes, Roger Taylor and Simon Le Bon © 1981, reproduced by permission of Gloucester Music Place Ltd/EMI Music Publishing UK Ltd, London W1F 9LD.

"The Hunter Gets Captured by the Game" words and music by William Robinson Junior © 1966, reproduced by permission of Jobete Music Co INC/EMI Music Publishing UK Ltd, London W1F 9LD.

"I Can't Help Myself (sugar pie honey munch)" words and music by Brian Holland, Edward Junior Holland and Lamont Dozier © 1965, reproduced by permission of Stone Agate Music/EMI Music Publishing UK Ltd, London W1F 9LD.

"Ain't No Mountain High Enough" words and music by Nickolas Ashford and Valerie Simpson © 1967, reproduced by permission of Jobete Music Co INC/EMI Music Publishing UK Ltd, London W1F 9LD.

"Hungry Like the Wolf" words and music by Andy Taylor, John Taylor, Nick Rhodes, Roger Taylor and Simon Le Bon © 1982, reproduced by permission of Gloucester Music Place Ltd/EMI Music Publishing UK Ltd, London W1F 9LD.

"The Tracks of my Tears" words and music by Marvin Tarplin, Warren Moore and William Robinson Junior © 1965, reproduced by permission of Jobete Music Co INC/EMI Music Publishing UK Ltd, London W1F 9LD.